Behind the Moon

Behind the Moon

Hsu-Ming Teo

SOHO

Fiction
Teo

First published in Australia in 2005 by Allen & Unwin Pty, Ltd
First published in the United States of America in 2007 by

Soho Press, Inc.
853 Broadway
New York, NY 10003

Library of Congress Cataloging in Publication Data

Teo, Hsu-Ming, 1970-
Behind the moon / Hsu-Ming Teo.
p. cm.
"First published in Australia in 2005 by Allen & Unwin"--T.p. verso.
ISBN-10: 1-56947-440-0; ISBN-13: 978-1-56947-440-2
1. Vietnamese—Australia—-Fiction. 2. Parent and child—-Fiction.
3. Best friends—Fiction. 4. Male friendship—Fiction.
5. Domestic fiction. I. Title.

PR9619.3.T43B44 2007
823'.92--dc22
2006042299

10 9 8 7 6 5 4 3 2 1

For Thi Kim Uyen Truong—the best friend anyone could hope to have—and in memory of my late cousin, Raelene Hui Hoon Teo (1977–2004), who was much loved by family and friends, and who died during the writing of this novel.

A hundred years—in this life span on earth
talent and destiny are apt to feud.
You must go through a play of ebb and flow
and watch such things as make you sick at heart.
Is it so strange that losses balance gains? . . .
By lamplight turn these scented leaves and read
a tale of love recorded in old books.

Nguyen Du, *The Tale of Kieu*

The Truth Found in Toilets

As you must weigh and choose between your love
and filial duty, which will turn the scale?
She put aside all vows of love and troth—
a child first pays the debts of birth and care.

Nguyen Du, *The Tale of Kieu*

Justin Cheong believed in the truth that was to be found in toilets.

His earliest childhood memory was of going to a public toilet with his mother. Perhaps they were at McDonald's, or perhaps they were in a food court in some suburban shopping centre where the glare of overhead fluorescent lights glanced off the laminated surfaces of tables and chairs, and the smell of sweet-and-sour Asian takeaway mingled with sizzling onions, chicken tikka and doner kebabs. Above the cacophony of conversations swelling in a maelstrom of noise, Annabelle screeched out, 'Jay-Jay! Do you need to shee-shee?'

He shook his head vigorously. His neck swivelled like
a periscope as he looked around to see whether anyone
had heard Annabelle. Already, he was starting to develop
the habit of censoring his mother in his head; eavesdrop-
ping on their conversation from an imaginary non-Asian
point of view and marking out her oddness.

'You better shee-shee now,' Annabelle insisted. 'I'm
not going to stop the car afterwards if you need to go.'

The tips of his ears reddened with shame. Annabelle
grasped his hand and hauled him off to the ladies'. She
locked them both into a cubicle and heaved him up so
that he was standing balanced precariously on the rim of
the toilet. She pulled down his trousers and held on to his
little body with a pincer-like grip so that he wouldn't slip
into the bowl. She flushed the toilet once so that no-one
would hear the happy tinkle of his urine hitting water.

'Aim properly and don't make a mess for other people
to clean up,' she admonished him.

She tore off a couple of sheets of toilet paper and
threw them down the loo. Who knew what had contaminated them? Then she wadded a few more sheets
together, grasped the warm dough of his penis with her
cold fingers, shook it carefully and patted it dry.

After she'd dressed him, yanking up the metal zip of his
trousers with a speed that had him wincing even at that age,
she tore off more toilet paper and wiped the rim clean
before flushing. They stood there and watched the gush of
water and the gurgling swirl of paper sucked down into the
S-bend. She could not endure the shame of strangers
thinking she had fouled the toilet. She and her husband Tek
lived their lives to one mantra: what would people say?

'If I ever catch you not washing your hands after going to the toilet, I'm going to twist your ear off,' she told her son as she soaped and scoured their hands under the tap and blasted them under the hot breath of the hand-dryer. He nodded obediently; he was a good boy.

By the time Justin started primary school, he had begun to develop the thigh and calf muscles of a rugby league player from crouching over public toilets. He was small for a six-year-old so Annabelle still persisted in accompanying him to public toilets. To her great annoyance, however, he now refused to let her into the cubicle.

'I can do it myself, Mummy,' he insisted. 'I can't go if you're in there.'

She tapped urgently on the locked door with her wedding and engagement rings. 'Jay-Jay, don't touch anything you don't have to, you hear me? And don't sit on the toilet seat!'

'But I have to do a number two,' he protested.

The tapping on the cubicle door grew more frantic, like a woodpecker on amphetamines.

'You crouch, okay?' Annabelle cried. 'You listen to Mummy like a good boy. Don't you dare sit on the toilet seat. If you do, I'll wring your neck when you come out. You hear me? Are you sitting? Are you?'

Annabelle was hysterically clean. She disinfected the toilets in her house every day and kept aerosol cans of air freshener in her bathrooms. She was meticulous about personal hygiene. She showered twice a day, and after sex.

In his childhood, Justin was occasionally jerked out of deep sleep by the sound of the water pipes shuddering to life in the darkness. He'd roll over and check the luminous green hands of his Winnie the Pooh alarm clock. It would be nearly midnight. He could hear his mother showering in the bathroom next door. He'd ask her the following morning, 'Mummy, how come you showered again last night?'

She'd reply, 'Because Mummy got hot and sweaty changing the bedsheets.'

'You're always changing the sheets,' he would say with a slow, sly smile.

She'd frown slightly and say, 'Your daddy has an oily head. All that Brylcreem to keep his fringe back. It leaves stains on the pillowcase.'

Annabelle kept a toilet roll in her bedside drawer, next to lubricating creams and other sex aids. She was a woman who used a lot of toilet paper. Tons of timber were logged, entire forests felled, just to feed this habit. She judged relatives and friends, restaurants and hotels by the cleanliness of their toilets and the quality of their toilet paper.

Once, the Cheongs made the long drive from Strathfield all the way over to the eastern suburbs of Sydney to visit one of Tek's colleagues who lived in Bellevue Hill. Annabelle marvelled at the white mansion with its slate-grey roof and the Daimler in the driveway. A timber-decked pool sheltered behind a brushwood fence in the backyard. Inside the house, her eyes goggled at the sight of Turkish carpets—too expensive to be laid on the polished jarrah floorboards and trodden underfoot—warming the walls alongside the artwork. Chandeliers glimmered overhead in the hallway and lounge; recessed downlights glowed softly from the ceiling in other rooms. Antique occasional tables, inlaid wood cabinets and tallboys bore the weight of

sculptures—some traditional and immediately recognis-
able; others funkily modern, their plasticated forms
impressive to Annabelle largely because of the price tag
imparted by the hostess in a discreet murmur upon
Annabelle's inquiry. On a marble mantelpiece, a pair of
bronze chimpanzee hands clutched the air.

'They were cast from the chopped-off hands of a real
live chimpanzee,' the hostess said. 'There are only three of
its kind in the world.'

'*Wah*,' Annabelle said.

Then, before they left, she visited the guest bathroom.
When she came out, her mouth was pinched in disapproval.
She could barely wait until Tek navigated his way onto New
South Head Road to twist around in her car seat and tell
him indignantly, incredulously, 'You know what? With all
that money and art and antiques and monkey's hands, you
know what kind of toilet paper they use? One ply!'

'Maybe it's the rich *ang mors*. I read the Queen uses
cheap toilet paper in Buckingham Palace also,' Tek said.
'Better bring our own next time.'

'You can tell a lot about a person by what goes on in
their toilets,' Annabelle declared.

Justin would remember this nearly a decade later
when, at the age of fifteen, he first had sex in the men's
toilet in Strathfield Plaza.

He was twelve years old when he first wondered whether
he was gay. He sat in a history class watching a video of
Gallipoli, staring at the Anzac soldiers swimming naked in
translucent green water while shells exploded all around

them. He was mesmerised. He could not take his eyes off those lithe white male bodies rippling in the sea, suspended in a water ballet of blood and carnage. At the end of the movie, his heart pounded painfully against his chest and his throat was sore with suppressed tears at the sight of Mark Lee frozen at the moment of death. Later, he hunted down a poster of the film and Blu-Tacked the picture of Mel Gibson and Mark Lee to his bedroom wall.

His father nodded approvingly. It was a sign, Tek thought, that Justin was growing up an Australian.

When Annabelle saw the semen stains on Justin's sheets, she frowned and made him change them. She knew about wet dreams, of course. She was a doctor's wife, after all. The involuntary oozings of her son's adolescent body distressed her, but she sat him down and told him with kindly resignation that it wasn't unusual if he couldn't control it.

'Jay-Jay is growing up,' she sighed. 'Can't be helped, poor thing.'

Justin did not dare tell her it was deliberate. She was already in mourning for the armful of soft flesh she had once bathed, powdered and hugged to her face, drawing in a deep breath of its clean baby smell. Her son's hard, hormonal body was suddenly alien to her. For a brief moment, she realised that she did not know him.

Then she said, 'Must always change the sheets, *hor*? Otherwise *ho lah-cha*. Don't let Mummy have to tell you again.'

She did not want to know about her son's nocturnal imaginings. Sex was a four-letter word to Annabelle and it spelt DIRT.

This was a woman who tried to censor her son's movie-watching habits, who, if she could, would have restricted him to Disney films featuring doe-eyed animals that chirruped and sang. She was fiercely protective of his innocence. Even when he was fifteen, Annabelle automatically slapped her hand over his eyes whenever a sex scene came on the TV screen. She ordered, 'Don't watch, Jay-Jay. Dirty things going on.'

Worst of all were the annual televised snippets of the Sydney Gay and Lesbian Mardi Gras. Try as she might, Annabelle could not remain oblivious because, on some Sunday evening in March, she might turn on the television for the news and, suddenly, she'd be ambushed by the sight of the previous night's parade. The moment she caught a glimpse of those floats and feathers, the glittering costumes and all that prancing flesh, she was riveted. She would stand there, paralysed with prurient shock, the remote control in her hand, repeating in fascinated horror, '*Ai-yoh*, look at all those *hum sup lohs*!'

'Terrible,' Tek agreed. He frowned ferociously at the screen. 'They shouldn't show it on prime time television when children might be watching.'

Annabelle noticed that her son was in the living room. She pushed him out of the room and warned him, 'Don't look, Jay. Dirty like anything.'

Justin looked back over his shoulder at his parents and, loving them, did not say a word. He dropped his eyes to veil his shame. That night, in the dark, he huddled on the floor of his bedroom and steadily battered his head against the wall. He punched his arms and thighs over and over again until bruises bloomed on his body and he throbbed with pain. 'I'm going to be good,' he croaked. 'I swear it.' He wanted to cry, only there was nothing inside him but a parched wasteland of regret for the choices he was too afraid to make. At last, exhausted, he crawled into bed. In the loneliness of the night, he could not help reaching for his groin to make himself feel better. Orgasm was an agony of pleasure that made him feel dirty like anything. He knew he was too unclean for his family or his friends.

Nigel 'Gibbo' Gibson was Justin's oldest and best friend. The two boys had met when they were six at Saturday afternoon piano lessons with Miss Yipsoon. They bonded immediately over a mutual lack of practice and a regular smack of Miss Yipsoon's twelve-inch wooden ruler across small knuckles where the bones knotted through thin skin.

Disgrace inevitably attended each lesson. Justin forgot to trim his fingernails and the yellowed keys of the old Beale piano (they were not allowed to touch the glossy black Yamaha upright grand until they reached Grade 6) were in great danger of being *clawed*. Those nails were long enough to be a *girl's*. And as for Gibbo, his wrists drooped wilfully when he fingered his scales. The heavy dodecagons of fifty-cent coins were placed on the backs of Gibbo's hands and his fingers were forced to crawl crab-like up and down the keyboard. The wooden ruler hovered menacingly as his fingers marched rightwards, then left, descending sharply whenever a coin fell off the back of his hand.

The trauma of shared humiliation was as good a basis for friendship as any at that age, and it certainly helped that their mothers got along so well. Annabelle was enchanted by the vestiges of Gillian Gibson's English accent, and Gillian preened under her Asian friend's admiration.

'*Wah*, Jay. See how Mrs Gibson speak so good English! Got standard, *leh*.'

'Well,' Gillian said modestly, 'I *am* an elocutionist and a singing teacher. My own teacher learned from Julie Andrews' teacher. Diction is everything. The separation of consonants, and clear, crisp vowels.'

'I tell you what, Jay. You should learn to speak from her, you know. Then you can teach Mummy and Daddy, *hor*? You want to take speech lessons with Mrs Gibson?'

'I thought you and Dad migrated to escape the *kiasu* culture of Singapore,' he complained. 'I don't wanna take speech lessons.'

'Must want. Cannot don't want,' Annabelle insisted.

Justin shrugged in resignation. It was inevitable. To the long list of after-school activities he was already enrolled in—tennis lessons, maths tutoring, Chinese classes—Annabelle added speech lessons with Gillian.

Gillian spent most of her mornings teaching aspiring opera singers diction and her afternoons tutoring NESB kids like Tien Ho in English. Tien was a Vietnamese refugee who had become friends with Gibbo when she was repeating Year 3 and she joined Gibbo's class at school. Justin had met her a couple of times at the Gibsons', but he did not get to know her until he went to school with her and Gibbo in Year 8.

By then, he had been expelled from his prestigiously expensive and hideously conservative private school for mysterious reasons that Tek Cheong angrily refused to believe. Tek did not once ask Justin if there was any truth to the scandalous allegations which were so appalling that of course no son of his could be involved. After all, this was the son who, as a three-year-old, had stood quiescent between Tek's hairy legs after he had returned from work and slumped onto the sofa in his undershirt and shorts. When he commanded his son, 'Lift legs, Jay-Jay,' Justin bent down, wrapped his chubby arms around Tek's shins and valiantly hauled up his father's legs to the level of his own armpits. The toddler's face grew redder. He bled sweat and his full rosy lips firmed into a constipated line as the minutes passed and his father warned, 'Not yet, Jay. Don't put them down yet.' Justin's little body quivered and strained and his arms were hot with pain. Finally, he could bear the weight no longer. He let go. His father's slippered feet thudded down to the carpet. Justin hung his head in shame.

'What? Still so weak, ah!' Tek marvelled, and his son burst into tears. Only then did the father relent. Tek said, 'There now. No more crying, okay? Only sissies cry. Come. Climb onto Papa's lap.'

And that was the moment his son had been waiting for. Justin scrambled eagerly onto Tek's lap and rubbed his wet face against his father's chest. He could feel the ribbing of the white singlet impressed on his warm cheek. Tek's arms closed around him and Justin turned his face to burrow towards his father's armpit, curiously sniffing in the human smell of musky sweat and slowly sloughing skin that his mother could not bear. He sighed deeply and felt content. Safe. His father's arms tightened around him and rocked him briefly. Then Tek lifted his son off his lap and put him down.

'Try harder tomorrow, okay?' Tek said.

As always, his son nodded obediently. There was nothing his son would not have done for him, nor he for his son. Justin was a *good boy*. And now, this good son of his had been expelled from school. Without the benefits of a private school, how would he get into a medical course at university?

'Those damn racists,' Tek fumed to Annabelle. 'I should write to the government about this.'

Being Singaporean by birth and education, if no longer by nationality, he did no such thing. He dared not draw attention to himself.

What made the incident even more frustrating for Tek was that he was denied the consolation of complaining about the expulsion to friends and colleagues. He was unable to defend his own son because that would entail an explanation of what had allegedly taken place, and he simply could not bring himself to mention it.

Instead, he told everyone, 'Annabelle and I realised we believe in public education. Better to spend the money on after-school tutoring than on private school fees. Even if you go to private school, you have to go for tutoring anyway.'

To Justin, he said, 'Daddy believes in you. We don't have to talk about this again. Just be a good boy and study hard in future.'

So he did. Justin wanted to make sure that his father would never again have a reason to be disappointed in him. No shade of uneasy suspicion should furrow his father's brow, no recoil of horror spring into those gold-bespectacled eyes. Justin put the whole incident behind him and vowed to make a fresh start at his new school. He was happy to be with Gibbo, even if he had to share him with Tien.

He soon counted Gibbo and Tien as his best friends. They did everything together after school and on weekends. He spent hours on the phone talking to them in the evenings. They came over for dinner and his mother taught them how to cook. He loved them. They thought they knew him. They were wrong.

Gibbo and Tien looked at him and saw a tall, slender Chinese boy with blond-streaked shaggy hair (grudgingly allowed by Tek, on account of his son's 'adolescent phase') that he tied back with a red rubber band when he played the piano. They knew the idiosyncracies of his parents. They knew his musical and movie tastes; they knocked him about the Michael Jackson dance steps he mimicked in front of video-clips and the Michael Jordan basketball moves he practised on the Cheongs' concrete driveway. He simply smiled, and everyone liked him for that. He could take a joke, good old Justo.

He was athletic without being a jock, playing in the B-grade basketball, cricket and tennis teams at school. He was good at being B-grade. Tek proudly nailed a wooden shelf over Justin's bed to hold the ribbons and trophies his son had accumulated. The shelf broke off from the gyprock wall one night and an avalanche of second-rate sporting triumphs cascaded down onto his head. He emerged from the rubble with a deep cut over his left eye. Blood ran down his face, nearly sending Annabelle into

cardiac arrest. As vigilant as she had been over the eye-
poking possibilities of compass, pencils and assorted
kitchen utensils, she had never envisioned this. She took
him to the optometrist and demanded regularly over the
next fortnight, 'Can see or not?' When the cut healed, it
left a thin white scar slashing his eyebrow, and the sight of
it became as familiar to Gibbo and Tien as the reflection
of their own faces in the mirror.

As for the rest of him, he was just ordinary: such a
stereotypical Australian-born Chinese boy that he was vir-
tually invisible. To his friends, he was *nice*; there was
nothing more to be said. His slightly pimpled face
was serene and beautifully blank. His easygoing smile hid
the thoughts he did not utter. They touched him and
clutched a skinful of flesh and bone that did not connect
to the feelings or fantasies he harboured. He did not tell
them because he loved them. He was protecting them
from himself, for he knew he was a dirty boy. And perhaps
he was also protecting himself from them.

On Saturday, 17 August 1991, Justin had a late lunch with
his best friends at the Coffee Pot café inside Strathfield
Plaza shopping centre. They ordered soup and toasted
sandwiches, then Gibbo and Tien began a pointless
argument of the sort they both frequently engaged in over
some rock band they disagreed about. Justin eased back
into the settee and distanced himself from his friends. He
arranged his face into an expression of bland interest and
tuned out of the conversation. His heart beat a rapid tattoo
and his hands were trembling, for he had made up his

mind about what he was going to do that afternoon. He had made an assignation earlier that week; at last he would know the taste and texture of a man's kiss. This was the day he would learn something about love. He was almost sick with anticipation and dread.

After lunch Tien wanted to buy some things from the supermarket. Gibbo was, as ever, eager to accompany her. Justin smiled and shrugged in resignation. He had always known that Gibbo preferred Tien's company to his own. On several occasions, he had half seriously, half playfully accused Gibbo of having a crush on Tien—a charge that Gibbo vigorously denied.

'Yuck. All that love stuff's so gross,' Gibbo had said, shifting uncomfortably. 'It just messes everything up. Anyway, I don't think of people that way.'

But Justin was unable to believe in his best friend's asexuality. And even if it was true, that made things worse because it meant that Gibbo simply preferred Tien as a person to himself. Justin refused to think about it. He swept up his jealousy and tidied it away, shrugged on his habitual good-natured normality instead.

'I'll wait here for you,' Justin said to Tien. 'Half an hour max, guys, then I'm going home if you're not out by then. I don't want to hang around here the whole afternoon while you dither over which brand of hairspray to buy and Gibbo agonises over a Mars Bar or a Milky Way.'

He waited until they left, then he got up and settled the bill. He was at once exhilarated and terrified. He felt anxiety pressing on his bladder, gripping his bowels. He wanted to pee and he felt a phantom need to shit. He checked his watch, then he went to the men's toilet tucked away at the back of the Plaza. As he stood at the urinal, he heard the door opening. Footsteps echoed around the corner. At first he kept his gaze in front of him as he heard trousers being unzipped. He was breathing hard and sweating profusely, as though he'd just run a marathon. Finally, he mustered the courage to slide a quick glance upwards and he saw that the man was watching him, a questioning half-smile on his lips.

'Hey,' Justin mumbled in greeting. The tips of his ears burned. Slowly, helplessly, his gaze drifted downwards towards their mutual tumescence.

Nothing terrible ever happened in Strathfield except perhaps car theft, which made car insurance premiums one of the highest in the state of New South Wales. It was a staid suburb of middle-class homes and middle-class private schools churning out neatly uniformed kids. By the early 1980s, Anglos and Eastern Europeans had been joined by Indian and Chinese families who moved into the suburb and left their unmistakable imprint in the form of yum-cha restaurants, Indian spice shops and abandoned shopping trolleys nestled against rough-barked tree trunks and cracked telegraph poles. They were followed a decade later by Koreans who opened up cute shops with cute clothing and ever cuter accessories. They introduced karaoke clubs and lifted the culinary profile of the suburb with marvellous restaurants which bled the mouth-watering barbecued aroma of *pulgogi* and the sour tang of *kimchi* into the air.

In time, the red-brick façades of high-rise apartments would mushroom around this transport hub. Buses groaned and rumbled through the maze of the main square. Trains snaked regularly into the eight-platform station where children flocculated in the early mornings and weekday afternoons, scoffing down sausage rolls, hot chips and potato scallops. Schoolbags littered the train platforms for annoyed adults to stumble into or trip over, and they would spend the rest of the train journey composing letters of complaint to various school principals.

But on the whole they were not a fearsome crowd, these children, for they were mostly dressed in the regalia of private school uniforms. They did not menace the middle-aged with the sight of basketball boots, baseball caps twisted backwards and baggy tracksuit tops over school trousers. Nor did the girls offend the intolerant with the Muslim modesty of elegantly arranged headscarves. Such sights were more common further west, out in Auburn, Lidcombe or Lakemba, driving a spike of fear—the culturally different mistaken for the criminally dangerous—into the tidal wash of Greek, Eastern European and Anglo-Australians whose lives had sedimented in those suburbs.

In Strathfield children shrilled and squawked like cockatoos at sunset but they looked affluent and orderly. Surging down the ramps from the train platform in the late 1980s, they ignored the advertisement overhead telling them: 'If you've got time to kill, relax at Strathfield Plaza.'

On the afternoon of Saturday, 17 August 1991, while Tien and Gibbo killed time by relaxing in the supermarket, Justin was locked in the single cubicle of the men's toilet having his first sexual encounter. He was not entirely certain whether it was consensual, for he did not dare to know what he truly desired. He hid in his passivity and refused both volition and responsibility. Pain was twisted with pleasure, he felt simultaneously thrilled and ashamed. He closed his eyes and gritted his teeth to savour the sensation, but the experience was fractured by too many thoughts. Part of him was terrified that someone would come into the toilet. In another, more detached substratum of his mind, he imagined himself watching a B-grade movie that had never been made; a vastly inferior and bathetic rehash of the moment Grace Kelly kissed Cary Grant in Hitchcock's *To Catch a Thief*. Even if there were no brilliant starbursts, only the flickering fluorescent glare overhead, he could have sworn that he heard firecrackers exploding as if it were Chinese new year.

Later, when he was alone in the cubicle, he ritualistically tore off two sheets of toilet paper, dropped them into the bowl, wadded more sheets together and cleaned himself up, wincing slightly as he wiped his tender genitals. His mother burst out of her cage and rampaged back into his head. Although he tried to shut out her voice, he could hear her reproach. 'Ee-yer! Dirty boy! How could you? I'm going to twist your ear!'

Defiantly, he told himself that whatever happened, at least he had not touched the toilet seat. And before he left, he made sure that he washed his hands thoroughly with soap and hot water.

He swung out of the men's toilet, mentally rehearsing what to say to Tien and Gibbo if they should ask where he'd been. And that was when he saw the people crouched in terror on the floor, the blood and broken glass. He did not fully understand what he was looking at; he had to hear it explained on the television news later that night. He had to read about it in the newspapers the following day.

Shortly after two thirty that afternoon, a Caucasian man in his early thirties wearing a grey beanie entered the Coffee Pot café and sat down in a booth. He lounged there for nearly an hour, drinking four coffees slowly. At 3.30 pm, he signalled to a waiter and asked for the bill. He got up, paid his bill and headed towards the door, making his way between the plush booths of the café. Then he whipped out a knife and plunged it into the back of a fifteen-year-old schoolgirl.

He pulled an SKS 7.62mm semi-automatic rifle from his bag and opened fire on customers in the café, shooting dead four people and wounding others. The owner of the Coffee Pot, George Mavris, heard the gunshots in the kitchen and ran into the shop to see what was going on. The gunman shot and killed George. He then left the café and stalked through the Plaza, firing randomly at plate-glass windows and screaming shoppers.

Greg Read was a retired naval officer who had served in Vietnam. That afternoon, he was in the Plaza's newsagency when he heard the rapid rattle of the semi-automatic rifle. He raced out of the newsagency and a woman screamed, 'Look out. A man's gone berserk with a gun.' He could see the gunman heading his way, so he ran ahead, yelling out warnings to other shoppers. He saw the gunman heading for the escalators to the car park. Greg ran outside and bounded up the external stairs to the car park to warn others there.

Inside the Plaza, the gunman killed a man at the foot of the escalators. He made his way up the escalators, then ran up the ramp to the upper rooftop level of the car park. He leaned his rifle on the concrete balustrade, trained it on the town square, and fired at the buses and trains and shops. A volley of shots shattered the windows of a taxi, the railway ticket office, and a milk bar.

By this time, Greg Read had reached the rooftop level of the car park. He saw a woman driving out of the car park and yelled at her to lie low. She looked at him. 'It's too late,' she whispered. 'He's already behind you.'

Greg turned and saw the gunman. He dived under a car and felt a searing sting as bullets slammed into his feet.

The gunman then wrenched open the door of the station wagon and jumped into the car of the terrified woman. 'Where are you going?' he demanded as she drove down the ramp to the lower level of the car park. She stammered out a reply and he said, 'I don't want to go where you're heading.'

She stopped the car and he looked at her.

'I'm sorry,' he muttered as he thrust open the car door and got out. Moments later, he turned the rifle on himself and shot himself through the head.

He had already killed seven people and wounded another six that afternoon.

Justin pushed past the turnstile and ran through the supermarket, searching aisle after aisle for Tien and Gibbo. He felt a rising tide of panic as he failed to find them anywhere. He shoved his way out of the check-out lanes and scrambled through the shopping centre, ducking in and out of shops, dodging people crouched sobbing beside the wounded and the stunned. He could barely hear the swelling police sirens for the beat of blood in his ears. It took him nearly twenty minutes to find Tien and Gibbo in the Symonds Arcade leading out of the north side of the plaza. They huddled together wordlessly, wrapping their arms around each other, rocking slowly for comfort.

'We didn't know what happened to you,' Gibbo said. 'We thought you were still waiting in the Coffee Pot.'

Tien was crying silently. He could feel her tears soaking into cool wetness on his T-shirt. She hugged him so tightly that, when at last she drew away and fumbled for a crumpled handkerchief, the medallion he wore under his T-shirt was imprinted on her cheek.

'I couldn't bear it if anything happened to you,' she said. Her eyelids were swollen and the tip of her nose glistened with traces of teary mucus. She was not a girl who wept gracefully; she was ugly with fear and shock.

Justin simply looked at her and shook his head. He was overwhelmed by her concern for him. He was still sore from sex. He did not deserve her friendship. He stepped towards her and clasped her close. He felt such love for her in that moment.

'It's okay,' he said. He felt like an adult, full of meaningless reassurance that his friends did not believe but took comfort from. 'It's okay.'

For a moment, Gibbo stood beside them uncertainly, locked out of their circle of twined arms and braided bodies. Then he too threw his arms around them.

'Yeah, we're all right,' he said. And he tried not to think of those who were not.

On Saturday, 17 August 1991, Justin lost his virginity in a public toilet and, because of this, was saved from the massacre which began at the Coffee Pot, where he should have been waiting for Gibbo and Tien. Survival brought its own guilt. He was still young enough to place himself at the centre of all that happened around him. Through his mind ran the refrain: 'Dirty boy. It's my fault. It should have been me. Dirty boy.'

He vowed to himself that what happened was a one-off lapse. It wouldn't happen again. He would be a good boy. He would not grow up to be gay. He looked towards Tien, and wondered if she could save him.

A Surfeit of Mothers

Within a stranger's gate Kieu slaved and lived,
confiding in her shadow or her heart . . .
All heaven was one white expanse of clouds—
she peered far into space: where was her home?

Nguyen Du, *The Tale of Kieu*

Tien Ho would never outgrow *The Wizard of Oz*. She saw it for the first time when Gillian Gibson took her and Gibbo to see a special screening at a community centre during the school holidays. Later, she asked Gibbo to videotape it when it was broadcast on television. They watched it over and over again. Even when she was a teenager, she was transfixed by it.

Once, she was serving in Uncle Duc's restaurant when, suddenly, on the small black television mounted above the cash register, she caught a glimpse of the familiar sepia-stained barnyard a-clatter with activity, all the adults scurrying around doing important adult things while the little girl and her dog just got in the way. Tien simply stood there with a bowl of steaming *pho bo* in her hands, ignoring customers' gestures for attention and Auntie Phi-Phuong's annoyed hiss.

She looked at Dorothy, and she knew just how she felt. She'd been that little girl. They told her to get out of their way, the adults; to find some place where she wouldn't get into any trouble. She knew they loved her. Of course they did. But sometimes their love was so hard-lacquered with impatience and obligation that maybe her heart was cracked with doubt because, after all, they were not really her parents. They were only Auntie Em and Uncle Henry, and the only one who truly belonged to her was Toto.

Growing up, Tien had Auntie Ai-Van and Uncle Duong and their three daughters who formed a closed circle against her because they were already a family. They didn't need another daughter, especially one whose different skin colour attested to dubious parentage and the sins of her missing mother. But Uncle Duong and Auntie Ai-Van took her in because they were obligated to, and because they were basically kind people. She was not mistreated; she had a well-cared-for childhood. She loved her Auntie Ai-Van and Uncle Duong. Dutifully.

But whenever she watched *The Wizard of Oz*, her dark round eyes bored into the screen as though, by sheer willpower, she could thrust herself through the static-charged pane into that vibrant Technicolor world. And she swore to herself that if, by some miracle, she should ever succeed, unlike Dorothy she would never click her red heels together to return to a land bleached brown and white. No.

She would stay with her friends in Oz because however
much your family might love you, they were not sufficient;
they could not make you heart-whole and happy.

All her life she felt as if there was a Tien-shaped
treasure box inside her that she could never quite manage
to prise open. But if she could, she would find whatever
it was she needed to make life feel just right. As she
grew older, however, she began to wonder whether there
was anything inside this box but air. Or, even worse,
perhaps there was just another, smaller Tien-shaped box
nested inside the first, and yet another inside that. An
infinite progression of Tien-shaped boxes locked inside
each other like Russian *matryoshka* dolls.

She looked at the television screen and whispered the
words along with Dorothy. 'Some place where there isn't
any trouble,' she said. 'Do you suppose there is such a
place, Toto? There must be. It's not a place you can get to
by a boat or a train. It's far, far away. Behind the moon.
Beyond the rain. Somewhere over the rainbow . . .'

Tien Ho had arrived in Australia from a refugee camp
in the Philippines in 1982. She was nearly eight. For nine
months she stayed in a refugee hostel in East Hills with
her relations who had escaped with her from Vietnam.
There was her grandfather Ong Ngoai, Uncle Duong,
Auntie Ai-Van and their three daughers: a dactylic triplet
of pretty, hair-tossing girls who came to be known collectively as Stephanie-Tiffany-Melanie. They were much
older than she was. They did not play with her. They
rolled their eyes and giggled when they looked at her, and
they linked themselves with secrets breathed behind
cupped hands. Then there was Uncle Duc, Auntie Phi-

Phuong and their two sons, Van and Thuy, who were too bitterly engaged in their own intense rivalry to pretend any interest in her.

Her mother Ly-Linh, Tien was brusquely told, had not escaped from Vietnam. When she asked why not, the adults refused to discuss the matter further. It was left to Stephanie-Tiffany-Melanie to tell her that her mother had given up her place in the boat for Ong Ngoai.

'He begged her to escape,' Tiffany volunteered. 'He said you needed her to look after you.'

'She didn't want to, I suppose.'

'She didn't look after you very much even when we were in Vietnam.'

'She left you with our mother and went out to work.'

'As a bar-girl. She knew lots of American men.'

'Maybe she had a boyfriend waiting for her. That's why she didn't want to get on the boat and come with you.'

'She had many boyfriends in Saigon.'

'Even *black* American ones. Like your father. They were not married when they had you, you know.'

'She did not behave well during the war.'

The girls giggled. They were not deliberately cruel; they were at an age when the sexual exploits of adults provoked avid curiosity and half-mocking, half-uneasy laughter.

Tien did not say anything, but she felt the stirrings of shame for her mother. Later, she asked Auntie Ai-Van what had happened to Ly-Linh.

'Duong wrote to our neighbours in Cholon, but we never heard from her. The communists came and got her, I suppose,' Auntie Ai-Van said in Vietnamese. 'Better not talk about her, Tien. You just be a good girl. Life is hard enough without fighting ghosts as well.'

Eventually, Uncle Duong's family moved into a small, red-brick, white-trimmed 1960s apartment block in Auburn along a fissured bitumen street near the train station. Further down the road, halal butchers and kebab eateries nestled next to Chinese poultry shops, Vietnamese grocery stores and narrow doorways where bright-coloured bolts of cheap synthetic cloth angled out of cardboard boxes. The Hos were invisible in the multicultural mix. They felt safe.

The family argued long and hard over who should be responsible for bringing up Tien: Duong, with his three girls, or Duc, with his two sons. In the end, Duong got Tien, and Ong Ngoai went to live with his younger son, Duc.

'You can come stay with us, Tien,' Auntie Ai-Van said kindly, and Tien said thank you politely.

She knew that she had debts to repay, but she was only eight. There was nothing she could give this family which was almost-but-not-quite hers. There was nothing she could lay down at their feet like a puppy plopping down a well-chewed bone, mouth open and tongue lolling in the hope of eliciting a laugh and a pat. She tried to keep out of Stephanie-Tiffany-Melanie's way whenever she could. When she could not, she sucked in her stomach, tucked her things tightly around her and tried to take up as little space as possible in their shared bedroom. She never lost her temper and she never showed her hurt. She kept her feelings to herself and tried to efface herself from their lives. They did not mean to be unkind, but there was a shortage of mothers, and not enough of Auntie Ai-Van to go around.

Then Tien had to repeat Year 3 and, because of that, she met Nigel Gibson and acquired her second surrogate mother.

Tien's new classroom was a demountable aluminium cage which steamed in summer and froze in winter. The desks were arranged in pairs. At the start of the school year, the children were allowed to choose whom they wished to sit next to. Tien stood at the front of the class and watched as everyone else partnered up. Finally, there was no-one left but a fat, freckled kid with muddy brown eyes and a thick thatch of coffee-coloured hair. A birthmark in the shape of Tasmania drifted southwards under his right cheekbone towards the isthmus of his ear. His meaty shoulders, swelling under a too-tight grey school shirt, were slumped in the expectation of rejection. Even when the teacher introduced him as Nigel Gibson, he barely looked up from the polished gloss of his large black school shoes.

They were the two class rejects. They had no choice but to sit next to each other. Tien did not talk to him much at first, and he kept his face carefully turned away from her. Even when he forgot his red pen which he used to rule the margins in his exercise book, he did not ask to borrow hers although it was in plain sight. He just sat there, growing red-faced with silent anxiety.

Gibbo was a bubble boy, a hungry soul encased in a stout body. Trapped behind his physical and social ineptitude, he looked out longingly at the world that passed him by. At lunchtime he sat by himself, breathing heavily as he turned the pages of a picture book wedged between the folds of his stomach and his thighs. He cast occasional furtive glances at boys roughing each other up, girls skipping or swinging from the monkey bars, kids swapping the toy fad of the month. Nobody ever played with him. The only notice they tossed his way came via the occasional well-aimed missile—a scrunched-up brown paper bag, an empty drink carton, a browning apple core— hurtling towards his head.

By Year 3, he had learnt that school was about survival. All he had to do was survive until the last bell rang and he could scurry back home, safe. He couldn't afford to look ahead to the long years of primary and high school that stretched before him. One day at a time was best and, by the age of eight, Gibbo knew that he could live through almost anything, even the scatalogical atrocities children were sometimes driven to perpetrate. He didn't need to reach Year 9 and read *The Lord of the Flies* in order to learn the cruelty that lurked inside kids. He was used to being the schoolyard reject, the fat kid everyone picked on. He even resigned himself to a weekly wedgie.

Then one day, Tien walked across the playground and sat down beside him. He looked at her in faint alarm. He knew she was supposed to have come from Vietnam, but she did not look properly Asian. She was repeating Year 3 and she was two years older than everyone else. In winter, her skin was the warm colour of a piece of KFC chicken, freckled with those eleven secret herbs and spices. In summer, she tanned to a crisp dark shade of honey-soy chicken wings. Her black hair kinked wildly around a raw-boned face.

She had enormous cow eyes and a big, wide mouth like Whoopi Goldberg. When she laughed, she looked like a Muppet. Her nose was large and flat. Stephanie-Tiffany-Melanie insisted that she sleep with a wooden peg pinned to her nose in order to raise the bridge. They had seen it on *Little Women*. For a year and a half, she did as they demanded and she got used to breathing through her mouth, panting like an over-grown mongrel.

She wasn't Asian, she wasn't even Eurasian. The other Asian girls whispered that so-and-so heard someone say that Tien's father had been a black man. One day a few of the older boys yelled at her crudely, 'Hey, Abo! Whatcha doin' here?'

After her shower that night, she wiped away the steam from the mirror and stared at herself, running her water-wrinkled fingers over the homely reflection. Then she padded out to the living room in her pyjamas and asked Uncle Duong, 'Was my father a black man?'

He was embarrassed so he pretended not to hear. She asked again, but still he ignored her. Finally, Ong Ngoai, who was having dinner with them that night, beckoned to her.

'He was only half black. *Un métis*,' her grandfather said. He rarely spoke to Tien but when he did, it was usually in French. The French might have vacated Vietnam more than three decades ago, but they had never vacated Ong Ngoai's head. '*Il était Américain*.'

Tien was delighted. 'Cool,' she pronounced care-fully, still prodding her way through the idiom of casual conversation.

But Auntie Ai-Van frowned disapprovingly. 'We shouldn't talk about your father or mother.'

Tien went around telling everybody that her father was American. She watched *The Cosby Show* on television and fell in love with the family. She imagined her father as a Bill Cosby look-alike, loping along the skyscrapered streets of a blindingly bright American city that held out the promise of everything she could ever ask for or even dream of. Some day, he would return and claim her. He would take her back to America, and at last she would go home.

Had she not been two years older and taller than most of her classmates, she would have been bullied mercilessly. As it was, kids sidled around her and left her alone. By default, she was thrown together with Gibbo for every activity where a partner was needed, and so he became her first friend. There was nobody else. And when Gibbo saw her struggling with English, he mentioned hesitantly that his mother was an English teacher and an elocutionist; perhaps Tien could have some after-school tutoring. Desperate not to live through Year 3 a third time, Tien asked Uncle Duong and Auntie Ai-Van if she could have after-school lessons with Mrs Gibson.

'Why should she have lessons specially?' Stephanie-Tiffany-Melanie protested.

'So expense,' Auntie Ai-Van agreed doubtfully, but Ong Ngoai overruled them. They had to make up for Tien's mother's sacrifice, he reminded his son and daughter-in-law. They had a debt to repay.

'What sacrifice?' Tien asked, but as usual the child's question was ignored.

Tien was allowed to go home with Gibbo three times a week. She had her English lesson for an hour, then she did her homework with Gibbo. Uncle Duong picked her up afterwards. The first time he came to fetch Tien, he stared in amazement at Gibbo's father and blinked hard. 'Oh, it is really Bob Gibson!' he said, clasping the other man's hand warmly and pumping it up and down. Then Bob's eyes bulged in alarm as he was enfolded in the ropey arms of a skinny man a full head shorter than himself and probably half his weight. 'Thank you, thank you very much.'

Gillian was surprised. She later asked her husband curiously, 'Do you know Tien's uncle then?'

He reddened a little and, looking away from her, mumbled, 'Yeah. Knew the family when I was in Saigon.'

'Imagine that,' Gillian marvelled. 'A small world indeed!'

She nagged Bob to invite the Hos over for a barbecue lunch. He only said, 'Give it a rest. They won't want to come. Things were different back then.'

Tien was afraid of Bob at first. He was a thickset, red-faced man who clipped his hair military-short and snorted and stamped around his house, grizzling at everyone when his sciatica pained him. It seemed that his favourite pastime was baiting his wife. They argued constantly about things that did not matter to Tien.

One evening, when Gillian invited Tien to stay for dinner after an English lesson, she said, 'Your father was a soldier, wasn't he, Tien? I wonder whether he ever came across Bob. Bob was called up to be in the war, you know. They drew the marble with his birth date on it, so he went and did his duty.'

'Bloody thanks I got for it,' Bob grouched. He got up from the dinner table and hunched himself into his easy chair. His hand snaked around the cluttered coffee table, groping for the remote control.

'You could have conscientiously objected, like my brother did,' Gillian pointed out. She said to Tien, 'I myself marched in the Sydney moratorium. We met at the Roundhouse at New South Wales uni and then we marched down George Street. It was one of the most exciting times of my life.'

Bob looked away from the footy on the TV. 'You know what they ask you when you object?' he said. 'You go to court and then they ask you how you'd feel if you came home and found your sister being raped by an Asian because you didn't do your duty. I wonder what your brother had to say to that.'

'Bob, shush,' Gillian said. She frowned and jerked her head in Tien's direction. She was always alert to the slightest hint of perceived racism from Bob or anyone else. She sped to that place of hurt feelings before Tien had even lifted her foot to start the journey.

'Don't you shush me,' Bob said. 'I got a right to say what I want to say and if Tina listened, she'd learn something about this country.'

They started arguing again. Tien shifted uncomfortably. She had never heard Auntie Ai-Van or Auntie Phi-Phuong disagreeing so heatedly with their husbands. She did not know whether to be shocked at Gillian, or to admire her.

She looked down at the roast Gillian had made for dinner and tried to ignore the Gibsons. She did not want to remember Vietnam. She did not want to hear about the

American war. As far as she was concerned, her life began in the refugee camp in the Philippines and even those memories were fading rapidly. In a few more years, she would finally forget everything that had happened to her and her family before they came to Australia. Maybe then she would stop grinding her teeth in her sleep at night.

Tien wanted to be like everyone else, but with Gillian Gibson it was hard to forget that she was a refugee. Gillian was a curious woman. She wanted to know about the war, about Tien's experience as a refugee, and she was always looking out for discriminatory newspaper articles about Cabramatta—Vietnamatta, the schoolkids called it—to show Tien so that they could get upset together.

'I'm really going to have to write to the *Herald* again,' Gillian would say, looking annoyed and tapping the newspaper which was neatly folded open at a particular article. 'They've gone too far this time with all these articles about Vietnamese crime gangs. I remember back in the seventies there were plenty of silly scruffy young lads running around in surfie gangs. It's racist, that's what it is.'

When Gillian said those things, she made Tien feel like a Cause, as though she was being diluted into a group she didn't really want to belong to: the South Vietnamese who suffered during the war. Those unfortunate boat people—who did not necessarily accept Tien as one of themselves. Gillian made Tien aware of problems she didn't want to know about, because all she wanted was to be a normal, everyday Australian. She wanted to be Bob Gibson's 'Tina' who came around and played with Gibbo, learned to broaden her speech and toss in the odd slang word as she listened to Bob grouching about pollies and people in general. She wanted to be an ordinary Aussie girl who learned to cook chops and make chocolate crackles with Gillian.

'My mother used to do this with me when I was a child,' Gillian said to her one Saturday afternoon as they pored over a folder full of yellowing recipes together.

Tien looked at her and wondered if Gillian understood how important it was for her to do these mundane mother–daughter things with this white Australian woman. When Gillian didn't go on and on about Vietnam and refugees, there was nobody Tien loved more. This was the woman who taught her English, tested her spelling, accompanied her to parent–teacher meetings and took her to swimming lessons with Gibbo. She sewed Tien costumes for the school musical, threw a birthday party for her, and even bought Tien her first white cotton triple-A cup bra at the age of eleven. Tien wore her new bra all the time, even when she was sleeping, until it grew limp and grey. She would not take it off to let Auntie Ai-Van wash it and she got scolded for that.

A few months later, Gillian gave Tien a slightly battered copy of *Where Did I Come From?* and showed her a video—borrowed from the local library—about menstruation and sex education. It featured coltish long-haired girls asking innocent questions of their knowing older sisters and comfortably smiling mothers. It was a short film oozing oestrogen. There were female hugs and laughter and lots of butterflies and a pony in a meadow at the end. Sitting in Gillian's bedroom watching this video, Tien dreamed about slipping her hand into the older woman's. She longed for the intimacy of mother–daughter chats. She looked at Gillian, but she was shy and could not think of a single thing to say.

Then Gillian rewound the tape, opened her linen cupboard and gave Tien a fat pink plastic bag of bulky sanitary pads and a small floral box of tampons which, Gillian warned, were only to be used during swimming season. Tien put the pads and tampons into her backpack and hugged it to herself like a secret. It made her feel good when she went back home to Uncle Duong's flat. She kept them in her bag and carried them to school for the next fortnight until she found a hiding place to stash her treasure. At night, she lay on her mattress on the floor and as she listened to the regular breathing of Stephanie-Tiffany-Melanie deep in sleep, she thought about Gillian and silently tested the word on her lips: 'Mum'.

One Saturday morning in early May, Tien caught a train to the Flemington markets and bought some flowers. The next day, she begged Uncle Duong to drop her off at the Gibsons' house in Homebush. Gillian opened the door and welcomed her with a big smile when she saw the yellow chrysanthemums Tien held out to her.

'Oh, how lovely, Tien!'

'Happy Mother's Day,' Tien said. There was an awkward pause. Gillian looked at her and Tien suddenly felt she had made a terrible mistake. Perhaps this was a stranger after all; nothing more than the mother of her best friend.

Then she saw the tip of Gillian's nose reddening with emotion. Gillian took the flowers. She bent down and hugged Tien. She hadn't hugged anybody for such a long time, not since her son started primary school. She had not realised how much she'd missed the comfort of close contact with a child's sturdy body. 'Thank you.'

'You're welcome,' Tien said. Silently, she added, 'Mum.'

'Tell you what. Why don't you spend the day with us if your Auntie Ai-Van doesn't mind?'

'All right.' And she could not remember being happier.

When Tien was thirteen her mother reappeared in her life. That was the winter Gibbo's piano teacher, Miss Yipsoon, developed pneumonia and had to be hospitalised. Gillian brought Miss Yipsoon's mother her meals and took her out for regular walks.

Old Mrs Yipsoon had already had one hip replacement. She lived at the top of a hill near Strathfield train station and she liked to walk down to the shopping centre, sit in the square for a while, then toddle off home. It was the return journey that took the longest time, for Mrs Yipsoon had a bad heart and that, coupled with arthritis and the dodgy hip, made the climb uphill seem interminable. Furthermore, she was a squat woman shaped like a butternut pumpkin, so it was a huge effort to haul that bulk uphill. Gillian had to push or tug her while she puffed all the way.

Tien was having her English lesson one Thursday afternoon when Gillian suddenly remembered that she could not take old Mrs Yipsoon for a walk on Friday morning because she had to go for a mammogram.

'And I can't take her on Saturday because Bob and I have a wedding to attend. Then my sister is coming to stay with us next week so we'll be busy then. I won't have

the time to take her for a walk until the week after,'
Gillian said, getting up to look at the calendar which was
stuck on the fridge door. 'Poor thing. Her knees will get
so stiff without the exercise.'

'We'll take her, Mrs Gibson,' Tien volunteered.
Immediately, Gibbo kicked her foot under the table.

'We can't,' he said. 'We've got exams coming up.
Remember? We have to study on the weekend.'

Gillian said, 'That's very kind of you, Tien. But Nigel
is right. You should study. I mustn't put you kids out.'

'It's okay, Mrs Gibson. In Asian culture we respect the
elderly and treat them with consideration,' Tien said vir-
tuously. 'We can study after we come back.'

'Crawler,' Gibbo muttered under his breath, but she
just smiled smugly.

She was uplifted by the novelty of her altruism until
she, Gibbo and Mrs Yipsoon started the return journey up
the steep slope.

'One of you kids get in front of me and start pulling.
The other get behind me and push,' panted Mrs Yipsoon.
'Go on. Push! Put some effort into it. Aaah! Stupid kids.
Not so hard!'

Progress was slow. People were beginning to stare at
the spectacle they made. Shopkeepers wandered out into the
street to look and grin. Traffic slowed and the occasional
car honked cheekily.

Then Tien was dazzled by inspiration. 'Mrs Yipsoon,'
she said. 'I know what's wrong. You're not doing it right.'

'I've been walking since before you or your mother
was born,' Mrs Yipsoon snapped. 'I've just about mastered
it by now.'

'No, what I mean is, you don't have any problems going *down*hill, do you?'

'No. Of course not. Downhill's easy.'

'Well then,' Tien said triumphantly. 'What you need to do is to fool your body into thinking you're going downhill when you're actually going uphill.'

'Huh?'

'You need to turn around and walk up the hill backwards. The knee and ankle motion will then be the same as if you're going downhill.'

Gibbo started to make gobbling noises like a turkey. 'Hang on, hang on,' he started, but Tien was on a roll and she ignored him.

'Trust me, Mrs Yipsoon,' Tien said earnestly. 'This is scientifically proven. I've seen it done before. In fact, there's an old woman round the corner from where I live and I help her to walk backwards all the time.'

Gibbo snorted derisively. 'Yeah, right, you dag,' he muttered, elbowing Tien. 'And her name is the invisible woman.'

'Is that right?' Mrs Yipsoon asked suspiciously, but Tien could see that she was struck by the idea.

'Every week. Swear to god.'

'Well, if you're sure . . .'

A few minutes later, old Mrs Yipsoon was squawking in alarm and swatting at Tien and Gibbo with her walking cane. 'You kids are crazy!' she screeched. 'You have no respect for the elderly. I'm going to ring your mothers and tell them about this. I'm going to report you to the police!'

'But you're making great progress,' Tien insisted stubbornly. 'You have to keep going.'

By now Gibbo had got into the sheer fun of making Mrs Yipsoon walk backwards. 'Go on, Mrs Yipsoon. There's no other way we can get you up the hill. You're too fat otherwise.'

Mrs Yipsoon grew red-faced in alarm as they surged towards her and, to their great delight, she retreated a few steps backwards up the hill. They shouted out encouragements and whooped and danced around her. Flustered and angry, she brandished her walking stick at them while lifting her foot to take another step back. For a split-second, they caught a glimpse of the pavement without either of her feet on it. For a moment of liquified time she was suspended in midair like the coyote in the Roadrunner cartoon.

And then the old woman's shriek was a whiplash on Tien's conscience. She felt the sickening crunch of bone as it hit the pavement, as though it was her own hip that had fractured. She screamed along with Mrs Yipsoon and rushed to her side. The old woman had passed out.

Tien wanted to be punished by Gillian. She needed to feel a pain so bad—the pain of a broken hip and fractured wrist— that it would make her pass out with relief. Perhaps only then would Gillian talk to her; perhaps only then would she begin to feel better about herself again. She needed to atone but there was nothing she could do. The Gibsons did not want her at the hospital. Bob sent her home in disgrace.

She climbed up to Uncle Duong's apartment, toed off her running shoes and placed them neatly among the flock of shoes herded onto a clear plastic sheet by the doorway. And she noticed a pair of shoes she had never seen before.

Pointy red court shoes, badly scuffed. They had a visitor. She was relieved. That ought to delay her showdown with Auntie Ai-Van.

She stepped into the living room. Uncle Duong was there. So were Uncle Duc and Auntie Phi-Phuong and their two sons. And, seated on the sofa beside Uncle Duong, who had his arm wrapped around her shoulders, was a thin woman whose shoulder-length black hair was liberally streaked with grey. Her face was gaunt and expressionless, but Tien realised that the shape of her eyes was familiar. She looked at those eyes every day when she stared in the bathroom mirror.

Nobody said anything. Then Auntie Ai-Van came in from the kitchen carrying a tray of *che ba mau* drinks. She stopped, looked around, and carefully placed the tray on the table. Then she came towards Tien, put her hands on the girl's shoulders and shook her.

'Mrs Gibson rang. You are so naughty,' she sighed. Then she took Tien's hand and led her towards the sofa.

'Tien,' she said. 'This is Linh. Your mother.'

The woman stood up and looked at her. 'I have to punish you, Tien,' she said. 'The first time I see you in eight years, I have to punish you. Do you understand?'

Tien simply stood there and stared at the carpet. This was the woman who had given up a place in the refugee boat even though it meant giving up her daughter. She would not look at this stranger who claimed to be her mother.

Tien was grounded. She had to come straight home after school, do her homework by herself and help Auntie Ai-Van with the housework. Auntie Ai-Van had never talked much to her, but now she seemed embarrassed and uneasy. Every time she spoke to Tien, she cast a quick glance over her shoulder towards the living room where the woman Linh was sleeping in a corner. Linh slept a lot at first. Then, eventually, she roused herself and tried to talk to Tien. She poked and pried into Tien's life. Tien answered her politely but briefly, and she took care to avoid the woman's gaze.

After a month, Tien was allowed to resume her visits to Gibbo's house. One Saturday morning, she helped Gibbo and Bob rake up the leaves in the garden, then they washed Bob's car. After that, she and Gibbo went inside the house and poured themselves a drink. Gillian was ironing a pair of trousers. Tien said to Gillian, 'Mrs Gibson, is there anything I can help you with now?'

Gillian finished the trouser leg, then rested the iron precisely on its stand. She looked at Tien and said, 'It's very nice of you to come around and help us, Tien, but I think you'd better go home now. Your mother just rang to ask if you were still here. In fact, you should probably spend more time at home. Your mother might need some help too.'

The words were innocuous but the implied rejection was swift and stunning, a lightning-quick punch to the solar plexus. Tien looked at Gillian and told herself she did not care. Her lips thinned and twisted into a cynical smile. She shrugged and said carelessly, 'Yeah, you're probably right, Mrs Gibson.'

By the time she got home, she had magnified the tiny incident in her mind. She smashed her mental idol of

Gillian and dragged it through the mire of her bitter thoughts. There was something in her which shored up pain and exulted in hurt. She lashed herself into a frenzy of self-pity and wanted to feel sorrier still. That night, while Stephanie-Tiffany-Melanie were out with their Vietnamese friends, she shut herself into her bedroom and cried in the dark. She wept for a mother, any mother. For the first time, she wanted the woman Linh to scratch on the door and push into the bedroom. She wanted her mother to sit on her bed and enfold her in a hug. She wanted Linh to ferret out what was wrong with her.

'What's the matter?'

'Nothing.'

'Something's the matter. Why are you crying?'

'It's nothing.'

'Tell me.'

'No.'

'I love you. I won't go away until you tell me what's wrong.'

'All right then. Only if you really want to know.'

She raised the volume of her sobs so that Linh might hear her through the closed door. She waited and waited, but Linh never came, and neither did Auntie Ai-Van.

The next day, she took the pink bag of sanitary pads Gillian had given her, tore open the pack and slowly began to shred the fat pads one by one. When it proved slow going, she took a knife from the kitchen and locked herself in the bathroom while she slashed the pads to pieces. Then she stuffed the scraps back into the bag and dumped it in the communal rubbish bins behind the apartment block.

An Ignorance of
Hieu Thao

'A home where love and concord reign,' Kieu said,
'whose heart won't yearn for it?'

Nguyen Du, *The Tale of Kieu*

Ho Ly-Linh was not a woman given to self-reflection, but if she thought about her life at all, the thing that amazed her most was not that she had survived, but how quickly and easily she could forget.

In her days of listlessness, prostrated on the sofa in her brother Duong's living room, she watched daytime television and forgot herself in other people's pain. There were those on television talk shows who revelled in remembered traumas; who believed that by recovering the past and reliving pain, they could conjure up the meaning of their lives. They told and retold their autobiographies in the hope that, this time, the end result would be something different from the disappointment life generally turned out to

43

be. This time there would be healing. There would be wholeness. They would at last achieve normality.

Linh wanted nothing to do with this process. In the dark humidity of hot summer nights in western Sydney, when the desk-fan rattled and wheezed in its steel cage beside her mattress and the apartment exhaled the stale breath of fish sauce and fried garlic from the night's dinner, she sometimes tossed in restless sleep and was chased by nightmares of long hours spent hacking fruitlessly at a feral jungle, nothing to fill her stomach at the end of the day but a fistful of boiled bamboo.

She dreamed of lying atop hessian sacks of manure in a cargo hold, less than half a foot of rank air between her body and the splintered underside of the boat deck, knees drawn up to her chest for hours on end, cramping in pain until numbness set in and she could no longer straighten her limbs to climb up for air, even if there had been room for one more in the crush of bodies above deck. She had squeezed her eyes shut, pinched her nose closed, and inhaled through gritted teeth, but still she tasted shit in her mouth. She told herself over and over that survival was a matter of one slow breath after another.

Snared in sleep, she dreamed of the shuddering collision of wooden boats, heard the heavy splash of bodies hitting the South China Sea and the shrieks of women overhead. She felt her heart jump into her mouth as she was dragged off the manure heap and she whimpered into sudden wake-fulness. She slid her trembling hand between her thighs and cupped her crotch to reassure herself that her nightmares had not violated her body. She rolled off her mattress and waited in silence to see whether she had woken anyone up.

Then she levered herself off the carpet and staggered to the bathroom to boil herself clean under the shower.

Who wanted to relive such things? Who wanted to remember the bloated bodies of the dead gently bumping the boat, or eyes like lychees which stared up blindly into a glazed ceramic sky? She believed that her best chance of becoming normal lay in forgetting the past.

One day, she woke up and felt inexplicably energised. She donned a pair of black and white checked trousers, pulled a pink sweatshirt over her head, crammed a white lawn-bowls hat over her untidy hair and let herself out of the apartment. She strode briskly past brick and weather-board houses with their lolling tongues of parched lawn and the bare antlers of thorny rose bushes. She headed for the local shops and bought a sackful of groceries so that she could prepare dinner for Duong's family that night. Then she stopped in front of a hairdressing salon. After slight hesitation, she stepped inside and immediately felt comforted by the clean smell of hair chemicals and the warm gusts of air from the huffing dryers. She had her hair cut to a shoulder-length bob and a henna rinse put through it. When she stared at her reflection in the long mirrors that lined the salon she fancied that, apart from her eyes, she looked Korean or Japanese rather than Viet-namese. It made her smile self-consciously. She had her nails manicured and, when she caught sight of her scarlet toenails peeping through her strappy sandals, she felt that she was ready to take on the world.

Two months later, she got herself a job at Lidcombe hospital, then she rented an apartment in Flemington and moved in there with Tien, despite her daughter's protests.

'Why do you complain?' Linh demanded. As usual, Tien winced at the sound of her mother's voice. Unlike Auntie Ai-Van and Auntie Phi-Phuong, Linh did not often speak Vietnamese to her family. Instead, she spoke rather formal English tainted with a faint American accent—evidence, Stephanie-Tiffany-Melanie claimed gleefully, of all those American GIs.

'Stephanie said you do not like sharing the bedroom with them. You will have more space now.'

'I want to live with Auntie Ai-Van and Uncle Duong,' Tien muttered.

'Well, you cannot do that. You have to live with me,' Linh said, and she was compelled to remind Tien, 'I *am* your mother, Tien. Where is your respect?'

You haven't earned it, Tien decided, but the thought did not sit comfortably with her because a large part of her was still Vietnamese, however much she might flail against it. She felt guilty, for she could not deny the ties of blood and the claims of family. Only in the West did respect need to be earned; to her mother, it ought to be automatically given. She was miserable in her confusion. She watched *The Wizard of Oz* again and read *Anne of Green Gables*. Sometimes she wished she was still an orphan.

Linh tried to be a good mother. She went to Cabramatta and bought material to sew dresses that Tien refused to wear. She got up early in the morning to cook *pho* for Tien's breakfast, but Tien went out to the corner store and returned with Coco Pops and a carton of milk. She made Tien come straight home from school instead of going over to the Gibsons', and when she was not on nightshift at the hospital, she sat at the kitchen table opposite Tien and watched her daughter doing her homework. Sometimes she wanted to reach out and touch her daughter's face; to trace her fingers over those jutting cheekbones and that wide mouth. But she kept her hands to herself and drove her daughter hard. There was nothing to be gained by softness and leniency; she had survived a tough world and she would bring her daughter up to do the same.

'I don't see why I have to do this on a Friday night,' Tien whined. She pushed petulantly at her textbooks and felt pleased when they tilted off the table and slapped onto the tiled kitchen floor.

'You have exams coming up.'

'In eight weeks.'

'You have to make sacrifices and work hard if you want to get anywhere in this country. Life is difficult and you won't survive unless you study.'

'You're the only one making my life difficult,' Tien grumbled. 'I never get to hang out with Gibbo anymore.'

'Why don't you have any female friends?' Her mother's tone was almost accusing.

Tien shook her head incredulously. It was the hypocrisy which galled her. This was the woman who had worked as a bar-girl and hung out with American soldiers, who got knocked up by a Bill Cosby look-alike (perhaps). She was in no position to criticise. Still, there were many things a Vietnamese daughter could not say.

'I don't like girls. They don't like me. Anyway, Gibbo was my first friend. I had him when I didn't have anyone else.'

Linh looked at her daughter and was filled with feelings of guilt and inadequacy. She had not been there for her daughter. She said, 'You can hang out with Gibbo if you bring him here.'

'No way. There's nothing to do here.'

'I want to meet him,' her mother insisted. 'If you're going to hang around with a boy, I want to know who he is.'

The first time Tien brought Gibbo to meet her mother, Linh was kneeling beside a vegetable bed in the common garden of the apartment block. He couldn't really see what she looked like. Linh was wearing a navy-blue baseball cap with NY emblazoned in white. The lower half of her face was hidden by a pink bandanna with blue teddy bears on it, folded diagonally and secured across her nose and cheekbones so that her eyes were the only part of her face that peeked out from under the bill of the cap. She wore a long-sleeved blue gingham shirt and hot pink dish-washing gloves that reached halfway up her forearms. She clutched a trowel in one hand and the straggly roots of Vietnamese mint in the other.

Tien stopped short and rolled her eyes at the sight of her mother. Embarrassment was fast becoming a reflex where her mother was concerned.

'Mum, this is Gibbo,' Tien muttered.

'*Chao co*,' he uttered carefully. He'd been pestering Tien for Vietnamese phrases all the way from Flemington station where she'd met his train. 'It's great to meet you, Mrs—' He flushed as he suddenly realised he didn't know what to call her. He knew that she had not been married to Tien's father.

'You can call me Miss Ho.'

Gibbo liked her immediately. Her voice was soft and

her eyes were friendly. They crinkled up in a smile as she shook Gibbo's hand.

'All right,' he said obligingly. 'Hey, you've got Tien's eyes, you know that?' He nudged Tien and grinned at her. 'Isn't that great?'

'Yeah, well, her eyes are all you can see,' Tien said acidly. 'Mum, what do you think you're doing? Take off your gloves. You look ridiculous.'

'I protect my skin from sunburn,' Linh explained. 'I do not want my skin to get dark from the sun. You must cover up too, Tien. Look at your skin!'

Tien had always been sensitive about the swarthiness of her complexion. She glared at Linh and snorted rudely. She thought of Bob Gibson and channelled him into her speech. 'Fair dinkum? You look bloody ridiculous. You're not in Vietnam anymore, you know.'

Her mother's eyes hardened. 'But I am still Vietnamese and you cannot speak to me like that. Do you not understand *hieu thao*?'

'No, because I don't speak Vietnamese,' Tien said defiantly. 'I'm Australian.'

'Hey, c'mon, Tien,' Gibbo said uncomfortably. He shuffled his feet and could not think of anything to say that would diffuse the tension in the air. He said tritely, 'Tien has told me a lot about you, Miss Ho.'

'Is that so?' Linh said. She gave her daughter a quick, measured glance. 'That is difficult for me to believe. What have you told him, Tien?'

'Nothing. He's just being a dag,' Tien said. She turned away and tugged Gibbo's arm. 'C'mon, Gibbo. Let's walk down to the shops. I feel like some *goi cuon*.'

'Tien, I cannot allow you to go anywhere until you apologise,' Linh said. She added, 'You know I don't want to punish you, but when you are disrespectful . . .'

'Jeez, all right, all right. Sorry. Didn't mean to be disrespectful, blah, blah. Now can I go?'

'You know, I can make some *goi cuon* for you and Gibbo, if you like,' Linh said. Holding out her olive branch.

Tien felt a pinprick of remorse. She tried to soften her tone. 'It's okay,' she said. 'I feel like a walk anyway. We'll drop in at Uncle Duc's restaurant and get something to eat.'

She grabbed Gibbo's arm and dragged him away. They walked down The Crescent towards the shops and he said, 'What's wrong with you? You didn't even give me a chance to talk or say goodbye to your mum properly.'

Tien knew she had behaved badly in front of Gibbo but she felt angry with him for commenting on it. She said shortly, 'Nothing's wrong. I'm just hungry, that's all.'

'Yeah, right. Anyway, I don't reckon you ought to talk that way to your mum, even if you've got a beef with her.'

Something cracked inside Tien's head. She stopped and flung off Gibbo's arm. 'What would you know about it? Just because you haven't the guts to stand up to your old man doesn't mean I'm the same. And where the fuck do you get off telling me how to act and what to do?'

Gibbo hated raised voices and hostile confrontations. She knew that. His face was hot and his eyes watered a little. He turned away and sniffed. She felt a small nudge of shame but shook it off.

'Go ahead and cry like a baby then,' she said unkindly. 'You're such a wuss.'

'I'm going home,' he said.

'Go on, then. I'm not stopping you.'

She watched as he shuffled down The Crescent, past the shops, towards Homebush. He was a hundred metres away when she started sprinting after him.

'Gibbo! I'm sorry. Wait up!'

He stopped immediately and waited until she caught up with him. That was Gibbo all over. He could never hold a grudge and he didn't have it in him to make her earn his forgiveness.

She flung her arms around him and said, 'I'm really sorry. I shouldn't have yelled at you like that.'

They were near Airey Park now so they cut across the grass and sat down on the swings. She shut her eyes and twisted her seat round and round, then lifted her legs off the ground, spinning rhythmically as the swing unwound.

'You all right?' he asked. He put a diffident hand on her shoulder, wanting to comfort, afraid of being thrust away.

'I don't know what's wrong with me these days,' she confessed, scuffing the dirt to stop the motion of the swing. She bent over and buried her face in her hands. 'It's scary, what I feel. She's my mum. I'm supposed to love her, but mostly I hate her and I don't even know why. I wish she'd never come back. Sometimes I wish she'd just stayed dead.'

Then she sat up, fished in her backpack for a tissue and blew her nose.

'Damn. I really hate crying. My eyes get puffed up and I look like a freak. Or more of one than usual.' She turned to Gibbo and said, 'I really am sorry, you know. Don't hate me, okay? You're my best friend. I didn't mean to take it out on you like that.'

''s all right,' he said. He rubbed her shoulder. 'Want to tell me about it?'

'Nah. Doesn't help. It's just Vietnamese mother–daughter shit, you know? Anyway, I don't want to talk about her anymore, all right?'

'Yeah, sure.'

She swiped the tissue under her nose again and said, 'I just wish I could have a normal family like yours, you know.'

He looked away and kept silent.

Later that afternoon, Tien went home and tried to make it up to Linh. She unpegged the clothes from the communal clothes lines, folded underwear and ironed shirts. She vacuumed the carpet in the living room and bedrooms, cleaned the bathroom and scrubbed the shower cubicle free of mould. She checked the fridge and saw that the little glass jar of *nuoc cham* was nearly empty, so she made more of the dipping sauce. She washed and shredded the mint leaves that her mother had gathered that morning and prepared *rau thom*, arranging it neatly on two plates. She cooked *bun thit bo xao* and, as she waited for her mother to return from the hospital, she felt satisfied with her act of atonement.

Her mother was late. In the end, Tien ate by herself in front of the television.

Linh was exhausted by the time she got home. She was surprised at the trouble Tien had taken to prepare dinner but she did not have much of an appetite. She ate the stir-fried beef with rice vermicelli desultorily and said, 'Whose recipe did you use for the *nuoc cham*, Tien? The proportions of fish sauce and lemon juice aren't quite right.'

'Auntie Ai-Van's,' Tien said sulkily. 'We like it this way.'

Belatedly, Linh remembered to say, 'Thank you for

preparing dinner.' Her daughter did not answer, so she said, 'I like Gibbo. You can invite him over whenever you want to.'

Gibbo needed no second invitation. He liked Tien's mother and was comfortable with her. He came over almost every weekend and sat at the table talking to Linh, entertaining her with tales of Aussie life, helping her to cook and clean.

'Jeez, I'm bored,' Tien interrupted one morning. 'Let's go out and do something, Gibbo. Let's go to the movies or something.'

'In a minute,' he said, and continued a tedious tale he was recounting to Linh. Then he said, 'I know. Let's go to Chinatown for yum cha. Hey, Miss Ho, why don't you come along?'

Tien watched the two of them with hostile eyes. Linh was a woman who was good with men, she remembered. She had stolen Gibbo away from Tien.

The Urge to be Asian

Once in a thousand years! Is that the most
the best of friends may ever hope to meet?
Two wanderers will part ways—where shall I find
the crane, the cloud that roams the wilds and heights?

Nguyen Du, *The Tale of Kieu*

As long as Gibbo could remember, he wanted to be thinner and he wanted to be Chinese, just like Justin.

He had been ecstatic when Justin was expelled from his private school and joined him and Tien midway through high school. His two best friends—his two only friends—with him in school, fortifying him against his own oddness, demonstrating to the rest of his classmates that he was no longer an outsider. Two could still be the class rejects; three were a *gang*! He belonged to a group. Reading Dumas at the time, he liked to think of them as the Three Musketeers! All for one and one for all!

He mentioned this once, and the following afternoon Justin fashioned a pair of big black cardboard ears, stuck them onto Gibbo's head and pranced around chanting: 'M-I-C-K-E-Y M-O-U-S-E!' Then, in a pinched falsetto: 'Hello, mouseketeers. I have a message from the Mouse. He can't be with us today because he's eaten stinking blue cheese and has got the runs. For those of you hoping for a personal appearance, stiff shit. So long, boys and girls.'

'*Hi-yah*, you *chee sin lo*,' Gibbo said, laughing. He yanked off the ears and jammed them onto Justin's head.

'Oh god, here we go again.' Tien rolled her eyes.

'Your accent's terrible,' Justin said, pulling off the ears. He crushed them into a ball and tossed them from hand to hand. 'My mum'd have a fit if she heard your pronunciation.'

'Why do you keep pretending to be Chinese?' Tien said, exasperated.

'Because I am,' Gibbo said.

'It's ridiculous.'

'It's true. My great-grandfather came over from China during the gold rush. He opened a grocery store at Ballarat but they eventually moved to Sydney. Then my great-grandfather fell in love with this Anglo woman and they had an affair. When she got pregnant, her brother and their neighbours found out and they beat him up. He died in the streets, right where they left him. She had the kid but gave it up for adoption. That was my grandfather. He anglicised his name to "Gibson" and covered up his Chinese roots. But I'm actually fourth or fifth generation Chinese. My piano teacher, Miss Yipsoon, is some kind of cousin to Dad. That's the only reason why he sends me for piano lessons. It'd be too wussy otherwise.'

'Well you don't look Chinese,' Tien said, as she always did whenever Gibbo made this claim.

'But I am,' he insisted stubbornly.

Gibbo wanted so desperately to be Asian while Justin and Tien tried so hard not to be. Even as Justin had speech lessons with Gillian so that he could talk like a ponce and Tien tried her best to imitate Bob's ocker Strine, Gibbo was busy patterning his speech after Annabelle Cheong's Singlish. He peppered his speech with inappropriately placed '*lahs*', sighed '*hi-yah*', marvelled, '*Wah*, so good!' and exclaimed '*Ai-yo!*' He learned to request chillies with every meal ('*Lay pey ngor laht chiu see*,' he'd enunciate carefully in his broad Australian accent to bewildered waiters in the Vietnamese restaurants at Flemington) and asked his mother, 'Where's the *choy?*' when she brought out the chops and mashed potato.

'What *choy?*' Gillian asked, puzzled.

'Green veggies,' Gibbo explained.

'Bloody idiot,' Bob growled. 'Speak English, why can't you. And you eat what your mother puts on the table.'

Gibbo ate it, but he didn't like it. He had discovered a passion for yum cha. He loved pork and prawn dumplings and he forced himself to develop a taste for pork knuckle, braised tripe and chicken's feet. He sucked the skin off the claws, spat out the bones and looked pleased with himself when Annabelle said, '*Wah*, look. Gibbo knows how to eat *foong chow*. So clever!'

'That's because I've got a bit of Chinese in me, Auntie,' he said.

'Is it? True or not?' Gullible Annabelle, in characteristic wide-eyed wonder.

'True, you know.'

Tien just looked at him and shook her head, never able to understand why he did not want to reap the rewards of being an Aussie male.

One weekend not too long after Justin joined them in high school, they met at Gibbo's house in Homebush and cycled down Arthur Street then turned onto Centenary Drive. They made a right into Weeroona Street and thrust their bikes through the rusting iron gates of Rookwood Cemetery. Hot asphalt melted beneath soft tyres. Summer clutched them in its sweaty fist and they panted heavily as they flung their bikes aside and gained the cool concrete shelter of the green-roofed pavilion amid the Chinese gravestones. They sucked on plastic bottles of cordial and snacked on Twisties and Tim Tams, scattering their homework over the stone tables. Glancing up from algebra equations and English essays, they saw a woman stooping over a tombstone with an armful of flowers. When she straightened up, the boys saw it was Miss Yipsoon with a bag of joss sticks and plastic daffodils. She recognised them and beckoned them over.

'What are you kids doing here?' she asked. 'It's not safe to play among the dead, you know. The spirits are always watching. They might follow you home one day.'

'Dad's singing karaoke again. He thinks he can do the best Dean Martin impersonation this side of the Great Dividing Range. There's nowhere else to go where there's a bit of peace and quiet,' Justin said. 'Who are you visiting?'

'My grandmother's tomb,' Miss Yipsoon said. She moved slightly to one side and they crowded round to read: 'Mary "Chookie" Yipsoon. Died 1954. Beloved wife of Sam Ah Seng Yipsoon. Mother of Lily, Thomas and Jimmy, tragically dead at age 32.'

'Why Chookie?' they wanted to know.

'I don't know,' Miss Yipsoon said. 'I never asked my mother. All us kids just called her Por anyway. Maybe her Chinese name was Choo-Kee or something. Or maybe she raised chooks. I know one time they had a farm out Fairfield way.'

'Why was Jimmy tragically dead?'

'He was beaten to death in Surry Hills one night. Nobody knows what happened. Por never got over it. She loved him best, I think, because he was the youngest. He was really talented, Auntie Lily says. An entertainer. He did a gig at the old Tivoli once. Por wanted to bring Uncle Jimmy's body back to the ancestral homeland in China, but those were the days of the White Australia Policy and Goong, my grandfather, was never really sure that she would be allowed back into the country, so they never went.'

All this time Gibbo kept nudging Tien with his elbow. 'See! I told you how it was.' He was bursting with ancestral pride at Jimmy Yipsoon's bloody death. He wanted to say something to graft himself into the Yipsoon family, but he didn't get the chance.

Justin said facetiously, 'They could have paid the Walkers of the Dead to come and walk his corpse all the way back to China.'

'What are the Walkers of the Dead?' Gibbo wanted to know. He looked slightly crestfallen at this gap in his knowledge about Chinese culture.

'They're these really powerful mediums who are paid to make dead people get up and walk back to the ancestral burial ground so that families don't have to go to all the hassle of transporting the corpses back themselves,' Justin explained. 'My grandmother told me about them. She said that in her village, when they heard that a Walker of the Dead was coming through, everybody would rush inside their houses and bar the windows and doors until the medium and the corpse had passed through the village. If you look at the corpse, you'll drop dead.'

'Wow,' Gibbo said, suitably impressed. Then he remembered himself. 'I mean, *wah*.'

'Honestly, you kids are so silly,' Miss Yipsoon said. She pointed to a small patch on the right where modest white headstones had been washed nearly anonymous with the passage of time and the caress of the weather.

'Uncle Jimmy used to be buried over there somewhere. But a few years back Auntie Lily decided she wanted to keep the family together so she applied for the bodies to be exhumed. She bought this plot and got the Italians to make a fancy tomb for us all. Look at it.'

They surveyed the red marble tomb in silence. It was a massive slab, measuring just over a metre and a half, with sloping sides that hugged the grave like a fat mother's arms. The whole thing was enclosed by an ornamental white concrete balustrade. The front of the tomb announced ITALIAN FUNERALS in gold-leaf sans serif type. More gold leaf sprouted up each side of the gravestone, twisting into elaborate birds and flowers intertwined with Chinese characters. On the flat surface of the marble, the joss sticks which smouldered in the metal cage of a built-in censer were now joined by a pale blue vase sprouting plastic flowers.

'Isn't it a beauty?' Miss Yipsoon said. 'One day I'll also be buried here and my nephews and nieces will do what I'm doing now.' She contemplated the prospect with profound satisfaction.

'I'll definitely come and pay my respects,' Gibbo said, nodding earnestly.

'Well, I wouldn't want to be buried with my parents,' Justin said. 'I've never even had to share my room.'

'Silly kids,' Miss Yipsoon repeated, but without any real heat. She shook her head as she gathered up her bag and turned to leave. 'Don't be so careless among the dead. And you boys, don't forget to practise. B flat major and G sharp minor scales. The Clementi sonatina. Practise right and left hands separately. And don't drop your wrists!'

As she walked away, Justin looked up the gently rising ground and said, 'I'd rather be a Jew buried in the Jewish plot. They have nicer epitaphs and better taste in tomb-stones. But Asians . . .' He just shook his head, wanting, even then, to be anything but Asian.

Tien ran after the piano teacher. 'Miss Yipsoon, can I ask you something?'

'Yes, what is it?'

'Is Gibbo related to you?'

'Has he been telling you he's Chinese again?'

'Yes. Is he?'

'What do you think?'

'Well, he looks Aussie to me.'

'We're all Australians now,' Miss Yipsoon said as she walked away. 'Even if Nigel doesn't feel like one.'

For Gibbo it was never a simple matter of nationality or ethnicity or culture. It was all about friendship. When Justin first joined them in high school, he called them the multicultural reject group. He meant it in a self-disparaging way, but Gibbo revelled in the title. In their casually racist playground, there were the skips who played rugby, the wogs who played soccer, the slopes who hung out at the basketball courts, and then there was them: the multicultural reject group, who were such dags they could even encompass him. But as he watched Tien and Justin drawing closer together in the later years of high school, he felt the panicky sensation of being left out. He began to fear that it was because he was not Asian.

It bewildered him, for when he looked at Tien, he did not really see a Vietnamese. She hardly spoke Vietnamese anymore. In any case, she was a half-American . . . something. Who knew what her father was? Some of the Asian parents looked down on her, so why would she want to identify with them? Unless ethnicity was bred into your bones by the thousand daily rituals and the million different meals you ate throughout your life. Unless identity was like a radio wave that pulsed through the ether until it found an available channel which decoded it as ethnicity and broadcast that to all the world. Did Tien think of herself as Vietnamese or Australian or some hyphenated mixture? More worryingly, was there some intrinsic Asianness that would bind Tien and Justin more closely together, cutting him out of the loop and leaving him alone once again in his not-quite-Australianness?

He would have given anything to be Asian when she climbed into Justin's boat instead of his and the two of them pedalled off together during a summer holiday in Adelaide . . .

Bob was attending a medical conference in Glenelg and Gillian had persuaded him to bring the kids along because they never went anywhere. And besides, the kids would provide a buffer between husband and wife. There were moments when Gillian could not stand her husband. He was a provocative man; an educated man—a doctor— who therefore had no excuse for mocking her desire for class and culture, constantly pushing his deliberate vulgar- ities in her face. She could not forgive him for holding his own son in contempt even though, if she were honest, Nigel was something of a disappointment to her too. Gillian had always wanted a daughter. She liked the imagined neatness of little girls. She thought she had one in Tien until Linh arrived in Sydney. Still, she tried hard to be a good mother to Nigel—but boys needed fathers and Bob was not much of one. That he had agreed to take the children on holiday was a major victory for her.

It was their first trip out of Sydney together and it had taken them three days to drive to Adelaide, stopping at Mildura and the Barossa Valley on the way. Adelaide was sti- flingly hot but Gibbo, Tien and Justin loved Glenelg. They kicked around in the sand during the day, dipped into the purling waves, then walked to the end of the pier to watch the sun bleed into the sea. As deepening shadows washed over the sky, they climbed into a Ferris wheel carriage and felt the wind whipping through their hair as they jumped and rocked wildly at the zenith of the arc. They were still laughing when they were thrown off by the exasperated operator. Fairy lights flickered like a thread of stars.

As he pushed his face into a pink cloud of spun floss and tasted sugar fizzing on his tongue, Gibbo knew that this was the happiest day of his life. A feeling of melancholy followed later that night as he shut his ears to his parents' habitual bickering. He tossed in his bed and kicked at the tightly cocooned sheets. Life had been so sweet in that moment on the pier that he was afraid he would have to forfeit something precious for that feeling of perfect friendship. And therefore he was not surprised at the kick in the heart he received the following day.

Tien was already in a foul mood when they clambered onto the Glenelg Tram, riding down King William Street to Victoria Square.

'What's up?' he kept bleating anxiously.

'Shut up, Gibbo,' Tien said.

He was hurt. He noticed that she never vented her temper on anyone else but him. '*Hi-yah. Lay ho mung-chung, lah,*' he said and grinned at Justin.

'She really is irritable,' Justin agreed.

'Jeez, give it a rest, why don't you,' Tien snapped at Gibbo. 'Your accent's terrible and you're not fooling anyone that you're Chinese.'

'Come on, Tien,' Justin said, kicking her foot lightly. 'Give him a break. Let's not spoil the day, okay?'

A dishevelled young man wearing a badly stained plaid shirt, stinking of beer and urine, staggered onto the tram. He sat opposite Justin and Tien.

Justin immediately held up his left hand to his nose and pressed his fist against his nostrils. He breathed through his teeth and muttered, '*Chow toh say!*' He exchanged a quick grin with Gibbo. Tien looked bored and Gibbo felt sorry that she was being left out. He leaned towards her and explained, 'Justo says the smell will kill us.' She ignored him and smiled at Justin.

'What're you lookin' at?' the young man demanded. 'Hey! I'm talkin' to you. Bloody chink.'

'Nut case,' Justin whispered to Tien. 'We'd best ignore him.'

'What're you fuckin' whisperin'? You talkin' 'bout me? You think yer fuckin' better'n me, you fuckin' slope? Fuckin' slanty-eyed boatie. Bloody fish-breath gook.'

Tien looked at Justin. He stared fixedly at his feet and the tips of his ears were bright red. She looked around the tram and all the passengers were looking out the window or just looking away. Gibbo stared back at her, mouth clamped shut, white-faced with fright.

'Four-eyed. Yer all fuckin' four-eyed. Can't see nothin' so yer no use here. We don't want youse here. Go back to where you came from, you commie bastard boatie.'

Tien could bear it no longer. She said with exaggerated politeness, 'Excuse me. I should point out that he doesn't wear glasses and he's actually not from Vietnam. I'm the Vietnamese one here and I can assure you it's not really possible to be a commie bastard and a boatie at the same time.'

'I wasn't talkin' to you,' he snarled. 'You want me to start on you? Is that what you want, you fuckin' boong? You want me to smash this bottle an' cut ya? Go climb back up ya tree and take fuckin' four-eyes with ya.'

Justin pinched her hard and shook his head. She

nodded reluctantly and held her tongue. Two more stops to go. They had to sit there and endure it.

'Fuckin' cocksuckin' motherfuckin' slope. Stealin' our jobs. Kill youse all. Bang bang. Get rid of all you chinks.'

Gibbo couldn't stand it any longer. He pulled the cord and jumped off at the next stop, and the others scrambled down after him. He was so angry and ashamed that he was trembling. Tears ran down his face and slime dripped from his nostrils. He felt humiliated for Justin and Tien and himself and every single person on that tram. In the weeks to come, he would replay the incident over and over again in his head. Next time, he swore to himself, he would be prepared. Next time he would do something. He would not just sit there, dumb with shock and fright. And embarrassment. How could embarrassment be so paralysing?

'What are you crying about?' Tien said nastily. 'It didn't happen to you. You didn't do anything. You just sat there.'

'Tien, don't,' Justin said, pulling her arm gently. 'Gibbo couldn't have done anything. It might've made things worse.'

She burst into tears and Justin hugged her, patting her back and soothing her. She cried because, for a moment, when it all started, she was simply glad that it was Justin who had been targeted and not her. She was not certain that she would have spoken up if she hadn't known Justin. If he were a complete stranger, she might just have sat there and looked out the window; she would have thanked god it wasn't her and pretended it wasn't happening. Just like the other passengers.

'Come on. Let's walk,' Justin said.

They wandered along North Terrace until they reached the Torrens River. They had to split up there because Tien wanted to try out the pedal boats, which only seated two people. Gibbo clambered into a yellow boat and held out his hand for Tien. She avoided his eyes and climbed into Justin's boat instead.

Gibbo sat in his boat and watched as they pulled away from him, their two black-haired heads bending towards each other. A south-to-north magnetic attraction of Asians. He could claim to be Chinese and toss off Cantonese phrases and Singaporean exclamations, but he knew he would never be picked on like Justin or Tien because, no matter how Asian he felt inside, he looked white.

It wasn't a turning point in their friendship. Not exactly. Nor a defining moment, either. Life simply did not have sufficient clarity. Perhaps it was just the onset of awkwardness among them and the feeling that, for whatever reason, he was being left behind.

A Fistful of Happiness in the Front Seat of a Car

We chanced to meet—and ever since
I have in secret yearned and pined for you.
My slender frame has wasted—who'd have thought
that I could linger on to see this day?
For months I dreamt my goddess in the clouds;
lovelorn, I hugged my post, prepared to drown.

Nguyen Du, *The Tale of Kieu*

Linh was jealous of Annabelle Cheong in a way she hadn't been of Gillian Gibson, even though Tien continued to give Gillian Mother's Day cards. She knew that Tien gave lots of women Mother's Day cards: herself, Gillian, Ai-Van, Phi-Phuong, and Annabelle. Her daughter was sweet that way. Gillian might have tutored Tien and thrown her birthday parties as a child, but Gillian was white; she was too different to be a threat. Annabelle, however, was Asian. Linh compared herself to Annabelle, and she felt inferior.

Annabelle was not as educated as Linh, but she was still middle-class. She and Tek had migrated as much-needed professionals; they had not arrived on sufferance as refugees. She lived in an amazingly ugly, spacious, air-conditioned concrete mansion in Strathfield and employed a cleaner and a gardener. Linh did her own cleaning and gardening. Once a week, she went and cleaned other people's homes for extra cash. She was not bitter about this, but she felt wounded that Tien should esteem the Cheongs so highly and prefer their company to her own.

'After all, she cannot help you with your homework the way Mrs Gibson does,' Linh told Tien. 'The woman's English is awful.'

'She's so cool. I love the way she talks *lah*,' Tien said. 'So does Gibbo.'

'Ong Ngoai will be disappointed,' Linh said. 'He was always particular about our language. You come from educated people. Our family was well respected in Saigon.'

But Tien did not want to know about the past. 'Ancient history,' she said impatiently, waving it away with a dismissive gesture. 'Anyway, the Cheongs are not running a school. I'm not going over there to be educated. I just like hanging out there. Mr Cheong has the most amazing gadgets. Huge TV. Video camera. Computer and video games. Even a karaoke machine.'

'Why would anyone want a karaoke machine?' her mother wondered. Then she added doggedly, 'You should be studying.'

After that, Tien did not see much of her mother for the next six months. Linh did a lot of overtime at the hospital, and Tien resented her mother for telling her she had to stay at home when there was nobody else around.

She dreaded going to sleep in the silent, empty flat. She hated being alone.

Then Linh woke her early one Saturday morning. 'Come. I have a surprise for you,' said her mother excitedly. She grabbed Tien's hand, dragged her out of bed and pulled her into the living room. The carpet was strewn with plastic, packing tape, ripped cardboard and moulded polystyrene frames. Out of this wreckage rose a huge Korean-made television mounted on a grey glass cabinet. 'There. What do you think?'

'It's big,' Tien admitted. It was of such mammoth proportions that the rest of the furniture in the small living room had to be crammed together to make room for it. She stubbed her toe as she clambered over the coffee table to get to it.

'The driver came and delivered it half an hour ago. I read the instructions and connected it myself,' Linh said proudly. 'It works. Look.'

'Yeah, great.' Tien picked up the remote control and flicked on the television. She yawned. 'Nothing but cartoons and *Video Hits*. I'm going back to bed.'

Linh stared at the closed bedroom door and her lips thinned into a hard, angry line. Where was the gratitude, she wondered. Couldn't her daughter see how hard she was working so that they could enjoy the luxuries that other people—the Cheongs—enjoyed? She tried again. She did more overtime and bought a video machine but Tien still kept going over to the Cheongs'. Finally, Linh couldn't stop herself from telling Tien, 'I don't want you going over so often. If you want to watch TV, you can do it here. You shouldn't watch so much of it anyway. You must have homework to do.'

'I don't watch telly all the time. There's nothing to watch these days. I just hang out with Annabelle. She's teaching me how to cook.'

'Oh, cooking. I did not know you wanted to cook. I can teach you,' Linh offered. Then, too late, she realised that this was another one of those verbal traps her daughter delighted in setting.

'Thanks, but I won't put you to the trouble. You don't have time anyway, and I only like to eat the stuff Annabelle cooks.'

'You are not allowed to go there on school days,' Linh said. 'I forbid you.'

Tien simply said, 'How? You won't be around to do anything about it.'

They looked at each other and realised that their unacknowledged war had escalated. Tien had been rude before, but she usually apologised. She had never challenged her mother's authority outright. Her declaration of rebellion exhilarated her, yet she could not escape a quick surge of guilt because it sometimes seemed as though *hieu thao* was tattooed on her DNA. She could not excise it without destroying some part of herself.

'You will not get away with this,' Linh said finally. She resented her daughter for putting her in a position where she had to be stern and forbid and mete out punishments. She was afraid that she had brought it on herself because of her past actions. *My name is marked in the* Book of the Damned. *We both reap what we sowed in our past lives.*

Linh took a week off work. She waited for Tien outside the school gate and walked her home. She ignored Tien's complaint that at her age she looked ridiculous being walked home by her mother. But Linh had to return to work the following week and when she rang home at five, Tien was not there to pick up the phone.

'What are you going to do?' Tien said, and her smile was insolent. 'You going to ground me? Well, you can't enforce it. You going to stop my pocket money? I don't need it. I work at Uncle Duc's. You tell him not to employ me, I can just go to the restaurant next door. You going to throw me out of home? Great. I'll move back in with Uncle Duong. The shame will be on you as well. Auntie Ai-Van will know what kind of a mother you are.'

'And just what kind of mother am I?' Linh cried in frustration.

But Tien could not answer her, for she did not know herself. She only knew that Linh was to blame for all the things that were wrong in her life, from the distance between her and Gillian, to her unsuitability to be Justin's girlfriend because she was two years older than him and she did not look sufficiently Asian.

Tien realised that she was too dark-skinned. She took to wearing hats and long sleeves in summer, but it didn't stop Annabelle from exclaiming, '*Wah*! How come you so dark one when your mummy so fair?'

Tien shrugged, but Annabelle was not to be deterred. 'Must be your daddy.'

'Don't know. Maybe.'

'How come you don't know anything about your daddy, Tien?'

'He was like Bill Cosby.'

'What! Bill Cosby was your daddy?'

Annabelle could be an amazingly gullible woman. For a moment, Tien debated whether she should try to lay claim to Hollywood parentage. Then she sighed and said, 'No, not really. But he might be sort of related, I suppose.'

'*Wah*, so good one *lah*! Does he know about you?'

'Yes.' No. Tien simply didn't know. She told herself she had to be nice to Annabelle otherwise she would not be allowed to hang around the house with Justin.

'How come you never go and live with him?'

'He's an American. Visa problems, I suppose. You know how hard it is to get a green card and everything. One day it'll be sorted out and then he'll come and get me.'

'Oh.' Tien could see the pity and disbelief in Annabelle's eyes and she was angry with Annabelle and everyone else like her who kept twisting her mongrel roots around her neck. Most of all, she was angry with Linh for having been a bar-girl who knew lots of American GIs— even *black* ones! An awkward adolescence made Tien unforgiving in her rigid morality.

'Your mummy must have been very broad-minded, *leh*?'

'Broad-minded?'

'You know. Your daddy was a black man, isn't it?'

'Only half. Blacks are the coolest people in America. They're funny, they've got great fashion sense and they dominate *Video Hits*. I'm black and I'm proud. But what are you saying anyway? You think it's not okay to have mixed-race relations?'

'*Hi-yah*. No need to be so sensitive. I'm only asking. I'm not racist, you know. Of course it's okay to us, but some people mind, you know. I remember Jay-Jay's third great-auntie warned him not to marry an Indian or a black woman or she cut him out of her will. She's very rich, you know. From Jakarta. Of course we were very shocked, but what to do? She's very traditional, *leh*. Anyway, Tek told her that Jay will marry a nice Chinese girl of course. No need to worry.'

Tien anxiously scrutinised Annabelle's face but could not tell whether that was a hint to her to stay away from Justin.

By the time Tien had completed her School Certificate and gone on to Year 11, she had to admit to herself that she was in love with Justin. It took the Strathfield Plaza massacre for her to realise how much she cared about him. Love made her embarrassed and insecure; she didn't want him or anyone else to know. After all, he was only sixteen—two years younger than her—and nothing like the fantasies of romantic heroes she'd dreamt about in her early adolescence.

There was nothing particularly remarkable about him. He was simply Justin Cheong, B-grade pianist and athlete who played basketball and cricket for the B-team at school. He was nice enough in an ordinary sort of way. But to Tien, he was beautiful. She loved his long, lean body and the flat planes of his face. After the Strathfield shootings, he began to hang out with her more often. He never had very much to say to her, so she was able to read her dreams into his silence.

Tien couldn't get over her crush on Justin. She thought about him constantly and rang him as often as she dared. She tried to make herself acceptable to his parents. She sat with Tek in his karaoke den as he belted out 'My Way' and other Sinatra songs. She hung around with Annabelle and endured her reproaches—'How come your mummy never teach you how to cook rice properly?'—just to be near Justin.

She waited for two years. She bided her time, borrowed and read outdated issues of *Dolly* and *Cleo*, then psyched herself up to ask him to the Year 12 formal. He said yes, and she felt as ecstatic as if he'd agreed to marry her. She saved up her earnings from Uncle Duc's restaurant and bought herself lace underwear, plucked her eyebrows and waxed herself in all the requisite places in order to prepare herself for love. She was determined to lose her virginity that night.

Justin borrowed his mother's blue Toyota Camry to pick Tien up for the Year 12 formal. He handed her a corsage—yellow Singaporean orchids—and barely looked to notice that it clashed with the traditional Vietnamese silk *ao dai* she was wearing.

'You look good,' Tien told him. He shrugged and did not return the compliment so she was forced to ask diffidently, 'Do I look okay? I mean, I don't look stupid in this get-up, do I? Maybe I should've got a normal dress instead of letting the mothers talk me into this thing.'

'You look fine,' he said automatically as he waited for her to buckle up in the car. He glanced at her and was surprised to realise that she did indeed look all right. He'd always thought of her as a rather ugly girl; now he saw that there was a certain exotic beauty to her strong-boned features. He said, almost wonderingly, 'You look really good, Tien.'

She beamed at him with that big wide mouth, and the momentary illusion of beauty was dispelled. He sighed and started the car. He did not know what to say to her as they drove to a hotel in the city. He parked the car and they walked inside to the function room where their classmates thronged, already half pissed. He felt depressed because it was only now that he realised how much more he'd wanted from his school life than this, and although he liked Tien and had been reciting her virtues to himself on a nightly basis to coax himself into attraction, he wished he was with Gibbo instead.

'Why can't you just come along?' he'd begged Gibbo. 'Don't make me go to this alone, mate. We can be a three-some, as usual.'

'Tien asked you, not me. And I won't turn up without a partner.'

'Who cares if you go solo?'

'I care. I'm not going to play the loser for the whole year to see, even if I *am* one.'

'Fuck.' That was the problem with school formals, Justin thought bitterly. Everybody marched into that Noah's Ark teamed up two by two. What did you do if you'd always been a threesome and there was nobody else to even it all out? He was angry with Tien. She had placed him and Gibbo in the position of being rivals. Instead of best friends, they were now winner and loser; the chosen and the rejected.

Justin made an effort to shake off his mood, but he couldn't. They sat at a table and he only asked Tien to dance once. Few people came up and talked to them. They did not talk to each other.

Finally, he said to her, 'Do you want to get out of here? Maybe go to Macca's and grab something to eat?'

'Yeah, all right,' she said, and she thought that perhaps something of this night might be salvaged after all. He seemed to cheer up once they left the hotel. He loosened his tie, unbuttoned his collar and said, 'Sorry to spoil it for you, Tien. I just really hate that kind of thing. Bores me shitless.'

'Yeah, me too,' she agreed heartily, although she had been looking forward to this night with Justin for months. She had pored over magazines, spun daydreams, practised dance moves and rehearsed conversational gambits which would never be used now. But she did not care because she was out with Justin, alone, on her first real date.

They went to a McDonald's along Parramatta Road and ordered takeaway from the drive-through window. Then they sat in the car park and ate their burgers and fries, and Tien was finally happy. For the first time in months, it was just the two of them, without Gibbo. They talked about the HSC, what they wanted to do during the summer holidays, and what they hoped to do when university started.

'Hey, you know what? It's been so long since we've really had a good chat,' Tien said.

'Yeah, you're right. We should do this more.' He grinned at her and, just like that, her night was suddenly perfect. She wanted to extend this moment of intimacy.

'You want to get some VBs and go somewhere else?' she asked.

'We could do that,' he considered. Then he said, 'Nah. I'm buggered. I just wanna get out of these clothes and crawl into bed. Feel like I'm choking. Take a raincheck, eh?'

'Sure.' She hid her disappointment behind a smile and was rewarded with a light, friendly punch on her arm.

It was not even eleven when Justin pulled up to the kerb outside the apartment block where she lived. He put the car into 'park', leaving the engine running and the headlights on.

'Well,' he said, drumming his fingers lightly on the steering wheel. 'That was all right, wasn't it? Thank god it's only once in a lifetime.'

'Yeah,' Tien said. She unclipped her seatbelt and wriggled around to face him. 'It was a really great night. I had such a good time, Justin.'

'Yeah, good. Me too. Specially Macca's! Not.'

'Yeah.'

He waited for her to say goodnight, but she didn't.

Tien sat there in the darkness, expectant. Throughout her HSC preparations, even during the exams, she had obsessed about this night. This was the night when something was meant to happen between her and Justin. There had to be more to it than this.

The street was quiet, the darkness pierced only by the lit windows of houses and apartments. The car engine sputtered and she could feel the framework vibrating. An empty cassette case shivered on the dashboard. The digital clock glowed eerily green. Minutes flickered by. Still she did not say anything. She just scraped up all the love and yearning inside her and focused it into a gaze so concentrated she was nearly cross-eyed. After all this time, he simply had to see how she felt about him.

Justin shifted in his seat and looked away. 'Well,' he said with forced cheerfulness. 'Getting late. Thanks for a great evening, Tien.'

And she remembered that this was Annabelle Cheong's son. He would never initiate 'dirty things' with a girl unless she showed him that she was sexed up and seducible. She would have to make the first move. Tien cleared her throat.

'Justin,' she murmured in her best husky voice. And she began to undress in the front seat of Annabelle's car.

Tien realised something almost immediately: if you're not used to wearing an *ao dai*, never attempt to seduce someone while trying to take it off. Her zip ran off its track and locked into the fabric halfway down the zipper but, in her excitement and nervousness, she did not notice. So when she tried to pull the long skirt up and over her head to expose her breasts, the narrow sleeves got caught at her elbows. She sat there in a silk dress that had suddenly transformed into a straitjacket. Her dress was over her head, and her arms were crossed in front of her face, entangled in the material she was trying to tug off. She struggled in vain for several seconds. It was hot under all that fabric. Her arms felt wrenched out of their sockets. She began to think she was suffocating. Panic gushed up swiftly.

'Justin, help me,' Tien begged.

For a moment, she thrashed on by herself, wondering whether Justin had left the car in disgust. Then she heard him sigh, and she felt his hands gripping the fabric near her pinioned arms. After a lot of tugging and the sound of ripping silk, her arms were free. She sat there in the loose white silk trousers of her *ao dai* and a matching white lace bra that contrasted starkly with her dark skin.

At this moment, she reached a point of no return. She had humiliated herself so completely that she had nothing left to lose. So she took a deep breath, reached around her back and unhooked her bra. She forced her lips to tilt up into a smile, turned to Justin and said, 'Okay. Let's try this again.'

And that was when she noticed the look of horror on Justin's face. He wrenched open the car door and stumbled out.

Tien sat there in the front seat of Annabelle Cheong's car, her bra hanging loosely from its shoulder straps. She closed her eyes for a moment, and when she opened them, they were wet with tears. She dashed them away and swiped her hand under her nose like a little kid.

'What's wrong with me?' she whispered.

'Hey. Don't cry.'

Tien heard the car door opening. Justin climbed back in. She could not look at him. She remembered that she only had her trousers and bra on. She crossed her arms over her breasts and turned her back to him.

Justin shrugged off his dinner jacket and wrapped it around Tien. He hugged her and said, 'I'm sorry.'

'I feel so stupid,' she sniffed. 'I don't know what to say to you now.'

'Me neither,' he admitted.

'I guess you think I'm a slut.'

'Nah, no way. I was just, I don't know, taken by surprise. Yeah.'

She dashed the tears away from her eyes and looked out the side window. 'I know I'm not pretty or anything. It's just that I thought you'd want to. I mean, I thought all guys want to if they get a chance. And it's not like I'm expecting, you know, anything after.'

He looked at her and recognised her low expectations of life in himself. For the first time since he'd known her, he felt that he understood her—this twin soul who believed she could snatch a fistful of happiness in the front seat of a car and that it might just be enough to get her through. In understanding, he loved her a little and his voice was tender as he uttered the age-old cliché: 'It's not you, Tien. It's me. It was just such a shock. I'm sorry I didn't handle it better.'

He shut his eyes for a moment and thought of his parents. He took a deep breath and said, 'You looked really beautiful tonight, Tien. You sure you want to do this with me?'

She turned around slowly and, even through the darkness, he could see that she was radiant with incredulous hope. Hesitantly, she reached for his hand and gripped it tightly. 'Of course I want to. If you want to, that is.'

'Yeah, me too.' He could do this, he told himself. He would make himself want her, like any normal guy. 'I just don't want you to be sorry after.'

'No! I couldn't be. I want you to be the first. I l—'

He put his hand over her mouth quickly and said, 'Don't say it, okay? In fact, let's agree right now that we won't say anything. We'll just do it but we won't talk about it 'cos we don't need words. Okay?'

She nodded silently and he kissed her on that full wide mouth smudged with lipstick. The car was still running. He shifted the gear. 'Let's go somewhere more private, eh?'

They drove towards the Potts Hill reservoirs near the Chullora railway workshops where steel skeletons of electricity towers hulked overhead, dragging thick black power lines like musical staves across the sky.

Justin nosed the car into deep shadows and parked it. Silently, he unclipped his seatbelt and she did the same. He leaned towards her and locked his arms around her body. He hugged her for a long moment and turned his nose to sniff at her stiff sprayed hair. He did not move.

She couldn't gauge his mood. She didn't understand him.

'Are you crying?' she asked uncertainly.

'No. Course not.' Grimly, doggedly, he began to kiss her. Their mouths opened and tongues melded. He ran his hands over her back and across her breasts, patting and kneading mechanically.

It was not what she had expected. Where was the epiphany of passion, the thrill and the ache in belly and breasts? Arousal was intermittent. Lust flared and fizzled out. Her nipples pinched in the cool night air but she remained stubbornly dry. She had waited so long to make love with Justin. Now she had to squeeze her eyes shut and block out the reality of the man so that she could focus on the fantasy that had stirred love's desire in the yearning dark of lonely nights. She ran her fingertips across his smooth skin and marvelled at the liberty he granted her. Her flesh pressed into his, she breathed in his air. They had never been closer, never more intimate.

And she felt so alone. She could not break past his skin to touch the essence of him. It was such hard work with so little reward. At last she pulled away from him and said, 'It's not going to work, is it?'

'No, I guess not.' He sighed and felt sorry for her. 'Um. There are other things we can do.'

He reached under the loose elastic of her trousers to try to masturbate her, but she pushed his hand away. She sat back in her seat and pleaded, 'What's wrong with me?'

'Nothing. It's not you.'

'What is it then?'

He kept silent. He badly wanted to take her into his confidence but he did not dare. He groped for her hand and squeezed it gently, hoping that in this pulse of flesh there would be some measure of comfort and the faint hope of friendship.

But she refused to be comforted. She bleated the phrase he did not want to hear. 'Justin, I love you.'

He fumbled for words, but anything he clutched at was bound to be inadequate. He was learning that in the wide range of human experiences, the ones that truly mattered had the narrowest of vocabularies; the emotions that were most deeply and individually felt found expression through the quotation of other people's clichés.

'I love you too,' he said. 'But just as a friend. I'm sorry.'

She couldn't let it go. She said hopefully, 'But we had a good time tonight, right? Maybe if we just give it a go again some time, something'll happen. I mean, I really love you.'

Why did she have to keep thrusting her love at him until he had no choice but to lie? In his desperation to give her what she wanted so that he could get away, he said, 'Yeah, sure. We can give it a go. See what happens.' When he dropped her home shortly afterwards, he promised, 'I'll call you.'

Tien said she didn't expect anything from Justin. She lied. Over the next week she waited for him to phone her but he didn't. Finally she rang him. He wasn't home. Annabelle said he'd gone away with Gibbo.

'Camping with *Gibbo*?' They hadn't mentioned anything about it to her. Her heart cramped with hurt and jealousy. She felt betrayed. How could it be that Justin meant everything to her, and yet she was only ever the friend of his best friend? She loved him until she was sick with yearning, but he always put Gibbo first. She blamed Gibbo. She said to Annabelle, 'Can you ask Justin to ring me when he gets back, please? It's important.'

She waited, but he did not call. Then, just before Christmas, she got a tacky card with a Christmas tree on it. *Gone to Singapore to visit the rels. Have a good Xmas. See you when I get back. Luv ya! Justin.*

She knew better by then but she could not help re-reading the card and clutching that last sentence like a lifeline. 'Luv ya!' At nights she hugged her pillow to her chest, squeezed her thighs together to ease her sexual ache and repeated the words to herself: 'Luv ya!'

In early January she heard from Gibbo that Justin was back. She tested him with silence. Still he did not call. She took his Christmas card out, tore it into tiny pieces and dropped it into the large garbage bin behind Uncle Duc's restaurant. She dumped the remains of pork and duck bones on top of it.

Justin finally phoned her in February, a few weeks before university started.

'I'm really sorry I didn't call sooner,' he said. He sounded tense and upset. 'I'd like to try and explain and make it up to you.'

'Nothing to explain or make up for. No expectations, remember?' she said breezily. 'Hope you had a great summer. I've been so busy at Uncle Duc's restaurant I don't know where this summer's gone.'

'Oh. Well, can I take you out for lunch? I'd really like to have a chat with you.'

'Not this week. I've got heaps of stuff to do.'

There was one of those long, awkward pauses between them, like a rubber band stretched too taut. She could feel their friendship snapping. It wasn't her fault, she told herself. He couldn't expect forgiveness that easily. He had to earn it. She wanted him to prove that he was truly sorry. She wanted to be wooed away from her grudge and back into friendship, but he didn't know how to make things right.

'Um. Are you okay?' he asked diffidently.

'Sure,' she said. 'Why wouldn't I be?'

'You're not mad at me?'

'Why should I be?'

Another pause. Still he did not tell her what she needed to hear.

He should have recognised that in her deep hurt,

she flung out words like a barrier he had to break
through. He was supposed to say, 'I know you're not all
right. You can't be. I was so mean to you and I'm sorry.
Talk to me. Let me make it up to you.' And if he said it
often enough, if he really persisted in grovelling, she
would know that their friendship meant something to
him; she would know that she was important. Only then
would she unbend and forgive him. But he was a guy and
he compounded his crime by taking her at her word.

'Well, some other time then. Give us a call when
you're free, okay?'

'Sure thing,' she said carelessly. With Justin she had
always found it difficult to express what she felt. Now she
had reached a stage where her words conveyed the
opposite of what she actually meant.

Best Friends at the Beach

He yearned and pined—he seemed to have his soul
inside a kiln, his heart beneath a plow.
The silkworm, spinning, wasted day by day;
the gaunt cicada, bit by frost, shrank more.
He languished, half alive, half dead—he'd weep
real tears of blood, but lose his soul to dreams.

Nguyen Du, *The Tale of Kieu*

A few days after the Year 12 formal Justin rang Gibbo and asked him whether he was game to go camping somewhere around Reef Beach. 'I need to get away for a bit.'

'I don't think we're allowed to camp there overnight, are we?' Gibbo said doubtfully.

'Who's going to know?'

'All right then. You're on. Is Tien coming as well?'

'Don't be stupid,' Justin said shortly. 'D'you think her mum would let her go camping with two guys? My own mum wouldn't be too happy about it either.'

In fact, Annabelle was unhappy about the whole trip, but Tek encouraged them. He said, 'You should

86

do it. It'll toughen you up. If you were Singaporean citizens you'd both have to do your National Service now that you've finished school. I tell you, they'd make NS-men out of you. You have to camp in the most terrible conditions with the heat and humidity and mosquitoes and thunderstorms. My nephew got a fungal infection in his feet because he couldn't change his socks for a week and he had to tramp through mud during the rainy season.'

'Ee-yer,' Annabelle exclaimed. 'So *lah-cha*. Dirty like anything.'

One of the reasons Justin was so fond of Gibbo was that Gibbo had known Tek and Annabelle since he was a child. There was no need to explain his parents to Gibbo, no need to feel embarrassed or ashamed of the things they said or did. Gibbo accepted with equanimity Tek's obsession with karaoke and made no comment when he came over for dinner and, immediately after the meal, Tek pushed back his chair and disappeared down into the rumpus room to transform himself into Frank Sinatra getting a kick out of you.

Neither did Gibbo raise his eyebrows or take offence when Annabelle knocked on the toilet door and called out, 'Gibbo, are you doing a *berak*? Use the Harpic powder after you flush and don't forget to open the window. So stinko otherwise.'

'Mum!' Justin said, highly embarrassed.

'But he has that cheesy-lamby smell like all the *ang mors*,' Annabelle protested.

'That's so racist,' Justin accused angrily.

She said, bewildered, 'But it's true, you know. I can smell it.'

Gibbo just replied obligingly, 'Okay *lah*, Auntie.'

He loved Annabelle more than his own parents. Whatever she might say, her actions demonstrated her kindness. She was ever-willing to teach him and Tien how to cook. She was always eager to chat with them and she met them on their level effortlessly. He adored the way she spoke because there was something about Singlish that precluded the polite formality that maintained emotional distance. His mother's precise English was a language that kept others in the visitors' lounge; Annabelle's Singlish hauled him right into her kitchen, sat him down on a stool and fed him food to welcome him. After that, she could comment tactlessly on his *ang mor* smell all she wanted; he knew it was not personal and he did not mind. But Justin did not understand this.

Justin had often wondered how any other friend of his, let alone any future partner, would deal with his parents. He loved them, but he simply could not envisage inviting anyone home to meet them. He did not see how anyone could like him enough to distinguish him from his parents' behaviour. He could not step outside his own wincing reaction to Tek and Annabelle long enough to imagine that other people might genuinely like them, idiosyncracies and all. Their perceived transgressions loomed large in his mind and he could not see them clearly for their imagined faults. Guiltily, he struggled against their Asian oddness and resented the knowledge that he was contaminated. In feeling ashamed of them, he also felt ashamed of himself. He did not want to be Asian and he did not want to be gay.

Ever since the Strathfield Plaza massacre and his first sexual experience in the toilets two and a half years ago, Justin had maintained a certain distance from Gibbo because he was afraid of what he might start to feel if he were to get too close to him. Yet he did not see how he would ever be accepted by anyone else because Gibbo had known the Cheongs almost all his life and was practically a part of the family. Gibbo not only accepted them, he emulated them.

So when Annabelle turned to the boys and said, 'You better make sure you don't forget to bring toilet paper and disinfectant,' all Gibbo said in reply was, 'Okay *lah*, Auntie.'

They didn't forget, as it happened. Neither did they forget their sleeping bags, a slab of beer, two cigars that Justin had bought from the tobacconist in Strathfield Plaza and a couple of joints he had acquired somewhere else, a plastic cigarette lighter, a mammoth bag of corn chips and two limp rump steaks they picked up from a boutique butcher which were so expensive they couldn't afford anything else. They caught the ferry from Circular Quay over to Manly and did the Esplanade walk along the north harbour coast towards The Spit, lugging their loot down to Reef Beach and dumping it where seaweed was scribbled along the high-tide strand.

In a few weeks' time it would be Christmas. Justin would fly to Singapore and face the annual gathering of the Cheong relatives—all the successful uncles and studious cousins who would have heart attacks if they really knew who he was and what he'd done. Gibbo would have Christmas lunch with his parents and spend the rest of the day hiding in his bedroom and nurturing his loneliness.

But for now it was a perfect, warm and bright December day. The HSC was over and the rest of their lives had yet to begin. For the first time in years it was just the two of them again: Gibbo and Justin. Kicking sand into each other's faces, dunking each other in the waves, it was as if time had concertinaed and they were simply kids once more, back on Miss Yipsoon's piano stool mucking around and consolidating their friendship through the rough and tumble of play like a couple of scrapping puppies.

When the bright afternoon smudged into dusk, they clambered carefully over sharp rocks and threw out a tangle of fishing lines with no hope of hooking anything more than Coke cans coughed out of the sea. They started to feel hungry so they gathered up twigs and soggy driftwood, trying to fire up the sorry pile with the cigarette lighter. After half an hour of scorching their fingers on the flickering flame, they still had no success, so they set alight individual sticks and tried to sear their raw pieces of rump steak with the smoking brands. It was a disgusting dinner, of course, with the meat half charred, half raw, but they laughed and were happy.

They consigned their steaks to fish bait, stuffed themselves with corn chips and got plastered on VB. They lit their cigars, choked and spluttered and puffed away with watery eyes, feeling rather grown-up before they lurched over to throw up on the rocks. Reaching into the depths of their backpacks for plastic boxes of Tic-Tacs (they'd remembered the toilet paper but not toothbrushes or toothpaste) to remove the taste of puke from their mouths, they grinned idiotically at each other and felt exhilarated by enacting the sheer normality of being two Aussie adolescents smashed at the beach.

At two in the morning, when the wind blew strong and cold over the surging waves, they wrapped their unzipped sleeping bags around themselves and smoked their joints in silence. Justin shivered and squirmed closer to Gibbo for warmth.

'That's one consolation for all this lard on me anyway,' Gibbo said thickly. 'Don't feel the cold much.'

'Come on, you're not that big.'

'Too fat for girls like Tien and her cousins,' Gibbo sighed. 'Too fat to be going anywhere. You ever notice that, Jus?'

'What?'

'People like us. You wanna move up and move out of the west, you have to shed the load and get built and fit. You're lucky 'cos you're not fat. There's a bell curve of fat between the Blue Mountains and the coast. People look at me in all my lard and think I'm going nowhere, and the sad thing is, they're probably right.'

'What a load of crap. Lots of big people are really successful and earn heaps more money than my dad. Anyway, you'll be glad of all that fat when you're middle-aged,' Justin said. 'Have you ever noticed how skinny people seem to age more quickly? I think the fat stretches out the wrinkles and keeps you looking young. Decades from now, when those trendy eastern suburbs types are cling-wrapping their wrinkled faces, you'll still be looking young.'

'But fat,' Gibbo objected. 'Anyway, years from now doesn't count. How'm I ever gonna get a girlfriend looking like this?'

'Now you're feeling sorry for yourself,' Justin scoffed. 'Fuck girls, eh?'

'That's the problem. Wish I could.'

Justin snorted with laughter. 'What are you worried about? I'm sure you'll get good marks in the HSC and you'll be off to uni next year where you'll meet lots of new people.'

'Yeah, but we'll all be split up and what'll happen to me then? Who's gonna wanna hang around me at uni?'

'Who gives a shit about people at uni? We're still friends, aren't we? Gibbo, mate, you're the best.' Justin flung his arms around Gibbo and hugged him tight. 'You're my best friend, you know that?'

Sloppily sentimental from too much unaccustomed booze and bong, distressed by his friend's dull gloom, he sought only to give comfort and take a little bit for himself. He turned his face towards Gibbo's—fleshy, familiar, and so loved by him just then—and stroked his thumb over the Tasmanian birthmark. He kissed Gibbo long and hard. Love detonated like dynamite through him. Like an explosion of fists on his face.

Tek and Annabelle were horrified to see the cuts and bruises smudged over their son's face when he returned the next day. Annabelle raced for the Dettol and began disinfecting Justin's wounds.

'What happened?' she demanded.

'I slipped and fell on some rocks,' Justin said.

She shot a seriously annoyed look at her husband. 'You see. I told you it's not safe. This is what happens when you try to make an NS-man out of your son and tell him to go camping.'

Gibbo picked up the phone to ring Justin several times but he was always too angry and too ashamed to dial Justin's number. He did not know what to say to his oldest friend. He rang Tien instead. He wanted to tell her what had happened. He felt that if only he could talk to her, they would be able to sort things out. But he could not reach her. She was never in and although he left several messages with her mother, she did not return his calls. He didn't know what he had done wrong. He did not have the courage to ask. It was the end of the Three Mouseketeers.

When university started they were scattered; different universities, different courses, different life directions. Gibbo made a number of acquaintances in his engineering classes and socialised in the most basic manner. He went to the pub with them after class, got blind drunk, and chanted collectively: 'Engineer! Rhymes with beer! Engineer! Rhymes with beer!' He thought he was enjoying himself; he was doing all right. Then he discovered that these were not the kind of friends to whom he could really talk, or the kind who would even ring him up to hang out on weekends. Nothing in his experience of watching cheesy American campus movies had prepared him for university life where, after classes and the pub, people just disappeared back into the suburbs from which they came. And when they moved on to different classes the following year, he didn't see them anymore.

That was when he realised that his friendships—such as they were—had congealed into a pattern of association by default, followed by the fragmentation of the group when the centrifugal forces of life circumstances flung them outside his physical orbit. He ached with fear that he would always be alone.

Saturday Night Phobia

All her emotions tangled like sleave silk
as dreams of home kept stirring sleep till dawn.
From her gauze-curtained window, at heaven's edge,
alone, forlorn, she'd watch dusk follow dusk.
While the moon hare and the sun crow whirled round,
she mourned all victims in the Sorrow League.

Nguyen Du, *The Tale of Kieu*

By the time he was halfway through his university course, Gibbo was convinced that weekends should never have been invented. Or if that was impossible, then mankind would have been better off sticking to the six-day working week. Saturdays were a humiliation, a taunt by malicious higher beings—both terrestrial and celestial—who delighted in demonstrating to him on a weekly basis his social ineptitude and consequent isolation.

Friday nights were all right. Just. He was so buggered by the end of the university week that it was as much as he could do to drag himself home through traffic jams and road rage, bolt down the dinner his mum had prepared for him, thrust his clothes into the washing machine and flop onto the bed to read in his Y-front underwear. Anything served his purpose; he did not differentiate between Tom Clancy or Thomas Mann, *Tom Jones* or Thomas the Tank Engine.

Out the back of the flame-brick house, in the dun-grey fibro extension that now served as the TV room, he could hear his father exclaiming angrily at Friday night football on the television. If Gibbo had a Groundhog Day in his life, Friday night footy was it. Friday nights hummed with the muted buzz of barracking crowds, his father's pugnacious critique of the game punctuated by the occasional 'Yes!' and the more frequent disbelieving demand, 'Did you see that? I mean, come on!' To which his mother would reply irritably, 'What now, Bob? Can't you see I'm reading?' as she flicked through the pages of *Woman's Day*.

Little changed over the years, except these days her lips pursed into a disapproving prune more frequently as features on new knitting patterns gave way to chatty, sycophantic articles about the Royals, and these were in turn superseded by celebrity scandals that pierced her consciousness in high-pitched, girlish, twenty-something exclamations. HOW PRINCESS ANNE ESCAPES THE LONELY NIGHTS! WOW! AMAZING DIET—NEW SLIM FERGIE DROPS 16KG! WOW! MADONNA'S UNCENSORED KINKY SEX ROMPS WITH LOTS OF SUPERSTARS! WOW! WOW! WOW!

'You're an English teacher. Don't know how you can stand to read that garbage,' Bob Gibson would grouch predictably, but Gillian noticed that he listened attentively enough to the short snippets of gossip she read out to him.

'It's a bloody disgrace,' he pronounced, and she flicked him a look of annoyance because she was reading him gossip so that they would have something to talk about, not so that he could pass judgement on her and the whole world of celebrities. Then he raised his voice and said, 'Just as it's a dis-*grace* to this household that your son coops himself up in his room with a book on the weekends. Can't get a bloody date and no wonder. Not even interested in the footy.'

His father's voice had a stentorian quality that sent it pulsing down the short hallway to Gibbo's bedroom at the front of the house. He slammed the bedroom door shut and willed himself to refuse the lash of hurt and the balm of self-pity, but they came anyway.

He had been four years old when his father started chucking all kinds of balls at him: footballs, cricket balls, volleyballs, tennis balls. 'You're a little tiger, aren'tcha,' Bob insisted over the next ten years. He'd nodded, swallowed phlegm and sniffed back tears as an asteroid of a football punched into his chest; as his ear was smacked by the red blur of a cricket ball; as the volleyball cracked his brand-new wristwatch and hammered the metal strap into his flesh; as his father's tennis ball stung his nose and bounced to the far corner of a rundown asphalt court. 'Ace. Forty–love. Game, set and match.'

By the time he was fourteen, even Bob gave way to the inevitable. 'Bloody girl,' he snorted as he stored the sporting equipment away in the attic with forbidding finality. How was he going to get to know his son without the aid of a ball shuttling effortlessly between them, knitting them together in blokey camaraderie? Delete the language of scores, tries, wickets, LBWs, and run-outs, omit the lengthy debates about top five batsmen and top five spin or fast bowlers of all time and how were you going to lob serious man-to-man topics into the conversation? Without sport, how did you touch on subjects like sex, drugs and career choices? How could you paddle your way around these potentially emotional boulders without the smooth-flowing current of great sporting moments? You couldn't. You were shipwrecked conversationally and then there was a whole lot of awkwardness between you and your son. Love him as much as you did, he didn't seem a proper man, a real Aussie.

But manumission from Australian masculinity brought many rewards for Gibbo, disinterest from Bob and freedom from Friday night football being two of the most immediate effects. No longer did he have to sit on the sagging sofa, wedged between his growling father and purse-mouthed mother, staring miserably at the ascending flight of wooden ducks on the cork-lined wall above the TV as thick-necked players dodged and wove their tribal dance on the convex screen.

The unexpected restitution of his Friday nights was a wonderful gift while he was still in school and had no expectations of a social life. In his university years, however, Friday nights acquired the rime of dreary depression because there was nothing to look forward to in the coming wasteland of his weekend.

Gibbo would have liked to sleep in on Saturday mornings, to be unconscious for as much of the day as possible. But even without the benefit of his army years, his father was an early-to-bed, early-to-rise kind of man. No son of his was going to laze in bed like a bludger as long as he had any say in the matter. Yet Saturday mornings were actually made bearable by the structure of household chores. Gibbo washed the car, swept the driveway free of rusty liquidambar leaves, cleaned out the gutters, trimmed errant tree branches, spread manure in the azalea and camellia beds. In the garden, fragile basil and mint seedlings—the tiny buds not even half the size of his thumbnail when he tucked them into the soil—bloomed into thick-leafed fragrance and bled the nostalgic smell of an imaginary home into his earth-stained fingers.

He was meticulous, careful. On Saturdays he fixed leaking taps and creaking doors, wound out the metal measuring tape, drilled, screwed, hammered and generally felt reasonably competent as a human being, even as a man. Lumbering around the house with various tools of wood and iron clutched in his massive fists, he felt in harmony with his limbs. He felt in control of his life. There was nothing around the house he could not fix.

But he was too efficient, and the chores petered out as morning slid away into sleepy noon, leaving him with nothing to do and too much time to think. The slowly creeping afternoon sapped his self-assurance and his sense of being at home in his body. By the time streetlights rubbed their eyes and blinked awake in the early evening, he was bloated with self-hatred. He resented the tonnage of his body. His rotund trunk and limbs, the fleshiness of his arms, the thick meat of his thighs, seemed a Sisyphean burden he was too weary to roll through life. He gripped a fistful of flank and wished he had a sculptor's knife to carve it down to the bone. He would watch his flesh fall off in slippery glistening slices as the blood flowed free.

Yet it was even more than that, for fat men in history had overcome their weight with their wit. A fat man could be funny and, therefore, popular. Anything could be forgiven a funny man, even murder; witness the literary and filmic success of the convicted murderer Chopper Read.

Gibbo's problem was his tongue, that swollen muscle lodged like a lump of unbaked dough in the tepid oven of his mouth. His tongue would not obey his thoughts. He knew he was not unintelligent. He was, in fact, quite well-read, thanks to his English-teacher mother and a combined arts/engineering degree at the university. In his head he could hold scintillating conversations with people he'd just met. He could use words as his foil to fence with the world. The essence of Gibbo, he felt, the person who was really Nigel Gibson, was erudite and unflappable inside the carcass of his body. But the essence of Gibbo was entombed within all that flesh and could not fight his way free. He willed his tongue to obey the increasingly frustrated orders of the inner Nigel Gibson, but his heart drummed loudly and furiously and caused his vocal chords to quake, his tongue to trip and stutter. Fear was like a butcher's hand around his abdomen, squeezing his heart like a sausage until it exploded through his lungs or shot up his oesophagus to lodge in his mouth. Blood thumped like a timpani in his brain.

So in the company of others, especially those of his own age, he was fat and dull, a social dead weight. The kind of person people tried to edge away from as quickly as possible at parties. The kind of person whose eyes jittered in desperate panic and flickered around the room seeking eye contact with someone with a social conscience who would come and rescue him. He depended on the kindness of strangers and was always let down.

Gibbo was the kind of person who then hovered around the food and drinks table, guzzling cheap beer, taking as long as possible to dip corn chips in plastic tubs of salsa, and who then spent half the night locked in the toilet so that he would not have to face his social failure. He was, in fact, the kind of person who no longer got invited to parties. The last party he'd been to was Tien's twenty-first, and what he remembered most was that first slash of hurt that he had not been asked to make a speech when he was the oldest, the first friend she'd ever had in Australia. Since then, his Saturday nights had been desolate.

On the verge of turning twenty-one himself, Gibbo decided that it was time to take positive steps towards acquiring his first girlfriend. He had no idea how to go about it, so he looked at the personal ads in the local paper:

Lonely European widow, 79, slim, attractive and healthy, n/s, very active, financially independent. Seeking intelligent financially secure man for lasting, genuine, loving relationship 69–82yo.

Never married, black sense of humour, not much into pubs and clubs, seeking someone to make funeral plans with.

Compatibility? Could be you are aged 30–46 profes-
sional/business. Free of ties. 37yo dusky sleek sporty
features, happy and heart motivated. Let's talk.

White charger/accompanying knight sought by
romantic and passionate 24yo just back from Europe
but with no bad habits or baggage or money.

Stunning classy nondancing transsexual with internet
dating phobia seeks sane and stable Greek/Italian gen-
tleman over 40.

He thought it might be easier to go to one of those
group dinners where he could meet people. That way,
even if he didn't manage to hook up with a woman any
time soon, he would be able to observe and learn the
dating and mating habits of the average Aussie male.

He took a deep breath, rang the group dinner
company and paid his fifty-dollar membership fee. A fortnight later, some chirpy-voiced secretary rang to tell him
that a dinner had been organised for Saturday night at an
Italian restaurant in Parramatta. The hostess would meet
them at the bar at seven thirty and collect the special
forty-five dollar three-course dinner fee. She advised him
to wear a shirt and tie.

He was the first to arrive, even before the hostess. He
felt a panic attack coming on because he was there too
early, or perhaps he was at the wrong restaurant. He eased
out the folded piece of notepaper on which he'd scribbled
the instructions. It was creased and grubby from countless
checking. The address and time were right.

He went to the bar and ordered a bourbon and coke. Waited. Ordered another. Eventually, the hostess turned up and made small talk. He panicked again and mumbled his excuses as he fled to his usual refuge: the toilet. When he came back, he was calmer and had a pleasant, friendly, 'hey, how's it goin'?' smile pinned to his lips. Everyone had arrived by now. They shook hands and he saw, with a small jolt of surprise, that one of the women was Tien's mother, Miss Ho. Linh, she'd asked him to call her the last time they met, at Tien's twenty-first. He didn't know whether Linh was equally surprised to see him there because his own insecurities were blooming so brilliantly in his head that he was beyond registering anybody else's reactions by then. As the group was led to the table, Linh tugged on his arm and held him back.

'Wha'?' he said, his tongue thick and his head woozy from the drinks he'd had earlier on.

'Gibbo, your fly is undone,' Linh whispered. She stood in front of him and her hands swung behind her back to gesture at him to fix the problem while no-one was looking.

Embarrassment spiked. He tugged up the zipper of his black jeans quickly and snagged the flesh of his index finger. A bead of blood popped out and he automatically shoved his finger in his mouth to suck on it as he followed Linh to the table.

'Hungry, are ya?' one of the guys said.

Gibbo blushed and mumbled something about cutting his finger.

'Gee, how'd you do that?' A frizzy blonde who could have been a potential, but he rather thought he was more attracted to Asians even though her sun-speckled cleavage was hypnotic. His brain sloshed inside his skull.

He felt his whole face engulfed in flames as he stuttered and subsided into an incoherent mumble. Not that it mattered because some other guy was being funny so the centre of attention had shifted away from him. That was it. He'd lost his chance to be interesting. He ordered another bourbon and coke and remembered little else about the evening. Bruschetta came and went and he vaguely remembered picking it up and being unable to find his open mouth with any reasonable degree of accuracy. Bits of roma tomato and basil fell off and he tried and failed to scrape them back onto the soggy bread. Conversation ebbed and flowed around him but he felt cocooned in the Cone of Silence from *Get Smart*. He drank two glasses of a rather acidic red wine with his veal parmigiana, and dessert was a complete blank.

He woke up just before midnight, sitting in the passenger seat of his car as Linh watched him from the driver's side.

'Wha'?' he asked her stupidly for the second time that night.

'You stink,' she said, wrinkling her nose and holding her hand up to sniff her perfumed wrist. 'You had better get to bed, Gibbo.'

He rubbed his burning eyes and slowly realised that they were parked outside his parents' house. All he had to do was unlock the car door, push it open, stumble up the neat paved path to the front door, unlock it, and he was home. He shut his eyes, groaned, and his head flopped back onto the headrest.

'Too drunk,' he said.

'You're telling me.'

'Engineer. Rhymes with beer.'

'Go on, Gibbo,' Linh said, giving him a light shove. 'You should go in.'

He cracked open an eye to look at her, felt a rumbling in his gut, and nausea was like a tsunami swamping him. Huge peristaltic waves of sick juddered in reverse along his alimentary canal. He tried to hold it in. His cheeks ballooned like a blowfish. Vomit erupted from his mouth, spraying the dashboard, windshield, landing on Linh's left shoulder and spattering the fake Louis Vuitton handbag on her lap.

The next morning, his car had been cleaned up and the windows rolled down. The stink of puke would take several days and multiple sprays of Glen 20 to eliminate. He didn't know how he was ever going to face Linh again. He needed a buffer zone of several years. Instead, he would have to meet her at the Cheongs' Dead Diana Dinner a couple of weeks later.

On Saturday, 6 September 1997, Gibbo turned twenty-one.

In houses all over the city and in bedrooms everywhere, young people were showering, spritzing on deodorant or anti-perspirant, tugging and teasing hair, blow-torching follicles, shaving and waxing faces, legs, arms and other body surfaces and crevices he preferred not to think about unless they looked like the airbrushed layouts in his pitiful porn collection. He imagined the musical clink of metal hangers, the susurration of synthetic fabrics yanked out of overfull closets and dumped, rejected, in gaudy hills on unmade beds. There was never anything to wear. Hair was carefully arranged into casual disarray and sprayed into armoured stiffness. Earrings, nose rings, eyebrow rings were attached. Beer was swigged, pills were popped and bodies then rotated in front of mirrors with inadequate length and lighting while heads twisted to gain anatomically impossible viewing angles. The arse always looked too big in the mirror.

All over the city, all over the world as Saturday night lapped the spinning globe from east to west, young people—normal people—were getting ready to go out and party with friends. How much more, then, should this have applied to Gibbo on the night of his twenty-first birthday.

Had he been in any way normal, he might have arranged for a piss-up at the pub with his friends. Or perhaps his parents might have hired a hall and a sound system, scraped together a few CDs, platters of finger food, lots of booze, and arranged for a slide show of embarrassing baby photographs, followed by speeches from family and friends inducing even more delightful discomfiture.

But Nigel Gibson, self-confessed friendless loner and lard-arse freak, an athletic philistine who tripped over his tongue as well as his feet, buttoned his twelve-dollar blue and yellow floral Hawaiian shirt over a white Bonds T-shirt, shrugged on an over-zippered, over-seamed tan leather jacket and prepared to accompany his parents to their friends' house for dinner. Why? Not because they had remembered his birthday, but because Princess Diana had died and that was the momentous event they were marking. Even his mother had overlooked him and, really, he should have refused this dinner out of pique so that they would realise how terrible it was that they had *forgotten*, how much he had been *hurt*, and they would have to make it up to him.

Yet he said nothing and glumly agreed to go because he had nothing better to do and no-one better to do it with. At dinner, Annabelle Cheong would undoubtedly ask, with characteristic Singaporean bluntness, '*Wah*, Nigel, how come you so fat?', followed by a contradictory exhortation to eat up and don't be shy. Justin would spend the entire dinner avoiding him because they hadn't talked since that appalling incident at Reef Beach. Tien would be artificially polite and over-friendly to him to hide the fact that they no longer knew each other. And as for her mother, he didn't even want to think about how, just a fortnight ago, he had puked all over Linh in the front seat of his car. To top it all off, they were going to spend the entire evening watching the live broadcast of Diana's funeral on television.

The Dead Diana Dinner

I fear that, if and when a storm breaks out,
it will wreak harm on you and grief on me.
Try for your freedom—run or fly away!
Our love has had its time—this is the end.
We two shall soon be traveling opposite paths

Nguyen Du, *The Tale of Kieu*

Bob Gibson was a bitter man who lived his life in a slow-simmering rage, perpetually pissed off by the world. He worked as a surgeon in a public hospital and the human race disgusted him. He resented his former registrars who raced ahead to take on more senior positions at prestigious hospitals in Sydney's northern and eastern suburbs while he was stuck out in the west. Not that he'd ever move; he knew where he belonged.

He was a westie—born and bred in Toongabbie—and proud of it. Anyone who couldn't hack him, well, they could just piss off. On the one occasion he attended a flash medical conference in Double Bay, sponsored by a multinational drug company, he wore his short-sleeved shirt with a fat, colour-slashed tie, broadened his Strine and sat by himself in belligerent silence. Bunch of wankers, he thought scornfully as he glanced around at his colleagues sipping cocktails before the conference dinner.

So he stayed out west and was driven apoplectic by patients who continued to smoke right up to the very hour of their surgery, and who then had the temerity to raise the issue of lawsuits if things went wrong. Any occasion at the Gibsons' was usually flavoured with revolting stories about the astonishing and imaginative variety of things men and women found to put up themselves, cautionary morality tales ending in ruptured colons, septicaemia and peritonitis. He had no time for the petty foibles of ordinary men and women and, most of all, he had no time for Diana.

He blamed her for everything that subsequently went wrong. In fact, as far as he was concerned, it all started when that tiresome woman died and they had to gather at the Cheongs' to mark her funeral even though she meant nothing to him.

Bob had been fuming for the best part of a week since the car crash. At first the news of her death bounced like a rubber ball off the solid wall of his indifference. Truth to tell, he didn't even remember where he was or what he was doing when he heard about it, although he later announced provocatively that he'd been busy taking a crap in the dunny.

'Too much bloody couscous along with all that other multicultural crap Gillian makes me eat these days,' he growled at anyone who would listen. 'Tells me I need more fibre in my diet,' he said, sliding his eyes sideways towards his wife. 'History of bowel cancer in the family. Got me eating All-Bran in the morning and food that tastes like soggy pillow stuffing. Helps keep me regular, she says. Well, I'll tell you what. That couscous went through my gut regular as an express train. Where, in all that, was there time to take in what had happened? Not that it mattered fuck-all to me. Diana's dead. So what?'

But it mattered to Gillian and Annabelle. The women had run into each other on Victoria Avenue, Chatswood, a week before Diana's accident. For a moment they just stared at each other in mutual surprise.

'Eh! What are you doing here?' Annabelle exclaimed.

Gillian tried to pull herself together. She air-kissed Annabelle's cheeks perfunctorily. 'What a surprise to see *you* here.'

'I came to buy Tek some thermal underwear,' Annabelle confided. 'And also to visit Mr Vitamin to buy Vitamin C and echinacea. So cheap, you know!'

They looked at each other and felt awkward. Their children had not been friends for some years now, not since high school. They did not know why. And they did not know whether they were still connected if their children were no longer friends.

'How is Gibbo?'

'He's fine. In his fourth year of engineering.'

'*Wah*! So clever.'

'How's Justin?'

'Doing architecture. *Ai-yah*, my boy never study hard enough. Otherwise he could be a doctor instead.'

'Oh.' Gillian could think of nothing else to say. She nodded and began to walk away but Annabelle's curiosity could not be satisfied so easily.

'So what are you doing here?' she repeated.

For a moment Gillian thought about lying. Then she said, 'I went to get my biopsy results. I didn't want Bob to know so I came to a GP in Chatswood.' And to her great embarrassment, she began to cry. 'I'm so sorry. I'm being silly.' She opened her handbag to grope for a handkerchief but Annabelle was already offering her a tissue. She took it, murmured her thanks and mopped herself up.

'Come,' Annabelle said, grabbing Gillian's arm. 'I take you for dim-sum at this special restaurant. *Ho sek*, ah— delicious, you know. Cannot say no!'

It was still early and the queues had not yet begun to form outside the Chinese restaurant. They were seated straight away. Annabelle ordered a pot of tea, then she leaned towards Gillian and asked quietly, 'Was it bad news?'

'No,' Gillian said. 'That's why I feel so silly. It was good news. It was benign. But for a few days there I wondered.'

'Yah, I know,' Annabelle nodded. 'I had a scare a while back. There was this lump on my head and I had all these headaches so I thought it was a tumour, *lor*. Actually it turned out to be a big pimple that nearly got infected. And also I had to change my specs to bifocals. But I tell you what, *lah*, I was so scared before I found out. I thought, what will happen to Ah Tek and my Jay?'

That was just it, Gillian thought. Annabelle held her husband and her son in the iron grip of her love. They were her first concern. How could Annabelle possibly understand what it felt like to realise that she'd lived most of her life on a famine of affection, indifferent to—if not actually irritated by—her husband, obligated to her son, and the one creature she'd felt any overwhelming fondness for was that strange refugee girl, Tien, whom she'd pushed away before there was any trouble with the mother? She was a good woman; she had helped many people. But was she incapable of loving? Where were the people who really mattered to her?

She looked at Annabelle and felt a strong need to connect with someone. She said, 'I really miss having the kids around. I haven't seen Tien and Justin for so many years.'

'*Yah lah*. Me also. One moment they such good friends and now look! Never see them anymore. I don't know what happened. So sad, you know.'

'Maybe we should do something,' Gillian said slowly.

'What to do?'

'I don't know. But we've got to do something.'

A week later they turned on their televisions to learn that Diana had been in a car accident in the Pont D'Alma tunnel in Paris. Annabelle rang Gillian at midday. 'Eh! Come over and watch with me. Got CNN, you know. Also BBC,' she added as a concession to Gillian's English sensibilities.

As long as Gillian had been alone, it had been a mildly shocking piece of news. Once she was with the Cheongs, however, the emotional reality of other people, the presence of an audience to act and react with, transformed the event into a communal melodrama staged in Annabelle's plastic-shrouded living room. In Annabelle's obsession with cleanliness, clear plastic sheeting covered the sofa—although lace doilies were placed over the head-rests—plastic squares were cut out to fit the coffee and side tables, plastic jackets hugged the hi-fi system, and the lampshades were still entombed in plastic. The house was redolent with the synthetic lemon scent of Ajax Spray 'n' Wipe.

Shock and grief were cultivated within this antiseptic atmosphere. The two women sat in front of the television sipping tea and nibbling on the pineapple tarts that Tek had brought back from a recent trip to Singapore. The news coverage of the accident was unremitting, cutting rapidly from the commentary of grave-faced anchors perched in front of bustling news rooms, to the latest updates from European correspondents 'on the ground'. They watched the Parisian night sky pale into dawn and gasped at the mangled metal of the car, the scatter of glass winking in the pewter light.

By evening their eyes were red-rimmed and puffy. A gentle hill of soggy pink tissues bulged from the waste basket. Tek shuffled and looked distinctly uncomfortable.

'What's it got to do with us?' he asked.

The answer lay in the avalanche of tributes; the rapidly assembled hagiographies; the sight, on television, of ordinary people on the street—mums and dads with their little kids—as well as dignitaries and celebrities sorrowfully launching forth their hearts to those poor boys who must be so traumatised; and even the sight of the overweight black man in Muslim garb prostrating himself at the foot of the black iron gates of Buckingham Palace, wailing, 'There is no justice!', as if his heart were breaking.

As though her life, let alone her death, could possibly matter to him.

This was a personal tragedy on a global scale, and Gillian felt particularly proprietorial towards the event, for had she not been born in England and come out to Sydney in the late 1950s as a ten-pound immigrant? As for Annabelle, she was an avid collector of women's magazines with Diana on the cover and her hair was still styled like Diana's. So the world mourned, and Gillian and Annabelle along with it. Hugging each other at the end of the evening, they cradled their grief and agreed to nurture it by getting together for dinner on the day of the funeral.

'We'll get all the families together,' Gillian said. 'And you know what? This will be a great chance for the children to meet again.'

'Yes! They can friend each other again over food,' Annabelle said excitedly. The two women beamed in satisfaction.

'You've got to be joking,' Bob grumbled when Gillian told him about it later that night. 'Diana's dead and you want to hold a dinner? A Dead Diana Dinner. Bloody hell.'

The three families, plus appendages, were at the Cheongs' just after six that evening: Annabelle, Tek and Justin; Gillian, Bob and Gibbo; Tien, her mother Linh and her fiancé Stanley Wong. Introductions were made and, like the first time Tien had met him in their Year 3 classroom, Gibbo stared fixedly at his feet and avoided meeting anyone's eyes. When she greeted him, he looked past her shoulder and nodded in awkward greeting. There was nothing but a residual embarrassment. It would have been easier if they had never been friends.

'Good to see you,' Justin managed, but the words rang phoney even to his own ears.

Gillian and Annabelle's enthusiasm camouflaged the tension. Gillian had made a pot of curry and a pavlova which she now gave to Annabelle. '*Ai-yah*, I told you no need! So kind of you. Tek, see how kind Gillian is. She made us curry.'

Her husband looked unenthusiastically at the porcelain bowl Annabelle held. 'Great. Thanks.'

'*Ai-yoh*! *Ai-yoh*! You all so grown-up already!' Annabelle said as she hugged and kissed Gibbo and Tien. 'So good to have the three best friends here for dinner once again. Remember how you used to come over all the time? Mustn't be a stranger now, you know.'

She made them take off their shoes by the front door. She stooped to arrange the shoes neatly on the plastic hall runner so that stray dirt from the soles would not contaminate her cream carpet. Then she ushered them into the dining room and got them seated. Tek rolled his 80-centimetre television into the dining room so that they could have dinner while they watched. Annabelle darted out into the kitchen and returned with huge platters of something that looked like burnt boots and discs of hardened lard.

'Roast beef and Yorkshire pudding,' she told them triumphantly. 'Made especially for Diana's funeral. Oh, and Gillian's curry.'

'I'm afraid it doesn't quite go,' Gillian said apologetically. 'I thought you'd make something Asian.'

'You should have,' Tek muttered as he sawed away at the roast beef.

It was a dismal meal. Chewing doggedly on chunks of over-roasted meat and unyielding pudding, they waited for the awkwardness to dissipate, but the atmosphere simply grew more stilted and unnatural. They were overwhelmed by indigestion and everything in the universe seemed to circle back to this: the acutely uncomfortable feeling of fullness, of massive solidity, nudging insistently against the heart.

Only Bob seemed satisfied, perversely cheered by the obvious failure of the Dead Diana Dinner. He squirted tomato sauce until his dinner plate was a massacre of meat and bleeding pudding, defoliated of wilted greens which he had brazenly dumped onto his son's plate.

Tek opened more bottles of red wine and topped up glasses. They would need it to get through the meal, let alone the evening.

Annabelle, who ordinarily prided herself on her culinary skills, fibrillated with embarrassment and slid apprehensive glances around the table. If only someone would let her catch their eye so that she could apologise profusely for the meal. But all eyes were fixed on the TV screen featuring the flower-decked coffin bearing the white envelope inscribed 'MUMMY', while all mouth muscles were involved in the unrewarding task of mastication.

Because the television was his and he had paid nearly ten thousand dollars for its behemothic mass and booming sound, and simply because he was a man, Tek would not relinquish his right to the remote control. In his role as host, he reluctantly deferred to Gillian's wishes and stifled a yawn at the BBC's dignified but silent camera work, zooming in on the carriage until the bobbing envelope filled the screen. Nobody said anything but the bleeding obvious, punctuated by long pauses. 'And there we have . . . on the gun carriage . . . a poignant card . . . from the young prince . . . Mummy.' They could see that for themselves. It was boring. Were they going to watch the jogging coffin the whole night? For God's sake, why didn't the commentators *comment*? That was what they were paid for.

Tek craved garrulous American sentimentalism, a flood of soothing banality to fill the silent space in which only the clink of cutlery could be heard in the dining room. He wanted the comfort of noise.

He flicked the channel and ignored the deliberate hiss of Gillian's inhalation. That was better. They knew how to liven up a funeral, the Americans, with their wide-angled shots of the gun carriage and the tripping horses, the zoom-ins on the teary, sporadically applauding crowd swarming from Kensington Palace to Westminster Abbey. Then it was 'Over to you, Dan', and a cut to the studio for commonplace observations from the sculpted faces of immaculate presenters wearing their Serious and Distinguished looks, followed by a live satellite feed from London for a comment from the bouffant-haired thirty-something woman in the street: 'You know what? I flew all the way from Chicago to be here? It's like, such a tragedy and I'm, like, how could I miss this last chance to say goodbye? I'd kill myself if I didn't come. She was so special, you know? She was like someone you felt you could pick up the phone and talk to and say, hey, come over and we'll bitch about men, you know? I feel so sorry for those poor boys. My heart just goes out to them and I'm, like, I feel your pain, you know?' At that point her young friend with the beaded hair, who had been hovering impatiently next to her, stuck her heavily made-up face into the camera and shouted, 'I just wanna say one thing. Princess Diana, if you can hear me out there and I know you can 'cos you is an *angel*. Yes ma'am, an *angel*. You go, girl!'

Later, they wouldn't remember exactly how or when the argument started. The cameras swept Westminster Abbey and picked out celebrities like snipers. The waiting was interminable. The choir started singing Verdi's *Requiem*. Perhaps it was then that Bob said (everyone was sure that it was Bob who started it), 'I can't believe we're watching this crap. I can't believe the whole world is so bloody stupid that people actually imagine this is important.'

'It *is* important.'

'Why?'

'Because. Because she cared for kids and landmines and people with AIDS. Because she was a special woman and we won't see the likes of her among royalty again.'

'Special? Come on. A woolly-minded, starry-eyed teenager who married upwards and didn't like the deal she made. Who was spoilt enough to demand that her life be a fairytale, and then when it wasn't, she threw a tantrum, told a lot of nasty stuff to the media and had it off with any number of other stupid dickheads just to prove that whatever else money and fame can buy, it can't buy good taste. Special my arse.'

'Lovely. Thanks for that. Obviously good taste is beyond the reach of some here at the table.' Gillian dabbed her lipstick delicately with her napkin to emphasise her point.

'No, actually, I agree with Bob.'

'Even if he's right, her death is still tragic.'

'What her death is, is unoriginal.' That was Stanley the doctor, striving to demonstrate his artistic side as usual, Tien thought. Always on a quest for innovation.

'Too right,' Justin agreed. 'Hundreds of Hollywood dickheads have achieved an inglorious death by drug overdose or car accident.'

'Yeah, when you come to think of it, even Grace Kelly beat her to it.'

'Don't you women see? This silly woman, with all her fantasies and affairs, was just a pathetic, ordinary woman with the heart of a Noelene Donaher from Sylvania Waters. The People's Princess indeed.'

'Doesn't say much about the people, does it?' Stanley, being sophisticated and amused at the hoi polloi.

'Nup. A vain, ignorant woman who knew how to preen for the cameras and who had the morals of an alley cat.'

'Oh, come on. If she did, it was Charles's fault. She was only nineteen. She was only a child.'

'She didn't stay nineteen, did she?'

'She was a slut, all right. At least Charles was faithful to one woman. How many lovers did she have?'

'He started it first.'

'Just because he had an affair doesn't mean she can go ahead and have one too. Nice women don't do that.'

'Nice women, Tek? Talk about a double standard!'

'You chauvinist Asian men—'

'Cut the racist feminist crap, Gillian.'

'What the hell does it all matter anyway? Who gives a stuff?'

The men shook their heads. Their women had gone stark, staring mad. There was no other credible explanation. It was inconceivable that their mothers, wives and lovers should identify so deeply with this woman. It had to be some kind of princess pathology, an insanity that infected ordinary decent women.

So Diana found she didn't have much in common with her husband. Well boo-hoo! Welcome to the real world of marriage. So she found out her husband had been having an affair from practically the honeymoon or something like that. Well, lots of wives—especially in Asia, Tek opined—coped without sticking their fingers down their throats and having it off with who knew how many men. Didn't they? Because if women thought this sort of thing was all right, was understandable, was even forgivable—well, what did that say about the women they had married? Would their wives do the same thing under similar circumstances?

To care so deeply—what did that tell you? Could Diana really be the apotheosis of womankind? And if nothing could satisfy this woman who had everything—not fame, fortune, nor fabulous fashion; neither hot cars nor cool holidays—then what hope had the ordinary bloke of ever fixing things right for his woman? Because what the hell more did a woman want on top of all that?

Then Gibbo spoke up unexpectedly, his voice rusty from disuse. 'I think what she wanted was not to feel alone.'

'Ah, come on,' Bob said, embarrassed and annoyed that this son of his should always somehow be so touchy-feely, so unmanly. 'She wasn't alone. Or if she was, she didn't have to be. She had more friends, lovers and hangers-on than you could poke a stick at.'

'Not being alone,' Gibbo said. 'Feeling alone. You know. Lonely.'

Hostility diffused into general awkwardness and mental feet shuffling, because surely Gibbo was revealing something that nobody should be meant to witness. Bob huffed out an irritated sigh. His son was still the poor, bullied kid who had been shoved roughly onto the asphalt playground, who then came limping home to peel back the bandaid and expose tattered shreds of skin and flesh scraped hideously raw. 'Look,' he demanded with quivering lip and tear-filled eyes that pleaded for something no-one could give. He was not like other kids. You didn't know how to comfort him, and those eyes left you feeling inadequate and guilty. 'All right, all right. There's nothing to get worked up about. We'll just put some Mercuro-chrome on it and fix it right up. No worries.' He was an emotional suction hole that you had to scramble away from before he vacuumed everything out of you. He didn't have the decency to make a valiant pretence at being normal. Surely he should realise, at the age of twenty-one . . . and that was when it hit Bob. 'Fuck. It's your birthday today.'

'Oh my god,' Gillian uttered, horrified. Her eyes swung to Gibbo's and she reached out a hand towards him. 'Nigel. I am *so* sorry, darling. I completely forgot. Your birthday! Oh my god.'

'Happy birthday, son,' Bob said gruffly. The tips of his ears were red with embarrassment and perhaps even shame. How was it that he could never do right by this son of his, whom he loved so much but with whom he could never connect? They blundered about like blind-folded sumo wrestlers, occasionally thudding into each other with stunning force, but more often than not stumbling past one another and crashing into the walls of their relationship instead. The fault was wholly his this time. There was no denying it. But there was no apology forthcoming from Bob Gibson either. Instead, he punched Gibbo lightly on the shoulder. 'Getting on, aren'tcha, mate?'

'Happy twenty-first, Gibbo,' Tien said, and the others mumbled their congratulations self-consciously. It was an uncomfortable situation and although nobody voiced it, they could not help feeling that Gibbo was largely to blame for creating this faux pas on their part. Any normal guy would have been making a fuss about his twenty-first for weeks, so that you couldn't help but remember it. Gibbo, however, kept silent and this was the result. This feeling of guilt that, in the busyness of everyone's lives, he had been forgotten and he didn't deserve that because he was actually a pretty good bloke.

'I've got some candles somewhere,' Annabelle said brightly. 'I'll go stick them on Gillian's pavlova. Better late than never, isn't it?'

'I'll come help,' Tien muttered, wanting to escape the awfulness of this dinner party for just a moment. She put her hand lightly on Gibbo's shoulder as she passed. 'Sorry, Gibbo. I'll send you your present during the week.'

'Ditto that, Gibbo,' Justin said, leaning back. He inhaled deeply and massaged his temples. 'What shit-house friends you've got, hey? I'm really sorry.'

'No worries, guys,' he said miserably, aware that the awkwardness was somehow his doing.

The women returned with five pink and blue striped candles flickering uncertainly atop the white crust of the pavlova.

'Happy birthday, Gibbo,' Annabelle cried triumphantly. They sang a discordant 'Happy birthday' to him, gave three half-hearted cheers and urged him to blow out the candles.

'Let's drink *yum sing* to Gibbo,' Tek declared, and they toasted the birthday boy. '*Yu-u-u-u-m sing!*'

'Well, we all wish you the very best, Gibbo,' Annabelle said, the whiplash of her glance flicking around the table to coerce her family and friends into happy harmony once more. 'Diana might have been lonely, but at least you never have to be alone. All of us love you, you know.'

Into the muttering of assent obtruded Elton John, warbling his revamped version of 'Candle in the Wind'. They sat in silence and watched his shut-eyed, crack-voiced performance. Like everything else about this televised production, there was a sense of deflation at the end, a feeling that things were proceeding so smoothly, so mechanically, that time seemed to speed up like a metronome progressively picking up its pace, so that the end came galloping towards you, leaving you with no time to take it all in.

That was it, then. The coffin now in the hearse, wending its way out of London through the stems of scattered flowers and the shotgun bursts of applause. On the largely deserted verge of the motorway, the hearse stopped. The driver got out and flicked flowers off the windscreen, climbed back in, and the hearse rolled onto the motorway. The television cameras zoomed into the hearse and caught the reflection of grey clouds smoking over the rear window. It was over. Back to the studio for desultory comments and more American-accented solemnity.

Tek turned down the volume of the television. Bob drained his glass of wine and reached for the bottle. If they had been religious, if they had shared any one religion, they might have prayed and ended the evening with ritual and at least that would have been something to do. As it was, they were left with the inedible remains of the dinner and nothing to say to each other. It was his responsibility as the host, Tek felt, to break the sullen silence.

'Well, I'm sure I speak for Annabelle and my Jay here when I say that it's so good to see all the families and friends here tonight, sharing a meal. You know, in Chinese culture, eating together is a very important thing. Westerners go to the pub for a drink, but we Chinese always invite people to our homes to eat with us. In the old days, whenever we meet someone we don't say, "Good day, mate. How you going?" We say, "*Sek pau may?*", which means "Have you eaten yet?" But actually, it just occurs to me that when we call someone to the table, like this evening when Annabelle invited you all to sit down, we say, "*sek farn*", which means "eat rice", because of course we Chinese eat rice with every meal. In fact, if I don't have rice with a meal I don't feel properly full, as though I've really eaten a proper meal. But of course now that I have lived in Australia for so long, I am used to the Aussie meal, like barbecue. And Annabelle is so multicultural she always likes to experiment with other cuisines. Like tonight she cooked an English dinner for Diana's funeral.'

He looked forlornly at the remains of the meal.

'*Hi-yah*, Tek! *Lao sai!*' Annabelle exclaimed. 'Hurry up. Nobody wants to hear you talk and talk and talk. How come you always got so much to say?'

'No, it's all right, Annabelle,' Gillian said hastily. 'Let him finish.'

'So anyway,' Tek continued, 'we Chinese always ask, *Sek pau may*? Because we are concerned about each other's health and well-being. So here we are: all the families brought together because our children have been friends since their childhood. Hey, Gibbo? Hey, Tien? And Jay, of course. Always thinking about his good friends and wondering whether they already *sek pau may*! So what I think is that we would all agree that although we don't always see eye to eye where Princess Diana is concerned, the one thing we can learn from her death is how important it is to eat together. To all *sek farn*.'

'Because she was bulimic, you mean,' Bob said, burping loudly.

'Huh?'

It was so typical of Bob to try to spoil everything, Annabelle thought. She aimed a sympathetic smile at Gillian for having to put up with such a difficult husband.

Gillian interrupted testily. 'Oh, grow up, Bob. Why do you always have to act so superior and try to put people down? You know perfectly well what Tek meant.

Tek expressed some beautiful sentiments which happen to be very true, but as usual you have to sneer.' Slowly, to Tek: 'He understands you, Tek. There is no need to explain.' She looked around the table. 'Well, I agree with Tek. We should make a greater effort to maintain the friendship between our families. Quite right, Tek. Sake fan indeed.'

'Crap. It's a load of crap. What friendship is there to maintain?' Bob erupted. He slashed a furious glance at his son, then at Tien and Justin. How could Nigel just sit there politely while his friends ignored him all night? Friends indeed! When was the last time either one of them had called him or gone out with him? Those two Asian kids had run tame in his house. Why, he'd coached Justin at cricket and footy, even took him out for a spin in the old Holden Commodore when Justin first got his Ls. There was a boy who'd never been afraid of him, unlike his own son. And then the betrayal. Even worse than that, they acted as though it was all Nigel's fault. And the pity of it was that, in his heart, Bob could not help believing that Nigel was somehow to blame, because just look at him with his girly pansy ways despite the solid strength of his bulk. The irony of it all!

'Hey, Justo. Friends, your father says. Well, go on. Tell him the truth. Is my son your friend?'

Gillian squawked and flapped in her seat. 'Bob, what are you going on about? Please. Please don't make a scene.'

He ignored her. 'Answer me, dammit.'

'Yeah, of course,' Justin muttered. He couldn't meet that crazy bastard's eyes. He felt deeply ashamed, but more than that, he felt scared. What did Mr Gibson know? What had Gibbo told him?

'Tina? Is Nigel your friend?'

'Yeah, 'course,' she echoed. She looked at Justin for the first time that night and rolled her eyes. He grimaced back at her, and it was just that easy. The intervening years dropped away and they were back to being friends once again, united against the blustering fulminations, the sheer embarrassment, of Bob Gibson.

This was the last time she would ever come to dinner at the Gibsons', she swore to herself. She should have known better. In fact, she *did* know better, but Linh had insisted because she felt sorry for Gibbo. 'You and Justin must go,' Linh said. 'Don't let Gibbo be the only one of you to turn up. And besides, it will be such a great opportunity to announce your engagement to Stanley.'

Now look what had happened. She could have spent a romantic evening with Stan having dinner somewhere chic and expensive. Stan would have known where. He liked to read the *Good Food Guide* and *Gourmet Traveller* in his spare time, and she liked the fact that every restaurant he chose was right at the other end of the city from where she grew up—a constant affirmation to her of her own success. She'd shrugged off those Vietnamese boat people roots and made the cultural and class migration eastwards into hip, cosmopolitan Sydney life. But after all that, to have to drag her fiancé back to this: the boredom, the humiliation, the sheer and utter daggyness of everything she'd come from and everything she was trying to flee, including her childhood friends. Before, when she realised she'd forgotten Gibbo's twenty-first birthday, she'd felt the strong tug of guilt, especially when she thought of Gibbo in his friendlessness. But in the midst of this new humiliation, there was no room for anything but the purity of white hot fury. She felt justified in her choices.

Still, childhood training held and she said placatingly, 'Gibbo and I will always be friends, Mr Gibson. But you must see that everybody is really busy these days, what with finishing uni and finding our feet in the workforce and everything. We all go through different phases of life and right now, many of us are in the process of establishing relationships. Settling down.'

She was quite pleased with how she'd prepared the groundwork for her big announcement. She turned to Stanley and saw that he was gone. Then Bob Gibson cut the ground from under her.

'Don't you talk to me in plurals, Tina Ho. I'm not interested in "many of us". I'm only interested in you and why you have no time for Nigel now that you're working. English teacher, huh! Grown too fine for us now you're living in Bondi? You've forgotten your roots.'

'Vietnam?' she said coolly. 'I don't think so.'

'Bob, calm down, please,' Linh said, placing a hand on his arm. 'Don't be so angry with Tien. You shouldn't speak to my daughter like that.'

'I'll speak to her any damn way I please. She could've been *my* daughter if things had been different. You'd have done better with me than that bloody Yank who fucked you over and then fucked off at the end of the war.'

He stopped short, aware that something had not come out right. He hadn't said what he'd meant to. It was the wine. He'd been diverted, sidetracked by other people's interruptions. He looked at his wife and felt disorientated.

'What are you telling us, Bob?' Gillian said. She was very calm as she looked at him. She didn't feel betrayed. Rather, an intoxicating sense of certainty, of vindication, welled up inside her, the knowledge that she had been right after all. There was a reason why she could not love him as she should. 'Did you have an affair with Linh? Is that what you're implying?'

Tien pushed back from the table and said slowly to Bob, 'How do you know what happened to my father? Did you know him? Why didn't you tell me? Mum, did you know Mr Gibson when you were in Vietnam?'

'Don't take any notice of him,' Linh said. Her face was flushed with deep embarrassment. 'Gillian, he doesn't mean what he's saying. Can't you see he's drunk?'

Gillian ignored her. 'You didn't answer my question, Bob. Did you have an affair with Linh?'

'No, dammit. Of course not. That's not what I meant.' He was furious at the filthy-mindedness of other people.

'I see. Excuse me.' Gillian got up from the table and went out into the hall to get to the bathroom.

'She's a bloody drama queen,' Bob accused. He looked at Annabelle. 'You both are. We wouldn't be here tonight if it weren't for your ridiculous antics. But oh, no! We've got to get together for this fucking Dead Diana Dinner.'

The bathroom door was closed. Gillian desperately needed a pee and a few moments to collect herself. How odd that phrase was, she thought irrelevantly. To collect herself, as though she had been dropped and scattered, like coins, and needed to be gathered up and put into a purse. Her breathing was shallow and she felt rather dizzy. She wondered whether she was having a stroke or a heart attack, then dismissed the thought. She just needed to sit down quietly.

She gripped the ceramic door knob and twisted. Locked. It was very annoying. She put her ear to the door. Silence. She got onto her hands and knees and peered through the crack between the base of the door and the cream pile of the hallway carpet. Darkness. Getting to her feet, she tapped on the door.

'Hello? Hello? Who's in there?' she called out. She could hear someone shuffling, shifting weight but trying not to make a sound. Maybe it was a burglar.

Quickly, she envisaged the toilet in her mind: pale green square tiles around the base of the commode, and a matching toilet seat cover in pale green carpet pile. Annabelle had told her long ago that she only put the cover on when company was coming, otherwise she'd have to wash it every week. On the whole, she said, her men weren't too messy because she had a No Standing policy in all her bathrooms and she'd trained her men well. To the right of the toilet bowl, a roll of toilet paper spawning blue shells and green starfish on its three-ply surface. To the left, a tiny white sink holding a squat clay jar with a white pump that squirted out antibacterial liquid soap. A paper towel dispenser above a bamboo wastebasket lined with a plastic bag. A stumpy little cactus bristling on top of the commode, next to a spare roll of toilet paper disguised as a fairy in a pink ballgown. And three and a half feet above the commode, a small fly-screened window that only the contorted body of a wriggling child could fit through. The burglar was trapped.

Later on, Gillian couldn't understand why she had not called out for help. She supposed that she was no longer capable of thinking. All she knew right then was that there was a burglar hiding in the Cheongs' mint green toilet. She was the only one aware of this fact, therefore it was up to her to handle this. Whatever else had happened that night, no matter how much Bob had embarrassed and humiliated her, she would not let the Cheongs be robbed blind without trying to do something. But what?

She glanced up the dimly lit hall and on the hall table, beside the telephone, she spotted three porcelain statues. The Three Immortals—Fuk, Luk and Sau—she thought, household gods found in many Chinese homes to bring health, wealth, happiness and longevity. In her stockinged feet, she stealthily tiptoed over to the table and contemplated the gods. She picked up the one on the left and tested its weight: twelve-inch high Sau, god of health and longevity, with his big bald head, rounded temples budding like apples, and long flowing white beard. He was dressed in an elaborately embroidered red and green Chinese robe trimmed in black, and he held in his left hand a walking stick with the head of a dragon. He would do just fine.

She carried Sau back down the hall and waited outside the toilet door. Her bladder was full and pushed uncomfortably against her uterus like a menstrual cramp. She pressed her thighs together, tried to refocus the feeling of urgency on the statue heavy in her hands, and thought inconsequentially of an ad she'd recently seen about incontinence pads. It couldn't be much longer, she assured herself, for how could he steal anything unless he came out of the toilet?

Then she heard it, the snick of the door unlocking. The ceramic knob turned and the door began to yawn open.

'Bob, I think you're a wee bit drunk.' Tek forced himself to smile jovially to show that he wasn't embarrassed for the poor *ang mor*'s tremendous loss of face.

'I'm not drunk,' Bob snapped. The effrontery of this Asian man to think that he needed placating; to take charge in this way—even if it *was* his house. To act as though he, Bob Gibson, was a problem—or had a problem—when, if only Tek Cheong could be brought to realise it, he was the one with the problem. 'I'm just telling people the way it is. Making you all face reality for once in your lives.'

'Maybe we don't want to face your reality, Bob.' Tek was starting to get annoyed. He cast an exasperated glance at Annabelle. Do something, he signalled. She was the one who'd insisted on having the Gibsons over for dinner. He knew how it would be, and now look at the crazy old man.

Annabelle said kindly, 'Bob, if you have problems with Gillian or Nigel, you know you can always come and talk to us?'

'Yes, we're here for your family,' Tek agreed a little too heartily. 'Fair dinkum, mate.'

Bob couldn't believe the insult. They sat there regarding him with such condescending patience as if their lives were perfect. The perfect Singaporean family who had made the perfect transition from pidgin-speaking migrants to perfectly acculturated Australianness. Perfectly multicultural, holding on to the best of the old Chinese ways—*sek farn* my arse!—and good-humouredly adopting the occasional ockerism, but always with that self-deprecating smile of awareness to show that they were quoting Australianness ironically; that they were cultured and sophisticated enough to play these multicultural games and win. Oh yes. My word, they actually believed they were winners and that he, Robert Gordon Gibson, had a problem. And now they'd made him feel belligerent and out of place, and there was nothing a man like him could do except push back and show them that he was as good as them. Or, at least, that their perfect little Asian family was just as fucked up as his own.

'I have a problem. Did I hear you right? Did you say I have a problem?' Slow and menacing now, drawing out each word, savouring the syllables, building up the drumroll to the frenzied crash and fury. 'I'm not the one with a problem, you fucking stupid . . . chinks. I'm not the one with a fucking faggot disgrace of a son who tries to feel up his best mate. You're the ones with the problem and here's some free advice for you. You'd best haul your poofter son in to the nearest hospital and get him checked out for HIV quick smart.'

He'd done it. He'd lobbed the grenade he'd been cradling in his hands for years, and the explosion should have been like an orgasm in its violent, no-holds-barred intensity. Instead, his throat constricted, his heart felt squeezed dry and all he wanted to do was cry. He raised his head in bewilderment. Was that the sound of his own weeping? He glanced confusedly around him and his gaze rested on Justin. Bob saw that tears were running down the young man's face, and right then he wanted nothing more than to rip out his own tongue until there was nothing but a bleeding mess in his foul mouth.

'God, what have I done? Justo,' he pleaded, but the words 'I'm sorry' stuck in his throat. He sat down heavily on his chair, breathing hard. He shook his head because there was nothing he could say that could possibly atone for what he had done.

'Justin, is it true?' Tek asked. 'Are you a—a *homo*?'

He didn't need the jerk of his son's head to confirm what the tears so obviously told him. He pushed back his chair and stumbled out of the room to do what he always did in times of stress. He retreated to his karaoke den in the rumpus room.

Bob gripped the table and leaned towards Justin. 'Justo, mate,' he begged, but Justin refused to look at him.

'Bob, I think you should go,' Annabelle said. She was white-faced with shock. She couldn't look at her son, couldn't bear the images that invaded her mind.

Bob looked at Annabelle, and all the remorse in the world was no use. 'Yeah, all right. Yeah. I'll just get Gillian—'

She came in at that moment, looking dazed and afraid. 'I've called 000,' she said breathlessly. 'I don't think I've killed him but he might be brain damaged. Tien, I'm so sorry.'

'Who?' Annabelle demanded, dabbing at her wet eyes.

'What?' Tien said.

'Stanley whatsisname. Your boyfriend. I'm afraid I hit him with the statue of Sau.'

'You *what?*'

'I thought he was a burglar hiding in the toilet. He's lying in the hallway now. I think he's still bleeding although I tried to stop it.'

'Fuck! Shit, shit, shit!' Tien pushed away from the table and ran into the hall, Annabelle hurrying after her.

'We meant it to be a good dinner for all of you,' Gillian said. 'We just wanted to help you become friends again.'

She turned and went outside to await the ambulance.

Justin stood up, walked over to the window and looked out. 'Did you tell him, Gibbo, you bastard?'

'I didn't mean to,' Gibbo said helplessly. 'It just sort of came out about that night. I'm sorry.'

'It just sort of came out,' Justin repeated. He couldn't stop the tears. He swiped the back of his hand under his nose and swung back round to the table, thumping it violently. A gold-edged plate slipped off and bounced on the thick pile of the carpet. Congealed brown gravy glistened like dog turd. 'I thought I loved you, you . . . fucking Judas. I'll never forgive you.'

He was still sobbing as he stormed out of the house.

Gibbo buried his face in his arms. He was twenty-one years old tonight. He hated his father, he hated his mother, and most of all he hated himself.

'Don't take it so hard.' Linh had moved from her place across the table to sit beside him. She put a hand on his shoulder and began to massage it gently.

'I fucked up,' he mumbled from under the mound of his arms.

'Yes, I suppose you did. So did everyone else, though.'

'He'll never forgive me.'

'Sure he will. Just give him time. Let's give everyone time to get over this.'

He raised his head and looked at her, his face red and mottled, smeared with tears. 'They despise me, Justin and Tien. They always have. I've been kidding myself we were friends all this time. They've never liked me. They couldn't possibly. I don't even like myself.'

She shook her head, moved by pity, and hugged him quickly. She gave his shoulder a comforting squeeze, then her hand dropped away. 'They don't like themselves either, and they take it out on you. Especially Tien. But the three of you are still friends, and that will never change.'

'Why not?'

'Well, maybe you need each other too much.'

'I don't believe you.'

'We'll see.'

Outside, a dog barked, then lifted its voice in a compulsive howl. One by one, dogs around the neighbourhood began to bay in a canine chorus. Seconds later, they heard the wail of a siren swelling in the night. Two blades of light sliced through the venetian blinds and angled away. The ambulance had arrived.

Linh picked up her handbag. 'Why don't you give me a lift home, Gibbo, since I drove you back the last time.'

He couldn't believe that she was smiling encouragingly at him. She'd brought a drunk home and he'd puked all over her. She'd cleaned him up, then mopped up his car.

And now, despite the tragedy and the farce of this evening, despite the sheer humiliation of it all, she was actually smiling at him.

His heart tumbled over in his chest and he said, 'Linh, I love you.'

B-grade Gay

'The breeze blows cool, the moon shines clear,' he said,
'but in my heart still burns a thirst unquenched.'

Nguyen Du, *The Tale of Kieu*

When Justin kissed Gibbo on the beach it wasn't because he
was all that attracted to his best friend; as a matter of fact,
he wasn't. He felt something that was deeper than attraction, stronger than sex. He didn't know what it was and he
didn't know how to convey it with words. All he knew was
that he wanted to comfort and he needed the intimacy.
Nobody was more important to him than Gibbo. He had
no memory of his life before they became friends.

There was a time in their friendship when there were
only the two of them messing around on the piano in his
parents' living room, playing 'Chopsticks' or 'Heart and
Soul' duets together. Their bums bumped on the piano
seat and they shoved and elbowed each other in rough

playfulness. Their hands reached across the other's half of the keyboard and each banged out false notes and tried to put the other off until they both collapsed in a fit of laughter, pushing each other off the seat.

Justin pretended that he dreaded piano lessons with Miss Yipsoon, but the truth was that he looked forward to those Saturday afternoons with Gibbo. He was realistic about his talent. He scraped through the Australian Music Examination Board exams with a B or B-plus and made his mother sigh over the certificates. 'Must practise harder, *leh*,' she chided him every year. 'You don't practise enough. That's why you don't get A-plus.'

When Annabelle listened to her son playing, she compared him with Brendel or Barenboim and noticed everything that wasn't right. She heard each false note, every stumbling arpeggio and ungraceful acciaccatura. She shook her head sadly over sonatas which seemed only to string together his mistakes. B-grade pianist only! He was never quite good enough for his mother.

Gibbo, on the other hand, made him feel great about himself. Everything he did—four octaves of D major arpeggios played with both hands; simple Clementi sonatinas; the thumping chordal satisfaction of 'Great Balls of Fire'; the tremendous skill it took to stand on the back porch and arc his piss so that the tip of the parabola fell with unerring accuracy into the small black pot of his mother's curry plant; breast-stroking in the Lidcombe public pool and letting out an underwater fart so sustained that bubbles trailed him halfway down the length of the pool—every single thing elicited awe-filled admiration from Gibbo and a dogged determination to emulate his achievements.

That was when there were only the two of them. Things changed when Gibbo was with Tien. One day, not long after the Strathfield Plaza massacre, Justin said to Gibbo, 'Supposing you, Tien and I were in a yacht sailing across Bass Strait. Maybe we're doing the Sydney to Hobart race, I don't know. Anyway, this storm blows up and the mast cracks and the yacht capsizes. What are you going to do? Do you rescue Tien or me?'

Gibbo frowned in confusion. 'But you're the one who's a good swimmer. You're better than both of us. In fact, didn't your mum make you do your lifesaving bronze medallion?'

'Yeah, but just suppose you're the only one with the life jacket but it can only support the weight of two people, max. Who do you choose?'

'Well, Tien, I guess, because you did your bronze medallion and she didn't.'

'Yeah, but what if I didn't?'

'But you did.'

'You're such a dag,' Justin said, exasperated. Then, grinning broadly so that it seemed like a joke, he punched Gibbo lightly on the arm and said, 'If it was me choosing who to save, I guess I'd have to choose you because you're my oldest friend.'

Gibbo reddened and looked embarrassed.

All through their friendship Justin had put Gibbo first, but after the incident at Reef Beach he realised that it wasn't worth it. Gibbo had no loyalty to him. He'd apologised over and over again, begged Gibbo to forgive him. But Gibbo couldn't. He never rang and, just like that, he cut Justin out of his life.

Justin had tried to make himself normal for his parents—the good son—and then he'd tried to make himself normal for his friends. He now realised that it was impossible because he didn't know what normality was. He wanted to be himself, but he didn't know who he was either. People said being gay wasn't a lifestyle, it was an orientation. But this wasn't entirely true as far as Justin could see. Being gay was a complicated affair. Gayness was an identity and, if you got it right, it was a means of belonging. If you didn't, if you were an Asian gay, it was practically an oxymoron.

He needed to acquire the accoutrements of a gay identity but he didn't know how to go about it. Nothing in his background—growing up as a first-generation Singaporean Australian in the western suburbs of Sydney—had prepared him for gay society. All he knew were the camp stereotypes that straight people assumed in their wilful ignorance: limp-wristed ponces who gestured eloquently, elegantly, and sounded like English thespians in the Royal Shakespeare Company; the Qantas trolley dollies satirised by Steve Vizard in his television comedy sketches; transvestites as in *The Adventures of Priscilla, Queen of the Desert*; or the annual Gay and Lesbian Mardi Gras which so horrified Tek and Annabelle.

He assumed that he would have to gravitate to Oxford Street or the Cross to explore his gayness, but he didn't feel confident enough to do it. A couple of times he'd ventured timidly to cafés in Darlinghurst and sat outside, slowly stirring his cappuccino, keeping an eye out for overtly gay men so that he could see what he was supposed to look and act like. All he knew was that he didn't look right because he was Asian. He did not have the right clothes or hair or the right body type. Despite years of elocution lessons with Gillian, he didn't speak properly either. His voice was not modulated correctly, his vocabulary was severely limited and he considered his conversational style lacking in droll wit and eyebrow-lifting irony. On top of being Asian, he wore the wrong clothes, had the wrong hairstyle and was altogether too much of a westie.

He experienced the familiar sense of inadequacy— B-grade gay only, must practise harder!—and was not comfortable venturing into the eastern suburbs. Instead, he stumbled upon a subterranean intervarsity Asian gay club and he despised himself both for this racial segregation and for his hateful feeling of superiority to the foreign students around him. It was safe and it was dull. There wasn't much booze at these affairs, what with the well-known low tolerance of Asians for alcohol: one drink and they all turned beetroot red. The best thing about club meetings was the food—long drawn-out dim-sums in Chinatown or lavish Thai dinners in a restaurant on King Street, Newtown, where the transvestite waiter tossed his hair and flirted with them as he recommended the house specialties that were not on the menu.

Justin did not feel as though he fitted in. He felt he had depressingly little in common with other Asian gays. He was about to give up when he met Jordie Kok, overseas student and jazz pianist extraordinaire. Like Justin, Jordie was studying architecture and, from his first year, was rarely seen strutting around campus without a grey plastic drawing cylinder tucked importantly under his arm. He shared a flat with three other Malaysian students in Randwick and they spent what little spare time they had playing mahjong and cooking fried rice, beef rendang and—their student special—chicken drumsticks braised in Coca-Cola.

Justin's infatuation with Jordie was fundamentally aural: before he ever set eyes on Jordie, he heard him ripping through jazz riffs on the piano at a university Asian fashion parade. He didn't remember anything about the clothes, but he kept wondering about the pianist who was hidden from sight behind a bank of plastic palms. Who was this guy (or girl; it was impossible to tell from the jeans and sneakers pedalling away, which was all he could see of the pianist) who effortlessly reproduced Herbie Hancock and Dave Brubeck, Errol Garner and Oscar Peterson?

After the show, when people clustered around the models, he made his way to the pianist—a slender, absurdly youthful-looking Chinese boy in a bronze silk shirt tucked into ripped jeans tightly girdled with a brown belt that accentuated his girlish waist. Two symmetrical floppy locks of hair, dyed orange, fell over his eyes from the bum-part in the middle of his forehead. Except for the ravages of acne scars, he had the dreamy good looks of a 1990s English boy-band member. As Justin introduced himself and paid him extravagant compliments on his piano playing, he looked up and smiled, and his fingers, still splayed over the piano keys, meandered into a sentimental improvisation of 'Misty'.

Justin fell in love.

It lasted nine months. They were inseparable in the first flush of love, though always careful in front of Jordie's flatmates and Justin's parents. It was easy to find excuses to be

ensconced in Jordie's room most weeknights and practically all weekend: they were in the same architectural
course and had a lot of group work to do together. They
flirted with each other over drawings and snatched
midnight kisses while building plywood models and
writing impenetrable, jargon-ridden postmodern architectural briefs. They spent a lot of time visiting art galleries,
wandering through city streets and criticising the unin-
spiring design of every high-rise building in Sydney's
CBD except for Harry Seidler's Australia Square, which
Justin felt obliged to defend for patriotic reasons.

Such was the power of love that Justin weaned himself
off Schwarzenegger-type blockbusters and abjured Mel
Gibson films unless they were of the *Mrs Soffel* type.
Instead, he made himself watch arthouse films like *Baraka*
and *Powaqqatsi* at the Valhalla cinema. He even forced
himself to hysterical heights of enthusiasm over an obscure
indie film about peasants from a tiny tribal village in Tibet
or Nepal who spent the entire film coaxing donkeys to
cart a dray of huge truck tyres up an impossibly steep
mountain goat track, only to see them all roll off into the
ravine on the other side of the Himalayan pass. 'So
profound,' Jordie sighed, and Justin agreed. There was
nothing he would not do for love.

He felt amply rewarded when Jordie came over to his
parents' house and played old Gershwin and Cole Porter
tunes. Tek wandered up from the rumpus room and
started singing along. Annabelle marvelled at Jordie's
piano skills—definitely A-plus! His parents loved Jordie
and Jordie, being Malaysian, understood 'Uncle' and
'Auntie'. He fitted right into Justin's family and there was

little need for an embarrassed exchange of glances or an agonised, long-suffering, reproachful 'Mu-um!'

Justin wondered why he had never before cultivated any Asian friends apart from Tien. He made up for it now. He befriended the Malaysian flatmates and was rewarded with steam boat dinners in winter and largely alcohol-free birthday parties where a state of intoxication was unnecessary for them to start squirting soy sauce and flinging flour at each other. He loved Asians! He loved their warmth, their easy intimacy, their hospitality, their slapstick sense of humour, their love of soft toys with big soulful eyes. He learned to appreciate Dr Mahathir. He wanted to be a Malaysian. He would go to Malaysia with Jordie over the Christmas break, buy a batik shirt and wear a sarong to sleep in summer.

He was feeling disgruntled and homesick in Penang when he first realised that although he and Jordie had been going out for eight and a half months, they had yet to have sex. He didn't know if it was mandatory; was it normal to be a celibate gay at the age of nineteen? he wondered. They kissed and touched a lot, but that was all. And even that was missing on the trip to Malaysia. He had not realised how schizophrenic so many Asians were—entirely different people in the presence of their parents than they were in the company of their peers—until he saw Jordie playing the filial son to his father. And then he realised that he himself was no different; he too had his separate masks, one for his friends and another for his family. He understood Jordie's servility even as he resented it.

Jordie's father was a successful architect who designed and developed hideous resort hotels polluting several

Malaysian beaches. On weekdays, Mr Kok insisted that Jordie accompany him to the office so that he could get practical, hands-on experience. 'Never too early to start learning to take over the company,' he said. 'I'm sure Justin can take care of himself. I'll leave him the keys to Mummy's Mercedes in case he wants to drive himself around.'

On weekends, the golf course beckoned. Mr Kok was obsessed with golf. He had swung his club around most of the famous fairways of the world. On the rare occasions when they had to queue for a table at dim-sum, he stood in line and visualised himself addressing the ball. He raised an imaginary driving iron in his clenched hands for the backswing, followed through with a twist of his torso and narrowly missed knocking out the people queuing in front of him. Jordie was compelled by his father to genuflect at the golfing green. He was incapable of saying no. One of the Indonesian maids woke him early on the weekends and he had to accompany his father to the golf club for a full 18-hole game. Justin was also invited but he had never played before.

'Never?' Mr Kok was dumbfounded. 'You must learn! How are you going to get on in life if you can't play golf?'

Jordie looked apologetic and tentatively suggested that Justin might like to accompany them to the golf course, carry the bag and act as their caddie. Mr Kok applauded this idea; he approved of young guests being useful. Justin looked appalled and said that he'd rather sleep in. He could see straight away that he'd embarrassed Jordie and displeased the father. He later overheard Mr Kok telling his son that it was a pity Justin's parents had not brought him up better, but that was the problem

with migrants who let their children get too Aussified.
They did not have manners.

Justin felt incredulous anger that this Malaysian
man had the gall to criticise an Australian. At the same
time, however, his resentment was laced with shame,
especially when he noted the way Jordie did not meet his
eyes. Until then Justin had always considered his Asian
parents the embarrassing factor in his social or love life;
he had not thought that an Asian might actually be
ashamed of him.

He stewed in his unhappiness for a week, then he
decided to force the issue. One night, after Mr and
Mrs Kok had retired to bed and he and Jordie were in
the study playing computer games, he leaned over and
fastened his mouth on Jordie's neck, his hand reaching for
the other man's thigh. Jordie squirmed and pushed him
away, casting a swift, scared glance over his shoulder.

'They're asleep,' Justin said impatiently.

'The maids might still be awake.'

'You know they're not.' He looked at Jordie's sulking
face and he felt angry, but he forced himself to say gently,
'I've hardly spent any time with you at all on this trip.
What's the point in me coming to Malaysia if we're not
going to do things together?'

Jordie said, 'I see you all the time in Sydney. My
parents never get to see me. Of course I have to spend
most of my time with them when I'm home. If you were
Asian, you would understand.'

'I *am* Asian,' Justin said, and he was surprised at how
hurt he felt by the accusation.

'No you're not. Not really. Asian-Australian, maybe.'

'All right. If I'm not, I'm not. But what about now? You never let me do anything more than touch you. And you hardly touch me anymore. Don't you want me?'

Jordie looked appalled. 'How can you ask me to do those things when I'm here under my parents' roof? My father would kill me if he knew.'

'He doesn't know. And everybody's asleep.'

'It's his house. I can't disrespect him like that.'

Justin shook his head. 'You don't want me, do you?'

'I don't want to have sex yet,' Jordie said. 'I'm not ready. I don't know why you guys always want to have sex. Why can't we just go on being friends?'

'We've been friends for nearly a year,' Justin pointed out. 'It's natural to take it to the next stage, don't you think? I love you, Jordie, you know that. I want you.'

'Now you're pressuring me,' Jordie complained. 'You don't understand my background. I come from a conservative Buddhist family, not like you westernised Chinese. My older sisters were both virgins until they got married. My parents didn't bring us up to sleep around, you know. We're not promiscuous.'

'What are you saying? You want to wait until we get *married*?'

'All you want from me is sex,' Jordie said. He looked hurt. 'If you really loved me, you wouldn't do this to me.'

Justin cut short his six-week holiday in Malaysia and flew back to Sydney. There was never an official break-up with Jordie where they said the words like a magical incantation and did the post-mortem on the relationship, promising to be good friends. They just stopped contacting each other and allowed the relationship to wither.

When the university semester started, they tried to avoid each other as much as possible. If they ran into each other in classes, they nodded and chatted superficially as though they had never been anything more than friendly acquaintances. The Malaysian flatmates ignored him. He suspected that Jordie had been telling tales. He swore to himself that he would never go out with an Asian again.

Justin was lonely. He longed to be in a relationship. He furtively bought gay magazines and responded to the classifieds. Nobody got back to him when he identified himself as Asian. He began to go to nightclubs in Darlinghurst. They were easier than bars, he figured, because they would be dark and his Asianness might be less obvious. The clubs were noisy and full of people. He would not have to undergo the humiliation of sitting on a bar stool by himself, nervous fingers clasped around a drink for god knew how long, sliding intermittent glances left and right, wondering whether anyone at all would come up to talk to him, because he was not attractive to other men and therefore not even worth the casual exchange of conversation. In the pulsing press of anonymous bodies gyrating in a nightclub he could pretend that he actually belonged to this community.

After a few weekends he was settled enough to start observing others. The first thing he needed to do, he realised, was to change his wardrobe. He got rid of the silk shirts he'd taken to wearing since he started going out with Jordie and he bought himself some tight white Bonds T-shirts and Armani jeans. He had his hair cut short and bought a set of electric clippers in anticipation of the day when he would have enough courage to shave his head. And then he went to the gym. He weight-trained four days a week and supplemented these sessions with aerobic exercises. He curled, kicked, squatted, crunched and lunged. He familiarised himself with barbell bench presses, dumbbell flies and cable crossovers. He jotted down all his exercises in a journal and recorded the six carb-rich meals he forced himself to eat each day. He waxed his legs and armpits but left his epicene chest alone. In winter his skin bubbled with goose-bumps and he looked like a plucked chicken. He went to the solarium, basted and roasted himself to a beautiful golden brown.

Fourteen months later he had an artificially tanned, gym-fit swimmer's body which produced satisfactory contours under his tight T-shirt. He scored his first approach from a white guy shortly after. Mal was a PhD student researching the history of male prostitution in China. He was a Muscle Mary with bleached blond hair, brown doe's eyes and the bulging mass-produced pectorals, flat stomach and tight six-pack of rigorous gym regimes. He was beautiful and, even more amazingly, he was friendly. He sat on an empty stool beside Justin. A short time later he was spouting Michel Foucault and informing Justin impressively that out of the twenty-four emperors of the Han dynasty in China, ten had had male lovers.

'Wow,' Justin said, mentally filing this information away for the time when he could actually use this tidbit of knowledge to prove conclusively to lamenting relatives that homosexuality was not a degenerate Western import into Asian society. In his mind, he constantly rehearsed endless conversations about his sexuality with his family and relatives. In reality, he had yet to rev up his courage to declare himself gay.

As he sat there and listened to Mal enthusing about the exquisite anal techniques of Asian queens recorded in nineteenth-century British colonial officers' diaries, nodding his head intermittently to show his attention was riveted, he could not help fantasising about the future. Here was a white man who actually appreciated Asians! Good old Muscle Mal, who loved Chinese culture and possibly felt that smooth brown bodies compensated for the stereotypical small dick. Enchanted with each other's company, they would leave the bar together and dine at a cosy restaurant nearby, proceeding back to Mal's place after that for their first fuck. Such was the physicality of this world (or so Justin thought) that without the first-date fuck, the possibility of finding true love might be remote.

Eventually they would move in together. He would complete his architectural studies and work for a big prestigious company—or even become another Glenn Murcutt—while Mal got a job teaching at one of the universities. He would design a quirkily modern, Philippe Starck-like apartment for them, making sure it had a studio for himself and his drafting table, and plenty of storage and shelving space for Mal's books. In the morning, Mal—who obviously wouldn't need to get to university until after ten o'clock, since he was in the arts faculty—would wake him with a cup of green tea and breakfast in bed. In turn, he would try to get home in time to cook a healthy Asian dinner for Mal. Then they would cuddle up on the couch and watch—he didn't know what gay historians might want to watch: 'South Park'? 'The Bill'? 'ER'? 'Four Corners'? He supposed he'd better start reading the newspapers and keeping up with current affairs. When they went out to one of Mal's book launches or to cocktails celebrating the opening of a breathtaking building he had designed, people would remark on what a lovely cosmopolitan couple they made, so devoted to each other, so eminently suited, the architect and the historian.

He'd just got them to the point where they were exchanging commitment rings in the gardens of Vaucluse House when Mal's monologue was interrupted by a short Chinese man in an ill-fitting double-breasted navy blue suit and cherry Doc Martens boots, shouldering a forest-green backpack so big it made him look like a Teenage Mutant Ninja Turtle.

'Mal, darling. So sorry I'm late. I was held up by a root canal,' the Chinese man said. He smiled and flashed orthodontically straightened teeth at Mal, then flicked a poisonous glance at Justin.

Introductions were made but Justin barely heard. All he could take in was the implosion of his dreams. Mal slid off his stool and said goodbye. As they walked away, the Chinese man paused, turned back to Justin and hissed in an undertone, 'Just fuck off and stay away from Mal. He's mine.'

Justin understood. Gorgeous white gays who were willing to look twice at Asians were not so common that those Asian gays who had one could afford to have others cut in. He felt sad but bore no ill will towards the other man. He just hoped for Mal's sake that the

Chinese dentist would get a decent haircut and a new set of clothes.

Still, he had made this important discovery: they were out there, those white gays who were attracted to Asians. It was just a matter of finding those rice eaters. When he did, he would at last be happy.

Then, a few months later, he met Dirk at the Sydney International Piano Competition at the Opera House.

The Rice Queen

'Along a lonesome, darkened path,' she said,
'for love of you I found my way to you.
Now we stand face to face—but who can tell
we shan't wake up and learn it was a dream?'

Nguyen Du, *The Tale of Kieu*

Dirk Merkel was an investment banker who loved Bach, Brahms and Billie Holiday. In the mornings, he fiddled expertly with his Krupps espresso machine and ate his breakfast of rye bread, Emmenthal cheese and cold meats to the exquisite polyphony of Bach's Brandenburg Concertos. On balmy summer evenings, when he came home from his high-rise office near Circular Quay, he poured himself a tequila—*reposado* or *anejo*, of course; no adolescent salt 'n' lemon slammers and definitely no worm-infested mescals for him. He'd picked up the taste for it in Mexico City on a work trip a few years back, when he'd also realised he was gay. He sat on the wooden deck overlooking the backyard of his renovated Balmain worker's cottage, slowly sipping his tequila to the sound of Billie mournfully singing 'You go to my head'. He leaned back in his deckchair, closed his eyes and felt an alcoholic warmth seep through his capillaries. He was so alone. He leaked self-pity.

It was his custom to sit thus for at least half an hour before stirring himself to venture into his tidy kitchen. He knotted an apron neatly around his spreading waist and cooked a simple meal for himself, did the dishes and put on the Brahms before logging on to the internet to study stock reports, consider company performances, or trawl the net for gay chat-rooms. At precisely ten forty-five, he logged off and shut down the computer, silenced Brahms and switched off the lights.

He padded to the bathroom to clean his teeth with methodical thoroughness. He looked in the mirror and saw thin brown hair framing an average, pleasant face which was in fairly good condition, although the pores were cracking open wider and the skin was no longer so taut. He had to breathe in deeply to still the sense of panic that this was all he could expect of life and, quite frankly, it was a big disappointment. How could someone who had so much love inside him, who had such a need to tend to others, be all alone? But he was a disciplined man; he would not give in to the panic that licked at him. He turned away from the mirror, climbed into bed and read a book—Don DeLillo or Philip Roth or Saul Bellow; he was seriously into serious American literature—for half an hour. Then he switched on the humidifier, turned off the reading lamp and lay awake in the dark.

He used to have a family. Now he saw his two children every second weekend and they were so polite to

him that it was unnatural. His ex-wife had kept the
Baulkham Hills house, married a plumber, and his
children were getting into the habit of calling their step-
father 'Dad'. He tried to accept his life, such as it was. His
weekends were occasionally varied by a visit to the opera
or the symphony with the handful of married friends who
had not divorced him along with his wife when they'd
found out he was gay. ('Poor Helena! How could he have
done this to her!') These days, however, melancholy was
his most frequent companion in his middle-aged solitude.

Justin was late for the Sydney International Piano Competition. He'd taken the train from Strathfield to Circular
Quay, but it had been delayed all the way because of
track work. From Circular Quay station, he'd stormed
along the footpath to the Opera House, bounding up the
two long flights of steps to the Concert Hall. He was
panting hard by the time he squeezed into his seat just
before the performance started. He hadn't had time to get
a program so he didn't know what he was listening to.
Hesitantly, he leaned over to his neighbour and whispered
the question.

'Brahms Piano Concerto Number One,' Dirk whispered back. They eyed each other for a moment in the
dim light of the hall. Each liked what he saw: the older
man neatly dressed in an expensive dark suit and tie, the
younger man in an arty black skivvy tucked into black
jeans, and boots. They eased back in their fuchsia-
coloured seats and fixed their eyes on the stage where
some impossibly young-looking Korean-Australian kid in

gold-rimmed glasses and a spiky thatch of Kim Jong Il hair was pounding away on the Steinway grand.

They swapped opinions between performers and had a coffee together during the intermission. After the concert Justin took him to a bar and they had a drink. Dirk did not like the gay scene. It was too loud, too outrageous, for a conservative family man like him. He paid for the drinks and offered Justin a lift home. They ended up in the Balmain cottage. Dirk fixed some rose hip tea which they did not drink. Instead, they fell in towards each other like a collapsing tent, kissed, and took each other to bed.

'I have to go home,' Justin said just after one in the morning. 'My parents will worry about me and wonder where I've been if I only turn up tomorrow morning.'

'Do they know?'

'No.'

'I'll drive you home,' Dirk offered. He raised himself from the bed and shoved off the covers, swinging his legs to the floorboards.

'No, don't worry,' Justin said. He pushed the older man back down on the bed and dragged the covers over him. 'It's too much trouble. I'll call for a cab.'

When the taxi came, Justin made Dirk stay indoors. 'It's too cold out there,' he said.

Dirk understood that Justin was not prepared to be openly gay even in front of a taxi driver. He accepted this and only said, 'I'd like to see you again. If you want to.'

'Yeah. That'd be great,' Justin said. He did not sound particularly enthusiastic, but he kissed Dirk before he left and it felt as though he meant it.

Dirk had formed a habit of loving very early on in his life. He'd married when he was only twenty. He yearned to love again. He wanted to have someone to call during the day, making up an excuse like 'Shall I buy takeaway tonight?' or 'Do we need milk?', just so that he could hear the beloved's voice. He wanted to come home and hear all about somebody else's day; to celebrate triumphs with a pop of the champagne cork or to soothe away frustrations with a soft kiss and a back-rub. He wanted to walk past a shop window and see something that he simply had to get for his beloved. He wanted to plan something special for anniversaries and public holidays—weekends away in quaint bed-and-breakfasts, horse-riding excursions, chartering a private yacht. He wanted to lavish affection, to spend and spoil, to tend and adore. He needed to serve. He needed to love.

And then there was Justin. To think that this exotic oriental youth with his beautiful dark looks and well-toned body actually desired him! He was ripe for love and he fell helplessly.

They'd been going out for nearly four months when the Diana dinner occurred. Justin turned up on his doorstep, drunk and distraught, just after midnight. Dirk couldn't work out what Justin was saying.

'Fucking bastard. I loved him. He was my best friend,' Justin sobbed against Dirk's pyjama top. 'To tell Bob and betray me like that. Fucking fucker.'

Dirk stood motionless in the hallway, his arms still around Justin. He felt tears forming in his eyes but he blinked them away. He'd always feared it was too good to be true. Those weekends that he spent with Peter and

Anna—what had Justin been doing? There must be another lover, of course. A younger, gorgeous man with a tight, toned body who bore Justin company in the gay bars and nightclubs that his older lover was too staid to enjoy. He swallowed hard and took a deep breath, steeling himself to deal with this betrayal.

'Don't take it so hard,' he murmured, rocking Justin like a child. The shock of infidelity could not override his basic urge to comfort, to care. 'It will be all right. We will make it all right somehow. Shh. Shh. Don't cry anymore.'

He led Justin into his bedroom, pulled off his socks and shoes, undressed him and put him to bed. He tucked him in, kissed him gently on the forehead and said, 'Get some sleep now. We will talk about this in the morning.'

He got up from the bed and walked to the door.

'Aren't you coming to bed?' Justin asked. He had raised himself up on one elbow.

Dirk stopped by the doorway and turned around. 'I can't, Justin. The children are here tonight. They are sleeping in the other bedroom.'

'Oh shit, I didn't realise. I thought they came last week.'

'They did, but Helena and Frank had tickets to a show tonight so I offered to take the children since . . .'

'Since I didn't want you to come to dinner tonight,' Justin said.

'You didn't want me to meet your family or friends,' Dirk said.

'No. I was ashamed of you. I was ashamed of myself. I'm sorry. I'm so damned sorry.'

'Get some sleep,' Dirk repeated. 'You will feel better in the morning.'

He closed the door behind him and went to the living room. He plumped up a few cushions, lay down on the sofa and pulled a mohair throw-rug over himself. He woke up to the muted sound of cartoons and when he knuckled sleep out of his eyes, he saw that Peter and Anna were sitting on the floor watching television, leaning back against the sofa.

Anna looked up at him. 'Oh. You're awake. Shall I make you a cup of coffee, Dad?'

He sat up and smoothed down his hair. He could feel a bald spot forming. It was vaguely worrying. He tried not to rub it. 'You two are up early,' he said. He glanced towards the hall and looked back to the children. 'I suppose you're wondering why I'm sleeping out here.'

'There's some guy in your bed,' Peter said. He scrambled up and went to the kitchen to pour out a bowl of Coco Pops, which he brought back to the living room. He ate it dry, not bothering with milk. 'We looked and stuff.'

'Peter, you must have a proper breakfast,' Dirk said, concerned. 'I shall cook you something after I have showered.'

'Yeah, thanks.'

'The man in my bedroom,' Dirk began. 'He is a good friend of mine. He was in trouble and he needed a place to stay.'

'Is he your boyfriend?' Anna asked. She took in her father's discomfiture and rolled her eyes. 'It's okay, Dad. We know about these things. So. Is he?'

'He is a very good friend,' Dirk repeated. He looked at his son. 'Peter? How do you feel about this?'

'About what? You being gay? Or the Chinese guy in your bed?' Peter shoved a handful of Coco Pops in his mouth and crunched. He shrugged. 'Free country. Your life.'

'I don't want to upset you,' Dirk said.

His son shot him a considering look. 'I'm not upset, Dad. I mean, yeah, if you asked me, I'd rather you weren't—you know. It was nice when we were a family. But Mum's got Frank now and he's pretty cool. And I guess you can't help it and stuff. Yeah.'

They tried so hard to be sophisticated and grown-up, his children. He wanted to gather them in his arms and hug them tightly to him but he was afraid of demanding something they might not be willing to give. He wasn't sure whether he had any right to expect anything from them except civility. When he looked at them, he felt guilty for the divorce, guilty for not being a normal father to them, for forcing them to understand his difference. And then he felt guilty for regretting his homosexuality because this was something he had to be proud of, otherwise he would become just another victim. He could be no other than the man he was, and surely he need not apologise for that.

He rolled his shoulders and pushed remorse away. Then he got up to love them in a way they could easily accept: he made them pancakes for breakfast.

Later, after Helena had picked up the children, he sat out on the deck with Justin and heard about the Dead Diana Dinner. He appreciated the magnitude of what had happened and he understood Justin's agitation, but all he could feel was overwhelming relief that he had not been betrayed. There was no other young lover. He reached out across the table and grasped Justin's hand.

'You still have me,' Dirk said. 'And you have a home here if you wish. You must know that I love you.'

Justin shook his head, unable to say anything for a moment. He could never have dreamed that anything good could come out of the Dead Diana Dinner. Yet here he was: accepted, wanted, *loved*, by a white man. He didn't deserve it.

He grasped Dirk's hand and said, 'I love you too. I'll do anything to make you happy.'

Coffee-coloured Venus

You raise a daughter wishing she might find
a fitting match, might wed a worthy mate.

Nguyen Du, *The Tale of Kieu*

Stanley Wong proposed to Tien a week before the Dead
Diana Dinner. They spent a Saturday morning doing the
cliff walk from Bondi to Coogee, stopping for a picnic lunch
around Gordons Bay. After lunch he told her he had a
present for her. He made her clamber down over the
knuckled rocks to where the sea bashed the cliffs and he told
her to look for a small wooden box which he had crafted
himself. Her fingernails tore and the skin of her palms
was scraped raw before she found it because he could not
remember exactly where he had placed it. They spent the
afternoon getting increasingly frustrated with the task and
with each other, but he would not let her give up. Finally,
she unearthed it and opened it triumphantly.

A diamond ring winked at her. Then, almost perfunctorily, exhausted by the afternoon's endeavour, he asked
her to marry him. She was moved by the trouble he had
taken to make this moment original. She said yes and
went home to flaunt her ring to her mother as a sign that
she was loved and wanted by a man. She was in such a
good mood that she later allowed Linh to persuade her to
attend the Dead Diana Dinner so that she could
announce her engagement. But instead of basking in the
congratulations of family and friends, she found herself
fielding their commiserations when Stan ended up in the
emergency ward of Westmead hospital waiting for the
two-inch gash in his left temple to be stitched up after
Gillian Gibson had smashed the statue of Sau over his
head. It was not a propitious start to their life together.

The damage went deeper than the scar on Stan's
temple. Gillian had wounded Stan's pride and cracked his
veneer of amiability. Weeks that should have been spent
mooning over bridal magazines, designing invitations and
daydreaming about their honeymoon were now squandered on Stan's thirst for revenge. Instead of planning
their wedding, Stan was planning to sue Gillian. He was
obsessed with the injury done to him.

'You can't sue Gillian,' Tien argued. 'You know she
didn't mean to do it. She was upset and not thinking
right. That night was just crazy.'

'You and your feral westie friends,' he said accusingly.
'I could have been brain damaged. It would have affected
my future earning capacity. It still might. I'm a doctor.
I need my brain cells.'

'But you're okay now. And Gillian is a good person.

She was like a mother to me when I was growing up. I can't let you do this to her.'

He pulled out his trump card. 'Who do you love? Her or me?'

Tien had practised her response often enough for it to roll out automatically. She twined her arms around his neck, kissed him deeply and said, 'You, of course.'

She slid the fingers of her right hand into the waistband of his black jeans, but he would not be distracted by sex.

'Then you should be on my side. I'm the one who loves you. If I can't trust you to support me now, how can I trust you after we're married?'

Love and betrayal walked hand in hand. Tien weighed up her options and, although she chose Stan in the end, she wondered whether he was worth it.

Stanley Wong possessed the soul of an artist. His parents did not understand this. They knew nothing of art. They had never set foot inside the Art Gallery of New South Wales, let alone the Museum of Contemporary Art. Their only encounter with art was the Monet calendar his mother bought every year and the faded Mona Lisa tea towel that dangled from the fridge door. They were cultural philistines. They made him study medicine.

Tien met Stan through her cousin Van, Uncle Duc's eldest son, who was training to be an anaesthetist. Van interned at the same hospital where Stan was posted. He brought Stan back to his father's restaurant one evening when Tien was working there.

Stan was the first man to ask her out, so she accepted. She did not dare say no. Some girls crooked their fingers and men came running. Stephanie-Tiffany-Melanie always had more men than they knew what to do with. They ran through them like last year's fashion, then they went shopping for more. When the time came to settle down, they married successful Vietnamese businessmen and were happy to be imbricated in new webs of family relations. They lived next door to their in-laws and down the street from each other. They were a self-contained community, as they had always been. They were friendly towards her, but their carefully cultivated affability excluded her. As always, she did not fit in.

A few years earlier, Tek Cheong had gone through a Billie Holiday phase. One night, while Tien waited for Justin to come home, she sat in the karaoke den with Tek and sang 'God Bless the Child' with him. She learned that to those who had, more would be given; to those who didn't, well, they were simply losers throughout life. She was afraid that she would be among the latter.

Tien had thrown away her oldest friends only to find the new ones she made at university did not last. She was uncertain of the strength of new friendship and she did not dare test it in case it shattered under the weight of her emotional demands and her desire for intimacy. She liked her friends and they liked her, but they were missing that connection that would hold them all together when life got busy and they no longer saw each other at uni every day. She was afraid that they did not care enough about her to keep in contact. She peered into the future and could imagine little comfort in reading Germaine Greer in her forties and fifties with a vibrator in her bedside drawer if she was still alone. She yearned to get married so that she would have someone anchored to her.

Stanley Wong erupted into her life at this point, dazzling her with the brilliance of his artistic soul and the promised financial security of his medical studies.

'I should have studied art. I won an art competition at my local shopping centre when I was in school,' Stan told Tien. 'They gave me a book of de Kooning prints as a prize. A great man, de Kooning. Genius.' He was tinkering around with sculpture when Tien started hanging out with him. He'd just finished a piece he called *Multicultural Austral-Asia II*, which consisted of a tangle of piss-coloured plastic strips copulating on top of a badly soldered bronze box.

Stan told her that she had inspired him to turn to portraits and he asked her to let him paint her nude. He mentioned the Archibald Prize for portraiture. She was thrilled by the bohemianness of it all and willingly stripped for him in the middle of winter. She caught a bad cold and developed laryngitis, but he nursed her with Lemsip and echinacea and dosed her with antihistamines. She agreed that it was worth it for the sake of his art. When he finished his mixed-media painting, she found that he had Picassoed her, deconstructing her body and reconstructing it as a collage of condoms, diaphragms, tampons and twigs in the midst of violently rioting painted vegetation. She couldn't recognise herself. She was completely indistinguishable from the still life that surrounded her.

'That's the point,' Stan said impatiently. 'It's a postmodern intervention into the nature versus nurture debate where the liminal ambivalence of culturally constructed sexuality collides with an Armageddon of environmental concerns.'

On subsequent occasions he memorialised her naked body with abstract sculptures of corroding metal (he was really into rust) and rags of Vietnamese silk. He signified her sexuality with thick panes of spun glass imprisoning chunks of formaldehyde-preserved raw steak. For Christmas he presented her with a framed painting of her face realistically depicted with his body fluids. It was an expression of his devotion to her; he had collected nearly half a litre of his blood over a period of five months.

His mother, alarmed by his anaemic countenance, brewed him ginseng and chicken soup. She stir-fried pig's liver for his dinner every night to boost the iron levels of his red blood cells. And she could not forgive Tien for indirectly ruining her son's health. She began to wage a covert campaign against Tien, but Stan was oblivious at this stage, too caught up in his artwork and the muse who inspired it all.

Stan's focus on Tien was flattering. She tamed her hair with Frizz-Ease and did her best to turn herself into a docile Asian woman. She deferred to his opinions and preferences, making him feel manly even though he was nearly two inches shorter than her. In return, he took her out to expensive restaurants (he had his own souped-up Honda coupé and received a generous allowance from his parents, with whom he still resided) and promised her that they would get married after he finished his medical studies and internship.

'I need you. You're my artistic muse. My coffee-coloured Venus,' he proclaimed portentously. 'I see you with the eyes of an artist. Other people may see ugliness. They may find flaws. But you know what? I have a different aesthetic vision. I see opportunities!'

Tien hadn't really made up her mind about Stan until she met Justin again at her twenty-first birthday party. She had not seen Justin since high school. He walked towards her across the local community hall and her heart tripped and stumbled. He was even more beautiful than he'd been at school. Her stomach ached with love and she tasted a reflux of sorrow and rejection in her mouth. She wanted to cry. Instead, she threw her arms around him and hugged him enthusiastically, planting loud, noisy air-kisses on both his cheeks. He flinched a little and kissed her back, but his eyes flickered away from hers. He thrust a brightly wrapped box towards her and mumbled, 'Happy birthday'. She caught his arm and dragged him to her group of giggling university friends, proclaiming with an exaggerated roll of her eyes, 'This is one of my school friends, Justin Cheong. Hey, you guys wouldn't believe it but I used to have the most *massive* schoolgirl crush on him, the poor thing.'

They all laughed, Tien the loudest of them all.

Embarrassed, Justin extricated his arm from hers and she shrugged off this latest rebuff, waving him away carelessly. He did not stay long at the party. It gave her bitter satisfaction to note that he seemed to be avoiding Gibbo as well. She would not talk to either of them again, until the Dead Diana Dinner.

Later that night she made Stan drive her out west to the Chullora railway yards. She undressed in the front passenger seat like a schoolgirl changing for PE: quick and competent. There were no zips caught in their tracks this time, no skirts and sleeves straitjacketing her arms. She turned to Stan and said, 'I want you to fuck me and make it hurt.'

He winced at the crudity of her language and frowned at her. 'Well, how could I resist such a romantic invitation?'

'Please. Just do it.' She reclined the passenger seat and lay back, naked. 'I belong to you. Force me to realise that.'

She could see that the thought of it excited him. He climbed over her and unzipped his trousers. She yanked them down his thighs and he grunted as he thrust his erection between her cleft. And stopped.

'You're dry,' he said in accusing surprise.

'I don't care. Go!'

But he would not fuck her with violence and careless-ness. He withdrew from her gently and began to use lips, tongue, fingers and the rolling undulation of his hips and thighs to arouse her. He did not bring her to orgasm by the time he shuddered between her thighs, but she was slick with pleasure and she held him tight.

'You went all weird on me just now,' he said, stroking her hair away from her face. 'Are you all right?'

'Yeah.' She looked up at him and, in the darkness, she could only see a faint rim of white around his pupils. She could hear the hypnotic roar of a long freight train clubbing the silence. For the first time, she told him, 'I love you, Stan.'

'I know,' he said, cupping her face. 'I've painted you. I know you inside out. That's why I love you.'

She made herself believe him because, if she did not, she would always be alone.

. . .

Something fractured inside Tien after her first sexual experience with Justin. She felt unlovely. She feared she was unlovable.

When Justin rejected her, she wasn't simply hurt by unrequited love. She felt his rejection as a judgement on her as a woman. She later enrolled in a women's studies course and she despised herself for being unenlightened. But academic reading only penetrated her intellect; it did not persuade her emotions or break the reflex of social expectations that taught her what to see when she looked in the mirror. She told herself she shouldn't care whether Justin or any other man wanted her, but she did.

As a child, Tien would overhear Auntie Ai-Van and Auntie Phi-Phuong issuing hysterical warnings to Stepanie-Tiffany-Melanie about date-rape by all men, any man.

'You be careful,' they'd say whenever one of the girls started dating, especially if they were going out with an Anglo-Australian. 'All he wants is sex. Men always want sex.'

Auntie Phi-Phuong even went so far as to produce her own home-made Mace. She minced a packet of chillies, stirred them into water and funnelled the mixture into a small plastic spray bottle. 'You carry that in your handbag, darling. If he tries any funny business, you know what to do.'

Auntie Ai-Van agreed. 'Wait until you get that ring on your finger,' she advised. 'No marriage, no sex.'

In Auntie Ai-Van's mind a man could be redeemed from sexual harasser to husband with the acquisition of a ring. Men defined the parameters of their lives. They were sinister, but they also held out the hope of salvation. Sometimes it seemed to Tien as though men were just out there, randy and ready for sex anywhere, anytime, with any woman. Except for herself. She'd offered herself to Justin—a freebie; no strings attached. And still he didn't want her. Not even for sympathy sex. The familiar refrain of self-pity ran through her mind: what was wrong with her? Then, after the Dead Diana Dinner, she knew. It wasn't her; he was just *gay*. She did not stop to consider that, even if he hadn't been gay, he might not have been attracted to her. His gayness was a relief. It gave her an excuse to contact him and rekindle their friendship.

They met at a café in Newtown, ordered their coffees and sat there grinning at each other, ill at ease and embarrassed, but willing to make up and move on. They talked about the Dead Diana Dinner, then Justin told her about his sexual experiences, his struggle to accept his homosexuality, his confusion during the Year 12 formal, and the end of his friendship with Gibbo when he tried to hit on Gibbo and was bashed up for his pains.

'I thought, if that's how he reacts and he's supposed to be my best friend, what will happen if my family finds out? Well, I guess we know now.'

'It can't be that bad,' Tien said. 'Your father has always been so liberal-minded about all sorts of things. I mean, you expect homophobia from Bob, but not from your dad.'

'Yeah, it'd be all right if it was someone else's son. He'd be real open-minded then.'

Tien was gratified that Justin shared such confidences about himself; things she was sure nobody else knew. She hoarded his secrets as a sign of their intimacy. She thought that they would resume their interrupted friendship and everything would be the way it was in high school. Sure, Gibbo was out of the loop now, but she assumed that Justin would get to know Stan while she would get to know Justin's partner and his friends. They would all hang out together happily ever after.

She mentioned this to Stan and he was thrilled at the thought of having a couple of gay guys to add to his motley multicultural crew of arty friends, whom he acquired like cosmopolitan accessories. He couldn't stop talking about it.

'How fabulous! All we'd need to round off the group are some Koori friends. I don't know any Koori people, do you? Where does one go to meet interesting Koori people? We must ask Justin. Maybe he or his gay friends know some Kooris.'

But Tien only saw Justin a few more times before she got married and moved away. Justin never took to Stan, nor did he introduce Tien to his partner or his friends, gay or otherwise. He had a busy social life which did not include her. As in her late adolescence, she kept waiting for him to call but he didn't. In the end she just didn't understand the basis of friendship. How did people connect with each other in such a way that they achieved, at the very least, some sense of community, however evanescent or illusory? Try as she might, she could not figure out the requirements for a life-lasting friendship.

What were the overlaps that kept human beings adjacent and anchored to your life? Shared interests or occupation? Ethnicity, gender, sexuality, religion, the common experience of rejection or failure? How was it that some people managed to manacle others to their lives, bearing their childhood friendships with them triumphantly into the future towards death, whereas others found friendship as weak as water, sparkling and slipping away through cupped fingers, leaving only the impression of wetness and a thirst unquenched?

Tien tried hard to maintain the friendship. She needed to restore the sensation of closeness. Even though Justin did not call her, she rang him regularly. But she grew increasingly frustrated with their conversations. Despite Gibbo's betrayal, Justin never failed to ask her whether she had heard from him. And when he learned that Stan was suing Gillian Gibson, he was furious.

'I can't believe you're doing this. How's it going to make Gibbo feel?' he demanded.

'Quite frankly, I don't care,' Tien said. 'Fuck Gibbo. Why don't you think about how I feel for once? He's the one who let you down and yet it's always Gibbo first with you.'

She did not call Justin again and, this time, she was not surprised when he made no attempt to earn her forgiveness and friendship. She simply did not matter enough to him and, because of that, Stan's importance in her life was magnified. If she did not hold on to Stan, who would be there as her fallback when she grew older and everyone she knew married or moved out of her life? She was not even sure that her family would be there for her.

Tien never realised how much she wanted her family's approval until they withdrew it. They did not approve of the way she treated her mother. She was a daughter who did not show *hieu thao*, and even being engaged to an

Asian doctor could not make up for her lack of respect for her mother.

To Tien's way of thinking, she could never balance the scales with her mother once she'd wronged her. It didn't matter that Linh sighed and said she didn't mind; that there was nothing to forgive; that Tien was her daughter, no matter what, and she loved her anyway. Guilt hung heavy with the last word: *anyway.* That one word contained everything that was wrong between them. As Tien grew older, she became aware that there were things she had done which needed to be expiated, but she also realised that atonement was unending and guilt was unassuageable.

What she really needed, therefore, was for her mother to commit a crime against her. Tien needed Linh to do something so big and so bad to her that not only would the scales balance, they would tip in her favour and at last put her in a position of moral superiority—of utter, guilt-free rightness. She kept a mental list of her mother's major crimes:

1   She abandoned me to stay behind in Vietnam and let me think she was dead.
2   On the first day we met, she punished me for something I didn't mean to do.
3   She didn't have the right to punish me because she wasn't really my mother at the time. She was just a stranger. She hadn't *earned* any maternal authority.
4   Because of her, Gillian didn't want to be my mother anymore. She caused Gillian to abandon me.
5   She's a dictator; she made me stay at home and study through my school and uni years so I couldn't cultivate close friendships.

6   She wasn't there for me because she was too busy
     making money.
7   She doesn't approve of Stan.
8   She doesn't approve of me; maybe she doesn't really
     love me. Or if she does, it's only because she's my
     mother. She doesn't *like* me.

Tien reviewed this list in her mind from time to time and
felt depressed by its adolescent inadequacy. These hurts
loomed large in her mind, but they were invisible to
everyone else, particularly the family, who only saw a hardworking, long-suffering mother in Linh and a surly,
unappreciative daughter in Tien.

    One day, however, Linh finally shocked the family and
committed a significant sin against Tien: she began to
search for a husband after Tien started going out with Stan.
After all these years, Tien was proven right. Even if her
mother had not intentionally abandoned her, it was now
obvious that Linh was not content simply to be a mother
to her, and nothing else. All this time, Linh had been pretending to be a good mother, pretending to try to make up
for the missing years, when the truth was that having Tien
as a daughter was not enough. Linh was a woman who
needed a man in her life. ('Remember all those American
GIs?' Stephanie-Tiffany-Melanie said to Tien.) Linh wanted
to find love. She wanted to be married. She had the same
needs as Tien, and Tien despised her for it.

    Being a practical, focused woman, Linh went about it
systematically. She wanted a high-earning professional as a
husband, so she hung out in the lobbies of expensive hotels.
She sat on plush sofas and waited. She wandered over to the

bar and practised taking long slow sips of her mineral water. She donned her Chanel knock-off suit, entered expensive restaurants and ordered salads. She nibbled slowly on lettuce leaves and did her best to look available and interesting. No-one approached her. She paid her bill and left alone.

Then she put an ad in the local newspaper under 'Nice Asian Woman':

> Caring Asian lady, early 40s, looking for honest gentleman for loving marriage. Any nationality, professionals preferred. No time wasters.

Their answering machine blinked manically, inundated with messages for Linh. She replayed them with delight and Tien listened with disbelieving jealousy. Men wanted her mother. Linh was more popular than her.

Linh went out on several dates. She swatted away groping fingers, thrust out her left hand and firmly repeated Auntie Ai-Van's mantra: 'No engagement ring, no sex.' She did not see those men again. Eventually, she joined a dinner dating group and met up with Gibbo. She became friends with him even though the Gibsons had ruined the Dead Diana Dinner and Gibbo had betrayed Justin.

Tien could not believe it. She was engaged to Stan. This should have been *her* time to be pampered. She should have been the centre of attention. Linh should have been fussing over her like a *real* mother, picking out bridal clothes, arranging a band or DJ, booking ten-course banquets at some red-roomed, gold-chandeliered, dragon-festooned Chinese or Vietnamese restaurant. But

Linh was not there for Tien. Nobody was there for poor Tien except Stan.

Instead, Linh was out dating men and spending time with Gibbo, who had betrayed Justin. Tien knew. Even in the busyness of her work teaching English to foreign students preparing for university, even in the midst of her wedding preparations, she found time to keep tabs on her mother's relations with men. When she came back from Bondi once a week to visit Linh, she snooped through her mother's cupboards and drawers, and pawed through her mail. And when Linh began to be harassed by Gibbo, when his dogged devotion turned into the unheeding obsession of a stalker, Tien was appalled, but she also felt vindicated. Linh had not been a good mother and now she was paying the price.

Love is Coming
to Get You

His face yearned for her face, his heart her heart.
The study-room turned icy, metal-cold—
brushes lay dry, lute strings hung loose on frets . . .
Fast gate, high wall: no stream for his red leaf,
no passage for his bluebird bearing word.

Nguyen Du, *The Tale of Kieu*

7 September 1997

Dear Linh,

I am so grateful for your presence last night. I don't know how I could have got through that disaster of a dinner without you. You've been so good to me and I wish I could tell you how much I appreciate your kindness. You didn't condemn me for betraying Justin and you didn't side with Tien even though, as her mother, you'd be inclined to. Instead you held out the hope of future friendship. What a wonderful encouragement you are! In the midst of a nightmare I feel we forged a powerful bond. You are the first person to make me feel good about myself for such a long time. Thank you for your sympathy and support.

Love,
Gibbo

PS Will you call me? I need to talk to you.

10 September 1997

Dear Linh,

I've been thinking about you continuously for the past few days, waiting for you to call. Do you know what it's like to have all your hopes invested in the plastic handset of a Telstra phone? To pass by the phone a dozen times an hour? To look at it with intense concentration as though by sheer effort of will I could make it ring? To be housebound for fear that you would call in my absence?

I began to wonder if you would ever call. I began to lose hope. But I should have had more faith in you, for finally you did call. I wish I could write down how I feel but the poets have said it all and left me with nothing but trite clichés. In any case, words are inadequate to express how much your . . . well, friendship means to me. I guess you feel the same. You said so little yet I feel that beneath the silence our souls touched. After you hung up I held on to the receiver, unwilling to let go of that link with you.

I am filled with exhilaration at the thought of your existence. The memory of your face is like a blessing to me.

Love,
Gibbo

To: holylinh@yahoo.com
From: cyrano76@hotmail.com
Date: 12 September 1997
Subject: apology

Dear Linh,

I'm sorry if I made you uncomfortable when I rang yesterday. I didn't mean to. Offending you is the last thing I'd ever want to do. And I wasn't trying to tell you that you shouldn't attend the dinner-date sessions, or that you shouldn't be friends with all those men you meet. Please don't be angry with me. I was just concerned, that's all. We're friends. Aren't we?

I won't keep ringing you if it's not convenient for you at home. I understand. We'll just keep in touch via email. I hope you don't mind me ferreting out your email address. I trawled through Tien's last group email message and, as I suspected, she hadn't BCC'd the list of recipients and fortunately yours was there as well. Not bad detective work, eh?

Perhaps I should change email servers so that my messages are instantly transmitted to your account. Then I'll know that somewhere in the midst of fibre-optic cables or satellite signals, a part of us will have miraculously melded through the static of internet traffic.

Please, Linh, I just want us to be friends . . . if friendship is where you're at right now. I'm very good at waiting. I have waited all my life.

Love,
Gibbo

To: holylinh@yahoo.com
From: cyrano76@hotmail.com
Date: 14 September 1997
Subject: Re: apology

You're right, of course. It would be stupid to change servers
for such a dumb reason. Dumb, dumb, dumb. I can't
believe some of the dumb things that pop out of me
sometimes! I'm such an idiot. But you know I have only the
best intentions where you are concerned.

   You asked about my mother. As you can imagine, she's
pretty upset that Stan wants to sue her. Dad blew his top
when they got the solicitor's letter about damages and
emotional distress etc. They blame each other, and I can't
help blaming them. I know she was only trying to prevent
Mrs Cheong from being robbed. I'm just glad you were there
that night and that you're there for me now. I need you.
Things are pretty tense at home these days. They aren't
speaking to each other. Mum has even mentioned divorce.
Everything in my life is so awful right now but I can put
up with it as long as I have you as a friend. You make
everything all right again and I don't care what else is going
on as long as I have your emails to look forward to.

Love from your devoted friend,
Gibbo

To: holylinh@yahoo.com
From: cyrano76@hotmail.com
Date: 17 September 1997
Subject: Thank you for being you

Dear Linh,

Your support means a lot to me at this time. I feel so isolated. Mum and Dad seem to be on the verge of separating, and although I've tried to get in contact with Justin to apologise yet again, he's not speaking to me. I don't blame him, I suppose. I was never a good enough friend to him. I'm no good to anyone. Sometimes I don't know why you bother with me, especially when Tien hates my guts. I don't think she or Stan will ever forgive me. You don't know what that does to me. I know we haven't been close lately but she's my oldest and best friend. Losing her is like cutting off a limb.

Linh, I'm so glad we are friends. I'm content to be patient and wait for your friendship to grow. I need your friendship. I need you. I believe desperately in friendship . . . and even more in love.

In the meantime, let me know if there's anything I can do for you. No matter how big or small, I just want to make you happy.

Your true friend,
Gibbo

To: holylinh@yahoo.com
From: cyrano76@hotmail.com
Date: 18 September 1997
Subject: AFL game

Dear Linh,

I've done what you asked me to. You know I would do so much more for you than this. I've managed to get tix to an AFL game at the Sydney Football Stadium! I've never been there myself so it'll be quite an experience for me. I don't mean that I don't know anything about AFL, of course, because you couldn't grow up with Bob as a father and not know at least the basics of the game. I mean, I know quite a lot about it although I've never been a huge fan. Fortunately, living in Sydney, there's only one team for us to support. But you're quite right, as always: if you're going to take your friendship with any Aussie bloke (such as myself—just kidding, of course!) anywhere serious, you've got to know about all kinds of footy. Except soccer, I suppose. Dad says that's a wog's game, but you know how racist he is. I don't share his views, of course. I hate them, in fact. I'm nothing like him, as you no doubt realise.

He was such a bastard to suggest there was something between the two of you and get everyone all upset, especially Mum, at the DDD. That's just the kind of man he is. A real arsehole. You don't know what it was like to grow up with him as a father.

I'll pick you up this Saturday at 11.

Love,
Gibbo
PS I suppose we'd better wear red and white?

To: holylinh@yahoo.com
From: cyrano76@hotmail.com
Date: 21 September 1997
Subject: I love you!

Dearest Linh,

What a wicked game! And you. You are the most wonderful
person I've ever met. When I held your hand and led you
to the top of the stands, I knew that I'd been right to wait
and that patience must have its reward. I can't stop
thinking about our time together. I can't help wishing we
could do it again right now. I want to be with you always.

What can I say? I love you, I love you, I love you, I love
you, I love you, I love you, I love you—I could keep on
repeating those words eternally. I love you eternally.

Your Gibbo

To: holylinh@yahoo.com
From: cyrano76@hotmail.com
Date: 22 September 1997
Subject: Re: I love you!

Dearest Linh,

I suppose you didn't log on to the internet yesterday.
I suppose you were busy. I drove past your apartment block
after lunch but the curtains of your living room window were
drawn. I drove by again in the early evening but no lights
were on. I wanted to see you so much. I need contact with
you! I went back home for dinner because Mum had made a
roast, then I went out to your place again. The lights were

on this time, but I wasn't sure whether Tien was there and it occurred to me that she and Stanley might not want to see me at the moment, what with the lawsuit and everything. I wanted to ring you. Please say I can ring you. I want to hear your voice. I want to kiss you again. I want to press my lips to the phone receiver, knowing that your lips are at the other end. Your lips are life to me.

Your loving Gibbo.

To: holylinh@yahoo.com
From: cyrano76@hotmail.com
Date: 23 September 1997
Subject: I love you even more!

Dearest Linh,

I could not have been mistaken in what happened between us. I know you must feel what I do. Please, please, please check your email.

Love,
Gibbo

To: holylinh@yahoo.com
From: cyrano76@hotmail.com
Date: 25 September 1997
Subject: Re: I love you more than ever!

Dearest Linh,

Where are you? I need to see you, to speak to you. You haven't answered any of my emails and you don't pick up the phone . . . if you're in your apartment. I don't know. Are you there? I've left so many messages on your answering machine but you haven't called me back. Please, please call me. I need you. I love you.

Gibbo

To: holylinh@yahoo.com
From: cyrano76@hotmail.com
Date: 26 September 1997
Subject: Pick up the phone!

Dearest, darling Linh,

Don't hide from me. There's no need. I know you're there. I swung by your place yesterday after uni and I saw you getting out of the car with Stanley and Tien. You were wearing a navy blue pants suit and your hair was loose over your shoulders. You looked so elegant and feminine in your suit. You are the most beautiful woman I've ever seen. I know my words are trite, but they're true.

You looked right at me, across the street and into my car. I saw love in your eyes, but I also saw you signalling me not to come to you while Stan and Tien were around. You knew that I was there, waiting for you, loving you. You wanted to test my patience and my faithfulness. I passed the test once already, and I knew I would pass it again. I waited for them to leave. I waited there all night and finally I fell asleep in the car.

By the time I woke up the next morning, you'd gone to work. I know, because I went up to your flat and hammered on the door. I waited until I was sure you were not home. You must have gone to work by then. You work so hard. You're so dedicated to the patients you nurse. That's just another aspect of you that I love. There are so many things about you to love. I think about them—about you—all the time.

I don't know what to do with myself now. I'm in an internet café, around the corner from your apartment, waiting for you.

How many times do I have to say it? I love you and only you. I think of you and only you. Forever.

Gibbo

To: holylinh@yahoo.com
From: cyrano76@hotmail.com
Date: 28 September 1997
Subject: I'm on my way!

Darling Linh,

I went to uni because there was nothing else for me to do, but there was little point to it. Everyone's doing their major assignments but I can't focus. I feel so restless. I can't keep my thoughts off you. Nothing matters except you. I know that you must feel my love wrapping tightly around you although we are separated by half a city—you out in the west, and me here in town.

I can't stand being away from you. I'm going to send this email, then I'm driving out to find you.

Can you feel me? I'm getting closer to you all the time. You will look out the hospital window and wonder whether each car that whizzes by on the highway, each horn that sounds in the car park, each ping! of the lift, each swish of the doors sliding open, each step in the hallway, each tap on the shoulder—everything announces my imminent arrival at your side. Love is coming to get you. Love will find you. Love will not let you run or hide.

I love you.
Gibbo

To: holylinh@yahoo.com
From: cyrano76@hotmail.com
Date: 28 September 1997
Subject: Where are you?

Dearest Linh,

You weren't there at the hospital and you weren't at your apartment. Why weren't you there? Where were you? Where are you?

I NEED to talk to you. Please email me. Or pick up the phone.

LINH, PICK UP THE PHONE!

I love you. I love you forever. I'll never stop. I'll never let you down. I'll never let you go. You are mine and I am yours forever.

Gibbo

To: holylinh@yahoo.com
From: cyrano76@hotmail.com
Date: 1 October 1997
Subject: At last!

Dearest, wonderful, beautiful Linh,

I knew that you were testing me and boy did I pass it well or what! I hung in there and I didn't let go. I'll never let go.

I know how you think, how you feel, because I think about you all the time. I know you. You're insecure. You're afraid to believe in my love. You're afraid that I will let you down. Well take a good look at me! I'm still here, waiting for you. I'm not going anywhere. I haven't stopped calling you. I'm still reaching out to you. I WILL NEVER STOP.

You set the test, but I don't hold it against you. I know you just want to be certain, the way I am absolutely certain that we are meant to be together. I waited because I knew that my love would triumph, and at last I have my reward.

I look forward to seeing you tomorrow night. At last, we will be together. Do you know how that makes me feel? You don't at the moment, but you will. I'll show you. I'll prove to you that I can be everything you want me to be.

In loving anticipation,
Gibbo

To: holylinh@yahoo.com
From: cyrano76@hotmail.com
Date: 2 October 1997
Subject: I don't understand!?

Dearest Linh,

I got home over two hours ago but I haven't been able to get to sleep. It's now three in the morning but I feel I have to write to you.

Linh, I don't understand what tonight was all about. I had planned it to be something so special and I don't understand what went wrong. Did I do something wrong? Did you not like the pink tulips I gave you? You have to tell me how to please you! I would do anything to make you happy.

I thought you *were* happy. I've been saving up for weeks to take you somewhere grand. I thought you'd like the restaurant overlooking Circular Quay and the Opera House. I wanted it to be romantic and special for you. For us. You let me hold your hand and kiss you, then you tried to jerk away from me. I understood: you were shy in public. The modesty your cultural background instils in you is just one of the many things I adore about you.

I understand your background; I've read the Lonely Planet guide to Vietnam to catch up on the culture bit, and anyway, I'm sort of Asian too. I share your culture but sometimes the Anglo part of me gets carried away. Was I too exuberant in my affection for you publicly? I didn't mean to embarrass you. But when your heart is overflowing with love like mine, it's hard to keep it all bottled up inside.

I thought you enjoyed yourself at dinner. I thought you liked your meal. Maybe I didn't order the right wine for you? I'll do better next time. I'll learn more about it, and be as knowledgeable as Stanley, I promise. I'll do whatever it takes not to embarrass you socially or make you feel uncomfortable in any way.

But if it wasn't the meal, then what was it? One moment you're letting me hold your hand and kiss you. Then after dinner you say we have to talk, and you don't want me holding on to you. I can't believe you didn't want me to hold your hand! And then the things you said. I don't understand. How could you hurt me like that?

Linh, what's going on? I know you love me. I have to hold on to that knowledge. It's all I have in my life. You are everything that's good in my life.

I know what it is. You're being too noble as usual, thinking only of me and not of yourself. You said that you don't think of me in a romantic way and that in time I would come to see that you are much too old for me. Dearest, kindest Linh to be so concerned about how I feel! Always putting others' needs and feelings before your own! But don't you see, my darling? You don't have to! I love you with the kind of love that concertinas time and space and crushes all distinctions of age, erases all differences of race, and annihilates all opposition to the inexorable triumph of our love.

I drove you to Bronte and we sat by the beach, and you let me put my head in your lap and weep for the infinite emptiness inside me. I know it's inside you too. I see it in your sad eyes. Don't you realise it yet? Together, we have enough love to make each other whole. But you rejected that. You rejected me. Instead, you made me take you home and you said that I must never again tell you that I love you.

You may as well tell me to stop breathing! I love you. I love you. I love you.

And I know you love me. You must love me. With your words you tell me that we can only be friends, but with your eyes you show me that your soul is the other half of mine.

I won't give up. Perhaps you're confused right now, but I have enough certainty and clarity of vision for the two of us. I'll hold on to you no matter what. You will come to see that this is no passing infatuation on my part, but the type of love that comes once in a lifetime. And in the end you will come to me freely and tell me what is in your heart: that you love me too.

Forever yours,
Gibbo

To: cyrano76@hotmail.com
From: holylinh@yahoo.com
Date: 15 October 1997
Subject: PLEASE STOP CALLING ME!

It was a mistake to go out with you. Don't contact me anymore.

To: holylinh@yahoo.com
From: cyrano76@hotmail.com
Date: 16 October 1997
Subject: CAN'T YOU SEE HOW MUCH I LOVE YOU!

Dearest Linh,

I'm desperate for contact with you. You say I mustn't call you. All right, I'll stop for now. But at least email me.
I don't deserve to be treated like this. What's happening to you? What's happening to the wonderful, sweet, loving Linh that I know and love? How can you do this to me?

I feel so helpless and despairing. If this is another one of your tests, then I suppose I must just ride it out and hope that your true nature resurfaces. Please, please turn back into the sweet woman I adore.

What else can I do? Don't you understand? There is NOTHING ELSE in my life but loving you.

Gibbo

To: cyrano76@hotmail.com
From: holylinh@yahoo.com
Date: 26 October 1997
Subject: STOP SENDING ME ROSES EVERY DAY!

I don't want your bouquets of red roses at 7.15 in the
morning. I don't want your little presents on my doorstep when I get home, or your love letters in my mailbox.
I don't want anything from you. All I want is for you to
leave me alone! I don't want to hurt you, Gibbo, but you
must understand that I don't want you around.

To: holylinh@yahoo.com
From: cyrano76@hotmail.com
Date: 27 October 1997
Subject: Thank you!

Dearest Linh,

You are so sweet to me. You don't have to assure me that
you don't wish to hurt me. I know that it is not in your
generous, loving nature to hurt people. You're very kind to
be concerned, but you needn't worry that I can't afford the
things I give you. I've dropped out of uni and have got
myself a job. I'm working in a pub in Homebush and I earn
nearly $450 a week! Can you imagine? I'm saving up so
that I can take care of you. We'll be together very soon.

Your devoted
Gibbo

To: cyrano76@hotmail.com
From: holylinh@yahoo.com
Date: 7 November 1997
Subject: You're scaring me

Don't keep coming round. I will never open the door to you
again. Put it out of your mind and leave me alone.

To: holylinh@yahoo.com
From: cyrano76@hotmail.com
Date: 8 November 1997
Subject: I LOVE YOU!

Dearest, darling Linh,

Why are you doing this to me? Don't you understand how
much I love you? I would never hurt you. I want to take
care of you. I love you forever and ever.

Gibbo

To: cyrano76@hotmail.com
From: tien_ho@yahoo.com
Date: 15 November 1997
Subject: FUCK OFF!!!

Gibbo, you fat pathetic turd! How dare you stalk my
mother! How dare you even think of being in love with her!
You're sick. Just fuck off, do you understand me? I'm only
warning you this once. Stay away from her. Contact her
again and we're going to the police. Fuck off or I'll get her
to take out an AVO against you.

Mother and Daughter

Kieu said: 'You once bore me, you've brought me up,
a double debt I've not repaid one whit.'

Nguyen Du, *The Tale of Kieu*

There had been a time when Linh thought of nothing
else, asked for nothing else, but survival. Then she had
survived, and all she wanted after that was to be reunited
with her daughter so that they could live ordinary lives in
suburban mundanity.

She was so grateful to the universe at first. She noticed
little shocks of beauty all around her as she took her morning walk through the sleeping suburban streets. Brick and
weatherboard houses with low eaves hugging their crowns
like brown-rimmed hats, a garden splashed with paint-
daubs of pink azaleas. Two black crows stooped on a bare
branch. Cloud clots in the yawning blue. Vehicle-choked
Vietnamese auto-mechanics' yards adjoining cemeteries

of rusting steel and tumbled tyres, the pyramids of car bones piled skywards. Everything she noticed brought her kinetic joy.

Eventually, she got used to it and was no longer surprised. How quickly she then forgot the upheavals of her past and became accustomed to the torpor of the suburbs. Within a few years normality inflated her hopes even as it fuelled her restless dissatisfaction. Motherhood was unfulfilling and fear began to lap the edges of her life. She was determined that never again would she or her daughter be in a position where they had to flee their homes and have their fates determined by the impersonal bureaucracy of government organisations, where answers were rarely forthcoming because nobody seemed to be in charge and no-one wanted to know anything about her as an individual. She was determined never again to be another number which simply made up a statistic. Life had taught her that only the famous or the wealthy were safe from the rigid regulations of bureaucracy. To be safe, she needed to have money, and lots of it. For danger did not arise merely from war, famine, communist upheaval. It was all around her, right here in Middle Australia.

As she burrowed deeply into Australian life, she read the tabloids, watched current affairs programs on television and realised that she lived in a nation beset with fear. Australian life, she saw, was a patchwork of constantly dieting mums, shonky builders, tyrannous bank fees and branch closures, teenage crime and lax laws upheld (or not) by corrupt police. Occasionally the stormy surf of Australian current events was broken by the elation of sporting glory; the crime, corruption and incompetence featured in current affairs programs was interrupted by bedazzled interviews with swimmers and cricketers, or actors who had Made It Big in Hollywood.

But then the undertow of ordinary life sucked you down and the waters closed overhead, and as political parties ebbed and flowed on the beaches of the rich and powerful, the nation drowned in perverted morality tales of insurance scams, corporate takeovers and exorbitant payouts, rabid demutualisation of companies, ruthless shareholder profit-taking, vertiginous executive salaries, mass-scale retrenchments, unemployment figures that refused to diminish and welfare statistics that soared because there were too many single mums and dole bludgers out there who refused to get off their bums and go out and get a job.

Ordinary Australians teetered on the verge of victim-hood, clinging on with a death-grip to a nostalgic past when unity of race had ensured equality in the nation, and they cast panic-stricken glances around for someone to blame for all this gut-roiling fear. It was infectious, this deep anxiety that strangers were moving into the neigh-bourhood and now you had to lock your doors and barricade yourself into your home; that even in the midst of plenty, you hovered over the precipice of poverty.

Linh bought it all. She devoted herself to the pursuit of affluence. She believed she could win her daughter's love with a bigger TV and a new entertainment system. She joined the ranks of the Aspirational. Then one day she awoke to find herself in possession of a two-bedroom apartment in Flemington, a healthy bank account, an investment property out in Casula, two jobs, a seven-day working week, and not a single person she could really call her friend. Her daughter had already moved up in society and out of the west. Once a week, Tien would emerge from the eastern suburbs for stilted visits with the extended family. They had little to say to each other.

Linh searched the faces of Duong and Ai-Van, Duc and Phi-Phuong, and she discovered they were strangers to her, as she was to them. They had meals with each other several times a week, yet they did not realise how little they knew each other. The proximity and familiarity of each other's bodies gave rise to the illusion of soul-to-soul closeness, heart-to-heart intimacy. In fact, they pointed proudly to the strength of the Asian family and boasted that their remarkable prosperity arose from the bonds of blood.

The Anglo-Australians were envious and alarmed that so many Vietnamese migrants could afford to buy houses so soon, but they did not understand the extraordinary resilience and resourcefulness of the Asian family! People in the West, her brothers were fond of saying, could be independent individuals and break away from the family if they wanted, because they thought that, as a last resort, they could rely on the government to take care of them. People from the East, on the other hand, realised that few governments could be trusted and, in the end, they had to subordinate their independence and individuality to the will of the family, because their security in life arose from the prosperity of the family as a whole. It was the old story of the sticks: one stick could easily be broken, whereas a bundle of sticks had collective strength and could be used to bludgeon someone over the head.

And that was true enough if you were a stick, unani-
mated by individual dreams, unhaunted by loneliness,
untroubled by the desire not merely to be one stick among
many, but to merge your soul with another's and thereby
experience the miracle, the wonder, of being human. Being
in love. After a decade of living and thriving in Australia,
Linh woke up, wondered what the point of her life was,
and yearned for just such a miracle.

What she got instead was a persistent young boy—
younger even than her own daughter—who read love into
her words and actions when there had only been the vestiges
of pity. And perhaps the slightest, most hesitant reaching out
as loneliness kissed loneliness. Now look where her quest for
love had landed her. She shook aspirins out of a bottle,
inhaled slowly and deeply to calm herself, and could not
believe she was being stalked by Gibbo.

'You have to go to the police and report this,' Tien insisted.

One Sunday afternoon in December, when the air
was hazed with the siege of summer smoke from distant
bushfires and shadows drooped over listless streets, she
visited her mother and found herself with nothing to say
or do. She booted up the computer and logged on to her
mother's internet account. When she saw the long list of
emails from Gibbo clogging up the inbox she had no
scruples about reading them. With growing incredulity,
she noted his obsession with her mother.

It was ridiculous. It was laughable. It was pathetic. It was
utterly offensive, not just that he was stalking Linh, but that
he had the nerve to imagine himself in love with her mother.

Her reaction vaulted beyond mere concern for Linh. She felt nauseated at this turn of events and she didn't fully understand why. In some way, she felt violated. She felt that their friendship—such as it was these days—had been desecrated, that Gibbo had committed an unspeakable crime against her. And layered over that was her ever-present guilt.

She was responsible for this. Gibbo had been her friend and she had introduced him to her mother. Linh would not have met him otherwise. She had not been a good daughter or her mother would have been able to confide this problem to her. Why, half an hour ago they had sat at lunch, politely asking after each other's week, the silence of the meal broken only by Linh's occasional exhortation to eat some more, and take some back for Stanley too. She knew next to nothing about her mother's life. Linh remained a stranger to her, the path to familiarity and understanding barred by the mental list of maternal misdeeds she continued to review at regular intervals.

Guilt and shame made her determined to fix this problem for Linh. She wanted to act decisively to make up for her previous neglect; to show Linh just how strong and capable she now was in this country to which they had fled in confusion and fear. And she wanted to wreak vengeance on Gibbo for this terrible betrayal of their childhood friendship. She would sail in and set all things right.

'We'll get the local magistrate to issue an Apprehended Violence Order against Gibbo,' Tien said briskly. 'But you must report this to the police first.'

'You don't go to the police for this sort of thing. In fact, you shouldn't go to the police for anything.'

'Maybe not in Vietnam, but you do here.'

'Tien, what do I say? Excuse me, constable, but a young man has been sending me a dozen red roses every day and I don't like it? They will laugh at me! Anyway, I can handle it. It's not a big deal. I take the flowers to the hospital for the patients.'

'That's not the point. He's stalking you, and you've got evidence. You've got the emails.'

'Going to the police is too drastic. Even if they take it seriously.'

'You're the one who's not taking it seriously. Don't you know how dangerous this can be? He's a stalker. He's getting more desperate. His stalking might escalate and he might try to harm you one day.'

Her mother smiled tiredly. 'I don't think so. And I'm not going to get poor Gibbo in trouble with the police just because he thinks he's in love with me at the moment. It will pass. Just give him time.'

'And what if he gets more obsessed with time? What if the stalking gets worse and your life is in danger? Or do you actually like this? Maybe you're secretly flattered by his obsession. Maybe you like all the attention.' Tien looked resentfully at her mother and thought: *all the attention you never gave me, which you should be giving me now before I get married. It's too late. I don't know why I never learn. I don't know why I ever expect anything from you.*

Linh felt the sting of her daughter's disrespect like a slap in the face. She did not know why her daughter was so difficult. Even if love was grudgingly given, respect was always withheld. 'I think you should apologise, otherwise you should go. You're not helping matters at all. What kind of daughter says these things to her mother?'

'I'm sorry,' Tien said, but the apology was ungracious. She knew she was in the wrong, but still she felt angry. Her mother never missed a chance to fault her. She left soon after that. She had not been able to take control of the situation and protect her mother after all. She felt like a failure because she had perceived this as an opportunity to reach out to her mother. She had meant to be kind, supportive and mature in the face of this crisis; she'd meant to show her mother that she loved her. Instead, she had become rude and hectoring when her mother hadn't responded according to the script that was playing out in her head. The habitual pattern of mother–daughter relations was too strong to be so easily overcome. They fell back into the stock roles the family had assigned them: mother as saint, daughter as villain.

Tien determined to try harder the next time. She was an adult now, not a child to throw a temper tantrum because her mother hadn't done what she wanted. She would return next week to talk calmly and reasonably with Linh. Linh would come to see that Gibbo was indeed a danger to her, and that Tien was responsibly, thoughtfully, *respectfully*, looking out for her rather naïve mother. Linh had to see that Tien was a good daughter who did indeed know *hieu thao* (for, try as she might, she could not shrug off the filial expectations rubbed into her by the family's love). But Linh fluffed her lines again.

'Tien, where is your compassion for your friend?' her mother asked sadly. 'You and Gibbo have been friends since childhood and you want to ruin his life and bring this shame on Bob and Gillian by going to the police, on top of what Stanley is doing to Gillian by suing her? If you want to help, why don't you help Gillian by persuading Stanley to drop the lawsuit?'

'She's the one who assaulted him. Stan could have been killed or brain damaged. And anyway, Gibbo is not my friend,' Tien said. 'Not any longer. No friend of mine would be such a sicko as to go after my mum.'

'Is that it? Is that the crux of the problem? You're angry with him not so much for being a stalker, but for falling in love with me.'

'Don't talk rubbish. He doesn't love you. He doesn't know you.'

'Of course he doesn't know me. But neither do you. You made up your mind about what I was. The bad mother at first, and now the foolish mother. Why do you just come here and tell me what to do? Why don't you ask me what I think, or how I feel about all this? It is because you don't want to know. You just want to walk in here, do what you think is your duty, solve this problem and get on with your life with a clear conscience.'

It was so like Linh to try to turn the tables on her, to put her in the wrong once again. Tien took a deep breath and reminded herself that she was going to respond in a mature, adult way. 'Maybe that's true. I'll be the first to admit that I don't know you. I certainly don't understand why you're acting this way. But it's not just me. It's you. You don't allow anybody to know you. I've seen how you act with that guy you were going out with briefly. You nod and smile and you say nothing. You don't tell him what you think and feel. You don't tell me, or Ong Ngoai, and you also hold back with the rest of the family. So where does that leave you?'

'Alone,' Linh said. 'Just like you. When have you ever spoken your mind to Stan? We're more alike than you think. Maybe that's what you're afraid of.'

Linh turned away from her daughter and walked to the kitchen. After a moment, Tien followed.

'I don't want to argue with you over this. Maybe I'm not doing this right, but I really care, Mum. I hate seeing you like this,' Tien said helplessly as she watched her mother running water into a glass and shaking two charcoal tablets out of a bottle. 'You thought it was him, didn't you? When I knocked just now? And now you're so stressed you've got a stomach-ache.'

'I'm strong, and he can't keep this up forever,' Linh said. 'He'll get the message sooner or later. He's not a stupid boy.'

'Don't you see? He's not a boy at all. He's a man, and he's obsessed with you. How long are you going to dodge his phone calls and emails? How long can you barricade yourself in this apartment and not go out except for work, just in case he shows up? How long are you going to let him victimise you?'

Her mother did not answer. She gulped down her pills, rinsed her glass out and set it on the drying rack.

'God, why are you so damned Vietnamese? I've heard you and Ong Ngoai quoting *Kieu*, for all the good it does you. "How sorrowful is woman's lot . . . We all partake of woe, our common fate." Well fuck that. You're not in Vietnam anymore. You don't have to be a victim just because you're a woman.'

Linh sat down at the little kitchen table. She dragged her hands through her hair, then dropped her head onto her arms, too tired to keep up the pretence of strength in front of her daughter.

'Mum, please let me help you,' Tien pleaded. 'Let me do something for you.'

'How can you help me when all you show is disrespect?' Linh squeezed her eyes shut. If she was hard on her daughter, she was equally unforgiving with herself. She did not believe she deserved her daughter's respect even though she demanded it. Tien was right. She was too sexually needy. She wanted to feel the comfort of a man's weight on her. She wanted to feel alive and loved once more. It seemed as if it was only yesterday that she had been young and so much loved by Tien's father. Then she blinked and suddenly her bones ached on wintry days and she had to dye her hair. Time streaked by in her youth, then dragged out towards long, lonely old age. And though Tien might despise her, though she might despise herself, she was helpless against her desire to be loved and to make love once again. She buried her face in her arms and began to cry.

The old familiar guilt welled up in Tien. She sighed and sat down beside her mother. 'I'm sorry. I'm so sorry for everything,' she said. 'I don't know how to make things right.'

She put her arms around her mother and gave her a quick awkward hug. 'I don't want to fight with you any more, Mum. Let me help you. Let me take care of you.'

Tien rose up from the table and found some tissues in her handbag. Hesitantly, she lifted her mother's chin and began to blot away the tears. Linh was motionless under her touch. She did not jerk away. Tien took out a hair-brush and tugged it gently through her mother's hair.

'This feels strange,' Linh said after a while.

'Am I pulling too hard?' Tien asked anxiously.

'No. But I feel like I should be doing this for you. In fact, I used to when you were a toddler. When we were still in Vietnam, you stayed with Ong Ngoai and Uncle Duong and Auntie Ai-Van in Cholon. I had to go out to work but, whenever I came home, I would comb your hair. I sat on a stool and you stood wriggling impatiently between my knees. I dragged a fine-toothed comb through your curls to check for nits and afterwards I would give you a dry wash. I lathered your hair carefully, then I rinsed away the shampoo with a pot of water. Sometimes the water got into your ears, so I had to dry them out for you. Then I would take an ear scoop to clean out the wax from your ears.'

'The GP would have a fit,' Tien observed. '"Don't put anything smaller than your elbow in your ear," she always said.'

'You loved me doing it when you were little.'

'I don't remember any of it,' Tien said. She put down the hairbrush and looked at her mother. 'I don't remember anything about you before that day old Mrs Yipsoon broke her hip and you showed up and punished me. When we were talking just now, I guess you were right. I don't know much about you, but I'd like to.'

The Tale of Linh I

Spring feelings quivered hearts, spring wine turned heads.
A happy day is shorter than a span.

Nguyen Du, *The Tale of Kieu*

Ho Ly-Linh was married at the age of sixteen and abandoned a year later. Her grandmother was responsible for this.

When Linh was fifteen Grandmother took her north to meet the fourth son of a wealthy Chinese rice merchant. Linh would not normally have been acceptable even as a fourth son's wife, for she was not really a Hoa: a pure-blooded Chinese. Her father was half-Hoa, half-Viet, and her mother was pure Viet. But in 1956, when Linh was two years old, President Diem had decided to Vietnamise the Chinese. He introduced legislation forcing the Hoa to adopt Vietnamese citizenship or lose their businesses. The Tang family, arrogant in their unbroken heritage of Chineseness, disdained the Viet and refused to integrate. They did, however, make the concession of Vietnamising their name to Thanh, hiring Vietnamese sleeping partners in their business, and marrying their lesser sons to Vietnamese women.

Thanh Lam, whom Linh referred to respectfully as Ong Chong—Mr Husband—was forced into the marriage. Always sensitive to his less privileged position as the fourth son, Lam felt the indignity of marrying a Vietnamese. None of his three elder brothers had been forced to accept Viet wives; their father had sent for pure-blooded Chinese girls from the ancestral village in China. Lam threw a tantrum, got blind drunk in the local brothel and staggered back to submit resentfully to his father's will. What else could he do, in his position of youngest son, wholly dependent on his father's ferocious goodwill?

At the height of the Tet offensive in 1968, the relatives were informed of the betrothal. Gifts were exchanged, then husband and wife met for the second time at the Chinese ceremony a few months later. Lam was aggrieved by his bride's ordinary looks; he felt he deserved something more, for he was an extraordinarily handsome young man. Bridal photos showed a glowering bridegroom with glossy black hair oiled into an Elvis pompadour, lower lip petulantly thrust out, while a plain-faced, apprehensive bride drowned in a froth of white silk tulle, for the European colonisation of Asia had bred in the breasts of its women an unremitting love affair with Western bridal clothes.

Bride and groom returned to Cholon, the Chinese twin city of Saigon, to live. Lam soon discovered that, like

New York, Saigon—a mere five kilometres from his home in Cholon, the distance negligible on the old *xe lam* buses or the Honda scooters that coughed and spluttered through the thronging streets—was a city that never slept. The American war, the presence of Allied soldiers partying the night away on salaries of four or five hundred US dollars a month, imbued the city with a dazzling, neon-lit mardi-gras atmosphere.

He quickly became familiar with nightclubs where American rock 'n' roll screamed out of open doors and windows while dancers shuddered in frenzied joy within. He frequented various bars where bar-girls or prostitutes slid onto rickety stools next to him and sad songs drifted into dark corners. At 3 am, he staggered out of brothels, reeking of sex and cigarette smoke. He sniffed the fragrant odour of noodles frying over the charcoal braziers of roadside stalls, and threw up his dinner into the open gutter.

Unsurprisingly, he failed at the rice business he tried to set up. In Cholon, most people woke around five. Certainly by six o'clock Chinese merchants would be gathered in roadside stalls and coffee-houses, eating breakfast and exchanging the latest financial news and stock prices. Complex transactions worth millions of piastres were negotiated as they chomped on dumplings and slurped up noodles and soup. By the time Lam, nattily dressed and ready to be plied with potent cups of *café phin* and a bowl of *pho*, wandered out into the streets at midday, even the hawkers would be packing up their wares, ready to leave, while the merchants and other businessmen were nowhere to be seen. He was soon bankrupt. He sold the house that his father had given him as a wedding present, pocketed the money and moved into a dilapidated room at the end of a tiny, T-shaped alley near the Cholon Moi market. He was tired of working. He depended on his wife to support them.

In their dark little room, Linh made paper boxes and Chinese calendars which she sold once a month at the market. She sat on the low bed each night, wrapped the mosquito net around her and deftly folded sheets of paper and cardboard by the dim light of a single overhead bulb which yellowed during the frequent power fluctuations. In the early mornings, she hoisted a bamboo pole over her shoulders, filled the two big baskets on either end with *banh giay* and *banh chung* and wandered through the maze of alleys in Cholon to sell the glutinous rice puddings wrapped in bamboo leaves. She made the *banh giay* and *banh chung* in the afternoons, cooking them on a communal stove in the alley. On sunny afternoons, when the coffin lid of sky above the alley was filmed with smog tangling with the overhead electrical wires, children scattered around her, chasing each other, playing football, bouncing and kicking the brightly coloured feathers of shuttlecocks with skilled brown feet. Sometimes the boys helped her to cleave firewood to feed the stove while the girls learned how to wrap the rice dumplings.

Ten months after the marriage, Linh gave birth to a sickly girl and named her Thi-Lan. The baby would not stop crying. Lam was constantly irritated. On their first wedding anniversary, Lam packed his bags and told Linh that he was migrating to Hong Kong with his current Hoa mistress, whom he had decided to take as his second wife. There was no need for a divorce, he told Linh, for they had only gone through the Buddhist ceremony; their marriage had never been legally registered with the authorities.

'Ong Chong, how can you leave? What about little Lan?' she pleaded.

He snorted and replied: 'A hundred daughters aren't worth a single testicle.'

'Don't go,' she begged him. 'I will be a better wife to you starting today. Next time I will have a son.'

'Today?' he spat contemptuously. 'Today you become more Vietnamese. Tomorrow even more.' It was, in his Chinese eyes, an insult.

The baby Lan woke from her sleep and kicked at the mosquito net fretfully. She began to wail. Lam sucked his teeth in annoyance and clipped out of the small room into the alley, two brown suitcases swinging at the ends of his arms in measured rhythm like counterpointed metronomes.

'Ong Chong!' Linh cried from the doorway. Lam hesitated, turned around, and hefted up one suitcase in final farewell before proceeding down the street.

In her panic, Linh picked up the baby, hugged the whimpering child into the curve of her body as she curled up on the mattress and cried. She would never completely rid herself of the conviction that she was somehow to blame. If only she had been a better wife—better with money, better in bed, simply better—her husband would not have left her. She did not recognise that what she also felt was rage, for throughout her life she had not had many opportunities to vent her anger. She dragged herself up and peered into a small black-spotted mirror. She poured cold tea onto a towel and dabbed the compress to her swollen eyes. She said to daughter, 'You must never cry or your eyes will puff up and you will have piggy Chinese eyes like Thanh Lam.'

Linh told herself that Thanh Lam was nothing to her, merely a cell that spawned her child and a name that clung to her like sticky rice until she could wipe it off her fingers. She managed to look after the child for three months, then she woke one morning to find that she had rolled on top of the baby. Horrified, she put her fingers over Lan's mouth, but there was no breath and no sound when she shook the child. She knew from that moment on that suffering was her lot in life because she had killed her daughter.

Dry-eyed, she laid the dead child on a bamboo mat and placed a chopstick between lips still as pink as a camellia bud. She took one of Lan's tiny singlets and waved it over the corpse, calling for her daughter's soul to return to the body. Then she bathed the corpse, combed the straggly baby curls, dusted the body lightly with talcum powder, put her nose to her daughter's neck and sniffed deeply. How she loved the smell of her baby's skin. She took off her gold wedding ring and placed it carefully into Lan's mouth, together with a handful of cold rice.

She made a sturdy cardboard box, wrapped Lan in a white nappy and embraced her daughter one last time before laying her in the box. She fixed the lid over the box and secured it tightly. Then she caught a bus out to the countryside and buried the cardboard coffin under the dyke of a drained rice field. She went back to her little room in the alley, tied a black scarf around her head, piled her belongings onto a borrowed handcart and wheeled it down the winding streets to her father's house.

The Ho family lived on the top floor of a rickety-looking three-storey terrace which housed their printing firm on the ground floor. Mr Ho had three sons by his first wife, a Hoa woman who had died of dysentery when her youngest son had just been weaned. He then married a Viet woman who gave birth to Ly-Linh. Mr Ho's eldest son had been sent to Paris to study medicine, but Duyen returned to Vietnam infected with nationalist ideas of anti-colonialism. He had joined up with General Giap's army to fight the French at Dien Bien Phu. The French were defeated, Duyen was killed, and Mr Ho forbade his younger sons, Duong and Duc, to think about the war. Later, when the American war escalated and the South Vietnamese forces began recruiting young men, Mr Ho took a meat cleaver and hacked off his two sons' index fingers so that they would be unable to pull the trigger on a rifle.

Mr Ho married his two remaining sons to Viet women and set them to work in his printing shop, which churned out volumes of Vietnamese literature: the 'Self-Strength' novelists of the 1930s; medieval Nom poems; the eighteenth- and nineteenth-century luminaries of Viet-namese literature—Doan Thi Diem, Nguyen Gia Thieu, Nguyen Cong Tru; the cheeky proto-feminist verses of Ho Xuan Huong; and, of course, Nguyen Du's classic love story, *The Tale of Kieu*, large sections of which Mr Ho taught his daughter to recite by heart.

When Linh was a little girl, he would haul her onto his lap before bedtime, sniff her clean hair and assure her lovingly: 'Clouds could not shape the graceful fall of her hair and snow was no match for her complexion. The curve of her brows was like the dreamy line of mountains in the spring. A smile from her could rock empires and citadels. That is you, *con gai*, my lovely daughter.'

When Linh returned to her father's house, she found there was no room for her. Already crammed onto that third floor were her father, her mother, her brothers Duong and Duc, their wives, two daughters and one son—nine people in all. They welcomed Linh warmly, expressed shock and outrage at Thanh Lam's treatment of his family, grieved loudly at Lan's death (Linh did not explain how she had accidentally smothered the baby), heaped colourful curses on Lam's head, and offered her a bamboo mat in the kitchen—the only unoccupied space in that flat.

Whenever Mr Ho looked at his only daughter, guilt nagged at him because he had approved the useless Thanh Lam as her husband when his mother had insisted on marrying Linh off. How could he have known that an alliance with so wealthy a Chinese family could end in such disaster for his daughter? Late at night, when Linh curled like a comma on her bamboo mat, Mr Ho would shuffle to the kitchen and squat beside his daughter. He cupped his palm and his long elegant fingers slowly stroked the air above her black hair like blessing. He wanted to keep her safe and happy, but he was no longer sure he could even keep her fed. Wartime inflation had eroded his savings and his printing presses ceased their restless groanings, for who wanted to read long-dead poets in these years of war when American pop songs pounded across the airwaves and the young men felt that the next Tet would usher in a golden age of unbridled capitalist freedom or the conflagration of communistic apocalypse (nobody quite knew which)? In the end, he decided to

ask Mr Thieu for advice about what should be done
with Linh.

The second floor of the terrace had long ago been
sold to a school teacher who conducted French and
English classes. Each day a slow dirge of conjugated
verbs wafted up to the third floor, so that the Ho family
ate their lunch to the mournful chant of: '*Je veux le paix,
tu veux le paix, il veut le paix, nous voulons le paix, vous
voulez le paix, ils veulent le paix.*' In the early evenings,
the francophile Mr Ho would make his way down to the
second floor to join Mr Thieu—Mr Professor, they
called him—in a cup of *café phin*. The two men browsed
the dark wood shelves of the schoolroom and picked
out tattered copies of French poetry to read aloud to
each other.

Mr Professor had lost four sons in battle—first in the
French, and then the American war. He was half proud of
his anguish, half envious of Mr Ho's loving cowardice,
which kept Duong and Duc maimed but alive. Lately, Mr
Professor had taken to reciting with bitter humour André
Chénier's 'When the sombre slaughterhouse opens its
maws of death to a bleating sheep'. Slurping up the dregs
of his coffee, he removed his wire-rimmed spectacles,
wiped them carefully, waggled them at Mr Ho, and
intoned in French:

Perhaps in happier times
I myself, at the sight of the tears of the wretched,
Turned my gaze away distractedly;
Today, in turn, my misfortune is distressing.
Live, friends; live in peace.

'Haaargh.' Unbearably moved by his friend's late-won wisdom and the exquisite web of Mr Professor's sorrow, Mr Ho cleared his throat and projected his spit missile over the crumbling balcony onto the unsuspecting crowd that swirled in the street below.

Mr Thieu inclined his head slowly in acknowledge-ment of this expression of sympathy. '*Oui*,' he sighed. '*Trop tard*. Always too late.'

In the end, Mr Thieu arranged for Linh to take up a position as a companion and housekeeper to a middle-aged Eurasian woman living in Saigon.

'She is an educated woman. She reads Michel de Montaigne and is fond of Camus,' was Mr Professor's reassuring reply to Mr Ho's anxious queries about her character. 'I knew her father many, many years ago when we studied together in Paris. Ah, *les temps heureux quand la vie était bonne.*'

Madame Catinat was a short, spry woman with a huge head out of proportion to her thin limbs and hipless body. The bulk of her long black hair, quiffed over her unnatur-ally smooth forehead and disciplined into a formidably tight bun held together with two elegantly lacquered red and gold wooden pins, added to the overall impression of a dangerously enlarged head. Walking briskly down the street in her cream-coloured Jackie Kennedy suit, snake-skin handbag draped neatly over the crook of her left arm, she looked like a bobbing liquorice-flavoured lollipop. Her face was compelling, even bizarrely attractive, in its sheer ugliness. She had kohl-lined Picasso eyes which slid

constantly from side to side, a broad flat nose with long
nostrils, and a wide, thin-lipped mouth with an overbite.
She looked like a frog and could adopt the hypnotic
watchfulness of one as well. You constantly expected a
long tongue to flick out and whip the whining mosquitoes from the air, but like all the rich, she slept under
a gauze mosquito net swathed neatly around her four-
poster Louis Quinze bed.

Her grandfather was French and she often claimed
that the former rue Catinat—restyled Tu-Do, freedom,
after the French departed Vietnam—was so named in his
honour. When hesitantly challenged by a Vietnamese
officer who wondered whether the fashionable boulevard
might not perhaps have been named after a French
warship that had taken part in military operations in Da
Nang and Saigon during the mid-nineteenth century, she
was in no way discomposed. '*Mais oui*,' she replied swiftly,
the massive head inclining slightly in condescending
approval, like a teacher graciously smiling on an idiot
child who'd got it right for once. 'But that warship was, in
any event, named after Grandpère Catinat. *Voilà*.'

In the afternoons, like all the rich in Saigon after their
siesta, she liked to take long strolls along the boulevard,
window-shop, meet acquaintances, gossip. '*Alors, je vais
catinater maintenant*,' she would say to Linh as she pulled
on white gloves and fussed her handbag onto her arm. It
was her greatest source of pride that, so famous was the rue
Catinat (not until the late 1960s did the young Saigonese
call it Tu-Do), a verb, 'catinater', had been coined by the
Saigonese to describe their daily strolls to meet and greet
people, to meander to the cafés and chat.

Nobody knew exactly what Grandpère Catinat had done to acquire his fortune, still less from whence Madame Catinat's considerable income continued to flow. She held lavish soirées at her elegant colonial town house for diplomats and high-ranking officers, and wild raucous parties for junior officers and run-of-the-mill GIs. Linh was expected to serve at the former and savour the latter, when the gilded ballroom of Maison Catinat was transformed into a sauna of twisting, jiving bodies and ear-piercing giggles. Couples stamped hors d'oeuvres into the parquetry, slid in puddles of spilled Carlsberg and 33 beer, and hollered for faster, hotter songs as they scrounged remnants of spring rolls and *dau sanh vung* from garnished platters, shying the pieces of fried sticky rice balls at white-jacketed band members.

It was at one of these romps that Linh met Bucky Thibodeaux, love of her life. She had spent most of the evening creeping uncertainly around the perimeter of the ballroom, wishing that she was serving instead. She would have felt more comfortable slinking through the crowd with a tray of drinks or a platter of food in her hands. She had tried to do that earlier in the evening, but Madame Catinat spotted her and waved her over imperiously.

'*Non, non. Pas ce soir,*' she said as she gestured to a waiter to take the tray. 'You are to *enjoy* yourself tonight. You look beautiful. Now go. Dance. Meet people. Talk. Flirt. *Enjoy* yourself. Here.' She thrust a champagne flute into Linh's hands, slid her arm into her companion's, and pulled him onto the dance floor. They were swallowed up by the seething crowd and lost amid the screams. Craning her neck a few moments later, Linh could see that big head of black hair emerging at the far side of the room, companion still in tow. They disappeared through the large, gilded double doors.

Resigning herself to her orders, Linh backed towards the wall and tried to merge into invisibility, clasping the sweating glass of lukewarm champagne in both hands like a crucifix to comfort herself in her isolation while she warded off the embarrassment of social interaction with the Americans. She could read and understand English, thanks to Mr Professor, but she was too shy to speak to the big white men.

She cast her eyes down and wondered what her family was doing back in Cholon. It was nearly a month since she had seen them. Duc's wife, Phi-Phuong, was pregnant, she knew, and Duong's wife, Ai-Van, was trying to compete. She wanted to be able to fuss over Phi-Phuong, to give her a sponge bath and fan her in the humid afternoons just before the storm broke and dust boiled in the streets. She wanted to brew Phi-Phuong cups of tea and touch that slowly distending belly. She felt homesickness well up in her throat, a regurgitation of desolation, but she pressed her lips together firmly, steadied herself with a deep breath, and looked up. And that was when she saw him: a tall gangly scarecrow of a man with close-cropped curls, the profile of a crane, skin the colour of *café phin*, and buckteeth that jutted out like an awning over his lower lip when he grinned.

Étienne 'Bucky' Thibodeaux hadn't volunteered for the war in Vietnam but he hadn't tried to dodge the draft either. He was working on a submersible drilling rig in the Gulf of Mexico—just off the coast of Morgan City, Louisiana—when his orders flew in on the supply helicopter one afternoon so hot and still the wind barely ruffled the waves and the bright glare of the sun bounced off the brilliant water and hurt his eyes. He ripped open the envelope and scanned the unfamiliar words. Uncertainly, he read it through another couple of times.

'*Merde*,' he said, resigned and unsurprised, for bad luck never failed to find him. He went home to say goodbye to his Cajun father and Creole mother. 'Be a good boy, Bucky. We'll have a *fais do do* for you when you come home, *cher*,' she said. '*Reviens vite*.' Then he cut his hair and caught a Greyhound bus to boot camp.

He endured Parris Island and found himself doing tours of duty through Vietnamese villages whose names he could not pronounce let alone remember, ploughing his way across swamps where the sucking mud clung to his combat boots and it was all he could do to yank out one leg after another and trudge through the needling rain, let alone keep an eye out for the VC. On dry days, he choked down the rich red dust of dirt tracks, squinted up at helicopters whirling overhead like dragonflies, rested his eyes on the verdant green of lush jungles, and wondered how the rookie Tommy Dempsey was working out with the New Orleans Saints. Before he died, please god, he thought, he wanted to see Dempsey—born without toes on his right foot, so he'd heard!—scoring a field goal at Tulane Stadium. At night he scratched mosquito bites in his sleep and dreamed he was back home, sliding through silent cypress everglades in his pirogue, baiting crawfish traps and casting a line for catfish and striped bass. Once a week, he wrote cheerful chatty postcards back to his mother, but he did not expect to survive the war. 'Bad luck'll get me. You'll see,' he foretold laconically. He was astonished when he survived his first few months.

He could have spent his R&R anywhere in Asia but he chose to stay in Vietnam. He hitched a ride down to the Mekong Delta and hiked through rickety villages where thatched huts patched together from sheets of corrugated iron, ammunition boxes and unpressed Coca-Cola cans perched atop palm-wood platforms in the middle of brimming paddy fields. In the distance, white tombs rose out of the emerald-green rice, housing the bones of ancestors who watched impassively over their descendants. Red water buffaloes plashed and swished their tails placidly.

Bucky distributed gum and chocolate to swarms of big-eyed barefoot children who chanted '*Ong My! Ong My!*'—Mr American—and pranced beside him along a river track strewn with coconut husks and longan seeds. He goggled at slim young Vietnamese women in black trouser suits and white thongs who hurriedly covered their faces with their conical palm-leaf hats when they caught him staring. He grinned and scratched his head when a bare-chested young lad in faded pyjama trousers offered him a cocky grin and a grubby deck of 'feelthy peek-tures, monsieur! One dollah!'

And, for the first time in months, he felt something approaching contentment as he clambered aboard a wooden sampan which nosed along the riverine Mekong system, ducking under flimsy monkey bridges, dodging spiky palm fronds and pushing away from the rapidly proliferating water hyacinths that knotted along the banks. He sank a line but didn't catch anything, then happily stepped ashore to feast on fried fish and mint leaves rolled in rice paper.

When he made it back to Saigon without encountering an ambush, no-one was more surprised than him. He hunched himself into a cyclo and was hauled through the thronging streets by a rail-thin cyclist in a baseball cap who skilfully wove his way between bicycles, Vespas, yellow and blue Renault taxicabs, overloaded three-wheeled lambrettas with men hanging perilously off the sides, postie Hondas seating entire families, dark limousines, and a South Vietnamese official's BMW sedan, which bore a bumper sticker proudly proclaiming 'Ronnie Lau Trading Company. 273 Thomson Road Singapore. Specialists in buying, selling and exporting second-hand Mercedes-Benz, Jaguars and BMW cars'.

He was dislodged in front of La Pagode on Tu-Do, so he ambled inside for a beer and was waylaid by a bunch of Australians who had come in for the weekend from the base out at Nui Dat. After several rounds, he stumbled around the bar sentimentally hugging his new best friends. The next thing he knew, he was hanging out on the streets of Saigon with a certain Bob Gibson, waiting to crash a party at Maison Catinat. They stopped at a roadside stall and slurped up chicken soup and rice noodles, crouching over tables so low that back in the States they would only be found in kindergarten classrooms. Overhead, garish hoardings blinked giant neon-lit advertisements for Sanyo, 33 beer, cigarettes, aspirins, powdered milk and toothpaste.

'You don't want to eat too much, mate,' Bob told him. 'There's always plenty of tucker where we're going.'

'You've been there before?'

'Yeah. Couple of times with the other guys. She holds these do's every weekend. They get pretty wild.'

It was nothing less than the truth. He drank copiously, stuffed his face with food he'd never tasted before, danced with smartly turned-out women, managed to avoid the brightly made-up transvestites, snorted some coke, and stumbled to the toilet to throw everything up. He rinsed his mouth out and, when he emerged, Bob was waiting for him.

'You right?' he asked, looking doubtfully at the American.

'Yeah,' Bucky said and grinned weakly. He had a feeling that he wasn't coming out well at all in the masculinity stakes. 'Hey, come on. Let's party. *Laissez le bon temps rouler!*'

He sidled back onto the dance floor and bopped along with a couple of girls. They snaked their lovely hands all over him in languid caresses, ground their crotches against him and he was sandwiched between the unmistakable bulges of hard erections under their thin nylon dresses. 'Hi, GI. You buku handsome, yessir. You like same-same, baby-san?' He was horrified to feel his penis twitching in vague arousal and he felt sickened.

At that moment he looked up, locked eyes with Linh, and fell in love.

. . .

Vung Tau had its purely Vietnamese streets where names such as TÂN HƯNG, VĨNH-THO-DƯỜNG, and LIÊN-PHONG marched in an orderly row over shop terraces, and few white faces were to be seen. Then there was the relatively Anglicised section near the beach promenade where the gaudy lettering for HOLLYWOOD HAIR incongruously lorded it over HÓT TÓC—BĨNH-DÂN, flanked by large three-toned posters of men with short back and sides, and smaller signs announcing 'Hair cut short' or 'Cream hair soft'. The bars were ranged along these streets: Chikito Bar, Milano Bar, Hoáng Hotel (Air-Conditioned Bar and Restaurant), the Queen, and the Dong Tam Olympia Bar and Night Club. Not too far away, the Ly-Ly theatre stood opposite TÂY HỒ Photo, the Pharmacie, and a blue metal board announcing GASOIL, painted vertically, was nailed to a lamppost. In this section of town, an old man in a faded blue shirt, dark grey shorts, white thongs and a white cotton hat swept the streets each morning and afternoon with a palm branch, collecting rubbish in his wooden handcart. Brightly coloured fin-tailed American cars and the odd army truck could be seen here among the trishaws, bicycles and motorcycles. On the pavements outside the shop terraces, women wearing conical *non-la* hats sat on low wooden stools and cooked *pho* at kerbside stoves while children pranced around a hawker's huge pannier baskets yoked together with a long bamboo stick.

Linh stayed in a one-room apartment which Bucky rented for her in this quarter. It was only a few minutes' walk to the Dong Tam Olympia Bar where she now worked, and a short distance to the beach where he had taught her to swim. When he was not around, she shared the flat with a fellow bar-girl. Every piastre she saved went towards her trousseau, for there would be a marriage one day. She was sure of it. The only anxiety the future held for her was whether she'd have the right clothes to wear when she finally met his mother. She refused to consider the possibility that her father might object to him as a son-in-law because he was dark-skinned.

She and Bucky did not talk about these things because their love was not based on words but on laughter and kindness and, above all, the tactile pleasure of finger-tips smoothing over sweat-damp flesh, the ebb and flow of movement through and around each other's bodies, their love buoyant on a sea of sexual pleasure. They traced the outlines of each other's bones through slick skin. She wrapped herself around his back and kissed the vertex of his shoulderblade, watching it ripple under the skin, shaped like the wing of a duck in flight. He turned around and ran his fingers over her collarbone, so fragile that he sometimes feared he could snap it in his careless urgency when he needed so badly to be inside her, when he was chased by his unmentionable fear of the world beyond the circle of her arms.

One morning, Linh wriggled out from under the torn mosquito net and slipped on Bucky's green army T-shirt. Weak rays of light diffused through the shutters and fanned the room. She padded over to the window and opened it. As the wooden shutter creaked and scraped over the pitted concrete sill, flakes of paint rained down onto the street below. She was a woman who liked to look out of windows. She leaned her forearms on the ledge and gazed out to the distance.

Cap Saint Jacques hugged the ocean. Nestled among the lush greenery of the hill were the crumbling walls of old French villas, their terracotta roofs flashing in the sun. By the busy Vung Tau foreshore, grey naval vessels lolled together with the rusting hulls of container ships. On the shingles, net-draped fishermen's boats clustered, black eyes painted on the red planking just below the bow of each boat, so that it might see its way back to safe harbour. In the far distance, junks tilted and sampans oared out towards soft clouds. Children laughed as they played at the end of a rocky promontory, tumbling stones into the sea, clambering up onto the highest boulders and screaming gleefully as they flung themselves into the calm blue ripples. In that drop between sky and sea, they thought no more of war. Life was merely sweet with the honeyed warmth of holidays and the generous largesse of the Americans in the form of sweets, chocolates, gum, cards, and the occasional cast-off army hat. Down in the street below, hawkers were calling out '*pho*!' and rumpled heads poked out of apartment windows to order breakfast.

She turned around to look at Bucky dozing in her narrow bed, replete from early morning sex. She felt anew the marvelling delight that he could be hers, that he would want her in return. How she had yearned to belong to someone. As a young girl she had become accustomed to the pleasure of being safe, knowing she was owned and that she owned someone in return. It was the wonderful feeling of snuggling under a warm silk blanket during the monsoon season when rain sluiced down outside her bedroom window and the eaves dripped musically. She had missed the security of someone in authority over her, taking care of her

and telling her what to do. She had missed the giddy exhilaration of coaxing and cajoling until she gained her own way
because she was so extravagantly loved.

'All right, you shall have whatever your heart desires,
con gai, my little plum branch with your snow-pure soul,'
her father used to say indulgently. In the old days of
plenty, before the escalation of the American war, all
the men of her family—her father, her older brothers—
lavished love and trinkets on her unstintingly. She had
grown up accustomed to the pleasure of serving those she
loved. How they had appreciated her! She wanted to serve
her husband in the same way. She longed to fuss over
someone, to pluck some morsels of fish to drop into his
rice bowl, gently admonish him to take better care of
himself so that he would glance up from his meal, smile
at her and hold out his hand in tenderness.

She cooked Bucky an omelette for breakfast and as he
sat and ate, she asked in her careful English, 'You love me?'

'Yeah, sure thing. Don't worry so much, you.' He
reached for her hand and squeezed it reassuringly. 'I could
never leave you. I want a future with you as my wife one
day, when this war is over and we get to go home.'

'You marry me? Is true?'

'Of course. I'm not just taking you for a ride, *chère*.
I love you and nothing can change that. Believe me?'

She studied the ill-assorted features of his face and
found reassurance in his ugliness. 'Yeah, sure thing,' she
said, consciously adopting his casual American speech.
'I also love you.'

He rejoined his unit shortly after that. A few weeks
later she received a scrawled letter informing her that his

tour of duty would be up by the end of the year. He didn't
want to wait any longer; he had found a priest and was
making arrangements to marry her.

An AVO and
a Wedding

How much he toiled and strove to win my love!
But grown attached to me, he's marred his life.

Nguyen Du, *The Tale of Kieu*

Tien felt as though she was losing control of her own wedding. Her mother seemed barely interested in the preparations, while Stan and his mother were only too eager to hijack the whole thing. She hardly had any say in what she was going to wear or where they were going on their honeymoon. She felt a rising sense of panic that her life was being invaded and taken hostage.

It surprised her that, for a man, Stan was unnaturally interested in wedding matters. He had already decided on two wedding ceremonies: a traditional Chinese/Vietnamese one, and a Western white wedding. He relished the thought of seeing Tien decked out in a red *ao-dai* with the traditional red frisbee-shaped headpiece. He would invite his arty

Anglo friends along to the traditional ceremony so that they could marvel at the ritual and the spectacle, just as he had when he accompanied Tien to her cousin Van's wedding.

He could imagine his solemn arrival to the celebratory gunshots of stuttering firecrackers, accompanied by various uncles and relatives all bearing bridal gifts. He and Tien would bow to heaven, bow before the Ho family altar, ask the blessing of the ancestors as well as protection from that quaint god of marriage, the Old Man in the Moon, bow to her mother, then perform the tea ceremony in rooms decked out with red gladioli and red banners embossed with gold characters. He did not subscribe to the beliefs underlying such rituals; he firmly believed his ancestors were serenely interred in Hong Kong or long expired in thick plumes of smoke and coarse-grained ash. But he prided himself on being a man who appreciated the maintenance of tradition and culture. It appealed to him on an aesthetic level.

The white wedding in the afternoon was for his mother. Mrs Wong hankered after a ceremony in a sandstone cathedral and photo ops in front of the Sydney Opera House. She was already collecting faxed menus from various Chinese seafood restaurants in Chatswood and Chinatown for the wedding dinner. She did not know whether to order a set menu with lobster, or one with abalone. She felt stressed. She needed to go shopping. She haunted Double Bay boutiques and bought numerous outfits, handbags and shoes to suit all possible permutations of heat, cold, humidity and rain that might occur in the fickle autumn weather. She wanted to wear a corsage. She admired baby's breath and believed red and pink to be an entirely natural combination of colours for flowers and bridesmaids' dresses. When she met Tien's mother for the first time, she offered to take Linh shopping for a red or pink suit. When Linh politely declined, Mrs Wong was not so much *offended* as *hurt*. Her sensibilities were fragile. She was used to getting her own way.

'What's wrong with your mother?' Stan demanded, annoyed. 'You'd think she'd be happy her only daughter is getting married, but she's not into it at all.'

Tien privately agreed, but she felt compelled to defend Linh. Her newly brokered truce with her mother was still in its nascent stages and she did not want to do anything to jeopardise their relationship. She cast around for an excuse, came up blank and blurted out the truth.

'She's very stressed at the moment because she's being stalked. I think it's getting worse.'

'Stalked! Your mother has a stalker? I don't believe it. Who is it?' He was intrigued and incredulous, caught between the thrilling novelty of a stalking and the irritation of having something so outlandish interfering with his wedding plans.

Tien said reluctantly, 'Gibbo. Nigel Gibson.'

'Jeez, that figures. Your feral westie friends! Unbelievable.' But when he had cooled down and given it further consideration, he was determined to do his filial duty by his future mother-in-law. 'Leave it to me,' he ordered confidently. 'I'll speak to your mother and take care of things.'

Linh could not help feeling that she was partly to blame for Gibbo's infatuation. She had been lonely then, and

Gibbo needed a friend. She had always liked Gibbo. A woman who could find beauty in the distorted cubist features and jutting teeth of Bucky Thibodeaux could also look beyond a young man's blubbery body and flushed-faced fumbling ways to see the earnest desire for human connection underneath. She felt sorry for him, and she responded to his need for friendship.

She believed that she had handled their friendship deftly until the day he took her to the Swans game. They had both been so excited, their first AFL game, their shared baptism into Australian religiosity. She met him at a café in Oxford Street, Paddington, and they had lunch together. Eggs benedict for him, focaccia with bocconcini and tomato for her. Another first in her life. Even though Tien now lived in Bondi, she herself had not crossed the psychological barrier of the city to venture eastwards. It was a lovely sun-dappled spring afternoon. They walked over to the Sydney Football Stadium and Linh felt pleased with Gibbo's company, pleased that she had somebody to do these things with. It made her feel like a normal Australian.

Inside the stadium, people were milling about, buying fast food, hailing friends and acquaintances, finding their way to their seats. The air was sharp with the tang of salt, vinegar and tomato sauce. Gibbo grabbed hold of her hand. He did not want to lose her. She was so tiny that it would take him ages to find her again. She let her hand lie passively in his as they climbed up to the top of the stadium to their cheap seats.

After the game was over, when the dipping sun gilded the stadium and seagulls wheeled and squalled overhead, she let Gibbo take her hand once more as they climbed down from the stands and filed towards the exit gates. Even when they were clear of the crowds, he did not release her hand. She was surprised but not particularly alarmed or uncomfortable. It felt quite companionable.

Gibbo was raving on about the game. He understood for the first time its magnetic attraction for his own father, the way your whole life arrowed down to the tug and pull between two teams; the godlike hubris of your team winning, the feeling of exhilaration and invincibility, as though life finally mattered, incandescent with meaning because you were swallowed up by something bigger, something triumphant to which you belonged. He felt, for the first time, able to connect to something that mattered to Bob, and it was all because of Linh. He would never have considered going otherwise, he told her.

Linh listened absent-mindedly to his chatter and wondered what she should cook for her dinner. Mentally, she ran through the ingredients in her fridge: lemongrass, ginger, garlic, chillies, mint, bean sprouts. Did she have some meat, beef or chicken in the freezer? Perhaps she had some prawns and sugarcane to make *chao tom*.

'That was so great. We'll have to do it again soon,' he enthused as he dropped her off in front of her apartment. 'Shall I get tickets for another game?'

She looked at him with surprise then. She could not understand his exuberance over this game. Perhaps it was an Australian thing, she thought. It had been an enjoyable afternoon because of its novelty, but did he really expect her to go to another game with him?

'Thank you for taking me, Gibbo,' she said, one hand already on the door handle, poised for the transition from this interlude to real life. 'I had a very nice time.'

He leaned over to kiss her and she presented her cheek, for she knew this was what her daughter did with her Australian friends, both male and female.

What a shock it was, then, to find Gibbo sucking on her lips. Wet. He was a very wet kisser, was all she could think. It was like having your face mopped by the tongue of a golden retriever. But to her even greater surprise, she found herself yearning—not for him necessarily; just to be kissed. She had forgotten the flavour of a man's mouth, the taste of his tongue. She leaned back and let him in. He licked the ridge of her teeth, slowly slid his tongue around the smooth wet cave of her mouth. She closed her eyes and smiled, heart-softened by his clumsy fumbling.

A car backfired further up the street and Linh sat upright, pushing away from Gibbo. Flustered, she mumbled a quick thanks, then she scrambled out of the car and ran into her apartment. She thought of what Tien would say, how Ai-Van and Phi-Phuong would snigger behind her back. She was ashamed of herself. She was a tough woman; she'd had to be in order to survive. Why didn't she slap him?

But who could understand what it was like to be desired once more? She could not control the unexpected gush of soft feelings he'd uncorked. So when he'd kept bombarding her with messages of his devotion, she compounded her idiocy by agreeing to dinner with him in order to explain gently that she was not interested in him. She had been so apprehensive, so afraid of hurting his feelings if she didn't do it tactfully. How sorry she had been for him, with his trite declarations of love that sounded like a television commercial or a thousand B-grade films. I love you, I love you, I love you, he said, until the words twisted and tangled into a meaningless foreignness.

The worst thing was that the more he said or wrote it, the more she would be reminded of how she and Bucky used to wreathe the phrase around each other with their questing mouths and twining limbs. I love you. It was everything to her then, but now she didn't know what it signified and she began to doubt her relationship with Bucky. The great love story of her life wobbled and refused to stay fixed in its meaning. Gibbo had done this to her.

When Linh went to dinner with Gibbo ten days after the football game, a slight resentment was already simmering inside her, but she was determined to be nice. She sat in his car in long-suffering silence and let him peck sticky kisses on her lips and cheeks at every red light. She briefly debated whether she should say something to sort this out. It was not the best time; not when he was driving through the pouring rain, when the pain or anger of rejection might distract him into an accident. Then he was busy looking for a parking space in The Rocks and he was not paying attention to her.

It was even worse when they got to the restaurant because she could see that he had gone to a lot of trouble to make the evening romantic. Had she returned his feelings in any way, she would have been grateful. As it was, her heart sank and she lost her appetite. The waiters hovered by, drinks were served, the water glasses and bread basket were constantly replenished, entrée, main and dessert circulated efficiently from kitchen to table, and she was miserably

conscious of listening ears and watching eyes. In between
courses, he grabbed hold of her left hand and clasped it in his
sweaty palm. She wondered with growing exasperation how
he expected her to eat one-handed.

It was only when coffee came and the waiters finally left
them alone that she felt able to broach the subject. 'Gibbo,
I'm so sorry but I don't want to go out with you anymore. I'm too old for you and you should be hanging
around with people your own age.' He didn't want to listen.
He called for the bill and settled it, calculating the tip and
signing the credit card slip with an extravagant flourish.

They walked back to the car in silence and he grabbed
hold of her hand again. It was time to make a stand, she
thought. She tried to tug her hand away but he just tightened his grasp. Afraid of making a scene, perhaps even a
little afraid of him now and, above all, deeply embarrassed
for both of them, she desisted.

'I'm very tired, Gibbo, and I have an early start at the
hospital tomorrow. Can you please take me home now,'
she'd requested. Politely. She was always polite to men, no
matter how young or old.

She was so polite that, instead of driving her home, he
drove her to Bronte Beach. It had stopped raining by
then. He got out of the stuffy car and said, 'Let's talk on
the beach.' She had no choice but to follow. She tottered
across the grass in stilettos, felt the heels sinking into the
damp soil and balanced herself like a stork to slip them
off. She felt gritty wet sand slipping in between her
stockinged toes.

They sat on a park bench. He turned to her and
poured out another declaration of love. He would not

listen to her. He would not be diverted from his urgent compulsion to confess love repetitively, endlessly, excruciatingly. She was horrified to realise that love could be so boring. She told him tiredly that she could never love him in return, that he must stop bothering her like this. He burst into tears and buried his head in her lap, sobbing for all the women who had rejected him throughout his lifetime, conflating her with her daughter, mourning the loss of female friendship. Linh felt the seat of her panties soaking up water from the rain-wet bench, while the front of her skirt soaked up Gibbo's tears. His head was heavy on her lap, his snuffling breath hot on her thighs. Sighing, she closed her eyes and listened to the rhythmic roar of waves beating down on the beach. She would get through this. She was a woman who could get through anything.

Then she woke up one morning to the sound of fists thumping against the glass door of her balcony. She lived on the ground floor of her apartment block. She had always thought that was convenient. Now she realised she was vulnerable. She got out of bed, shoved her feet into slippers and shuffled over to the window. She tugged the curtain slightly and saw Gibbo knocking on her door. When he noticed her peeking out at him, he held out an armful of roses as red as a blood-gash in his chest.

'Why can't you see how much I love you?' he cried. 'I'd do anything for you.'

'The bastard! No woman deserves to be harassed like that,' Tien said when she found out. She was fuelled with righteous indignation and a need for vengeance. 'No means no. This is Australia, not Vietnam. Women have rights in this country, you know.'

In her eagerness to integrate into mainstream Australian society, Tien often disparaged her mother's culture in order to distance herself from her ethnic and cultural roots. She had never visited Vietnam and knew little of its history or culture, yet she felt herself qualified to pass judgement. It was true that she didn't speak Vietnamese very often now, but hadn't she grown up with Uncle Duong and Auntie Ai-Van? Didn't she celebrate all the festivals with the family? Hadn't she served in Uncle Duc's restaurant? Of course she knew Vietnamese culture!

Linh looked sadly at her daughter. 'Why are you so anti-Vietnamese?'

'I'm not,' Tien said impatiently. 'But I don't believe in being a downtrodden victimised Vietnamese woman either. This isn't the time or the land of *Kieu*, you know.'

'You're not a victimised Vietnamese woman? Why do you let Stan walk all over you then?' Linh hurried on before her daughter could interrupt. 'Anyway, you don't know anything about Vietnamese women, Tien. We're not victims. We're fighters. Like the Trung sisters. Did you know that in 40AD Trung Trac and Trung Nhi led twelve other women generals against the Chinese? The Trung sisters were pregnant but they still defeated the Chinese in battle at the Red River Delta. That's the kind of people you come from.'

'Ancient history, Mum. What's it got to do with now?'

'You're so Australian,' Linh complained. 'Australians are always moving on, always living in the present. Meanwhile the rest of the world walks hand in hand with the past, but you can't understand other people's grief and pain.'

'We may live in the present but at least we're living for the future,' Tien retorted.

Linh kept silent. She wouldn't argue with her daughter. She did not think their relationship was strong enough to withstand prolonged disagreement.

'Stan and I will make a deal with you,' Tien said one Sunday afternoon when she and her fiancé dropped by the Flemington apartment. 'We've talked it over and Stan is willing to drop his lawsuit against Gillian if you will protect yourself by applying for an AVO against Gibbo.'

'Tien, you can't be serious! How can you bargain like that with people's lives?'

'Your safety and well-being are more important to me, Auntie,' Stan said smugly. 'You must let us help you.' He placed his hand on Linh's shoulder and squeezed it, smiling conspiratorially at Tien. She smiled back and looked expectantly at her mother.

How things had changed, Linh thought. In the old days, the young would have looked to her for advice. She herself would have sought advice from her father. These days, her father dozed in his armchair by the window and barricaded himself behind books, while her daughter and this young man regarded their elders with impatience. They insisted on holding up the mirror of assimilated youth to demonstrate to their parents and elders a first-generation migrant helplessness and ineptitude. Don't speak; just listen to us, their attitude conveyed. Your old ways and beliefs don't count; things are different here.

'So we're agreed then?' Stan demanded. 'We'll file a police report and take Gibbo to court.'

'The poor Gibsons,' Linh said. But she agreed.

If Linh had had a better relationship with her daughter, she would not have felt the need to barter for her love. If Tien had chosen to mend her relationship with her mother earlier, Linh would not have clutched this new-found intimacy quite so desperately, willing to do whatever it took to maintain the link, willing to unite against a perceived external threat: Gibbo.

They went to the police station together: Linh, the victimised Vietnamese refugee; Tien, her triumphant competent daughter who believed that at last she could demonstrate *hieu thao* to the family (for as Australian as she claimed to be, she found she could not yank out her need for her family's approval); and Stanley, who, in a state of barely repressed excitement at this domestic drama, also did his duty as a future son-in-law and flicked Gibbo off like an irritating fly.

It was difficult to calibrate your maternal expectations in a different cultural milieu; to determine what was and was not reasonable. Linh had been seduced by the idea of inter-generational friendship. She leafed through women's magazines, watched Mother's Day ads on TV and listened to young Anglo women in their twenties talking about how their mothers were their best friends. In a culture where there was no automatic respect and deference towards the elderly, adult children met their parents on equal ground. The rudeness and impatience could be heart-stumbling, but the loss of authority was offset by the lure of intimacy. Equality held out the possibility of friendship with your children.

Linh thought she was working towards this point with her daughter. She would be the first to admit that she had made mistakes when Tien was a child. Perhaps she had been too distant and strict in her drive towards success. She had arrived in Australia with numbed emotions and she had had nothing to give Tien in those early years. But she was redeeming herself as a mother now. Wasn't this why she had, in the end, given in to Tien and Stan and applied for the AVO? She had consolidated her relationship with Tien by destroying the Gibsons.

And her reward? Glowing words of praise from Tien and Stan at their wedding reception. A tight hug from Tien as she whispered, 'I love you, Mum', and the glib assurance from Stan: 'We'll always take care of you.' Then the wedding was over. Tien and Stan departed for their honeymoon and disappeared from her life. They went to San Francisco so that Stan could pursue his postgraduate medical studies at the UCSF School of Medicine. They had barged in, solved the problem for poor victimised Linh, and walked off dusting their hands with satisfaction. Now all she had to look forward to was a weekly phone call from Tien, and they simply hadn't had enough time to build the kind of relationship whereby intimacy could be continued via long-distance phone lines. They expected so much each time the phone rang, but their conversation was stilted and they sounded like strangers to each other. Each hung up feeling frustrated that there was so little sense of connection to the other.

In Linh's loneliness, there was plenty of time to reflect on and regret what she had done. She thought about Tien and Stan, and while she told herself to be grateful for their concern, she wondered how life could have failed these children—for they were still children to her—to the extent that even in the midst of their success, they needed something like this, someone to crush, simply to make them feel better about themselves.

Still, it was done. She could not unspin the world on its axis and rewind her life. She hardened her heart and told herself that she didn't care; they would all have to live with it. Then, one afternoon, she received a letter from Bob, and she broke down and wept.

Linh,

I've never asked anything from you before, or from anyone else for that matter. It's hard for me to do it even now. It really goes against the grain, especially since I'm so bloody furious with you I wish I'd never clapped eyes on you or your family.

I've never been much of a father, god knows, but I have to do this for my son. So I'm asking, I'm begging you to do two things for me. (1) Remember what I did for you and yours in Vietnam and over here, and (2) go to the magistrate and drop the AVO against Nigel. Don't ruin his life.

I've been a good friend to you and your family. I've kept all your secrets. I didn't intrude on your lives when you settled here. I gave you space and left you to start afresh without continual reminders of the old days. Think about it. You owe me this.

Bob Gibson

The Tale of Linh II

But it's still there, the moon that we swore by:
not face to face, we shall stay heart to heart.
A day will last three winters far from you:
my tangled knot of grief won't soon unknit.

Nguyen Du, *The Tale of Kieu*

Linh was working in the Dong Tam Olympia Bar when the mama-san told her that a GI wanted to talk to her. She looked up and all she could see was his black silhouette in the doorway, the bright haze of afternoon sunlight blazing around him. She hastened towards him, arms eager to embrace.

'Bucky!' she cried.

He ducked under low-hanging nylon fishing nets and, when he stepped into the dim light, she saw that it was Bob Gibson. 'Oh, it's you.' She glanced around expectantly for Bucky, but he wasn't there.

'Sorry, love. Just me this time,' Bob said. His mouth twisted into a slight smile which did not reach his eyes. He took her arm and led her to a wooden table under a whirring ceiling fan. The waiter hurried over with a Saigon tea for Linh: a small shot-glass of amber liquid which might, by a long stretch of the imagination and a good deal of faith in humanity, have been the Cognac Coke, 120 piastres, cited on the bill but which was, in all probability, simply tea. Bob ordered a beer for himself and glugged it back thirstily, wiping his dripping mouth with the back of his hand when he'd drained half the bottle. Linh sat there, patiently waiting for him to begin their conversation.

'You're not a bar-girl, Linh,' Bob said abruptly, getting straight to the point. 'You don't belong here. Why don't you come back to Saigon? Madame Catinat will have you back. I've spoken to her.'

'She angry. I run away.'

'No. She understands. She's very fond of you. She just wants you to be safe.'

'I earn plenty more here. Pay in Saigon not so good.' Her lower lip jutted out obstinately. Her eyes slid away from his. 'In Saigon, family talk. Neighbours talk. Nobody like Bucky and me together. Bucky like here. More better for us. Nobody talk.'

'Yeah, but how often is he here? A few days every month, sometimes more? You're wasting your time just waiting for him here.'

She smiled to herself and said nothing. She armoured herself in the impermeably smug confidence of a woman who had been assured—in writing, no less—that she was getting married soon. Bob tried again.

'Listen, Linh. You've got to be realistic. Bucky's a great guy, I'm not denying that.'

'He very kind, yes,' she agreed readily.

'But do you really think he's going to marry you? Do you know how many girls get caught up in affairs with GIs thinking they're going to get married and live happily ever after in America? Most of them get left behind and forgotten. They're just young boys, they're not ready to settle down and get married. They're not serious, don't you understand?

'And even if they are, sometimes it's not up to them. My god, I just heard of a case not too long ago where an Aussie bloke took up with one of you girls. Someone working at the Beachcomber, I think. He promised to marry her but his captain vetoed it. Said she was a communist spy and a traitor to the South Vietnamese government. Said he'd got that from US intelligence. When we poked around and tried to find out if it was true, they shut us up pretty damn quick.'

'What happen?' Linh asked, politely interested.

'His tour ended and he went home without her. It wasn't worth the risk for him. He was told that if he continued in his relationship with this girl, he might be found shot dead at the perimeter one day. Nobody'd ask questions because it was a war zone.'

'I hate Viet Cong! I not communist spy.'

'She probably wasn't either, don't you get it?'

'Bucky love me. He Catholic. No funny business. Look, he gave me this.' She reached inside her blouse and pulled out a crucifix. 'Is his mama's. He write to me he find priest. Soon he marry me. We go to America. I give his god back to his mama.'

'Yes, he probably loves you. But that doesn't mean he's going to marry you. I mean, look at where you work, for god's sake. You're better off waiting for him in Saigon.'

'I not prostitute,' she said coldly. 'I only sit with GIs. Smile, talk. I not sleep with many men.'

'Yeah, I don't know if he'll believe that. What man would?'

'Bucky, he trust me,' she said angrily. She tapped her breast. 'He the one make me come to Vung Tau. He know my heart.'

Bob looked at her, and all he could think was how much he envied Bucky. Not so much for the girl, though he could imagine himself falling in love with her one day, given sufficient opportunity. Linh was fairly attractive and sweet and he liked her a lot, but there were many others like her. In any case, there was no future for a bloke like him and an Asian girl like Linh. What he envied, though, was the easy devotion Bucky elicited despite his cheerful ugliness. He was adept at making women feel safe and comfortable. He knew what to say to them, he knew how to show that he was listening. He had the knack of getting them to mother him. For once in his life, Bob thought, he would like to have a girl look at him just like that, as if he meant everything to her.

Bob cleared his throat and took out a letter. He pushed it across the table to Linh. 'Well, if you won't listen to me, maybe this'll change your mind.'

'What this?'

'Go on—open it.'

She slid her index finger along the gummed-down flap and exclaimed when her finger was cut. She pulled out the single sheet of paper and began to read the all-too-familiar Vietnamese verse, sucking the blood from her finger as she did so.

When comes the time for love, the marriage bond,
my parents' wish will tie it or will not.
You deign to care for me, but I'm too young
to know what's right and dare not give my word.

She raised her eyes and looked steadily at Bob. 'This
is from my father?'

He nodded. 'Yeah. I told him I was coming to see you.'

She pushed the piece of paper away from her angrily.
'Why you go see my father? You talk about me and Bucky.
You make me so shame to him.'

'No. God, Linh, I'd never do that.'

'Then why? And how you know where he live?'

'It was through Madame Catinat. People are worried
about you, don't you realise? She sent for Mr Thieu and
he asked people where to find you. I had to go with him
to see your dad.'

'You betray Bucky and me,' she said flatly.

His temper flared. 'The hell I did. And listen to yourself.
If everything was above board and proper with you and that
bloody Yank, you wouldn't have to hide your affair like this.'

'I not like see you anymore,' she said.

'All right. That's fine with me. Anyway, I'm going
home soon. My government—the Australian government—is starting to pull us out of here.'

She was diverted from her resentment. 'You go home?
This your last time in Vung Tau?'

'I'm not sure. I'm heading back to Saigon for one last
weekend there. Then I'll be at Nui Dat a bit longer.
Maybe I'll pass through here when I take the Vung Tau
ferry back to Australia. I don't know.'

'Vung Tau ferry?' Her brow wrinkled in puzzlement.

'Troop carrier,' he explained. 'Unless they fly us back. Anyway, I won't be seeing you again, Linh, but you ought to write to your dad. He's a real nice guy. Your brothers too. When I saw them, I could tell they were really worried about you.'

'I sorry I angry,' she said contritely. She put out a tentative hand and touched his fingers. 'Please, not to be angry with Linh.'

'I'm not angry with you, Linh,' he sighed. He returned the clasp of her fingers lightly, then let go. 'I just hope things work out for you.'

'Thank you. Everything A-okay, sure thing,' she predicted confidently. 'If you go Saigon, you take letter to my father?'

He nodded, and she reached for the letter, turned it over and scrawled a quick four lines in Vietnamese:

It blows one day and rains the next—
how often does chance favour us in spring?
If you ignore and scorn my desperate love,
you'll hurt me—yet what will it profit you?

'That's it? Bit short, isn't it?'

'Is from *Kieu*. He understand. He choose first to speak through *Kieu*.'

'Linh, he loves you, your dad.'

'Yes.'

'You're lucky to have so many people love you, then.'

Guilt arrowed swiftly into her heart and tears pricked her eyes, but she didn't say anything. She merely folded the sheet of paper precisely in two and slid it back into the torn envelope. Then she presented it to him with both hands. 'I so grateful, Mr Bob. Be safe and happy in *Uc chau*—your country. *Tam biet.*'

'If there's ever anything I can do for you . . .' He shrugged and slapped down some piastres to settle the bill. '*Tam biet*, Linh,' he said, and without another look at a woman he might have grown to love over time, he walked out of the bar.

She watched him leave and felt a tinge of fear and shame that, in choosing her own happiness, she had openly disobeyed her father. She was too much a Vietnamese daughter not to believe that there would one day be a reckoning. When the months passed and Bucky did not show up, she packed her things and returned to submit herself to her father's will. She hoped that her act of atonement would balance the scales and bring Bucky back to her.

In early April 1975 Linh yearned for snow even though she had never seen it before. When it rained in Saigon at dawn, she leaned out of the window and caught raindrops on the tip of her tongue. She closed her eyes and imagined silence and whiteness all around her, the cold crispness of snowflakes melting on her face. Winter would be like this in America, she thought, humming softly to herself. *White Christmas.* The Americans were whistling it, the armed forces radio broadcast it constantly.

Every day the American disc jockey called out, 'It's 105 outside and the temperature is rising!' Immediately after that, Bing Crosby crooned about a white Christmas just like the ones he used to know. Everyone in Saigon was singing that song in April 1975, from the taxi drivers to the cleaners and shoeshine boys. In hotel lobbies, when nervous American guests heard the song they hurried to their secret rendezvous points so that the buses could pick them up and take them out to Tan Son Nhut airport where American evacuation planes were waiting to whisk them away to safety.

Hooters and car horns sounded. People shouted in the street below. Puddles steamed in the humidity. A young man emerged from the terrace house opposite. He looked up and spotted Linh. '*Do di ngua*—bitch!' he spat. 'American whore.'

Linh hurriedly jerked back inside, glancing over her shoulder to see whether Ai-Van had heard. Her sister-in-law caught her eye and turned away. Linh dropped her own eyes in hot-faced shame. *I don't care*, she thought. *Bucky and I are engaged.* She dried and combed her hair, then leaned over the mattress where her daughter rolled so that her baby girl could grasp a handful of black silk in a chubby fist. 'Let me make your own hair pretty, *em be*.' She combed her daughter's wiry curls, plaited red and pink ribbons into them, and kissed the child. 'You play with your cousins now, Tien. Ma has to go to work.'

'You are spoiling the child. You wait and see,' Ai-Van said.

'No, I am not,' Linh said. 'When Bucky returns he will know she has been treated well.'

Ai-Van sniffed. 'You have heard from him then?'

Linh had not had any kind of contact with Bucky since she returned to Saigon. She had left messages for him with the other girls in the Dong Tam Olympia Bar and the Beachcomber. They told her that he had yet to return to Vung Tau. But she would not lose faith in their love. She clutched the crucifix around her neck and reminded herself that he was going to take her to meet his mother. In the meantime, he had entrusted his daughter to her. He would not abandon them. One day soon, when she least expected it, he would appear out of the blue and collect all that belonged to him, then he would carry them away to America and they would finally be happy. She had to hold on to this thought because, if she lost faith, she would not deserve to have a happy ending to her love story. So she said to Ai-Van, 'No. Not yet. He is busy fighting in the war.'

'The American war is over,' Ai-Van pointed out. 'Most of the American soldiers have left. More Americans are leaving Saigon every day and still you don't know where he is.'

Linh said nothing. She pinned up her hair and left for work. Mr Thieu had found her a position as an English teacher in a small high school in Saigon. As was her daily habit, she passed by the boarded-up doorway of Maison Catinat on Tu-Do and stopped in front of the pedlar cooking by the roadside. 'Good morning, Auntie. Have you seen the American soldier?'

The old woman shook her head and held out a baguette. Linh paid for it and thanked her, then continued on her way.

Linh worked in the school six days a week and redis-covered the pleasure of studying. She spent all her spare time devouring whatever meagre textbooks were left in the school. Eventually, she thought, she would sit for the *Tu Tai* examination herself so that she could be admitted to a university in Vietnam, or even acquire an exit visa to study abroad when Bucky returned. Perhaps she might be eligible to study at one of those American universities, the names of which she threaded through her memory like silver charms on a bracelet: Harvard, Princeton, Berkeley, Yale. In her iron-willed anticipation of Bucky's imminent return, no dream seemed too impossible, no desire hidden behind the moon.

A grubby calendar—rather like the ones she used to make in the forgotten days of her brief marriage to Thanh Lam—hung on the schoolroom wall. Pages were torn off and thrown into the unswept streets. Weeks ticked by like a time bomb. The children sat for their examinations. Many did badly and handed their report cards to their fathers, hanging their heads in shame. They could not study at night for the continuous rumbling of bombs and the rattling of machine gun fire from North Vietnamese fighters strafing the sky with red-hot coals. Smoke stung the air and the streets trembled.

Linh climbed right up to the rooftop of her father's house at night, and she saw that the horizon was bright with fire. She clutched her crucifix and prayed to Bucky's god to protect him if he were out there some-where. She did not dare to ask for his safe return to her; she asked only that he should survive. In the morning, newspaper headlines declared grimly that the South Vietnamese government did not have enough food or ammunition to fight on. Where, they demanded angrily, were the Americans now? Where was the help they had promised?

Many children did not return after the holidays. Those who attended school were too distracted to learn. One afternoon, the government suddenly announced over the radio that curfew hours had been extended. Panicking people thronged the streets and the children cried out in fear and confusion. They clung to Linh's hands and wept into her skirt. She huddled with them at the top of the short flight of steps just outside the front door of the school, waiting for parents, older brothers and sisters to ride down the streets on their motorcycles and pick up the children.

She looked down on faces pale with fear, eyes filled with bewilderment and growing resentment. Men and women shoved desperately through the crowded street. Others stood where they were, jostled and cursed by passers-by, their heads swivelling from side to side, their eyes wide with alarm as they searched frantically for the lost.

Among the swarm of people, she thought she spied a dark, curly-haired American soldier in army fatigues. He turned his face away and she could only see the back of his swarthy caramel neck.

'Bucky!' she shouted, for she was sure it had to be him. She tried to disentangle herself from the arms and legs of the children, swatting away their clinging limbs. 'Bucky! It is Linh! I am here!'

She tried to drag herself away, but the children wailed and she hesitated and looked back.

'Just wait here. Your parents will come for you soon,' she pleaded. But she looked at their faces and could not resist their terror. She thought of how she would feel if it were Tien standing there. Slowly, she remounted the steps and crouched down beside them, folding them in her arms. 'It is all right. Everything will be all right.'

Later, she wandered through the deserted streets of Saigon, stopped only by the occasional ARVN soldier—frightened young boys nervously fingering their rifles—at sandbagged posts. He was gone by that time, of course, the American soldier. If he was Bucky. He was. He had to be. She could not accept that Bucky was dead. She refused to consider that he might have abandoned her. She knew the man he was; she knew the man she loved. She walked up Tu-Do and stopped in front of the boarded-up entrance of Maison Catinat. She climbed the steps. She sat down on the top step and, nursing fierce love and desperate faith in her heart, she waited for Bucky to come.

In the days after Saigon fell to the communists, the tops of buildings fluttered with bright yellow and red propaganda banners, giving the city a rather festive look at odds with the new atmosphere of apprehension and sobriety. Bars, brothels and nightclubs were closed down. Many restaurants went out of business. Tu-Do was renamed Dong Khoi—'general uprising'. Loudspeakers were installed in the streets, crackling harshly into life at dawn to urge citizens to awake and perform their physical exercises in public squares.

Life for the Hos did not change much at first. Duong and Duc continued to work downstairs in their father's publishing house. Instead of Vietnamese classics, they now churned out thousands of communist pamphlets. They typeset and printed the entire works of Ho Chi

Minh, Mao, Marx, Engels and Lenin. They were kept busy. All school textbooks had to be rewritten to cull out reactionary rubbish. In the meantime, the schools closed down and Linh found herself out of a job once again. She bundled Madame Catinat's cast-off clothing into two large pannier baskets and went out to sell it in the streets.

Up on the third floor of the Ho house, the women—Ai-Van, Phi-Phuong and Mrs Ho—thought of ways to make a few extra piastres since all the banks were closed and no-one could get any money out. They made sweet dumplings and sewed clothes for Linh to sell, then they prepared meals for the men and looked after the children. There were six cousins now: Duc's two sons, Duong's three daughters, and Tien. Mr Ho escaped this excess of femininity by shuffling downstairs to the second floor and, together with Mr Thieu, he read Karl Marx for the first time.

'He writes quite beautifully,' Mr Ho said, turning a page of the book he held on his lap. 'Listen to this, Mr Professor: "All that is solid melts into air, all that is holy is profaned, and man is at last compelled to face with sober senses his real condition of life and his relations with his kind." Quite inspiring in its passion, isn't it? No wonder my own son Duyen was enthralled by the poetry of what he heard.'

'That may be true,' Mr Thieu replied, peering over his glasses. 'Still, one may read Nguyen Du's *Tale of Kieu* and appreciate the beauty of the story, the artistry of the language, without in any way desiring to live the life of Kieu.'

'You know about these things, of course, Mr Professor. Yet can't we cull lessons from the life of Kieu? Shouldn't literature inform our lives, enlighten our actions?'

'And what do we learn from Kieu?' Mr Thieu wondered. He sipped his coffee, leaned back in his fraying chair and quoted: 'Heaven appoints each human to a place. If doomed to roll in dust, we'll roll in dust.'

'True, very true,' Mr Ho said warmly. Whether communists or capitalists ruled, his world remained unshaken as long as he could indulge in these literary discussions with Mr Professor. 'Yet "let's stop decrying heaven's whims and quirks. Inside ourselves there lies the root of good: the heart outweighs all talents on this earth".'

'And that is why,' Mr Thieu replied, 'Linh waits for her American to return, your Duyen believed in Ho Chi Minh and went to die for utopia, while my poor sons died for a corrupt leader they did not believe in.'

'They had good hearts, our sons. They knew *hieu thao*, and although they went their separate ways, still they followed the righteous path—*dao duc* and *le nghia*.'

'All we can hope for is to protect those who are left to us now. It is the only thing left for you to do as a father.'

A few months later, police and hired thugs exploded through the door of the publishing house and began smashing printing presses, overturning tables, toppling stocks of paper, sweeping books off wooden shelves and display cabinets. The old men heard the commotion from the second floor and hurried downstairs. Mr Ho cried out in dismay when he saw cudgels swirling, machinery smashed, ink spilt, glass shattered, pages ripped and ground into the concrete floor.

'What are you doing?' he demanded as he flung himself into the fray, hunching protectively over a printing press. 'We are a good communist press.'

'We know what you published before Liberation. We are destroying the enslaving, reactionary culture of the enemy,' the young man said. He lifted his staff and brought it down heavily on the old man's back, then he kicked the white-haired head and blood bloomed like a red camellia on the fragile skin.

'*Cha*—Father!' Duong rushed over to the broken body.

'Have you no respect for the elderly?' Mr Thieu demanded angrily. 'Have you no respect for the culture you are destroying? Who gives you permission to do this?'

'The government. We are stamping out the corruption of reactionary dissidents.'

'But we publish Marx and Mao and Ho Chi Minh,' Duc protested.

'This publishing house carries a list of prohibited books. Look at these authors.' With his staff he poked at some battered books. 'Nguyen Tuong Tam. Khai Hung. Forbidden. All forbidden. This house is an indecent den of decadent propaganda.' He signalled to his men to proceed to the upper storeys of the house to search for more prohibited reading material.

A week later, they received a summons to attend political meetings after work. There were several such meetings each week, lasting up to four hours. The roll was called at the beginning and the end. On one occasion, a meeting was held at midnight to welcome a political leader from the north who told them that they needed to be re-educated, but this could not be done in the corrupting atmosphere of the city. Intellectuals like themselves could only be transformed into new people, desirable citizens, if they went out to the country to dig irrigation canals. By working to revitalise Vietnam's agriculture, they would redeem themselves.

It was, therefore, no surprise to them when, less than a year after Liberation, the younger members of the Ho family—Duong, Duc, Ai-Van, Phi-Phuong and Linh—were sent to a New Economic Zone. They left the children in Cholon with Mr and Mrs Ho and boarded a rickety green bus that still sported the sign SAIGON–VUNG TAU. Hours later, the bus stopped on a red dirt road in the middle of nowhere. They disembarked and an official came around to collect the bus fare. 'It's over there,' he directed, jerking his chin to point the group of thirty-five young men and women towards a stone-strewn path that disappeared into the long grass stretching out for miles to the distant hills.

'There is nothing there,' a young man grumbled.

'It is the New Economic Zone,' the official insisted. He boarded the bus and it rattled away.

They faced three pressing problems upon arrival. First of all, there was nowhere for them to stay. Secondly, none of them had ever farmed before. And then they had only brought along a couple of pots, pans and bowls, chopsticks, a paring knife and a meat cleaver. It took them two months to erect a hut. They had to use the cleaver to hew down bamboo trees to build some sort of dwelling. Most of this construction work was done by the women. Almost immediately, Duong and Duc, despite their maimed hands and missing index fingers, were drafted by the community leader to cut down trees and clear the land to plant rice.

Every morning, the two brothers woke at five o'clock and went out to work without breakfast, for there was nothing to eat. Together with their team, they felled trees, cleared weeds, collected pebbles and other rubbish, drained swamps and caught scorpions, millipedes, crabs and snakes in the drying mud. They learned to work in synchronised rhythm, one slashing at the long grass and reeds, the other raking up the material into huge heaps which would then be burnt as fuel. They dug canals and built up dykes, packing down the solid earthen walls with brown palms that seeped blood where dry skin cracked over the bone. They planted rice seedlings in shin-deep water and harvested it when the months drifted and the fields drained and rippled with gold. They dried their crop in the sun, then took it to the rice-treading yard.

Under the bright moonlight, they took turns leading two lean buffaloes round and round the dry mud yard until the heavy weight of cloven hoofs crushed the rice grains from the husks. One of the brothers led the animals while the other kept a watchful eye for the betraying twitch of the buffaloes' taut tails, rushing forward with a wooden scoop to collect the dung before it fell onto the grain. The rice was then hauled to a mill made of timber and clay to be ground by hand. It was left out in the sun on tarpaulins for the wind to winnow the chaff from the grain. After all that effort, they hauled the rice to the communal warehouse and the leader doled out their meagre ration. It was not enough to feed the five of them.

The women planted tomatoes and corn, but they were city-bred. They had never had to grow their own food before and they did not know how to tend the young plants properly. In the end, they cut down more bamboo, peeled away the woody outer layer and boiled the remains to supplement their meals. They were all emaciated, their bones protruding through their green-tinged skin. But the men fared worse because of their back-breaking physical work during the day. Each night they could hardly sleep for the hunger that stung them like a scorpion's tail. They crawled on the mud floor, scrabbling for scraps of the evening's meal, and when they could find nothing, they curled up painfully like cooked shrimps.

'We must get out,' Linh said as she gave her own small portion of rice to her brothers, 'or Duong and Duc will surely die.'

The following night, they stayed awake until one o'clock, then they crept out of the bamboo hut and stumbled through the jungle. In the darkness, lithe branches of saplings slashed their skins and grazed their faces. Time ceased, night was eternal. They focused only on one thing: heading towards the moon. Then, in the pearl grey light of dawn, they reached the edge of the jungle and found themselves on the verge of a sealed road that the Americans had constructed many years ago. With considerable trepidation, they stopped the next truck that passed and were lucky enough to hitch a lift back towards Saigon.

'The thing that grieved me most,' Mr Ho said to his children when he saw them again, 'was that I could not even organise a fitting funeral for your poor mother. Her soul flits restlessly because she was not sent off properly. I could not invite the neighbours around to perform the ceremonies because these are now forbidden. Everything that we used to do, our rituals, our culture, our harmony with those who are gone—all is forbidden. Marx was right. All that is solid melts into air.'

'Did Ma leave us any instructions?' Linh asked. She had been waiting for an upsurge of sorrow since she first heard that her mother had died while they were in the New Economic Zone, but grief refused to come. There was only numbness and a weary recognition that she had failed her mother in old age and death. She was a failure as a mother, for she had killed her first baby, Thi-Lan. Now she had failed as a daughter because she had not been there to tend to her mother. The debts that she could never repay were mounting sky-high. She hugged Tien in her arms and guilt oozed osmotically from mother to daughter.

'Before she died, she told us to go,' Mr Ho said.

'She understood,' Duong said. A filial son who had looked after his stepmother to the best of his ability while she was still alive, his heart was untroubled by self-reproach and the tears ran freely down his face. 'She knew we could no longer stay here. And, *Cha*, she is right. We have no money. The printing presses are smashed. How can we start up any sort of business? We can't get jobs for we have no papers. And if we are caught, we will be sent to prison, or back to the New Economic Zone. We must leave Vietnam.'

'Well, I hear that Mr Professor wants to escape to Paris,' Mr Ho said slowly. 'He knows a man with a boat. They will be leaving at the end of April. Perhaps we could join them.'

In separate groups of two and three, they loaded themselves with food and left for Cuu Long—the Mekong

Delta. They hid among the long grass and low sweeping palm branches of a sheltered inlet for two days until a sampan came to collect the thirteen of them: Mr Thieu and Mr Ho, Duong, Ai-Van and their three daughters, Duc, Phi-Phuong and their two sons, and Linh and Tien. Oars dipped with gentle gulps into glimmering water and the boat eased slowly towards the mouth of the estuary. A few hours later, they pulled up beside a thirty-three metre fishing trawler which, they realised to their dismay, was already crammed with too many people. Torchlights flashed and in the sweep of the beams they saw, propped up against the engine room, a large hand-painted sign: 'PLEASE HELP. WE WANT FREEDOM.'

A silhouette detached itself from the mass of humanity and straddled the edge of the boat, leaning down towards them. 'Where's the payment?'

'It's impossible,' Mr Thieu said angrily. 'This was not what we were promised. The boat will sink.'

'Take it or leave it,' the shadow shrugged. 'Not everybody will make it, if you are worried about space. Some will die along the way. You had better decide quickly. If you are not coming on board, we will leave now.'

'Uncle, we have no choice,' Duc whispered to Mr Thieu. 'Don't make him angry. He might take it out on us during the voyage. *Cha*, please give him the gold.'

'Very well then. Here is your payment.' Mr Ho reached inside his shirt and pulled out a soft cloth bag, handing it up to the grasping fingers above him. They waited in silence while torchlight flickered over the bag and the man took out the gold taels and jewellery that they had brought. He gave a derisive laugh.

'This is very funny. You are a bunch of jokers, yes? You think this will pay for the thirteen of you?'

'It's all we have,' Mr Ho said apprehensively. 'We sold everything we owned. There is nothing more.'

The man shook his head. 'See these people on board? Do you know how much they paid? Twenty taels per person! You have enough here for nine people only. Four of you will have to return.'

'That is impossible. We cannot split up.'

'Then I cannot take any of you. But I will keep a few taels as a fee for all my trouble arranging this pick-up.'

It was pitch-black under the moonless night, the only light coming from the pinpricks of stars now that the man had clicked off his torch. Those on board the trawler huddled together and said nothing, listening passively to this exchange. On the sampan, the Hos and Mr Thieu grasped each other's hands and felt panic coursing through their taut bodies. Seconds ticked by in agonising indecision. Ai-Van's youngest daughter broke the silence with a wail. She hugged the child and put her hand over the toddler's mouth, urgently ordering her silence.

'Last chance,' the man said. He lit a cigarette and they could see the orange tip glowing in the dark.

Mr Thieu spoke up. 'You say we have enough only for nine people, but please consider that we are not all adults. There are six young children here. They won't take up much space. If you won't take us all, I myself will remain behind, but please take these others.'

'Mr Professor, you cannot do this!' Mr Ho turned to face his best friend, blindly reaching a hand out to him.

'Trong, you have always respected me as a teacher and an elder brother. Do as I say now,' Mr Thieu said in a low voice.

'If anybody should board that boat, it must be you. This was all your plan.'

'My four sons are buried in this country, and my wife also. What reason do I have for leaving? Paris? Paris is the dream of my youth, not the reality of my old age. But you, you have your family with you. Your sons and daughters and grandchildren. Go and make a new life for yourselves. Old Thieu will stay and keep faith with his family.' He raised his voice and called out to the man on the boat. 'Sir. Will you take six tiny children and six adults?'

'Six children and five adults. That is all. You had better start climbing on board now if you are coming.'

Mr Ho touched Phi-Phuong's shoulder. 'Go,' he said. 'Start climbing the ladder.'

'Father, I'll stay behind,' Duong said. 'It's my duty as the eldest son.'

'No. It's precisely because you are the eldest son that you ought to go,' Duc argued. 'I'll stay.'

'No, Duong, Duc. You should both go with your wives and children. I'm ordering you. I will stay back with Mr Professor. We're just two old men. All of you are young with your lives ahead of you.'

Linh laid her hand on her father's arm, and he said at once, 'Don't challenge me on this. I forbid you to speak. Get on board that boat right now.'

He tried to push her roughly towards the rope, but she handed her child to Phi-Phuong and slid closer to her father, wrapping her arms around him. She whispered:

'If moved by love you won't let go of me,
I fear a storm will blow and blast our home.
You'd better sacrifice just me—one flower
will turn to shreds, but green will stay the leaves.
Whatever lot befalls me I accept—'

'No,' her father said violently. 'Stop it. Don't you dare quote *Kieu* at me. Not at such a time. I won't listen to you.'

He threw off her hand and stuck his fingers in his ears like a stubborn frightened child. She leaned forward, kissed the back of his hand and tugged it away from his ear.

Still she quoted: 'What is she worth, a stripling of a girl who's not repaid one whit a daughter's debts?'

He was weeping now, his thin shoulders shuddering under the gentle grip of her fingers. She had never seen her father shed a tear before. She slid her hands down his arms until she held his gnarled hands. He turned his own palms under hers and clasped her fingers. He laid his wrinkled wet cheek against hers. 'There is no debt. Don't you under-stand? No debt! Only love from the moment you drew your first breath. I don't care what the poets and the teachers say.'

'I have to do this. I know the shame I brought on the family, the gossip and the loss of face you endured because of my actions. I need to do this now, for you and for the family, but most of all for myself. Let me regain a little self-respect and repay my debt to heaven.'

'Not in this way,' he pleaded. 'Make it up some other way. Think about your daughter. She needs you now.'

'I need to do this,' she repeated. 'I won't get on that boat. Don't worry; I'll follow you.'

He drew his daughter to him and held her close, stroking her slim back, running his fingers lovingly down the thick braid of her hair. Then he eased away from her and looked at Mr Thieu. 'Dear Mr Professor,' he said. 'How can I ever repay—'

'There is no debt,' the other man echoed. 'You'd better go now. Linh is doing the right thing. Let your daughter follow the righteous path.'

Mr Ho hugged Linh one last time. She rubbed away the tears from his face with her fingers, then she sat calmly in the rocking sampan with Mr Thieu as her father, the last to board, grasped the lowest rung of the rope ladder and hauled himself up the trawler. He scissored his legs over the side of the boat and climbed in. He looked down at her and there were no words to convey what he wanted to say. His gut twisted in anguish and he felt as though he would vomit grief. He shook his head abruptly, for he knew that he had made a terrible mistake in giving in to her will. He reached out his hand to her and said, 'No, it mustn't be this way.'

The engine of the trawler roared into life. The fishing boat drew away from the sampan and sputtered towards the open sea.

Three years later, Linh sat in a listing boat and watched as a man called Binh, wearing nothing but his underwear, bailed water. The boat had been damaged in the second pirate attack and now the engine was disabled. The women coiled into each other's near-nakedness and closed their eyes. They did not know how many men and children were still alive and how many wounded. As the deck sank closer to the skin of the sea, swollen corpses nudged the creaking sides. A gentle visitation from the dead.

'We're sinking,' Binh snapped. 'Don't just sit there. Do something. Give me your clothes to stuff into this hole.'

Out of the darkness a voice said, 'We have no clothes.'

Linh ducked down into the cargo hold and emerged with pots and woks. She put a hand on a woman's shoulder and felt bare flesh shrinking away from her touch.

'We must help Binh or the boat will sink and we'll all drown,' she said urgently.

'We may as well drown,' the woman said. She buried her face on her raised knees, hugging herself into a tight ball and keening hysterically. Linh slapped her hard and she stopped.

'Where's your kindness?' she demanded tearfully.

'It's all used up,' Linh said flatly. She turned away and clambered over to Binh. She took the largest pot and started bailing. Some of the other men and women followed suit. They bailed water for hours. Or it could have been a few minutes. The reality of their lives microscoped into the mechanical motions of dunking vessels, scooping water and tossing their brimming loads back into the sea. Fingers wrinkled, arched spines ached and prickled with pain.

Perhaps around midnight, the bright lights of a huge ship surged over the horizon and bathed them in radiance. They wondered without much hope whether salvation was at hand. The silhouettes that emerged over the ship's edge scarcely seemed human, ringed as they were with a halo of light. Binh shouted up to the ship. After a quarter of an hour, a bundle was lowered over the ship's side. Binh caught it and unknotted the rope. He opened a sack of clothes, food, water, motor oil, mechanical tools, and about 200 Philippine pesos.

The deck of the ship was plunged abruptly into darkness. The engines rumbled loudly and the ship began to move away, the powerful thrust of its forward motion sending the rocking waves surging over the sides so that they had to bail twice as hard to stay afloat. They watched until the ship disappeared into darkness and they could see and hear nothing but the ocean. The night appeared blacker than before. Their boat had not seemed so frail, survival so impossible, until they had looked up and seen the towering steel mass of the ship looming far above them.

The women continued to bail water while two men accompanied Binh to the engine room. When they heard the engine coughing to life, they were neither astonished nor relieved. The boat began to push feebly against the weight of water. On the deck they bent, scooped, straightened, tossed. Bent, scooped, straightened and tossed for an eternity.

Drifting southwards, they raised their eyes and saw fire flaming the sky like a dragon's angry roar. Nothing could surprise them now. Instinctively, they headed towards the light. As they drew closer, the air was heavy with the stench of crude oil and rotten eggs, and they realised that they were looking at the massive pilot light of an offshore petroleum rig. Binh steered the boat towards it. Smaller lights perforated the side of the pontoons under the main barge and the whole contraption looked like a massive seaborne city elevated on ten steel piles. They sputtered fitfully

towards the production rig and, when they drew up by
one of the steel piles, Binh cut out the engine and tied
the boat to an offshore supply vessel moored alongside
the pile.

'Get out,' he said to them. 'I'm going to sink the boat.
We can't travel any further in this leaking thing.'

They began to climb onto the OSV but a guard
lurched out onto the deck and chased them off.

'Climb onto the pile,' Binh ordered. He was already
taking a hammer to the wooden deck of the boat. Grasping
hold of any strut that they could reach on the trussed pile,
they hauled themselves up to the first platform, then to the
second platform. When Binh saw them perching safely
there, he hammered a larger hole through the side of the
boat that had been rammed by Thai pirates. Water surged
in and it began to sink. He sprang from the deck and began
to climb the steel pile.

The guard on board the OSV had alerted the production platform by now. Lights flared and men shouted
down at them to get off the rig. It started to rain, huge
fat drops plopping onto the sea. They were drenched
within minutes. Thunder cracked and the sky was shattered with violent light. Below them, the ocean churned
and spat.

'We should climb higher,' Linh said, looking down fear-
fully at the boiling waves. Slowly, for the steel framework
was now slippery, they climbed to the platform just under
the pontoons, where they could go no further. They
huddled together for warmth and comfort against the
clubbing thunder and the lashing quills of rain. They
gripped each other's hands but nobody said a word. Bone-

drenched, they suddenly saw a huge nylon sheet descending, warping wildly in the wind.

'Go on and catch hold of it,' one of the workers on the deck above hollered down to them. 'Cover yourselves.'

They clutched at the sheet until they could drag it in safely without losing their balance and falling off the platform. They tucked the tarp around themselves and anchored it by sitting on the edges. There was nothing else to do but wait. By dawn, the storm had worn out its rage. The sea below was grey and flecked with foam. An hour later, a worker descended to the platform in a tugger. He opened the cage door and helped a few of the women to climb in, then the crane hauled it back up to the production platform. It took several trips before they were all winched up to safety.

'We've radioed our boss,' the worker said. 'We've got permission to take you to Malaysia in the OSV when it leaves in a couple of days. It's okay. You guys are safe now.'

Pulau Bidong refugee camp, Malaysia

Dear Mr Bob Gibson,

It is an honour to hear from you. I was surprised. Thank you for your letter and your encouraging news. It is very kind of you to write to UNHCR and Australian government for me. You are always kind to me.

I have only one wish now. I want to see my family again, especially my daughter Tien. They are all I think of now.

It is wonderful that my Tien is going to same school as your son. Heaven is looking after her. I did not know you had

*girlfriend when you were in Vietnam. I am happy for you
that you have found good wife and that you are blessed with
good son also. Mr Bob, you are doing very well!*

*I am also happy when you say that my brother Duong
looks after Tien so well. I am happy he sends her to your wife
for English lessons. I have had many English lessons from
Presbyterian minister here. I read English books all the time
to improve. I help him to teach English now. I teach other
Vietnamese people what they want to learn: asking questions
like, 'Can you take me to Grand Central Station?' or, 'Where
is Empire State Building?' or tell the taxi driver, 'Mott Street,
Chinatown, please.' Everybody wants to go to America.*

*Thank you for sending me Duong's address. I will write
to him but I will not write to my father until I know whether
I can come to Australia. He is so old now. I do not want to
disappoint him again. He has been so disappointed in his life.*

*You ask me how I escape from Vietnam. It is long story. I
tried to escape twice. The first time in 1979, Mr Thieu
arranged it. I met his cousin in Bac Lieu and he brought me
to small boat. We were betrayed and arrested by the communists. I was sent to prison in Bac Lieu. They kept me with political prisoners. They were tied up all the time but it was not too
bad for me. Better than life in New Economic Zone because
the work not so hard and we had something to eat every day.*

*After six months they let me out. I had to sign the paper
promising not to escape again. I went back to Saigon to look
after Mr Thieu but he died while I was in prison. I was very
sad because I had no more links to the old life. Every year I
burn joss sticks for him and my mother and my poor baby
daughter on the festival of Vu Lan. I want to honour their
death anniversaries but everything is so confused. Sometimes*

I don't know what day or month it is. Sometimes I do not remember when they died.

Life was very hard for me. I had nowhere to live because people had moved into our old house. I did not mind very much. I did not want to stay in Cholon anymore. Too many bad memories for me there. Also, I do not have good reputation because people remember that I was with Bucky during the American war so they look down on me and point at me in the streets now I have no father and Mr Thieu to protect me.

I went to Saigon and made little house for myself in poor part of town near river. There, anybody can put up shelter anywhere. Nobody says anything. The houses are built on stilts. They jut over muddy little stream that goes into river. When it rains heavily or tide comes in, then little stream floods and we paddled up and down streets in small boats. When it is dry season, there is no water, only mud with lots of filthy rubbish and dung and very bad smell.

I had to let police know where I was living. At first they came to visit me every few days. I was so scared. They made me go to political meetings three nights a week. It was hard for me to find work because I had black name since I tried to escape. Also because of my black name, I had no ration card for food. After few months I ran away because I was afraid I would be sent to New Economic Zone again. You may guess how I earned money. You were always kind to me when I was a bar-girl in Vung Tau so I hope you will not despise me. Please do not tell my family. You do not know the things I do to survive. I feel I am not myself, Ho Ly-Linh, anymore. It is somebody else do these things.

The second time I tried to escape, it was with some friends I made in shanty town. Most of them tried to escape before. They told me story of married man with six children who tried to leave Vietnam four times but he was caught every time and then he had to go to prison. His whole life was just trying to escape and going to prison, then trying to escape again.

This time we planned everything very well. We sent one fisherman down Saigon River many times to see how often he was stopped and to find out where were police checkpoints. We were very careful. When we left in May, we sailed down river in small cargo boat which carried manure. One engine was very weak, the other strong. We only used small engine so that nobody would think we had engine big enough to go out to sea. We changed the look of the boat many times between checkpoints. Sometimes we put up lots of clothes. Other times we hanged out dried fish and put up canvas cover painted two different colours on two sides so we could turn it over. There were very many of us on the boat and we had to hide below deck. It was very cramped.

I cannot tell you about our journey across the sea except many people died when we were attacked by Thai pirates. I cannot remember. I will tell you about this camp I am at instead.

Camp is very crowded because all buildings perch on the edge of island, near sea. Behind this small strip of land are very steep hills, green like Vietnamese countryside. The Presbyterian minister who runs English school says it is outrageous because there are nearly twenty thousand of us living in one square kilometre. But it is all right for me because I grew up in Cholon.

Actually, it reminds me very much of home. People live on top of each other, laundry is hanging out everywhere and everybody has something to sell. There are all kinds of cooks here. There are bakers and cakemakers, people who cook and sell noodles and dumplings. There are hairdressers, barbers and mechanics. There are tailors, pawnbrokers, watch repairers, artists, and Chinese doctors and acupuncturists. You can get anything on the black market if you have money. They say that Malaysian fishermen swim out to the island at night to make deals with Vietnamese ex-army men. Sometimes we are quite afraid of them. Mr Bob, I am so tired of being scared.

I have a lot of work to do here. In the daytime I help doctor look after sick people. There are so many sick people here, especially with skin trouble, influenza and dysentery. Doctor teaches me many things. He says I make good nurse. I like nursing. It makes me feel good about myself when I help other people, like I pay back heaven a little bit. If I come to Australia, I hope I can be nurse. In afternoon I help Presbyterian minister teach English. He has lots of books. I don't know how he got them. He lets me read after English classes. Lots of kind people here also.

I miss my daughter and my family very much but I glad they don't know what I do to survive. Maybe it is better they don't know I am alive. If they think of me, I want them to remember the old Linh, not this stranger inside my skin.

You are the only one I tell about these things. You are my only link to my old life in Saigon and with Bucky, and also with the life I hope to have in Australia one day. I am so grateful to you, Mr Bob. I hope I can repay you one day.

Sincere regards to you and your beautiful family,
Ho Ly-Linh

Father and Son

Pity the father facing his young child.
Looking at her, he bled and died within . . .
I would not mind the ax for these old bones,
but how can I endure my child's ordeal?

Nguyen Du, *The Tale of Kieu*

When Gibbo was a child, he used to shut himself in his bedroom after dinner and talk to himself. The window was usually open, the yellowing gauze curtains ghosting in the slight breeze. From far away came the sound of a backfiring car and the pock of a cricket ball connecting with a bat, followed by a child's high-pitched voice calling, 'Howzat!'

Bob passed by the bedroom one evening and was filled with irritation and pity as he heard his son talking to himself. Nigel should have been out there in the reserve playing with the neighbourhood kids, Bob thought. You had to play cricket or footy, or how could you get along with other kids?

'Nobody wants to play with me at school,' Gibbo confided to his favourite toy—a ragged dog missing a button eye and a floppy ear. 'Ben tripped me on the asphalt today and I grazed my knees until they bled. He said I was a pansy when I cried, but I had to go to the sick bay.'

'You don't need them when you've got me,' the dog barked back to Gibbo.

'Yeah, we don't need them,' Gibbo repeated defiantly.

Bob felt pain bite his chest like a heart attack. He wanted to do something, but he was paralysed by awkwardness. He never knew what to say to this son of his. Clearing his throat loudly, he stepped into the doorway and flipped on the light switch. Gibbo flinched and blinked owlishly at him. It aggravated Bob immediately, his son's fear, his gutlessness.

Sometimes he felt guilty about his reflexive contempt, but when he reached inside, he could no longer find the vestiges of whatever softness or patience had once existed. Resentment was sclerotic. He was a man accustomed to rehearsing the bitterness of his Vietnam experience and the disappointment his life and family had turned out to be. He had wanted so much more from life, once upon a time. Then he was sent to war and, unnerved by the constant face-to-face confrontation with death, he came home and got married as soon as possible in the delusion that he was returning to a normal life. After a few years of anaesthetised existence, he suddenly woke up to find himself middle-aged and trapped. He could not help venting his frustration on his spineless son.

'What're you doing sitting in the dark?' Bob asked gruffly. 'It's still light outside. How about we go bowl a few overs?'

Gibbo scrubbed the back of his hand over his eyes and looked away, saying nothing. It was a mistake to have come in, Bob thought. He was just making things worse for the boy. He wasn't welcome here, in his own son's room. He turned away.

'Ah, you'd best clean up your room,' he ordered as he shut the door behind him. Out in the hallway, he leaned against the wall and closed his eyes, rubbing his fist against his chest.

Inside the room, Gibbo chanted over and over to his dog, 'We don't need nobody. We've got us.'

Nearly fifteen years later, Bob experienced a sense of déjà vu as he lurked indecisively in the corridor outside his son's bedroom and listened to Gibbo's ragged sobs. The feeling of inadequacy that pulled at his gut was all too familiar. He could not bear the sound of his son's sorrow. He'd watched his son squirt out into the world, all wrinkled red and wriggling like a fish, and he'd started weaving the warm glow of father–son fantasies around them both. Even if none of that had come true, even if his son had disappointed his dreams and he couldn't help flogging Gibbo with dead hopes, Bob wanted to protect him still. And then to see him come to this!

He wanted to whip up fierce anger against someone— anyone—to obliterate the pain he endured along with his son. It was treachery, Bob thought. His son had been betrayed by all those Asians. First, Justin had tried to hit on Gibbo, then Tien and Stanley had tried to sue Gillian, and now Linh had taken out an AVO against his son.

All his life he'd had to contend with his father's virulent antagonism towards Asians. Bob had only to shut his eyes and tilt his head to one side to hear the late Gordon Gibson's voice hissing hatred in his ear: dirty chinks, fish-breathed gooks, bloody slopes. Can't trust them. Commie bastards, all of them. And yet the child Bob had been confused because his father, for all his professed hatred of the Yellow Peril, had made him visit the Yipsoons several times a year, particularly at Chinese new year, and he had maintained a sullen respect towards old Mrs Yipsoon.

'They're different, that's why,' Gordon Gibson said brusquely when Bob ventured to question him. 'They've been here since the gold rushes. They're practically Australian. They're the exception that proves the rule.'

Old Mrs Yipsoon just said, 'You ought to remember where you come from and who your people are. You have nothing to be ashamed of.'

Gordon Gibson looked as if he could have struck her down at that moment. He clenched his jaw and reined in his temper like a good man.

To the young Bob, his father was a man's man. Every cliché in the book was true about Gordon Gibson. Tough as old boots, he loved his country, did his stern duty in war and never failed to provide for his family. He was a man made for wearing an Akubra, slitted eyes squinting out to the hard blue heat of the horizon, striding tall and confident along the rusty flats of the landscape, even though he'd lived in the city all his life. He was harsh but fair to his kids. He disciplined them and instilled in them the self-respect to transcend their working-class roots and scramble into the ranks of the professions. There was nobody Bob admired more. Outright approval was always withheld by the old man, but in all his life he'd only expressed disappointment once: when Bob married a left-leaning hippie, Gillian Armitage, a year after he returned from Vietnam. His father wanted him to marry a sensible Australian woman, not a ten-pound Pom with women's lib ideas. 'Least she's not an Eye-talian or Asian, I suppose,' Gordon Gibson grumbled. Bob had looked away uneasily, ashamed of the tug of attraction he'd once felt towards Linh and other Vietnamese women.

When Bob was sent to Vietnam, he did his duty like his father before him even though he couldn't see the point of saving people like the Vietnamese. Why bother? The events of 1975 proved his point. The waste of Aussie lives for a people who couldn't be bothered to fight for freedom. And yet he hadn't been able to resist the gamin grins of valiant kids whose cheerful resilience never ceased to amaze him, whose wide-eyed awe never failed to flatter him. He became friends with Linh and, because of her and Bucky and Madame Catinat, he met the Ho family. The reality of the Asian family in Asia was different from anything he'd been led to expect. The cleanliness, for one thing. However dirty the streets might be, the meticulous washing, scrubbing, sweeping and cleaning of the interior of the home was daunting. He unlaced his boots before he stepped into the house and felt self-conscious about his big smelly feet and sweat-stained socks.

His intitial suspicions and prejudice were allayed by their hospitality. He knew that as professionals and intellectuals, the Hos had suffered greatly from the massive inflation created by the American war. They were not wealthy people. Mr Ho had to send his daughter out to earn her own living and the shame of it was crippling the old man. Yet when

Madame Catinat and Mr Thieu brought him to visit the Hos that first time, they invited him to join them for a meal. He noticed that they themselves ate little but steamed rice and vegetables, piling all the meat into his bowl. 'We already ate plenty,' Duong insisted cheerfully. Mrs Ho, who held the purse-strings of the family—as did most Vietnamese wives—gave Duc some money they could ill afford and instructed him to run downstairs to buy a beer for Bob. He was touched by their generosity.

But then there was the rudeness. Sometimes they slid their eyes away and chattered in Vietnamese to each other and he couldn't understand what they were saying. He was suspicious when they laughed because he knew they must be laughing at him. One moment he felt welcomed and he liked them immensely, then he felt out of place and resentful. He didn't trust them. He didn't know what he felt about these people after all. Because apart from them, there were also the ARVN soldiers whom he was taught to despise. They seemed too small in stature to occupy their own country, except there were so damn many of them, and they were, in the end, part of the same race of 'noggies' the Aussies had gone there to fight. There was also the dirt in the streets and the casual, careless expectoration of phlegm in public places, the stink of garlic and fish sauce and urine, the corruption of certain South Vietnamese officials, the tawdry brothels, massage parlours and prostitutes openly soliciting and, above all, the VC, who just didn't fight fair and how could you respect them for that?

He went home deeply confused and troubled, but he put it all behind him when he married Gillian and his son was born. Then Duong wrote to him from the refugee camp in Manila and, when he remembered the open-hearted generosity of the Hos towards him, he wanted to do whatever he could to help them. The Hos were the exception that proved the rule, he repeated to himself firmly. They were worthy people. He wrote letters. He met with politicians on their behalf. He did his best to ensure that they were comfortably settled in a housing commission apartment. All this he did without anyone's knowledge, for he did not want his own father to know that he had gone soft where Asians were concerned. After Gordon Gibson died, there was no reason to say anything. It would only have made everybody uncomfortable, him most of all.

How surprised and disconcerted he'd been when his son became friends with Linh Ho's daughter and brought her home for Gillian to tutor. When he met Tien for the first time, he looked into her face and saw Linh's eyes staring out of Bucky's features. For the sake of her parents, he would treat her like his own daughter, he decided. In time he grew closer to her than to his own son. Acceptance was easier when it wasn't your own kid, when she was a girl who did not have to live up to the impossible ideals of Australian masculinity laid down by Gordon Gibson—the ideals that even Bob himself failed to fulfil.

And then Tien had to go and reject everything that he stood for. She had assimilated so well—he'd seen to that; he'd tried to help her fit in, taught her to speak like an Aussie—and then she threw it all away and announced her solidarity with Asianness as if she were declaring war on him. She distanced herself from him and his son. She embraced a culture that wasn't even hers—Cantopop!

She didn't even speak their language. Only in a Western country could a half-Vietnamese, half-black American girl take one look at the dizzying permutations of inter-mingling Chinese, Koreans, Indonesians, Singaporeans, Malaysians, Indians, Sri Lankans, Filipinos and Japanese around her and define herself as generically, if not geneti-cally, Asian.

When she went to university, she shook the dust of the western suburbs—both Anglo and Asian—off her feet. On the rare occasions when she came over for a meal, she used the hyphenated jargon of fine dining (sun-dried, pan-fried, honey-glazed, wok-seared, oven-roasted, truffle-infused—and everything just so bloody more-ish) to demonstrate her effortless cultural chameleonism; to show Bob that he might belong to the old Australia where she'd had to have the rules explained to her, but the tables had turned and now she fitted right in to the new cosmopoli-tan culture in which he was just a gawky tourist visiting the big smoke.

Then she married that tosser Stan, moved to Cali-fornia and kicked away the country that had sheltered her and the man who'd made her a true-blue Aussie. Where was the gratitude in that? Bob couldn't help but feel bewildered by what had happened to this society, to the kids he once knew. And under his hurt and con-fusion there was a growing need to strike back and stake out his own territory, otherwise how was he ever going to feel at home again in the very place he'd lived all his life?

Bob realised people found him hard to take and he was perversely proud of that. But he also knew he was a good man. Fair. He was fair because he was able to set aside his father's prejudice and help people, even if they were Asians. He'd helped Linh because he had been a little infatuated with her—not that he would admit it even to himself—and he'd helped Tien because she was Linh's daughter and simply because, dammit, he just plain liked her. How did they repay him? They'd summoned Nigel to court and the magistrate looked down at his son, saw a stalker, and slapped out an AVO. Nigel wouldn't have a criminal record, they explained, not unless he breached the conditions and was charged and found guilty. But still it was there. On the police system. Nigel Gibson, stalker. Linh and Tien had done this to his son. Bob grieved because they'd proved that his father had been right all along when he'd wanted to believe otherwise. You just couldn't trust these Asians.

Gibbo stared in stunned disbelief at the AVO. He read it over and over again, bewildered by what it meant. He didn't fully understand its implications until he faced the magistrate. Then feeling returned, swamping him in a backwash of pain. He read the AVO again and his sense of himself dissolved.

This was what it felt like: he was stumbling through a maze of mirrors in a fun park when suddenly someone stepped up from behind and collared him, grabbing his hair and yanking it back violently, jerking up his chin and forcing his watering eyes to look into a mirror and face a reflection that might or might not have been his own. How could he possibly know what was true?

In his mind he was a lover. He had proved himself faithful through Linh's moody silence, doubts and absence. How could she—how could *anyone*—not see and appreciate his devotion? He loved the age-honed beauty of her features, her skin slightly slackened but still uncreased, protected from the sun by a weird assemblage of hats, gloves and long-sleeved shirts. He loved the neat petiteness of her, the way her sturdy body was beginning to pear out into rounded hips. It wasn't just that he wanted to make love to her, even though his penis stirred and twitched when he indulged in fantasies of sex with an older woman: the eroticism of her experience; the deliciously terrifying thrill of being straddled and used by a woman confident enough to please herself; the irresistible superiority of feeling that he was a man who looked beyond toned muscles and unwrinkled skin for sensuality. He was set apart from the usual run of lovers by his own discriminating taste for the subtly layered beauty of an ageing woman. He longed to be enfolded by her, to feel her unfurling around him. Safe.

It wasn't just about easy lust but about romantic longings and suburban dreams. He wanted to lay his devotion down at someone's feet. All he asked was the right to follow at her high heels and be petted from time to time. His needs had always been impossibly simple. He wanted to browse companionably through the homewares section at Kmart, picking out kitchen appliances. His ambition was to be the Barbecue King, wheeling out the new state-of-the-art barbecue, heating up the coals and slapping down the tangy marinated T-bones, a blue and white striped butcher's apron wrapped around his waist and a pair of tongs in his hand. Competent. He could imagine his wife and her friends sunbathing on the pool deck, sipping cask wine, tossing to him the occasional friendly comment about the salivating smell of spitting sausages. In the pool, his kids and their friends splashing and whooping with joy. Happy family friends all around. His happy family. He wanted to do with his kids all the things he'd never done as a child. If it was possible for his father to get married and have a family, if it was possible for someone to fall in love with Bob Gibson, of all people, how could this be so impossible for him?

Yet he was prepared to release these dreams from his sweaty clutch and let them float away if only Linh would return his love. He couldn't say exactly why he loved her. He only knew that he went to sleep jerking off to his fantasies of her. He said her name with a catch in his throat. Yearning squeezed out from the clutch in his gut and escaped his lips in a long slow groan. When he awoke, his first thoughts were of her. He tried to wrench his mind away so that he could concentrate—first on his studies, then on his job. But the yearning simply to be with her diffused like a gas leak in his mind. He was fired with the hot helium of his love for her, floating free of anything that might anchor him to a loveless reality.

Gibbo was programmed by popular culture to believe that love would overcome all obstacles and triumph in the end. Patience and persistence were all it took. Linh simply had to see that no-one else appreciated her the way he did. Others—like her own daughter—saw her impatience and severity and withdrew from the spiny carapace of her. But he alone could understand her kindness and generosity and strength. This was a woman he had puked all over and who then turned up two weeks later, placed a comforting hand on his shoulder and gave him a second chance.

He knew the greatness of her heart. What he didn't know, what he couldn't believe, was that she might glance at his love in that distorting hall of mirrors and recoil from a monstrous terror instead. That she might look at him and his desperate wooing and see not a lover but a stalker. Not the faithful hound but the ferocious hunter tracking her down for the kill.

It was this that he wept for, not just the order keeping him away from her, but her deformed view of him that warped him into a mould of frightening obsession when he had only intended unswerving devotion. She did not see him as he really was and, because of this misrecognition, she made him doubt himself.

Bob hulked outside his son's room and wondered how he was ever going to make things right when he couldn't remember the last time he'd had a conversation with his son. And he wondered how he was ever going to look at himself in the mirror and recognise a father, however flawed, if he didn't even try.

He shuffled into the room with the uncertain gait of a man who had no right to be where he was stepping. He closed the bedroom door behind him and hovered at the edge of the room, uncertain whether to move towards Gibbo, hunched up at one end of the bed. Father and son were both dumbstruck, gazing at each other in an eternity of acute awkwardness.

'What do you want?' Gibbo said at last. He rubbed the back of his hand under his dripping nose and wiped it on the bedcover, not caring that this brought a reflexive frown to his father's face.

'Ah. Just thought we might have a chat.'

'About what? If you're gonna tell me off, don't bother. After court today, I don't reckon you need to say anything more, do you?'

'No, I wasn't—I just thought it might help to talk about it, that's all. Yeah. Look, son. I'd, uh, like to help.'

'You wanna help? Go away and leave me alone then. Last thing I need right now is to talk to you.'

His son's hostility was like a whip-slash across the face. He flinched but didn't budge.

It was the easiest thing to do, Bob thought. It was what he'd always done before. He should just turn around, open that door and get the hell out of his son's life. Being here only made things worse. He'd never been able to do anything right by his boy. He started towards the door, then he hesitated. To their mutual surprise, he plonked himself down on Gibbo's bed and shifted his bum on the doona to make himself comfortable. He leaned back against the wall and closed his eyes.

'What d'you think you're doing?'

'Gonna sit right here till you feel like talking,' Bob said.

He was a stubborn man; he would put his stubbornness to good effect now. Night after night he came in and settled himself on the bed. His son ignored him and turned away. After a few hours, Bob would get up, stretch and yawn, then he'd say to Gibbo, 'Night, son. See you tomorrow.' It almost sounded like a threat.

After eight days, Gibbo said, 'Why should I talk to you anyway? Do you remember what happened the last time you made me tell you something?'

'No. When was that? What happened?'

'It was the day I came back from my camping trip with Justo. You took one look at my face and—'

'And I said what the fuck did you get up to 'cos your eye was all swollen and your lip was cut. You wouldn't tell me so I shook it out of you,' Bob remembered. He could not look at his son.

'You promised me you'd never tell.'

'I know. And then I told Tek his son was gay during that bloody dinner.'

'How can I trust you after that? You let me down.'

There were so many things Bob wanted to say in his own defence: *I was off my face, don't you see? It doesn't excuse what I did but still . . . And then there's you. Look, Nige, you may think I hate you but I don't. I'm your dad. I couldn't ever hate you. I mean, it's quite the opposite, really. Yeah. Don't you know how bloody mad it made me when those two kids dumped you after school was over and they moved on and got themselves new friends? You were chewed up and spat out but you did nothing. You just took it. Do you know what it does to me to see you all alone like this? That night, well, I couldn't take it anymore, son. I wanted to hurt them the way they hurt you. Instead, I just ended up twisting the knife in your pain. And that was after I forgot your twenty-first, too. So I guess I was mad at them and I was mad at myself.* He could hear the words in his head but his tongue refused to utter them. In the end, there was nothing to say in his own defence except, 'I'm sorry.'

Bob left his room then and Gibbo sat on his bed and stared at the closed door. He couldn't believe it. After all this time when he'd been winding himself up to speak, to finally confide, his father just up and left. All that bullshit about wanting to talk then, when he had to apologise, he couldn't take it. What kind of father was that? He should have known better than to let his heart crack open slightly. He'd know better next time. He turned out the bedside lamp and buried his face in his pillow. He understood dimly that he was reacting in an adolescent fashion, and this only served to further depress him.

But Bob was back the next night. It was one of those dreaded Saturday nights when all Gibbo could find to do was maybe walk down to the Horse and Jockey hotel where he now worked part-time, knock back a few schooners, then shuffle home to stretch out in bed and read in his underwear while feeling sorry for himself. Bob poked his head in and asked hesitantly, 'Don't suppose you wanna go out for a drive?'

His son looked up in surprise and faint suspicion. 'Where to?'

'Dunno. Goulburn, maybe.'

'You've gotta be joking. What for?'

'Aw, thought we might stop by Macca's or the Big Merino. Grab a bite to eat.'

Gibbo was silent for a moment. Was he going to be moron enough to give his dad another chance? He shouldn't. The old man didn't deserve it.

'Yeah, all right, I suppose,' Gibbo said unenthusi-astically.

It was better than he'd expected, Bob thought, satisfied. He'd been going about this talking business all wrong. Sitting there on the bed with nothing but air and silence between them, it was awkward. A man couldn't just sit there and look at his son and 'share'. He needed to be doing something. So fine. They'd do something. They'd go for a drive to Goulburn and even bloody Canberra if that's how long it took them to start talking.

Father and son came to look forward to those Saturday night drives out of Sydney. They went out west to Lithgow, up the coast to Newcastle, down to Wollongong and the Southern Highlands. They never saw anything much except the road unrolling before them and oncoming headlights slicing through the darkness; it was the novelty of each other's company they secretly enjoyed, although they'd never say as much. Gibbo stored up puke stories from the pub to relate. Bob retaliated with gruesome gynaecological horrors from the hospital. Sometimes they laughed and almost liked each other.

Then, one night, as they were driving home through Galston Gorge, Bob cleared his throat and was finally able to say, 'Uh, Nige. I just want you to know, mate, that I, uh, I really enjoy these drives. Yeah. I mean, whatever you've done, son, whatever's gonna happen, your mother and I, we're behind you. You're a good man. Yeah. I, uh, you know, love you and all that. So, yeah.'

Gibbo began to cry. He cried because this should have been a great moment of revelation; perhaps even of reconciliation between father and son. If this were a movie, he could hear the soundtrack in his mind: the swelling finale of some angst-filled father–son song. And it wasn't because he was ungrateful for Bob's efforts that he did not respond to his father's fumbling overtures of friendship. He realised fully the magnitude of Bob's words and actions, and was astonished and gratified by the evidence of his father's love.

But he also realised something else: in the end, your parents are your parents and, although the quest for their approval might bend and shape the pattern of your life, it could never fill the empty womb that grew within you still. So although Gibbo reached out, grasped Bob's free hand and felt thankful for this new-found connection with his father, he wept because he could not rid himself of the gnawing need to be chosen, to be loved by somebody else.

Making Amends

If you still care for what we both once felt,
let's turn it into friendship—let's be friends.

Nguyen Du, *The Tale of Kieu*

The storm blew in on boiling clouds one late summer afternoon. There was scant warning, only the eddies of scuttling leaves raked by the talons of a southerly wind. The sky cracked with lightning, lobbed down hailstones the size of a child's fist. Spears of rain drummed down on red-tiled roofs and creaking gutters spouted plumes of dirty water. Windowpanes shook and shattered. Pock-marked cars stalled along the kerbs of sloping streets awash with the water that spewed out of drains clogged with dog crap, dead leaves, cigarette butts, chip packets and plastic bags. The television news that night would show the aftermath: scragged branches of trees gashed by hail damage, a litter of sticky leaves everywhere, black overhead cables snaking crazily from a power pole snapped like a matchstick, neighbours in wet shorts and rubber thongs sloshing out of flooded houses, and State Emergency Services workers suspended from rooftops in canary-yellow cherry-pickers.

A quarter of an hour and it was all over. Brown squares of lawn were covered by hail that glistened eerily white under a pus-coloured sky. Light rain shimmered as the sun squinted through ragged clouds that were already pushing further east. The air snapped with sudden cold and the clean smell of ozone. Children burst forth into backyards to scoop up fistfuls of frozen ice, chucking them at each other in the nearest they would probably come to a snowball fight. And then, of course, the sting of ice on the skin and the yawning mouthfuls of wailing complaint.

When Linh returned home from the hospital, she found that the power lines to her apartment block were down. Across the road, neighbours were tying blue tarps over roof tiles. She lit some candles but there was not enough light to assess the damage caused by a window carelessly left open. Water ran along the ledges and dribbled rivulets of dirt down the beige walls. The carpet was soaked under her feet, the kitchen tiles gleamed wetly. She slid open the glass door to the balcony and saw that her terracotta pots of herbs were smashed. Shredded coriander, mint and basil leaves glowed greenly against the moist black soil that spilled and ran like cheap mascara across the tiles, smearing the pastel-coloured towels that had hung from a collapsed clothes-horse. Hailstones had slashed through a jacaranda tree and dumped purple petals like confetti over the mess. She shook her head wearily and stepped back inside. Everything could wait until the weekend.

Twenty-four hours later she found that the mess on the balcony was gone. Broken shards of pottery and soil had been swept up and removed. The tiles were scrubbed clean. Ranged neatly along the left wall were new pots of herbs. Her towels had been re-laundered, neatly folded, and left in a basket by the sliding door.

There was no note to say who had done this for her, but she knew nevertheless. She had seen him in his car, parked across the street in the evenings. She had been slightly alarmed when she first noticed his reappearance, but Gibbo never approached her or got out of his car. Before she went to bed, she twitched the curtain aside and glanced out into the street. He was always gone by then. She lay awake in the dark and thought about him.

Little things started to happen which might or might not have been good. She wasn't entirely sure at first. Each day her letterbox was cleared of gaudy pizza pamphlets and the clamour of real estate agents insisting they had found a buyer for the apartment she had no wish to sell. The local council collected the garbage on Thursday mornings, and Linh found that by Wednesday evening, the dark green wheelie bin would have been rolled out to the kerb. When she returned from work on Thursday afternoon, the garbage bin would be in its place around the back of the apartment block. Such little things he did for her, all the while keeping his distance. If Tien had been around to stoke the drama, Linh might have continued to be apprehensive. In her daughter's absence, she felt herself softening into a slow warm smile that someone should care enough to do these things for her. He never asked for anything in return these days. Not even acknowledgement of his presence.

She smoothed back the curtain and looked out the window one night. And there was his car. She couldn't see him in the dark. She watched for a while, then she slipped her stockinged feet into a worn pair of mules, took a folded sheet of paper out of her handbag and let herself out of her flat. She paused at the front entrance and cast a quick glance at the windows of the other apartments above. Then she shrugged, crossed the road to the car and stooped beside the rolled-down window.

'Hello, Gibbo,' Linh said.

'I'm not doing anything,' he said anxiously. He would not look at her directly. She saw his hand darting towards the keys bunching around the ignition, and suddenly she realised that he was afraid, not of arrest, but of the expected slap of rejection. It buoyed her like nothing else could, this sense of power over him. She was soothed by his fear. She felt the last vestiges of her desire for revenge dissolving.

'Thanks so much for clearing up the mess on my balcony the other day,' she said. 'It was kind of you.'

He remained silent. He stared at his knuckles plumping around the steering wheel.

'Would you like to come in for a cup of tea?' she said.

Gibbo finally looked up at Linh. 'What about the AVO?' he said.

She reached for the piece of paper she'd slipped into her pocket. She unfolded it and held it out in front of him. Then she ripped it to pieces.

'I'll go see the magistrate tomorrow,' she said. 'I'm sorry.'

She opened the car door and held out her hand, palm upwards in a hesitant question. After a moment he put his own hand into hers and let her draw him out of the car. They stood by his car and looked at each other.

'Why are you doing this?' he blurted out.

'I don't know,' she answered honestly. 'I guess I just feel like it.'

'Are we going to be friends?'

She said slowly, 'Yes. Maybe.'

'Don't let me hurt you again,' he said. She understood that he was pleading for himself as well.

'Things will be different this time,' she said, and she smiled tentatively. 'We're going to be friends.'

Gibbo decided to move out of home for the first time in his life.

'Are you sure you want to do this?' Gillian kept asking. She scanned his face anxiously for signs of psychological neuroses. After all, he had been stalking a woman more than twice his age eight months ago and, although Linh had recently had the AVO revoked, she did not know whether Nigel was normal now. Something had malfunctioned in his brain; what if it should happen again?

'Don't worry, Mum,' he said patiently. 'I'm all right now. I just need to make some changes. You know. Move on and all that.'

'What about your meals?'

'I know how to cook. Auntie Annabelle—Mrs Cheong—taught me and Tien, remember?'

She did. The first time Gibbo had tried to stir-fry choy sum, he'd heated the wok until it was smoking, poured out sesame oil and threw in minced garlic and waterlogged vegetables. The kitchen had nearly burnt down when he tried to douse the flames in the wok with the bottle of cheap brandy that he'd intended to use instead of rice wine. She doubted his ability to take care of himself.

'How are you going to pay the rent on your part-time job?'

'I'm flatting with three other guys. Don't worry,' he repeated.

'Quit nagging and just let him do it, Gill,' Bob said. 'It'll be good for him. Toughen him up and teach him to stand on his own two feet. We can help him out from time to time if he runs a bit short.'

Bob helped him to move his meagre belongings into an apartment in Auburn. He shared the flat with Tien's cousin Thuy—Uncle Duc's black-sheep son—Phil, a New Zealander who coached swimming at the Auburn pools, and John, a Lebanese intern working at Auburn hospital. Gibbo felt comfortable with the mix; it was his second multicultural reject group. They had their own lives and they did not expect much from him except the rent on time. He tried to do the same. He hung out with John and learned to identify body parts and recognise the symptoms of rare diseases, converted to vegetarianism because of Phil, lost weight, cooked bok choy for his flat-mates and did not set fire to the wok or the kitchen. He basked in their enjoyment of his cooking and seriously considered becoming a chef. He began to watch cooking programs on the ABC, jotting down the recipes solemnly and venturing all over the city in search of obscure ingredients.

One Sunday afternoon, as he was returning from a day in town, he got off at Strathfield station on impulse. He wandered through the piazza and the shopping centre and marvelled at how much it had changed since the Koreans moved in. He bought a cactus arrangement in a brightly painted clay pot, then he walked over to the Cheongs' and rang the doorbell. Sadness washed over him as he heard the familiar tinny tune of 'London Bridge is falling down' and he felt homesick for his youth. Annabelle answered the door.

'*Ai-yoh*, Gibbo! So long I never see you! *Wah*, you lost so much weight. So handsome now,' she said as she raised herself up on tiptoe to hug him and kiss his cheek. 'Come in, come in.'

She sat him down in her kitchen and poured him a glass of sweet chrysanthemum tea. 'So what happen?'

'You mean about the AVO?' he mumbled, reddening slightly. 'Linh had it revoked. It was . . . a misunderstanding.'

'No, no. I mean how you lose so much weight? Before you so fat. Must tell my sister-in-law. *Ai-yah*, I tell you, that woman likes to wear very short denim shorts. She thinks her legs still so nice but I tell you, from the backside, when she walks, look like two pigs fighting to get out of her pants.'

'I've only lost about five kilos, Auntie,' Gibbo said.

'Is it? How come I thought you so much fatter than that?'

'I've become vegetarian,' he volunteered. 'I cook a lot of those *choy* dishes you taught me.'

'*Wah!* So clever one, *lah?*'

'*Yah lah*,' he said, and they grinned at each other.

Her smile faded. She put out her hand and squeezed his arm. 'Honestly, it's so good to see you. I miss seeing you around. And Tien also. Remember? You all always hang around in the kitchen while I cook. And my poor Jay also.'

Gibbo cleared his throat. 'Um. Have you heard from him lately?'

'*Yah*. He rings me every week. He was always such a good boy.'

'Is Uncle Tek still angry with him?'

'No. Yes. Actually, I'm not sure. He got over being angry but then last Chinese new year, Jay turned up at my sister Isabelle's house and told everybody he's a homo. *Ai-yoh*, I tell you! Some of them are so nasty! Anyway, Jay thinks that his daddy should have defended him but Tek didn't say anything so Jay was rude to him. Now Jay won't talk to his daddy. He say Tek is still ashamed of him. And maybe Tek is still angry because Jay was so rude. He say Jay broke his heart.'

'Oh. What about you?'

'*Hi-yah*, what to do? If he likes men, he likes men, isn't it? I just tell him to make sure he use condoms and keep clean. Otherwise can get all kinds of infection. You also, you know. Must be careful. You got girlfriend or not?'

'Not.'

'Oh well. You still so young, isn't it? Got plenty of time. Or are you still in love with Tien's mummy?' When he dropped his eyes, she sighed and pushed her chair back. She walked over to him and rubbed his shoulder. 'All of you young people today. Fall in love here, fall in love there. What to do?'

He looked up at her. 'I never had the guts to ask you. Are you and Uncle still mad at me for what happened at the Dead Diana Dinner?'

'No! How come you think we're mad?'

'Well, I mean it was me who told my dad about Justin being gay and everything. I spoilt your dinner.'

'No, no. Not your fault. You so poor thing. We all forgot your birthday. It was your birthday that was spoilt. I tell you, we never blame you. True, you know. *Yah lah*, Tek was so cranky, but at your daddy and then my Jay, not at you.'

'Well, has Justin said anything about me?'

'No.' She leaned her hip against the edge of the table and looked down at him. 'You know, my Jay was always so quiet. Such a good boy. I didn't know he could hold a grudge for such a long time. I brought him up and I bathed him and washed his clothes and I cooked for him and I know what he likes and doesn't like to eat. I know him so well on the outside but not on the inside.'

'Me too, I guess.'

'So. Do you ever see Jay?'

'No.' Then Gibbo made up his mind. 'But I'm planning to get in touch with him soon. And Tien also. I'll write to her. I want to make things right with everyone.'

Gibbo met Justin at Miss Yipsoon's house—neutral territory. Miss Yipsoon waited in her kitchen with the door open slightly. She could hear nothing. After a while, she pushed the door open and poked her head in. She frowned. Gibbo and Justin sat on her mustard-coloured velvet sofa and stared down at the pink and green roses of her Chinese carpet. They were not talking. She stalked in, opened the lid of her old brown Beale piano and picked up the scarred wooden ruler. She marched over to the two young men and smacked them on their ears.

'Ow!'

'What the fuck was that for?'

She smacked Justin on his other ear. 'Swearing, for one thing. And for not talking to each other. You call me up and you tell me you want to make up with each other. You ask whether you can meet at my place, where you first met when you started piano lessons. Fine. I let you meet. I put out the rice crackers and prawn chips for you. And what do you do? You don't talk. You don't touch my rice crackers or prawn chips. You just stare at my carpet!'

'I don't know what to say to him,' Justin complained, rubbing his stinging ears. 'Shit, that hurts.'

Miss Yipsoon raised her ruler again and he jumped up and backed away, holding his hands out defensively. 'Okay, okay. Sorry.'

'If you don't know what to say, then this is what you'll do,' she decided. She walked over to her bookshelf, pulled out a battered yellow book of duets and placed it on the piano. 'You can both sit down and let me see how much practice you've been doing lately.'

'You gotta be kidding.'

'No way!'

She bullied them into compliance. They sat there on the piano bench, two 23-year-old young men, meekly sight-reading a duet score to the mechanical tick of the swaying metronome, getting verbally abused and smacked on the knuckles for their pains. After a while, the absurdity of the situation began to dawn on them both. Gibbo glanced sideways and saw that Justin was grinning. They caught each other's eyes and burst out laughing. Their fingers stumbled over the keys. They nudged and shoved each other. The metronome jolted and tumbled down, knocking the score off its ledge and bouncing onto a jangle of jarring keys. Gibbo and Justin yelped hysterically. Miss Yipsoon exclaimed in annoyance and wielded the ruler more vigorously. When they left her house, she had smacked them into tentative friendship once again.

In the City of the
Gaia Goddesses

But such delights she feigned and did not feel:
who can you love when no one knows your heart?
Wind in bamboos, rain on plum trees she ignored:
a hundred cares beset a single soul.
Her heart, evoking things long past or fresh,
became a raveled skein, a mass of sores.

Nguyen Du, *The Tale of Kieu*

Tien and Stan had been living in Oakland for just over a
year when he hit her. It never happened again, just as he
swore it wouldn't. But it left her watchful and wary, constantly assessing the barometer of his moods, careful not to
say anything that might offend. Careful not to say anything
at all. She wanted to make her marriage work.

Stan had brought her to California so that he could
further his medical studies at the University of California
San Francisco School of Medicine. He said he wanted to
be an oncologist. His mother was thrilled. She bullied his
father into paying his university fees. It wasn't as good as
going to Oxford or Cambridge, she said, but on the whole

she was satisfied with his choice. Even excited by it. She threatened to pay them an extended visit when they had settled in. She had never been to America before, although she had a half-sister who lived in Marin County. She insisted they stay near Stan's aunt, but they looked at the rental prices and decided to stay in Oakland for convenience as well as cost.

Stan and Tien found a modern one-bedroom apartment near Chinatown. They were happy initially. They spent the first two weeks taking the Bay Area Rapid Transit to San Francisco to do gawky tourist things, then they returned to their neighbourhood in the evening to explore the various Vietnamese, Cambodian and Lao markets and grocery stores along Eighth and Ninth streets, where Tien discovered baskets of fresh lemongrass, holy basil and kaffir lime leaves. She crushed the soft leaves of fragrant herbs between her fingers and lifted her hands to her nose. She sniffed deeply and felt right at home. She would be happy here in this land over the rainbow.

It took her several months to realise all was not well with Stan. He left the apartment early in the morning, walking to the station to catch the BART across the bay to Civic Centre, where he boarded a bus to the Parnassus Heights campus. He spent the whole day there, returning after eight each night. They ate dinner in front of the television, then went to bed. Tien assumed that he was busy with his studies and obtaining valuable clinical experience at the medical centre.

Then one morning, as she was cleaning the apartment, she lifted the toilet lid and shrieked when a large grey rat poked out its whiskered nose and twitched at her.

She slammed down the lid and sat on it, breathing heavily, her heart stuttering with fright. She could hear animal noises coming from the pipes. She did not know how many there were infesting her plumbing. She thought that if she got up from her seat, the rat might hurl itself against the lid and lift it, thus gaining access to the bathroom and the apartment. She manoeuvred herself around on the toilet lid so that she was kneeling on it, then she flushed the cistern repeatedly and listened for any sounds of drowning. All she could hear was the whoosh of wasted water sucked down into the pipes.

After twenty minutes, she made herself get off the toilet seat. She dashed to the kitchen and grabbed the heavy carbon steel wok from the stove and lugged it into the bathroom. She placed it on top of the toilet lid and tried to ring Stan at his research lab in the UCSF School of Medicine. He was not there. He hadn't been there for the last five weeks. She was disconcerted by that, but even more distressed about the rat. She went to the kitchen and picked up the large pumpkin she had bought for Halloween so that they could play at being Americans. She carried it into the bathroom and placed it carefully in the wok. She filled the rest of the wok with potatoes, then she grabbed a spare roll of gaffer tape they'd used when they were boxing up presents to send back to Stan's mother, and she ripped off long ribbons to seal the edges of the toilet lid and the rim of the bowl. Only then did she dare to leave the apartment. She walked to the nearest supermarket and bought a two-gallon tub of bleach. She brought it back to the apartment, peeled off the gaffer tape, removed the potatoes and pumpkin, heaved the wok off the toilet lid, flushed the toilet a few more times, then lifted the lid. There was no rat. She poured two gallons of bleach down the toilet and waited for Stan to return.

Stan was not interested in the rat. 'You should catch it and plunge it into boiling water,' he said. 'That's what my grandmother always said to do.'

When she asked him where he'd been when he was supposed to have been conducting research in the lab, he smirked at her and grew excited.

'Shall I tell you?' he considered. Then he smiled. 'All right, I will. But you have to keep the secret. Actually, I'll show you after dinner.'

He took her down to the wholesale produce markets around the estuary, stopping in front of an old wooden warehouse with a corrugated iron roof. He folded a handkerchief into a bandanna and tied it around her eyes. Then she heard him unlocking the padlock and hauling back the doors. He guided her inside and flipped on bright overhead lights. He pulled off the bandanna and gestured elaborately. 'Ta-dah!'

Tien faced the banality of her husband's artistic vision: spiny assemblages of corroding steel, large canvases slashed with faecal colour, a squat stump of terracotta turd and, in the centre of the room, a large perspex box containing a torn brown paper bag, a milk carton with a pink-striped straw protruding from its open lip, a rotting, half-eaten banana and a mould-encrusted sandwich among a scatter of Smarties. Tien walked up to the box and read its plaintive caption: *Where are the children now?*

'This is what you've been doing with your time,' she stated flatly.

'Yup.'

'What about the lab and your clinical work? Your graduate degree?'

'What about it?' He gave her what he imagined to be an engaging grin.

Tien looked at him and shook her head slowly. 'Your mother is paying thousands of dollars for you to study at the UCSF School of Medicine.'

'I know. How do you think I make the rent for our apartment and this place?' He took her by the shoulders, looked into her eyes and said earnestly, 'I'm an artist, Tien. When will the people I love understand that? I must create or wither!'

He hugged her close and rubbed a hand over her back. 'I've lined up a showing at a gallery. Then everyone will see. Anyway, I'm glad I don't have to lie to you anymore. I haven't enjoyed the experience.'

She didn't know what to say, and he took her silence for understanding and support. He was especially considerate in his lovemaking that night. There was no membrane of unfortunate but necessary lies separating them now, he told her sleepily. They could connect in total honesty.

Stan's exhibition took place just before Thanksgiving. Four people turned up and were unanimously rude. They made no effort to hide their contempt. Stan sent Tien home and went to a bar in the downtown district to get wasted. He staggered home after midnight and wanted sex, even though he could barely keep himself—let alone his penis—erect.

'Make me feel better, darling,' he slurred, planting a clumsy kiss on her neck.

She pushed him away angrily. 'Fuck that. You're pathetic, you know that? You deserved what you got tonight. Here you've been lying to your mother and me all these months, brazenly fleecing her of money she thinks she's investing in your future, and thinking you're so clever about it. And what have you to show for it? That crap you call your art. It's rubbish. I've always thought so all along, and now you know it too.'

The whip-crack across her cheek resounded in the silent apartment and she staggered back under the force of the blow. She put her left hand up to her cheek to rub it and when she drew it away, there was blood on her palm. He had cut her with his wedding ring. She simply stared at her husband in shock, and he hung his head and began to cry.

'I'm sorry,' he sobbed. 'I'm totally pissed. I didn't know what I was doing but you shouldn't have said that about my art. I swear it won't happen again.'

She cleaned him up and tucked him into bed, then she tended to the swelling bruise on her cheek. When she slipped into bed, he turned away from her and said sulkily, 'I thought you believed in my art. You made me think that you really *got* me. But you were lying to me all this time.'

She did not defend herself because, her outburst that night notwithstanding, she had gotten used to silence. The thoughts in her head no longer connected with her vocal cords. In any case, there was just enough truth in Stan's accusation to make her feel vaguely guilty. Somehow, he'd managed to make her the villain of their relationship.

. . .

Tien needed to get a job to pay their rent. She didn't have a green card so she had to work illegally for a Chinese restaurant in their neighbourhood. There were only two staff apart from the chef and his wife. Tien prepared ingredients and washed dishes while a young Hong Kong woman waited on the tables. Her name was Chang Tsui-Ling, but she wanted to be called Michiko because she thought Japanese girls were much sexier. Michiko was Tien's first friend in California. She came over to the apartment several times a week when Stan was late and watched TV with Tien. She wore round, yellow-lensed John Lennon glasses, pornographically short skirts festooned with silver chains and thigh-high black stiletto boots which resulted in weekly visits to the reflexologist, and she streaked her hair and the tips of her eyelashes blonde. After they had known each other for about six weeks she invited Tien to a Gaia Goddess evening. She gave Tien a leaflet advertising the event.

She is the sacred mystic womb of the universe which birthed Pontus and Uranus and all that exists, the transcendent void of knowing, being and feeling beyond your worst nightmares and wildest hopes. A chaotic alchemical interconnectedness of feminine mystery. The supreme joy of all genitalia, the mother of all pleasures, she is Gaia. She is Earth Goddess. She is you!

When you discover Gaia, you discover your Self. There are no leaders or teachers to tell you what you know by your own divine instinct. Our dedicated guides generously provide the psychic and spiritual protection you need as you

*journey deep within your uniquely individual, sacred
Woman-Self to encounter the goddess who will empower
you and break the boundaries of all your limitations to
fulfil your deepest longings.*

On a drab drizzly Monday evening when the restaurant was closed, Tien and Michiko climbed three flights
of bare concrete stairs and knocked on a door slathered
with thick brown paint. They were welcomed by an ath-
letically toned woman in a kimono whose dirty blonde
dreadlocks sprouted out from her fuchsia-flowered gypsy
scarf. She introduced herself as Maya, their Gaia guide,
and ushered them into a blood-red cave with a black
ceiling. Incense smoked in the stuffy, overheated room.
Tea-light candles flickered in a wide circle and two repro-
ductions of fertility goddesses—Venus of Willendorf with
her soccer-ball head, pendulous breasts and rounded belly,
and Venus of Lespugue, shaped like a penis fused with a
garlic bulb—were placed on opposite sides of the circle.
To Tien's amazement, she recognised the terracotta tumescence presiding in the centre of the circle. Stan's clay turd
had found a home after all.

'I went to this electrifying new exhibition by this
amazing up-and-coming Chinese-Australian artist,' Maya
explained when Tien mentioned the lump. 'I recognised
the feminine earth forces flowing through it immediately.
Very *yin*.'

They were joined by half a dozen other women—eerily
similar in form to the Willendorf—who had already
stripped naked. Tien and Michiko did likewise. They began
with a re-wombing experience, rolling around on the

synthetic shag pile of the red carpet to the shivering strains of Ravi Shankar while Maya repeatedly intoned that they were safely wombed in Gaia's space. After several minutes the music faded away. They lay somnolent on the carpet and listened to Maya's mesmeric voice.

'In Gaia's womb you are safe. You are loved. The universe is tender towards you. You have the answers within. In Gaia's womb you are in a spiritual space of transformation which awakens you to the essence of your powerful goddess self. Feel the wisdom of the universe welling up in you. Awaken the sacred force of Gaia within you!'

After fifteen minutes they were given razors to shave their pubic hair off. Mirrors were then handed out for them to squat over so that they could look at their vaginas and confront their femaleness without flinching in fear or embarrassment. Tien was astonished at how much she resembled a plucked chicken. She was acutely uncomfortable. She cast her mind back to one of Stan's anatomy textbooks and steadied herself by labelling what she saw: mons pubis; frenulum, prepuce and glans of clitoris; urethral opening; labia majora and minora, vestibule of vagina. Everything sounded so much more polite in Latin and medicalese. When they'd had sufficient time to accept their goddess femininity, the music came back on and they were ushered into the circle to sit cross-legged around Stan's deity.

'This is the Circle of Truth,' Maya informed them. 'A charmed and sacred gathering where safety is ensured. Within the circle, you can say anything, be completely honest. You can be yourself. Cry, scream, rage, swear. Let it all out. Whatever you say or do within the circle will not be held against you after this divine ritual is over. There is no-one to judge or to tell you what to think or feel or do. The Circle of Truth protects you.'

They took it in turns to introduce themselves, sharing and emoting volubly. A few of the women were coming off bad relationships. They swore vengeance against men and cried for fear of loneliness, and were comforted by the fleshy press of other women's bodies melded in a psychic sacred group hug. Then it was Tien's turn.

'Well,' she said nervously. 'I'm half-American, half-Vietnamese-Australian. My father was Cajun-Creole. I never met him. He was lost during the American— sorry, the Vietnam war. I guess I've sort of been missing him all my life and wondering about him. I don't know what happened to him. Anyway, I'm married now.' She jerked her chin towards the terracotta-clod goddess. 'In fact, my husband made that.'

She wanted to tell them how frustrated she was with Stan; how he had turned away from her ever since she stopped believing in his art. She hardly ever saw him because he was always in his warehouse studio. She had tried to persuade him to resume his studies but he'd become so hostile that she was afraid of further violence. She was always anxious now. She worried that they would run out of money. She worried that she would get caught and be deported for working illegally. She worried that Stan's mother would find out what he was doing and blame her. Most of all, she worried that her marriage was not working out the way she had imagined. She could not bear the thought of divorce: the shame in front of Uncle Duong and Auntie Ai-Van and Stephanie-Tiffany-Melanie's happily-ever-after married lives with husbands and children; the humiliation of admitting this particular failure to her mother.

She wanted to confess all to the Circle of Truth, but Maya and the other women were thrilled that Gaia had channelled her creative energies through Stan. They marvelled and questioned her about Stan's other work. They envied her for being married to an earth-sensitive artist so embedded in the matrix of the universe. And she found that she could not tell them the truth about him.

At the end of the evening, the women were urged to attend a weekend within the circle at a resort out at Sausalito—Gaia's Journey, Maya called it. They would explore these things in greater depth and learn how to touch their inner divinity. It would only cost four hundred and fifty dollars. It was money that Tien could ill afford, but she wrote out a cheque anyway because she was lonely and unhappy, and she needed the connection with strangers who might be potential friends.

She cooked enough food to feed Stan for a week, packed it into neatly labelled plastic containers and put them in the freezer. 'I'll miss you,' she said, still going through the motions of marriage in the hope that ritual would one day become reality. He didn't reply because he did not believe her. In his mind, he had already categorised her as a liar. She did not speak her true feelings to him, therefore he could not trust what she said. And in her heart, Tien believed that he was right. She had never been honest with him.

Nothing was solved by the Gaia's Journey weekend. Tien gained neither enlightenment nor intimacy with the goddesses but she continued to meet with them just for something to do. Stan encouraged her to keep going. He liked the Gaia goddesses. They appreciated his art. He even earned a few commissions from them.

After a few months, however, Tien felt herself being sucked into an enervating depression where she couldn't see the point of doing anything, even getting out of bed. She stopped going to the Gaia meetings, quit her illegal job and lounged around the apartment indulging her depression, for it gave her the licence not to worry about Stan, his studies, his mother, or their financial situation. She had a right not to care, she told herself; she was depressed.

It took Stan a while to notice, but when he finally did, he could not contain his irritation. 'What the hell's wrong with you these days? You're not the woman I married. You just lie there doing nothing and feeling sorry for yourself. You've let yourself go. Well, just snap out of it.'

So she did. Tien woke up early one morning and made Stan *pho* for breakfast. When he left for his studio, she went to the offices of the International Red Cross and the Salvation Army. She had decided to find out what happened to her father. She wrote letters to the US army and various Vietnam veterans' associations. She went to the public library every day and began to read about Étienne Thibodeaux's background. She learned to distinguish Cajun from Creole culture, and she researched oil production in the Gulf of Mexico. She found telephone directories for the state of Louisiana and began to compile a list of phone numbers and addresses for all Thibodeauxs. She knew that the family might have moved, but she had to start somewhere.

Finally, she received a letter from the International Red Cross telling her that Étienne Thibodeaux went missing in action shortly before his tour was due to end. He was presumed dead, but they had traced his family to an address in Lafayette, Louisiana. His parents—Tien's grandparents—were still alive, living with the younger of their two daughters.

Tien told Stan about her search for her father. She wanted him to accompany her to Lafayette. She had never travelled anywhere new by herself. She was afraid of the left-hand drive of the American car she would have to hire. She was afraid of driving on American roads. She was afraid of getting lost, and she was afraid that the Thibodeauxs would not believe that she was Bucky's daughter. She needed his help.

Stan was gratified. He agreed at first and she booked two tickets to Baton Rouge rather than Lafayette. She assumed that the airport would be bigger in the state capital, and interstate flights would therefore be more frequent. Then, five days before their trip, Stan pulled out. He'd just been inspired with an incredible idea for a performance art piece underpinned by the Gaia philosophy and he wanted to undergo guidance sessions with Maya and some of the other goddesses to develop his idea further.

'Phone me and let me know how it all went after you meet the Thibodeauxs,' he said. 'You can even reverse the call charges.'

Tien landed at Baton Rouge and hired a car. After getting lost trying to drive out of the rental-car parking lot, she managed to navigate her way onto the Interstate 10 highway. After a quarter of an hour, she realised that she was heading eastwards when she should have been going west. She exited the I-10 and after much panicking and honking from other irate drivers, managed to get back on in the right direction.

It was late afternoon by the time she found the Thibodeauxs' street. She parked the car opposite their house, unclipped her seatbelt and sat there, watching the house from across the road. She told herself to unlock the door and get out, but she found that she could not do it. She realised that she had not thought about what she was going to say to them. Neither had she brought any proof apart from the letter from the Red Cross that she was Bucky's child. They had no reason to believe her. She knew nothing about her father or what kind of people he came from. Linh had said that he was kind and easygoing, affectionate and gentle. But Linh had been in love with him; she was not objective. What if the Thibodeauxs were anything like Stan's family?

She sat there, tortured by indecision. There were very good reasons why she shouldn't just march straight up to the house and knock on the door. There was probably nobody home at this time of the day. She could see no car in the driveway. It would be better to wait a while until there was some sign of life.

A few minutes later the front door opened. A middle-aged woman and her teenage daughter stepped out onto the small porch, followed by an elderly white man and a black woman. They embraced and kissed on the porch, then the elderly couple waved the woman and her daughter goodbye and stepped back inside the house. The woman and daughter walked down the street and turned into a garden path four houses down from the Thibodeauxs'. The woman pushed the front door open, and they both disappeared inside.

Tien simply sat in the car and watched. *Get out of the damned car and go to the house, you wuss*, she told herself fiercely. *Go! Just fucking go.* But she couldn't do it. She slumped over the steering wheel and shut her eyes. She wanted Linh, she realised. She should have done this with her mother. She wanted Linh and Gillian and Annabelle and Justin and Gibbo and Tek and even Bob. She wanted her family with her. She didn't know how long she waited in the car. It was dusk by the time she sat up and wiped her face with her sleeve. She looked at the Thibodeaux house again. There was a light on in one of the windows now. Smoke curled up from behind the roof and she could smell the grilling meat of a barbecue.

She pulled her seatbelt across herself and fastened it. She turned the key in the ignition, switched on the headlights, signalled carefully, and pulled out onto the road. Checking the rear-view mirror for traffic, she swung the car into a U-turn and headed back towards Baton Rouge. She booked herself into a hotel near the airport and rang Stan at the Chinatown apartment, then his warehouse studio. There was no answer. She lay awake in the dark, then caught the earliest flight back to California the next morning.

Later, Tien would be glad that Stan put an end to their marriage. She even came to appreciate the farcical absurdity of its demise. She arrived in Oakland mid-afternoon and caught the AirBART shuttle into town, then took a taxi back to the apartment because she was exhausted and running on fumes. She hadn't slept properly for a long time. She unlocked the apartment and stepped straight into an extramarital cliché, except Stan wasn't fucking Michiko in bed or on the floor or, indeed, at all. He was slouched on a chair in white boxers, his head thrown back, right foot on the floor and bony left foot disappearing into Michiko's mouth. She knelt in front of him in nothing but a Hello Kitty! bra and sucked away noisily at his toes.

Tien realised then that you couldn't hang around Annabelle Cheong for half your adolescence without something rubbing off. The first thought that jumped into her mind was a revolted, 'Ee-yer! So *lah-cha*! Dirty like anything! Did he sterilise his feet with Dettol first?' And after that, her mind went beautifully blank. She watched unmoved as Stan jerked in panic and kicked Michiko in the face. They both scrambled to their feet, simultaneously alarmed and truculent, apologetic and accusing. She looked at them and felt nothing.

'I'm going to have a shower and then I'm going to go to bed,' she announced dully. 'I really need to sleep. Keep the noise down, okay?'

When she crawled under the covers, she slept peacefully for the first time in days.

Stan told Tien they needed some breathing space. He couldn't think about their marriage right then because he was working on another commission for the Gaia goddesses and helping them to set up a men's group. He suggested that Tien travel around the country. She agreed. Now that she had made her first solo journey to Louisiana, she felt more confident about organising her travel. She bought a backpack, took some of Stan's mother's money from their joint account and booked a Greyhound ticket to New York via the most circuitous route possible. She flew back from New York just before Christmas and found the apartment empty. Stan had moved in with Michiko.

Tien felt lonely, so one Monday evening she climbed the three flights of concrete stairs into the Gaia cave, stripped off her clothes, re-wombed herself, shaved off her pubic hair and examined herself with greater curiosity and enjoyment than before. Then she entered the Circle of Truth where she could be completely honest and there would be no-one to judge her or tell her what to think or feel because she would be protected by the Circle. She told the Gaia goddesses what an arsehole Stan was, and how his work had been disparaged by the few critics and artists who bothered to check it out. She told them about Michiko's affair with Stan. And she demanded that they do something about it. She wanted justice and sympathy from these women who, even if they weren't exactly friends, were the only people she knew in San Francisco apart from her husband and Michiko.

'I'm sorry, you've missed the entire point of the journey, Tien,' Maya said coldly. 'It is not our place to judge or to condemn. We can't tell others what to do or what not to do. Each woman must look within and follow her own divinity.' And she closed the circle.

The women got dressed and Tien stood around waiting to see what would happen next. They were supposed to offer her unconditional love and acceptance, for they were interconnected with her and the universe. Nobody talked to her. Everyone avoided her or slid her hostile glances. Michiko was well-liked among the goddesses. She fitted in. Tien did not.

'I thought I could be totally honest within the Circle of Truth,' Tien said softly. 'You're not supposed to hold what I say inside the Circle against me after it's closed.'

Nobody said anything. They turned away and ignored her, even Maya. Tien walked out and closed that chapter of her life.

Tien did not know what to do with herself. She didn't know what she wanted. There were some days when she couldn't wait for the divorce to be finalised; she was eager to slough off her marriage and get on with her life. On other days, she didn't know whether she wanted a divorce at all. How was she going to tell her family that she had failed? And although she didn't love Stan, she didn't want to be alone either, especially during the holiday season.

She guilted him into staying with her for Christmas, nagged him into taking her along to his relatives' house in Marin County for lunch even though everyone was awkward and uncomfortable because they knew about the pending divorce. But Tien was defiant. Her marriage wasn't officially over yet, and wasn't the primary reason for a partner so that you didn't have to spend public holidays alone? But then he'd snuck off after Boxing Day, the bastard, leaving her in Oakland to face New Year's Eve

1999—the most celebrated New Year's Eve of the last
millennium—utterly alone.

New Year's Eve is the loneliest night of the year; the one
night when everyone knows for certain who their friends
are and what their exact status is in their friends' lives.
Christmas is for family; New Year's Eve for friends. Tien
didn't have any by that time. Stan went off with Michiko to
a party in North Beach while Tien curled back into the
apartment like a mollusc drawing into its shell. She
sprawled on the couch with a bottle of gin and a bag of
chips. She turned on the television and watched the world
spinning into millennial celebrations—black skies sparked
with unfurling flowers of fireworks, the phallic Eiffel Tower
aflame, New Yorkers crammed awkwardly into the freezing
frame of Times Square waiting for that glitzy ball to drop.
Ten, nine, eight, seven, six . . . She saw a replay of the
Sydney Harbour Bridge, molten with cascading light, and
she wept. She longed to be back in Sydney. For the first
time in years she yearned for her childhood friends. She
wanted Gibbo and Justin and she mourned for the stupid-
ity of lost time and squandered friendships.

When Tien reflected on her marriage to Stan, she
couldn't help feeling that it was doomed from the start. It
didn't last because the Gibsons and Cheongs were absent.
They had been so much a part of her life, so much a part
of her, that huge chunks were missing from her marriage.
Stan wasn't blameless by any means, but neither was she.
When she went to the United States, she thought she was
finally making that journey over the rainbow. She would
be happy at last. Then she discovered that she hadn't
landed in Oz after all because she didn't have the

Scarecrow and Tinman and Cowardly Lion with her, and what use was Oz without her friends?

She was still trying to drum up the courage to return to Sydney to face the disapproval of her relatives over her failed marriage when she received a call from her mother just after the new year. Justin had been bashed up at Tamarama Beach and was in hospital requiring twenty-four hour care. Tien wrote a brief letter to Stan explaining what had happened, slipped it into an envelope together with all the outstanding bills, packed her life into a suitcase and caught the first available flight back to Sydney.

A Craving for Potatoes

He said: 'Your heart cares not for what I feel—
so long you've let love's fire burn to cold ash.
Sorrow and yearning I have felt by turns . . .'

Nguyen Du, *The Tale of Kieu*

After the Dead Diana Dinner Justin dyed his hair blond, honed his six-pack and tanned himself in solariums. The urge to reinvent himself was irresistible. He wanted to wipe away the first twenty-one years of his life and start afresh. He became a Europhile. He learned to make his own pasta and cooked it to al dente perfection. He went to the opera and ballet with Dirk and started basic German classes at the Goethe Institute.

He did not realise it, but he was like Tien in his desire to migrate away from the west. He wanted to move upwards into the casual cool of inner-city cosmopolitan life. He longed to inhabit the sphere of the cultural elites so sneered at and damned by talkback shock jocks and right-wing newspaper whingers. Here was safety, security, the self-assured articulation of opinions and the ability to fight back with words. Here was the subtle exercise of social power and prestige—defending not only himself, but advancing the various causes of the less fortunate; and yes, he suddenly realised they were out there. Here, ultimately, was the possibility of happiness. He need never feel uneasily inferior again if only he could truly belong in trendy Balmain.

He realised that Jordie was a mistake. He wanted to shake himself free from all Asians. He could still hear the loud-voiced condemnation of his uncles and aunts at the last Chinese new year lunch at Auntie Isabelle's when he'd defiantly announced that he was gay. His father looked away, ashamed.

'*Hi-yah*!' his mother exclaimed. 'Why you have to go and tell everybody?'

'Don't make a fuss,' Isabelle, his mother's older sister, warned. 'You spoil my lunch, I cong you on the head! Then you know.'

But his relatives were not to be so easily quelled. Curiosity spurred them on. They discussed him with scant regard for his feelings.

'What do you mean he is homosexual? Cannot be *lah*! He never act sissy or walk like a woman.'

'Jay, get up and show us how you walk, *lor*.'

'Maybe he is the boy and not the girl? Jay, do they have boys and girls in the relationship?'

'How can you be a homo with so many nice Chinese girls around? You never look properly.'

'I tell you, some girl jilt him, that's why. True or not, hah? Jay?'

'Don't talk such rubbish,' one of his cousins said. 'If he's gay, then obviously he's not attracted to girls in the first place. And that's perfectly fine with me. That's cool. Just leave him alone, why can't you?'

'Tek, you didn't bring him up properly, I'm telling you!' another aunt squawked. 'You let him drop out of Chinese school. You let him run around with all the Australians and now you see what happen! You shouldn't have given up your Singaporean citizenship. Then you can send him for NS. The army can make a man out of him.'

'Ee-yer! I don't think the Singapore army want all these homos training with all the other boys. So *gilly* one!'

'Does he hang around Kings Cross? I hope he's not a drug addict.'

'*Hi-yah*! Just because he is gay it doesn't mean he's also into drugs. But I'm telling you, you better draw the line if he wants to change his sex.'

'I don't think you can get it on Medicare, can you?'

'In Australia, anything is possible.'

'How come he wants to change his sex if he doesn't like girls?'

'I don't,' Justin said angrily. 'I can't believe you guys. I just—'

'Better send him for HIV test, Annabelle.'

Some of the aunties looked alarmed. They stared pointedly at the dishes on the lazy Susan and then at their own rice bowls. Someone muttered, 'Did he use his chopsticks to help himself? Is it safe to eat?'

'All of you talk such rubbish,' Tek's eldest brother interjected violently. 'I tell you what. If he was my son

I would give him one tight slap on the right cheek and one tight slap on the left and then he will know.'

Justin pushed his chair back. He shot one look across the table at his father who still would not meet his eyes, and then he left. His Auntie Isabelle hurried after him and caught up with him down the street. 'Don't take it too hard, darling,' she said. 'Sometimes they all very funny one *lah*.'

'They're a bunch of fucking self-righteous homophobes.'

'Yes, but I tell you something, Jay darling. You too picky about girls, that's why you go for boys. You know, there was this young man and he go for a walk in the forest. Then he think to himself, there might be some dangerous animal in the forest. I better pick up a stick so I can defend myself. He see a stick and pick it up, but he say to himself, it's only a twig. So he throw it away and he walk, walk, walk. Then he find another stick, but it's too skinny so he throw it away also. Then he walk, walk, walk and find another stick, but it's the wrong shape so he throw that away. Eventually he come to the end of the forest and still—no stick! So you see!'

'Yeah, but he didn't meet any dangerous animals either, so he didn't need a stick,' Justin pointed out. His aunt ignored him.

'We better look out for a girlfriend for you. Cannot be so fussy, you know. Cannot be gay. Must get married soon and give Mummy and Daddy grandchildren.'

'What if I don't want kids?' Justin said.

'Must want. Cannot don't want. Remember the stick!'

He took refuge in scornful superiority. He extrapolated homophobia from his extended family and learned to

despise Asianness. It was clear to him that there could be no
return to his traditional Asian roots via Malaysian students,
only a forward movement via Dirk into an empowering
white multiculturalism. Strolling down Darling Street each
day, sniffing the yeasty smell of fresh-baked bread, peeping
into boutique shops selling exotic homewares, scented
soaps and candles, clothes, shoes, bags, world music and
ethnic cuisine, his dreams and desires congealed into something tangible and acquired a price tag. Consumerism was
the price of belonging; his relationship with Dirk was the
currency he gladly paid.

He strolled through his new life with a smug sense of
triumph. Finally, he was with someone who overlooked
his Asian oddness and offered him unlimited sex, emotional understanding and financial security. He felt his life
was vindicated because at last he was loved by a white
man. He became confident in his gayness. He preened in
front of his handful of gay friends. He dragged Dirk to
dinner parties, pubs, bars and clubs, just to show him off.
He wanted people to see that he was coupled. He was
sexy. He was desired.

Then one night, while Dirk was attending Peter's
school production of *Oklahoma!*, Justin dropped in at his
usual haunt and seated himself at the bar. André Chai,
who'd been nominated Young Australian of the Year
while he was still in high school and who'd been hitting
on him for months, sauntered up and draped himself
over a bar stool.

'Justin! What are you doing at this Asian takeaway
by your lonesome? Darling, don't tell me you've finally
dumped your old Rice Queen and are now auditioning for

Chinatown night? You'd better take me on, gorgeous. I may not be your rice bowl but at least I'm young. You'll only end up with a fat old saggy fag if you insist on sticking to a diet of potatoes. Young white hunks our age aren't interested in cracking open fortune cookies, sweetie.'

Justin found he was no longer contained in his own skin. He seeped out into his surroundings and viewed himself from other people's perspectives. What did they think when they looked at him? Was his own particular Asianness distinct from all other Asians? Did they realise the solid middle-class affluence of his background? Did they see a successful cultured architect whose design briefs had won favourable comment from the industry? Did they *know* he wasn't like other Asians? Or did they simply see a boat person filling his rice bowl from his Rice Queen? Did they disdain him for a Rose Hancock looking for an Australian passport and a wealthy mining magnate in a wheelchair?

He became embarrassed, and then angry, whenever Dirk tried to hold his hand in public. He glanced around quickly to see if other young white gays had noticed, whether they were smirking at him. 'Don't paw at me like that,' he snapped, shaking off Dirk's light handclasp. 'I'm not a dog, you know.'

He felt ashamed when he saw the hurt in Dirk's eyes. Sometimes he would feel contrition and do his utmost to make up for his nastiness. He tried to be especially nice towards Dirk. He booked a table for two at a restaurant listed in the *Good Food Guide*, took pains to be as attentive and perfect as possible, then returned to the Balmain cottage to love him gently. He lay awake beside Dirk, listened to his soft snores and wondered why he could not accept what he had. Dirk loved him, he told himself, and his life was not so crowded with people who were fond of him that he could afford to kick away love in whatever form it took.

Most of the time, however, he simmered in guilt-induced anger instead. He told himself that Dirk could be a pain in the arse, always wanting to do mentally or culturally improving things. He didn't know how to relax and go with the flow. Dirk was old and he was dull. He didn't want to go anywhere or do anything. He wanted to have quiet dinner parties at home with a couple of friends who would discuss all kinds of intense things that nobody gave a shit about. He wanted to teach Justin how to cook *sauerbraten mit klöße*—a sour roast with potato dumplings—the way it was done in Germany. 'I'm not your Asian houseboy learning to make the master's favourite dishes,' Justin said cruelly, annoyed with Dirk and furious with himself. Dirk's kids were a pain because they lost two weekends every month doing things the kids would like. For chrissakes, Justin was only twenty-three—way too young to be playing uncle to a couple of teenagers. He was too young to spend Saturday nights at home.

'Do you want to break up?' Dirk said. 'Is that what you want?'

'I don't know,' Justin said. 'Perhaps I should move out and give us both space. We can still date.'

'Is that what you really want?'

'I don't know.'

'If you don't know what you want, how can anyone make you happy?'

. . .

'You need to purge your system, darling.' André blew a
stream of smoke past Justin's shoulder and returned the
cigarette to his lips.

'What do you mean?' Justin said.

'Gorge yourself on baked potatoes till you puke. Then
you'll realise that eating rice is healthier.' He smiled and
moved closer, running a flirtatious finger down Justin's
arm. 'I used to be like you. We Asians who grow up here
can't help it. We just want potatoes because all the magazines, all the videos flaunt these gorgeous white beefcakes.
Young, blue eyes, blond hair, muscle-bound in white T-
shirts and tight jeans, dancing at the clubs and shopping at
Ikea. How we long for them! Oooh!' He closed his eyes and
shuddered with mock desire. Then he opened them wide
and stared at Justin and his eyes were hard. 'But they don't
yearn for us in the same way. If they fantasise, they dream
of big black cocks, not skinny Asian noodles. They don't
want us unless they want a submissive foot-bound bitch.'

'That's utterly revolting. You're the most racist man
I know,' Justin said. 'I don't know why I even bother to
meet you for drinks.'

'That's because you're secretly attracted to sticky rice
like me but you're just stubborn. Anyway, don't blame me,
sweetie. I'm telling it like it is. I've pranced around the
block a lot longer and a lot more times than you. I know
what I'm talking about. In fact, I'm just trying to help you.
You want fresh potatoes, I'll lead you to the chip shop.'

Justin went with André to the private clubs, backroom
saunas and fuckhouses where he endured endless loops of

Kylie Minogue. More often than not he was told to fuck off but occasionally he came across a gym-toned under-thirty who was a closet rice eater. He carried around slips of paper with his mobile phone number printed on it but nobody ever called him back. Worse, when he next met them on the street or in a bar, they looked right through him and turned away like he was dirt, scum. Like he was just nobody. In one post-sauna session, he stood naked under the steaming shower, propped his arm against the tiles and dropped his head down onto his arm. His tears were washed away by the cascade of water gushing over his face. He straightened up to soap and scrub himself but he felt that he would never be clean. 'You dirty boy,' he could hear Annabelle saying reproachfully. 'Didn't Mummy teach you better than to play in the toilet!'

Inevitably, Dirk found out and asked him to leave. 'It's not that I don't love you anymore,' he said sadly. 'But I have to think about what is best for Peter and Anna.'

'You're a good father,' Justin said. 'They're lucky to have you.' He raised his head and looked Dirk in the eye. '*I* was lucky to have you. I know I didn't appreciate you and I was a real bastard, but I can't imagine my life without you in it somewhere.'

'Still you don't know what it is you want,' Dirk said. He drew Justin into his arms and for a moment they curled into each other like a Klimt Kiss. Then he released the young man and stepped back. 'Perhaps you don't know who you are. Who can help you in your confusion?'

In the end love was too complicated for him, desire the hollow drumbeat of his heart. He heard the thunder-clap of sound and felt its reverberation shudder through his whirling world. And then its echo died away, leaving nothing but silence and brittle skin stretched taut and dry across the void.

One evening, as dusk leaped into darkness, he stepped out of a toilet block near the beach. In the aftermath of satiation he teetered on a tightrope over an abyss of loneliness and despair. Why did he imagine he could find love in a toilet? Why did he think it was worth the effort of a blindly groping search? It was a comforting lie he told himself; the cheating promise of the pot of gold that nobody ever found at the rainbow's end. The closer he got, the further away it danced, those particles of white light refracted in a weeping sky.

His eyes adjusted to the gloom and he could see at once that they'd been waiting for him: three bullish men with the glint of hate in their eyes and the stale stench of beer on their breath. He read his fate in the knobbled knuckles of clenched fists and the angry orange burn of lip-clamped cigarettes.

'Fucking Asian faggot.'

He closed his eyes and, to his mild surprise, thought about Gibbo and Tien. That was what he really wanted, he thought. His friends. In the lilt and drag of his pummelled body he remembered the rocking motion of a Ferris-wheel cage in Glenelg and he would have given anything to be a child again.

He heard the snarl, 'What are you?'

Through cracked bleeding lips he said, 'I am me.'

And at last, for the first time in his life, he knew that this was true. He no longer needed the external markers of identity, the first thing people saw or learned about him and judged him by. He was not reducible to his ethnicity or his sexuality or his occupation or geographical location or even to his family. Somewhere between the surface of his skin and the creases of his soul, in the interstice of mind and matter, there was a void in which he simply was.

'I am me,' he said. He accepted it.

Pain was a starburst on his flesh. They said, 'What are you?'

He stretched his split lip into a ghastly grimace, clung on to the thought of Gibbo and Tien, and said, 'I'm a Mouseketeer. All for one, and one for all.'

'What are you?'

At last he gave in and croaked, 'I'm a fucking Asian faggot.'

Behind the Moon

'Wind's held me up, rain's kept me back—
I've hurt your feelings much against my wish.
I'm home alone today—I've come out here
to make amends repaying love for love.'

Nguyen Du, *The Tale of Kieu*

The doctor recited a list of cigarette burns, fractured ribs, broken left tibula, contusions, concussion, oedema of the brain and a ruptured spleen that had been removed. Blood loss had been severe. He hesitated. There was more, he said. There had been anal penetration, possibly with a broken beer bottle. The rectum had ruptured. Infection was likely so they were feeding him a strong dose of antibiotics. Justin had not yet recovered consciousness.

'Sodomised? With a fucking beer bottle?'

No-one had ever seen Bob Gibson broken with grief. In his line of work, he claimed he'd seen everything and there was nothing left to shock an old cynic like him. Vietnam vet, football-chucking tough bloke, in the face of trouble he lowered his head and became bullish, snorting, stamping and galloping head-on towards obstacles to trample them underfoot or toss them out of his way. He did not often allow himself to indulge in warm fuzzy feelings. He refused to be a sentimental man. He muscled his way through life with a dogged determination and an aggressiveness that might lose him friends but which, so he claimed, actually got things done.

Now he fell apart. He sank down onto the grey plastic chair in the hospital waiting room and sobbed into his hands. His shoulders quaked with sorrow. Only now did he realise how much he loved their children. All of them.

'Justo,' he groaned. 'God, how can these things happen to our kids? We tried to take such good care of them. We tried to make sure they were safe. What kind of fucked-up world do we live in where people can do these things?'

Gibbo cut down his hours of work at the pub. He came to sit with Justin every day and spent alternate nights at the hospital to give Tek and Annabelle a chance to sleep properly in their own beds. He steamed rice and cooked Chinese stir-fries, packed them into plastic boxes and brought them to the hospital for Tek and Annabelle, urging them to eat.

'Come, Auntie, Uncle. *Sek farn.*'

'*Wah*, you so clever one,' Annabelle said after she tasted his cooking.

'Well, you're the one who taught me, Auntie,' he said.

'Is it?' She gave him a tiny smile. 'Pass, you know. *Ho sek.*'

He felt good about himself then. He liked the feeling of being useful, being needed. Late at night, after everyone left, he sat on a chair by Justin's bed and leant his head against the mattress. He reached out his hand and touched Justin's bandaged, broken fingers lightly, careful not to exert too much pressure in case Justin could feel pain even in his coma.

'I swear I'll take care of your parents like they're my own if anything happens to you,' he said to Justin. Then he began to cry, his tears soaking the thin white sheet covering the plaster cast on Justin's left leg. 'But don't go yet. Not when we've just started to be friends again. I haven't had enough time with you. I wish I'd done so many things different.'

He could not help rewinding and replaying the past in his mind, and his memories always stuttered to a stop when they reached that night at Reef Beach. In a life strewn with mistakes, Gibbo had one major regret. He wished that he had kissed Justin just once that night. If he could go back, rub out the past and rewrite his life, this was the thing he would change. He wished he'd had the maturity, the compassion and courage to kiss Justin back, hug him tightly, then ease away and say with a smile, 'Jus, if I was gay you'd be it for me. Maybe in our next lives, mate. Let's drink to that, eh?'

Gibbo swore to himself that when all this was over and their lives returned to normal, he would make it up to Justin. And in the meantime, he would make things right with Tien when she returned from San Francisco.

Tien arrived in Sydney a few days later. She was surprised to see Gillian waiting for her at the airport.

'Welcome home, Tien,' Gillian said, and she sounded as though she really meant it. She kissed Tien on the cheek and took charge of the trolley, wheeling it out to her car. 'I'm picking you up because your mother has been helping Annabelle to look after Justin during the night. They've moved him out of intensive care so he no longer has a nurse attending to him all the time. Annabelle wants someone there continually so that he won't be alone when he wakes up.'

'Thanks for picking me up. It's really good to see you, Mrs Gibson,' Tien said. 'So. How are things with you and Gibbo and my mum then? You're obviously talking again.'

'Oh, well. We need to pull together for Tek and Annabelle, don't we?' Gillian sighed. 'We all seem to have gone slightly mad over the last few years. Anyway, dear, how is Stanley?'

'I don't know,' Tien said flatly. 'I haven't seen him for a couple of weeks now. We're getting divorced. I haven't told Mum yet.'

'Oh.' Gillian started the car and drove towards the car-park tollbooths.

Tien looked straight ahead and said, 'Mrs Gibson, you know that it was Stan and me who made Mum take out the AVO against Gibbo, don't you? Stan said he would drop his lawsuit against you if Mum would do it. I didn't do anything to stop him either time.'

Gillian glanced quickly at Tien, then turned her attention back to the road. 'Tien, I think we shouldn't talk about all that. Tek and Annabelle and Justin need us now. Let bygones be bygones, all right? Now, did they serve you breakfast on the plane?'

'I just don't want you to be angry with me,' Tien said. 'Although you have a right to be. I'm so sorry for everything.'

'Tien, I'm not angry,' Gillian sighed. 'I'm tired and distracted and stressed over Justin, and I just haven't got room for anger anymore. I want us to move on. Write off the last couple of years as an aberration and let's just put it behind us, okay? Now, I can take you out for breakfast or I can take you back to your mother's apartment. Unless you want to go straight to the hospital. Whatever suits you best, dear.'

Tien was silent for a moment. She remembered that she had once given Gillian flowers for Mother's Day. She said, 'Thank you. I'd like to see Justin first.'

Nothing could have prepared her for the sight of Justin lying there in a tangle of tubes, his pulpy face covered with hideous bruises, his slightly parted lips chapped and dry, and his body swathed in bandages. Unrecognisable.

She didn't know how long she stood by his bedside, staring down at him, her fingernails biting into the soft palms of her clenched fists, her breathing choppy with anger and a heart full of hurt. She bent to smooth back Justin's hair and whispered, 'I don't know how important I ever was to you, even as a friend. I know you're gay. But I want you to know that I've always loved you. I still do.'

'You're a good girl to fly all the way back from San Francisco, Tien,' Tek said when he saw her. He walked towards her with outstretched arms and folded her into a tight hug. Then he stepped back, blew his nose hard and tried to smile. 'Thank you for coming. Justin will appreciate this. He's so lucky to have such good friends. All our families, you know, no matter what happened in the past, everybody is here now for Jay. Bob and Gillian have been so good to us, and Gibbo cooks for us every day, you know. We're so lucky to have you all. Even him.'

Tek jerked his head towards one corner of the visitors' lounge where Dirk Merkel was sitting apart from everyone else, looking uncomfortable but determined to stay. 'They broke up, you know. But I tell you what. Gay or not, he really loves my Jay. He comes to visit every evening after work and stays for hours.'

It was the only thing he and Annabelle could take comfort in just then. The fact that their son meant something to these people who came day after day. All debts were cancelled, all offences forgiven, simply because Justin was loved.

Tien looked over at Dirk and thought how lucky Justin was because he could command such loyalty and affection even from an ex. Perhaps love was like a game of pick-up-sticks, she thought. You tossed up the coloured sticks and you couldn't predict where they would land, what kinds of patterns would be formed. If you had enough skill, you could extract a stick for yourself, but if your fingers shook, you brought the whole pile down and then you lost your turn. You were 'out'. Well, it was her turn to be 'out' now. She was out in so many ways; out of love, out of a job, out of a home and, as always, out of place.

Inevitably, everyone asked after Stan, and she had to sit there and tell them bluntly that she was getting a divorce.

'*Ai-yoh*, how come?' Annabelle lamented, momentarily diverted from her own worries. She gripped Tien's shoulder and shook it hard. 'Don't be so hasty. All marriage difficult in the first few years, you know, but then you get used to it. Like buying a nice new pair of shoes, isn't it? *Oi lang moi mang*, you know. You want beauty even if it costs you your life. At first new shoes pinch and hurt so much when you walk you think you'll die! Then you break them in and they're not so bad. Always make your feet look good, though. Marriage is the same.'

Tien smiled and something eased within her chest. She felt a small part of her locking back into its rightful place. 'But I can always buy a nice new pair of shoes, can't I?'

Annabelle surprised herself by laughing. Then she shook her head sadly. 'This generation! Always throw away and then buy new things. Just like my Jay. All of you don't know what you want. You don't know how to value what you have.' Her eyes filled with tears again and Tien stepped in close to hold her tightly.

'I don't know what to say, Auntie,' Tien whispered into Annabelle's hair. 'I want to do the right thing and say the right thing to you and Uncle Tek, but I don't know what to say.'

'No need to say anything,' Annabelle said. 'You always so strong. Put up with so many things. You be strong for us now, okay? You and Gibbo. Always my Jay's best friends no matter what.'

She held out her hand and Tien looked up to see Gibbo emerging from the lift, a cardboard tray of takeaway coffee in his hands. Tien met his gaze, then dropped her eyes. How could he not hate her, she thought, when he must know that she had coerced Linh into taking out the AVO against him—her best friend, her first friend in Australia.

But Gibbo merely handed out the coffee cups, then he came over and hugged Annabelle and Tien.

'You must be tired, Tien,' he said. 'Can I drive you back to Linh's so you can get some rest?'

And it was just that easy for him. No thunderhead of vengeance or even a passing grey cloud of resentment seemed to shadow his heart. Somehow, in the angst of self-absorbed adolescence and her jealousy over his closeness to Justin, she'd forgotten the sweetness of his heart and all the things that made him worth hanging on to as a friend.

He dropped her off at Linh's and before she got out of the car, she touched his hand and said, 'I'm really sorry, Gibbo. I've been a terrible friend to you.'

He turned his palm upwards to clasp her hand tightly. He said, 'It's okay. I'm sorry too. Anyway, the main thing now is that we've gotta be there for Justin and his family.'

That night, Tien told Linh that she and Stan were getting divorced. She edited out most of her marriage, merely explaining that Stan had found somebody else.

'So you were right in the end. I shouldn't have married Stan.' When Linh was silent, Tien became defensive. She pushed against the imagined weight of her mother's disapproval. 'I suppose you're going to say "I told you so"?'

Linh looked at her sadly. 'So even now you don't believe that I love you. You're my daughter. What do I have to do to prove that your joys are mine, and all your pain as well?'

'I believe you,' Tien said, not wanting to argue with her mother. But she did not feel loved. She told herself she didn't feel anything. She would not acknowledge the anger simmering inside her.

A few weeks after Tien returned to Sydney, Annabelle rang Linh early one morning but Linh had already left for work. She spoke to Tien instead.

'The police have made an arrest,' she said distractedly. 'Tek and I are going down to the station to find out more. You and your mummy come over for dinner tonight, okay? We see you later.'

Tien and her mother had dinner with the Gibsons and the Cheongs that night—the first time since the Dead Diana Dinner. The women each brought a dish, and if Tek shuddered inwardly when he spotted Gillian's attempted rendang, made from a bottle of curry sauce she'd bought at the supermarket, he said nothing but smiled and thanked her warmly.

'So kind of you to cook. You all so kind to us.' His voice shook and he blinked away tears, then coughed in embarrassment.

'Eat up, eat up,' Annabelle ordered, dolloping huge spoonfuls of Gillian's curry onto everyone's plate so that there was nothing left in the bowl. 'Must finish everything tonight. Cannot keep any leftovers in the fridge. Got no space.'

By unspoken agreement, they avoided the topic of Justin's condition and the police arrests during dinner.

'So tell us about America, Tien. You must have lots of funny stories,' Annabelle said, determined to have a cheerful meal. 'Did you go to Hollywood? Is it true all the women have nose jobs and boob jobs?'

Tien roused herself from her abstraction. She had to be strong for Annabelle, she reminded herself. She had to be there for Justin's family.

'Yeah, absolutely,' she said. 'In fact, once I was at this dinner party in LA and there was this blonde tanned Babewatch-type stunner of a woman with humungous stripper breasts just popping out of her red halter-neck top. It was impossible to hold a decent conversation with any of the men there that night. Their eyeballs were just zooming like Exocet missiles towards her cleavage.'

'Really, Tien. This isn't very tasteful conversation,' Gillian murmured.

'*Hi-yah*, never mind whether tasty or not,' Annabelle said impatiently. 'What happen?'

'Oh, she just lapped it up. She was in her element, flirting and not paying any attention to what she was doing, and neither were the men. They were oblivious to everything but those breasts. Our hostess got more and more annoyed. She hissed to her husband, who was sitting opposite this F-cup woman, to fill up our glasses with more champagne because we were running low. He very reluctantly ran to the kitchen, grabbed the champers from the fridge and ran back to the table because he didn't want to lose any gawking time. He sat back down at the table, twisted off the wire and eased off the cork.

'Now, as I said before, except for the other women at the table, nobody was paying any attention to what they were doing. This guy, our host, didn't realise that he'd aimed the bottle right at Miss F-Cup. When the cork popped, it shot out like a bullet and struck her on her left breast. She screamed and clutched her breast. The champers fountained out and drenched her across the table because it'd gotten all fizzed up while the host was jogging back from the kitchen. And then, right before our very eyes, we saw that big left breast deflating like a punctured balloon.'

'No!'

'Yes! The impact of that cork made the saline bag of the implant explode and it leaked out quickly. So there she was, the former Miss F-Cup, drenched in champagne, sobbing for her lawyer, cradling her chest, one big over-inflated soccer ball on her right and no left breast!'

Annabelle shrieked with delight. 'True or not?'

'True,' Tien said with a straight face. 'Absolutely true.'

'Bullshit,' Bob said, throwing Tien an exasperated glance. 'That's medically impossible. Isn't that right, Tek?'

Tek agreed, and the two doctors got into a technical discussion about the probable velocity of flying corks and the durability of breast implants. Gibbo looked at Tien and rolled his eyes, grinning widely.

But Linh looked at her daughter and felt troubled. Tien was not herself. She had changed. She went through the motions of normality. She was helpful and efficient and entertaining when she needed to be. She learned to comfort and to listen. She became adept at saying the right thing. In fact, this was a new and improved version of her daughter whom everyone liked. Yet something was missing. This new Tien said and did all the right things, but her eyes were lifeless and devoid of emotion. Linh did not know how to reach inside and pull out the real Tien—the difficult, guilt-ridden daughter swinging between angry rebellion and filial duty, whom she loved so much but was always hurting in a multitude of unintentional ways. Linh put her hand on her daughter's shoulder and squeezed it gently, and she felt her heart contract with pain when Tien glanced at her with those blank eyes and quickly turned her lips up into an automatic smile.

After dinner Linh and Tien helped Annabelle with the dishes, then they brewed a pot of Chinese tea and brought it into the living room. Only then did Tek tell them about the case.

Justin had been bashed up and left to die on Tamarama Beach. He'd been having sex in the public toilets. His partner was still missing and the police were searching the coastline for the body of a Caucasian male in his early twenties. Three men had been arrested and charged but while two had been remanded into custody, one had been released on bail.

'What do we do now?' Gillian said. 'One young man missing, presumably dead, and Justin still in a coma! It's preposterous that a murderer is out on bail. We must be able to do something. Surely we can write to our local MP or the newspapers?'

'What's the point? They won't do anything,' Tek said. 'All we can do is wait.'

'What about justice?' Gillian demanded. She reached for her handkerchief and blew her nose emphatically. 'That young man should be in jail.'

'Anyway, the main thing is Jay,' Annabelle said. 'I want to bring him home soon. I just know he'll wake up if he can come home and sleep in his own room.'

Tien said nothing. She lowered her eyes to hide the rage that blistered her heart. That night she dreamed of

Justin walking out of a toilet block into an ambush of brutal fists. As in her first days as a refugee in Australia, she began to grind her teeth in her sleep once again. When she woke up, her jaw was sore and her pillow was wet. She was almost surprised to find herself trembling with a deep and bitter fury. She took a few deep breaths to calm down, and she congratulated herself that by the time she appeared at breakfast, she looked completely normal.

Tien had not seen her cousin Thuy since her wedding to Stan. She was surprised when she learned that Gibbo was sharing an apartment with him. In his younger days, he'd run away from home to hang around Cabramatta and Canley Vale, terrorising shopkeepers with other teenagers. He'd since straightened himself out and was belatedly following in his elder brother Van's footsteps. Thuy went back to TAFE, sat for his HSC again and was now studying pharmacy at university—appropriately enough for a former small-time dope dealer. Tien arranged to meet him at Bankstown shopping centre on the weekend. They walked around for a bit, window-shopping and catching up, then she took him to a Vietnamese restaurant and bought him a bowl of *pho*.

Under the raucous din of cheerful family chatter, she asked him softly, 'Are you still in touch with your Five T friends?'

'Not really,' he said. 'A couple of them I see on special occasions. Birthdays and Tet, that kind of thing. But mostly I've left all that behind. I'm straight now. A good little Vietnamese son at long last. Why?'

She told him and he choked on his noodles, spluttering soup all over the table.

'Careful,' she said, pulling out tissues from her bag and handing them to him. 'New cardigan here.'

'You've gotta be kidding, right?' he asked.

She shook her head and his face settled into a frown. He looked remarkably like Uncle Duc and Ong Ngoai just then. She stared at him and recognised in that stern frown an auspicious future as an upright family man and pillar of the community. She couldn't help smiling at the irony of it all.

'That's the stupidest thing I've ever heard, Tien. You don't want to go down that road. Believe me. It's just not worth it.'

They argued about it all through lunch. Then they walked back to Linh's car, which Tien had left in the car park next door, and sat in the car, still arguing.

'All right,' Tien said at last. 'If you won't help me, then I'll go and find someone who can.'

'You're nuts. I'm going to tell your mother and Uncle Duong,' he decided.

'They'll never believe you. I'll just deny it. And even if they did, what could they do to stop me? You'd just be worrying them unnecessarily.'

He looked at his cousin. 'Look, if you're really set on this, let me get someone to do it for you. I'll even do it myself. Don't go messing up your life, Tien.'

'Too late. Anyway, I don't want you involved at all. Once you put me in touch with your friend, you're out of it. Besides, I need to do it myself. You needn't worry. Nobody will ever know if I do it the way I planned.'

When Tien dropped him off at Uncle Duc's, Thuy unclipped his seatbelt but he did not get out of the car. 'I'll give my friend a call, but I'm really not happy about this. Take some time to think it over, Tien. I'm serious. Look, we don't know each other that well, but for some reason you've always been my favourite cousin. Probably because you were a bit of a rebel. Like me.'

'Well ditto, and for the same reason too,' she said. 'Thank you.'

A few weeks later Tien invited Gibbo over for dinner at her mother's. The three of them ate together, then Linh left for her shift at the hospital.

Tien waited until she heard the front door lock, then she said to Gibbo, 'I can't stop thinking about that guy who's out on bail.' She stacked the plates and brought them over to the sink to wash them. Gibbo automatically got up, grabbed the tea towel and stood ready to dry the dishes. He'd been well trained by his mother and Annabelle. 'It's so unfair, you know? Justin's in a coma, his partner still hasn't been found, and this guy's just out there on bail until the trial, which won't be for another year. It's just not fair.'

'No, it's not. But we can't do anything about it,' Gibbo said.

'Yes, we can.' She paused what she was doing and turned to look at him. 'I know who he is, Gibbo. I found out. And I know where he hangs out too. I've followed him to his regular pub. We can do something. We can punish him, Gibbo. Look at Justin! Doesn't it just wreck you? Doesn't it make you so fucking furious you want to tear the world apart?'

He was shocked at the wildness that suddenly sprang into her eyes, the rancour in her voice. He put a placating hand on her sleeve. 'Don't take it so hard, Tien. I love Justin too and I'd give anything for him to wake up. But it's not up to us to take revenge for Justin. It wouldn't be right.'

'What's not right is for Justin to be in a fucking coma. And it's not revenge. It's justice. That guy, he needs to be punished now.'

'Come on. Don't talk that way. That's not justice. That's vigilantism,' Gibbo said. 'You'll only make yourself sick in the head if you go on like this, Tien.'

'Hear me out, okay? I know where he hangs around. What's wrong with slipping a little something into his drink? Something that'll, you know, just give him diar-rhoea or something. Perhaps make him vomit. What's so bad about that? It's not half what he deserves. Didn't you hear what the doctor said? Justin was sodomised with a fucking broken beer bottle! Who's going to pay for that?'

She took the tea towel from him and dried her hands with it, then she found a tissue and wiped her eyes and blew her nose inelegantly. Every time she thought about what had been done to Justin, something hot and tight and hard lodged at the back of her throat and breathing became difficult. Her heart twisted with viciousness.

'I can't sleep at night for thinking about it,' she said. 'I have these nightmares every time I go to sleep. I see what was done to him. I see his face. Every night. And I feel so fucking useless. I feel like I've failed him over and over again and there may not be another chance to make

it up to him. I need to do something to make things right
for him. And it's such a little thing. Please, Gibbo. It's
such a fucking small thing.'

He looked at her uncertainly. 'You're just gonna slip
something into his drink that'll give him diarrhoea but
it'll be fairly harmless otherwise? Kind of like Agarol?'

'Yeah.'

'And that'll be it?'

'Yeah.'

'You promise it'll be safe?'

'Yes, I already told you.' She busied herself with the
dishes and did not look at him.

He sighed heavily and gave in, as she knew he would
eventually. '*Hi-yah*. All right. What do you want me to do?'

'Just help me distract him so I can slip the laxative-
thing into his drink. I'll chat him up or something and
you keep watch that nobody sees me doing it. Okay?'

'That's the grand plan?'

'That's it.'

He shook his head but he said, 'All right.'

It was working beautifully. Tien didn't even have to chat
him up. All she had to do was wear something very tight
without a bra and he just homed in on her. They sat at
the bar, flirted, slugged back beer and crunched salted
nuts. She was completely calm. She was utterly convinced
by the rightness of what she was going to do. It
was justice.

The only thread of regret that ran through her mind
right then was the lie she'd told Gibbo to get his help, and

the shock of her family when she turned herself in to the police the following day for taking a life. She'd told Thuy that she could get away with murder and perhaps she could; but she wouldn't, because justice had to be done. Even as he had to pay for his crime, she would have to pay for hers. That was what made her act an execution of justice, she told herself self-righteously. In *The Tale of Kieu*, her namesake Dam Tien told Kieu: 'your name is marked in the *Book of the Damned*. We both reap what we sow in our past lives: of the same League, we ride the selfsame boat.' In her conscience, mitigating circumstances were no excuse; the ancients knew that from both East and West. Oedipus killed Laius and married Jocasta unwittingly, and still he stabbed his own eyes out with the pins from his mother's dress because he had to pay for his actions. How much more her act of premeditated murder—even though it was justice?

She saw Gibbo pulling out a stool. At her signal, he started a casual conversation with the other guy, successfully distracting him. Tien withdrew her right hand from her bag and felt the small phial warm and snug in her palm. She eased off the plastic lid with her thumbnail. She glanced around quickly to check that nobody was looking. And jolted when a gentle hand was laid upon her shoulder. She looked up, straight into her mother's eyes. Their gazes held for several long seconds, then Linh bent to kiss Tien's forehead.

'Hello, darling,' Linh said. '*Con gai*, will you give me a lift home?'

She felt her mother's hand grasping the wrist of her right hand and slipping her fingers into Tien's tightly clenched palm. Slowly, bending to her mother's will, Tien released the bottle. Linh slid it out and turned it upside down so that the clear liquid splashed onto her dress.

'Thank you,' she said softly. 'You are a good daughter who does indeed understand *hieu thao*.'

They did not speak until the three of them were back in Linh's apartment. As soon as Linh shut the door, Tien grabbed the nearest thing she could find—a heavy cut-glass bowl Linh put her keys in—and hurled it at the huge television screen. The shattering glass released something wild in her. Tien whirled around to face her mother, ready for battle. Instead, Linh handed her a pair of heavy winter boots from the shoe-rack beside the door. Tien threw those at window. They thumped harmlessly and thudded to the ground. Then Linh ran into the kitchen and raided the cupboard for china plates and porcelain soup bowls. Tien wrenched open the sliding door to the balcony and shattered the stoneware on the tiles. She picked up a cushion from the sofa and went berserk in the room, swiping at and smashing whatever she could see, and still it did not soothe or satisfy.

'Did you tell her?' Tien screamed at Gibbo. 'Did you betray me with your fucking big blabbermouth the way you betrayed Justin?'

'No, Tien. It was Thuy,' Linh said. 'Gibbo thought it was a harmless prank but Thuy told me what you'd bought and what you were going to do.'

'I don't get it,' Gibbo said, bewildered. 'What was in the bottle?'

'GHB—an anaesthetic. Ninety millilitres of it. More than enough to send him into a coma and kill him.'

Tien sank down onto the carpet by the badly damaged coffee table, buried her face in her arms and wept.

'I want him to pay,' she sobbed. 'How can people do these things and just get away with it? There's all this pain and rage inside me and it just keeps growing. Like it's been there all my life and I feel so fucking mad and I just don't know what to do.'

'I know. I've seen it in you.' Linh knelt beside her daughter and put her arm around Tien's shoulders.

'Help me.' Tien turned to her mother and clutched her tightly. 'I need you, Mum. Make it go away. Make it better.'

Linh slowly rocked her daughter back and forth, stroking her hair. 'I want to. I wish I could.'

Gibbo looked at them. He did not know what to say. Instead, he fetched a broom and dustpan. He stepped outside onto the balcony and made himself useful clearing up the mess that Tien had made.

Later, after Gibbo left, Linh put her daughter to bed and brought her a bowl of soup. She sat beside Tien and stroked her hair while Tien ate.

'There's something I should tell you,' Tien said. Her fingers bunched on the blanket. She took a deep breath and said, 'I went looking for my father when I was in the US.'

Linh said nothing. She took Tien's empty bowl and put it carefully on the dresser, then she sat back down and kept on stroking her daughter's hair. Tien looked at her.

'Mum, he's dead.'

'How do you know?'

'He went missing in action shortly after he wrote to you and has never been seen or heard from since. So he did love you, Mum.' It was important to Tien to be able to give her mother this. 'He wasn't just another Pinkerton to your Cho-Cho San. He did love you. He was really going to marry you.'

Linh nodded slowly. She would think about this later when she was alone in her room. Then Tien said, 'There's more. I found out where his parents and family live. They're in Lafayette. I flew there and drove to their house. I parked across the street and I saw them. But I couldn't get out of the car. I just couldn't.' She looked at her mother with exhausted eyes. 'I panicked and thought, what if they can't accept it? What if they don't believe me, or they hate me for telling them I exist? And I told myself that if it was you, you would've just marched up to the door to get it over and done with. But I didn't have the guts.'

'Maybe the timing wasn't right,' Linh said. 'Still, you did a lot to find them in the first place. That deserves credit, doesn't it? I never had the courage to find out for sure what happened to Bucky. You did.'

'I thought that if I could just meet my father and get to know him, then everything would fall into place. Life would be good. I'd know who I am and what I need to be normal. I thought he might be the key. Now I'll never know. I suppose it doesn't seem all that important at the moment, compared to what the Cheongs are going through. But I wanted to be happy. It should be enough just to be alive, but somehow it isn't.'

'Everybody wants to be happy, yet who really is?' Linh sighed. She pulled the covers around her daughter. 'Get

some rest now. I will tell you a folktale Ong Ngoai used
to tell me when I was a child.

'There was once a young boy called Cuoi who was born
into a very poor family. They were so poor he couldn't go to
school. Instead, he had to herd buffaloes for a rich farmer.
One day, while he was out gathering wood, he came across
a beautiful tiger cub. He picked it up and started to play
with it, but suddenly he heard the fierce growl of the mother
tiger in the jungle. Frightened, he threw down the cub and
quickly climbed up a banyan tree. When he looked down
from the branches, to his horror he found that he had
thrown the cub down with such force that the cub's head
was smashed. He feared the worst. Then he saw the most
amazing thing. The tigress gathered the fallen leaves of
the banyan tree, chewed them into a pulp and smoothed the
paste over the head of the cub. Immediately it jumped up
and ran away, as if it had never died.

'After the tigress and her cub disappeared into the
jungle, Cuoi climbed down from the banyan tree. He
realised that it had miraculous properties, so he up-
rooted a sapling to take home. He planted it in his
garden and warned his mother never to throw rubbish or
dirty water where the banyan tree was planted. "Otherwise the tree will shake itself free of the earth and fly up
to the sky." But his mother thought he was talking
nonsense, and she did exactly that. She threw rubbish
and dirty water around the tree.

'Then one day, when Cuoi was returning with his
buffaloes, he saw his miraculous banyan tree pulling itself
out of the soil, ready to rise into the air. He ran towards it
and grasped its roots to haul it back down, but he was so

slight in stature that the tree lifted him up into the sky instead. He managed to climb into its branches and they travelled for many days.

'Finally, they reached a place where there was no poverty or trouble, only permanent peace. When Cuoi climbed down and looked around, he realised that he was on the moon. The banyan tree sank its roots there. Cuoi sat at the foot of the tree and looked down on the earth. He saw poverty and suffering and war and injustice, but he also saw the ones he loved. Although he was not unhappy on the moon, he longed to return to earth but he could not. Vietnamese children say that on certain nights, they can see Cuoi sitting at the foot of the banyan tree in the curve of the moon. He turns his head towards them and smiles, but he cannot return to his ordinary life and the ones he loves.'

Linh looked down at her daughter, breathing heavily in her sleep. She bent and pressed her lips to Tien's forehead. 'I'll go with you to meet your grandparents if that's what you need,' she promised softly. Then she switched off the light and closed the bedroom door.

Before she climbed into her own bed that night, she drew aside the curtains and looked out into a black sky pricked with stars and scraped by the silver fingernail of a dying moon. She rested her elbows on the windowsill and thought about Bucky for a long while. Then she tilted her face towards the moon and said, 'Bucky, I hope you found your banyan tree.'

Summer passed in a blur of blinding light and heat-hazed days. Then there was a bite to the air, chimneys bleeding loops of smoke, and the friendly argot of flocking birds at dusk, wheeling and arrowing northwards in annual migration. An autumn moon swung and the Southern Cross spread-eagled over the night sky.

Justin was discharged from hospital. He was still in a coma when Tek and Annabelle brought him home. Linh volunteered to take time off work to help nurse him. They brought him up to his bedroom, and Tien and Gibbo were surprised to see that the blue bedroom was unchanged since their childhood.

His high school trophies still perched precariously over the bed on a mended shelf. Sporting paraphernalia was tucked in a corner next to a cupboard crammed with clothes he'd given up wearing after high school. A pine bookcase still held his HSC and university textbooks along with a few paperbacks with pistols or planes on the cover, the complete Narnia series, and a plastic snow-dome with an improbable Germanic nativity scene: snowy pine forests framing a frozen lake where mittened and scarfed children skated adjacent to a quaintly pretty wooden hut enclosing Joseph, Mary, baby Jesus in the manger and a few bored cows looking on. If you held it upside down, you could trace your finger over the words 'Made in China' on the white plastic base. When you tipped it the right way up again, everyone perished in a blizzard. Tien had given it to him one Christmas as a kitsch joke. On the wall, giant black and white posters of Humphrey Bogart and James Dean were beginning to fade from long exposure to the afternoon sun while Mel Gibson and Mark Lee were frozen in immortal youth within the framed poster of *Gallipoli*.

'How could I know, Tien?' Annabelle asked, and Tien nodded in agreement.

This was the bedroom of a stranger. She felt sad for its bland innocence. There was nothing which revealed the boy who grew up in this bedroom: his fears, hopes and sweaty desires. Nothing seemed connected to him as a person. Looking anew at this room, she realised that it was a room carefully constructed to reflect the good Asian son: hardworking, studious, healthily athletic, with no hint of unusual interests to disturb his parents' normal ambitions for the personal and professional success of their child. It was a room which masked the person that he really was; the person who was, in effect, a stranger to his family and friends because he had been hiding from them for so long.

'I want a second chance,' Annabelle sighed. 'You think you know your children but you never do when they're adults. If only he'll wake up, I want to get to know him this time.'

Later, after Annabelle went downstairs to make lunch for them, Tien said to Gibbo, 'Do you think we really knew him at all?'

Gibbo looked at her and said slowly, 'I don't know if I ever knew him or you. Not really. Do we ever know anybody completely? You're both my oldest and best friends, yet after a lifetime together we still shocked each other.'

'I shock myself,' she admitted. Then she asked, 'Are you still angry with me? I wouldn't blame you if you were.'

'No. Why should I be?'

'That incident in the pub—you know. And Mum. The AVO. I could go on.'

'Well, you always had a hell of a temper,' he said, and grinned.

'And I always took it out on you. Sometimes Mum, but mostly you. I'm sorry. It was so slack because you were my best friend.'

Gibbo looked at her over Justin's sleeping form. 'So here we are again. The Three Mouseketeers back in Justin's room. All for one and one for all. Where do we go from here?'

'I'm not sure,' Tien said. 'But I'd like to think we're still friends of sorts. That we have something to build on.' She tried to smile. 'I mean, nobody else could put up with me. Just ask Stan. He couldn't. And now I'm back to plain old Tien Ho again.'

'Well, if you ask me, plain old Tien Ho is a pretty good thing to be,' Gibbo said. 'Plain old Tien Ho was my best friend. Still is.'

Right at that moment, Tien knew that she would never find another friend like Gibbo. She walked around Justin's bed to Gibbo and hugged him. 'Gibbo, I really love you,' she said. 'You're the best friend anyone could ever ask for. I'll never let you down again. I'm always here for you now. I swear it.'

Gibbo nodded and squeezed her tightly. He knew that she meant it at that moment, and he accepted her good intentions. But their friendship could not be snap-frozen at this point. When Justin woke up and healed—and Gibbo was clinging determinedly to that hope—there would be an inevitable loosening of the strands of their lives as new friends and lovers were hooked and looped in. For whatever the strength of their friendship now, he knew they would not resist the pull of romantic love and the promise of that special partner if and when one came along.

The saddest myth the world ever told itself was the story of Hermaphroditus, he thought. Lonely people like him believed they would be whole once they found a soul-mate they could merge with. Full connection. Not just sexual, but mental and emotional intimacy. He knew it was an impossible fantasy but, like everyone else, he was helpless to resist it even though it seemed to him that the people all around him—even those he was closest to—only ever presented amputated selves to him. He would never see them as they really were. He thought about himself and realised he was no different. But he also realised that this was something that he could live with. There would never be a merging and a wholeness, only the quiet thrill of sharing ordinary lives and a patient waiting for an occasional glimpse of slivers of the self.

Life rutted into a routine of sorts. The Gibsons went over to visit the Cheongs several times a week. Gibbo and Tien sat upstairs with Justin while Bob and Tek bickered over everything for half the night, then trooped down to Tek's karaoke den to fight over the microphone, sing at each other, and disparage the other's musical tastes and talents. Everyone was surprised and appalled when Bob was converted to karaoke. He was blessed with a terrible, honking voice and a tuneless ear.

'There ought to be a UN statute banning him from singing for the sake of human rights,' Gibbo said, wincing at the sound of his father bellowing out Cold Chisel's 'Khe Sanh'.

Eventually, Tek and Annabelle started inviting Dirk Merkel around for dinner. It was not only an act of reconciliation with Justin's sexuality; it was also an offering of faith. This was the partner their son had loved above all others. When Justin woke up, he would know that the man he'd loved was welcomed by his parents. He would know that he was fully accepted, that their love came without strings.

'All my life, until the Dead Diana Dinner, my son never gave me any trouble,' Tek said to Dirk one night. 'From the time he was a baby, he was always such a good boy. He was always so good-natured and obedient. He studied hard and tried his best in everything. Whatever he is, I know that he is a good son.'

'True, you know,' Annabelle said. 'Jay is *ho tai sek* and *ho kwai*. So lovable and such a good boy. You know, I never have to tell him to clean up his room or sit down when he use the toilet at home so he doesn't shee-shee everywhere. And then, when he learn how to drive, he always fetch me where I want to go. He never complain, *lor*. Always help me around the house, not like young people today. Except for Tien and Gibbo, of course. My Jay is very lucky to have his friends here, like before when they were young. He'll be so happy when he wakes up and sees all the people he loves around him.'

In the end there's simply the Cheongs and the Gibsons and the Hos. Waiting. Watching. When they look back on their lives, they are acutely conscious of how often they've messed up. There's no doubt they'll do so again.

And yet if you offered them a fresh start, they wouldn't take it because, even if such a thing were possible, it would unravel the thick threads that knit them together, making a messy but meaningful pattern of their lives. When they're all together, even if they're steeped in fear and pain and confusion, they are no longer living on the fraying fringes of a difficult and hostile world; they are at the stable centre of the universe and life is simply the way it should be.

So they stumble through their joys and sorrows together, lurching past the heart-stabbing treacheries that sometimes go with a lifetime of love and friendship. When they slip and fall, they clamber back onto the same path of the social cripples and the lamed in love. They lean and groan and cheer each other on, arms entwined around each other's shoulders. Limping along the yellow brick road towards that place where there will be no trouble. Never getting there.

Glossary

ai-yah	Singaporean exclamation
ai-yoh	Singaporean exclamation
ang mors	Cantonese term for white people
banh giay	Vietnamese glutinous rice pudding
banh chung	Vietnamese glutinous rice pudding
berak	Malay term for faeces
bun thit bo xao	Vietnamese stir-fried beef with rice vermicelli
café phin	Vietnamese coffee sweetened with condensed milk
cha	Vietnamese word for father
chao co	Vietnamese greeting for a woman
chao tom	Vietnamese prawns with sugarcane and rice vermicelli
che ba mau	Vietnamese drink of coconut milk with red beans, tapioca pearls, jellies and lychees

chee sin lo	Cantonese term for crazy old man
choy	Cantonese word for green vegetables
con gai	Vietnamese term for daughter
dao duc	Vietnamese concept of morality and social order
dau sanh vung	Vietnamese sticky rice balls
do di ngua	Vietnamese equivalent of bitch
em be	Vietnamese term for baby
foong chow	Cantonese dish of chicken's feet
gilly	Singaporean term for something revolting which makes one cringe
goi cuon	Vietnamese rice paper rolls
hieu thao	Vietnamese concept of filial piety and moral debt to one's parents
hi-yah	Singaporean exclamation
ho kwai	Cantonese term for well-behaved and obedient
ho lah-cha	Cantonese term for very dirty
ho sek	Cantonese term for delicious
ho tai sek	Cantonese term for very lovable
hor	Singaporean exclamation
hum sup loh	Cantonese term for dirty old men
kiasu	Singaporean concept meaning competitive; a 'keeping up with the Joneses' mentality

kimchi	Korean cabbage dish
lah	Singaporean exclamation
lao sai	Hokkien expression for defecate, also used to convey the idea of verbal diarrhoea
le nghia	Vietnamese concept of the 'righteous path'
leh	Singaporean exclamation
lor	Singaporean exclamation
non-la	Vietnamese conical hat
nuoc cham	Vietnamese dipping sauce made of fish sauce, sugar, water, lemon juice, chillies and garlic
Oi lang moimang	You want beauty so badly that you don't want life. Cantonese proverb
Ong My	Vietnamese term meaning Mr American
pho	Vietnamese rice noodle soup
pho bo	Vietnamese beef rice noodle soup
pulgogi	Korean grilled beef dish
rau thom	Vietnamese herb salad of mint, coriander and basil
sauerbraten mit klöße	German sour roast with potato dumplings
sek farn	Cantonese invitation to dine, literally meaning eat rice

sek pau may	Cantonese expression meaning have you eaten yet?
tam biet	Vietnamese for goodbye
Tet	Vietnamese term for the lunar new year
Tu Tai	Final high school examination determining admittance to university
Uc chau	Australia
wah	Singaporean exclamation
xe lam	type of bus in Vietnam
yah lah	Singaporean exclamation
yum sing	a Chinese toast

Author's Note

Excerpts from Nguyen Du's *The Tale of Kieu* come from Yale University Press's bilingual edition of *Truyen Kieu*, translated and annotated by Huynh Sanh Thong, New Haven and London, 1983. The André Chénier poem referred to in the text is 'Quand au mouton bêlant la sombre boucherie ouvre ses cavernes de mort'. The novel contains my translation of the following lines:

> Peut-être en de plus heureux temps
> J'ai moi-même, à l'aspect des pleurs de l'infortune,
> Détourné mes regards distraits;
> A mon tour aujourd'hui mon malheur importune.
> Vivez, amis; vivez en paix.

I believe 333 beer, famous throughout Vietnam nowadays, used to be 33 beer during the era in which Linh's story is set. The tale of Cuoi comes from 'The Buffalo Boy and the Banyan Tree', *Vietnam Legends and Folk Tales*, The Gioi Publishers, Hanoi 2002.

Acknowledgements

My heartfelt thanks to:

Annette Barlow, Christa Munns and Colette Vella of Allen & Unwin for their great patience in waiting for and believing in this novel. I am grateful to Allen & Unwin for giving me the time to develop this story through its various incarnations and for their investment in early-career writers.

Jo Jarrah, for her encouragement, insight and thoughtful editorial work.

Yale University Press for their kind permission to reprint Huynh Sanh Thong's translation of Nguyen Du's *The Tale of Kieu*.

Mr Van Uu Nguyen and Mr Phung Do, for their generosity and time spent checking the Vietnamese background of this story in earlier drafts—any remaining mistakes in the final draft are entirely my responsibility. Mr Dung Van Ma, of Vietnam Promotions and Public Relations, for kindly putting me into contact with the relevant people. Nguyen Dat Truong, for being an excellent and informative guide in Vietnam.

Hoa Pham, for her insightful reading and comments on an earlier draft. Stuart Ward, for his feedback on certain sections of this novel. Kim Truong, for checking my French and corroborating some Vietnamese details. Annemarie Lopez—a meticulous research assistant—and Guy Perrine, for their friendship and encouragement through various dinners and diversions during the long writing of this novel.

My colleagues in the Department of Modern History, Macquarie University, who have been so supportive of both my academic and literary careers.

My sister, Hsu-Li Teo, who always regales me with bizarre and outrageous anecdotes.

And, as always, my parents, for loving and putting up with me.